P9-AQM-034

BEFORE
I LET GO

Darren Coleman

**BEFORE
I LET GO**

A Novel

Amistad An imprint of HarperCollins*Publishers*

BEFORE I LET GO. Copyright © 2004 by Darren Coleman. All rights reserved. Printed in the United States of America. No part of this book may be used or reproduced in any manner whatsoever without permission except in the case of brief quotations embodied in critical articles and reviews. For information, address HarperCollins Publishers Inc., 10 East 53rd Street, New York, NY 10022.

HarperCollins books may be purchased for educational, business, or sales promotional use. For information, please write: Special Markets Department, HarperCollins Publishers Inc., 10 East 53rd Street, New York, NY 10022.

FIRST EDITION

Designed by Chris Welch

Printed on acid-free paper

Library of Congress Cataloging-in-Publication Data
Coleman, Darren.
    Before I let go : a novel / Darren Coleman.—1st ed.
      p. cm.
   ISBN 0-06-059484-5
    1. African American men—Fiction. I. Title

   PS3603.O433B44 2004   2004041130
   813'.6—dc22

04 05 06 07 08 BVG/RRD 10 9 8 7 6 5 4 3 2 1

In Memory of
Ella Ridley, Sara Carroll, and Meg Chaney

Dedication,
The skills, the creativity, and the drive are all gifts from my creator. All
thanks are directed to Him. It has been my mother, Doris, however, who
has nurtured, taught, and encouraged me from day one. For your
support, love, and unyielding devotion, I dedicate this book to you. You
are the wind beneath my wings.

Special Thank You,
Chiquita Martin, though we are no longer together you must know that
you will forever be a part of me. It would take too many words to describe
the impact that our relationship had on me writing this novel. Do you
remember the song that the deejay played on 12-23-93 as we danced
the night away?

ACKNOWLEDGMENTS

Many *people to thank*. First off, I want to thank Sheryl Hicks. You were there for me from the time when this book was just an idea. Your friendship has meant the world to me. I love you always. Derek Lowe, thanks for pushing me to bring my dreams to fruition. Your support of my work and Nvision Publishing has been INVALUABLE.

As you remind me, brother, steel sharpens steel. We all need that friend who tells us when we are smelling ourselves. Thanks to Michelle Lowe for being such a sweetie all the time. Now look at you, reading and whatnot.

For all the people who invested their energy and time into helping me reach this point, I want to offer you my most sincere appreciation. My test readers and good friends Endrea Frazier, Lynn Thomas, Bridgette Roy, and Bekisha McWilliams. Tracy Turner, thanks for all the love, support, and patience. You always believed in me and that meant a lot.

My big sis, Tanya Ross. Thank you for waiting patiently for the book. You spoke my destiny into existence many years ago when I was headed in the wrong direction . . . you may not remember what you said to me, but I do. You are the best sister in the world and you finally remembered my birthday! Thanks for taking such good care of my little man the same way you took care of me. I love you.

Patty Rice, I am so proud to call you a friend. You have been such a positive force in my life. It's just a matter of time before we introduce the world to our work. You are an outstanding author. *Simpatico!*

Shannon Holmes. I remember that first night you called me and told me that you were feeling *Before I Let Go*, you gave me a lot of needed energy. *B-More Careful* hadn't even come out yet. Now look at you. You are just as humble today as you were then and that's *"what's really good."* This industry doesn't allow friendships to grow, but ours was written. Thanks for all your help and advice.

V.S., the one and only Vickie Stringer. What is the world gonna do with us? Pay us! I am so glad to claim you as a dear friend and colleague. You mean so much to me and I wish you nothing but continued success.

Zachary Tate, author of *No Way Out*, *Lost and Turned Out*, and *Ain't No Half Steppin'*. The world has no idea what you are putting down on those pages. But they will! You have three of the best books I have ever read and more on the way.

Anthony Carr, you are brilliant. Thank you for bringing my characters to life on the covers. Thanks to your wife, Renee, for always making me feel welcome. Thanks to my photographer, Curtis Catrell at Emagine Studios. Thanks also to my daaaaawg, Les Green at Green Scorpion Web Design.

Kim Lee, you are so premiere with your makeup artistry. You have been such a big help. I wish you twice the success you desire for yourself. You are truly one of the most special people to ever enter my life. Angelique at WHUR and the entire WHUR Family, thanks for your help and giving me my first on-air experience.

Much love to my homegirls Michelle Wright and Rane at WPGC. Shout out to EZ, Joi, Prince DeJour, and Huggie Lowdown. A special thanks to a woman I go to bed with often, Justine Love. Thanks for the spot on *Love Talk*. I also want to shout out Russ Parr, Jeannie Jones, Natalie Case, Mike Chase, Alvin Waples, and the entire Radio One Family.

I want to thank all of my friends and family who have lent an ear, support, and prayers. To the entire Ridley family, aunts, uncles, cousins, in-laws—remember *it's* in the genes. My cousin-brothers Chuck Bishop, Ted Ridley, Damien Lyles, and Marcus Bishop, stay focused. James Chaney, how many people can maintain friendships that form at ages four and five? We are brothers forever. To the entire

Chaney family, especially Skip, much love. Darrell and James Munson, and Tre' Chaney—don't fake, who taught you? Mike Davis, thanks so much for having my back all these years. Mike's Barbershop in Landover Hills, Maryland, is number one. All my fam at the shop, My Barber E., aka Eric Carter; my adopted friend-brother Anthony McCrae—keep the chess board ready; Ed Walker; Mr. Hackley; Terry; Big Pete & Shelly; Tee; and my man Nice.

My road dawg and top-flight security, Shaka. Reginald (BBD) Miles; Marcus Benefield, aka Butter; Kenny Campbell; Daren B.; Graham Cracker (D.C.'s number one deejay); my main man Big Al— it's always great talking to you. The Glendale Lake Crew, Delfis Worthy, Mike Bullock, Derek Fikes, Chris Cason, and Harold Bullock R.I.P. Steve Armstrong, Renaldo Williams, Darren Clark, and Show Place Records. Pierre Fletcher at Radical Art Clothing, thanks for the gear and for helping me coach the youngsters. Kevin Moore, you've been a good dude forever. Tony Carter and everyone in Covington, Virginia, I miss y'all. Chad Cunningham, it's great to have you as a friend, Braveheart. I got your back. June, a reason, a season, a lifetime—you know what's up.

Alex, you are my reason, I am proud to have you as a son. Mykala, my princess, Uncle D loves you. To all my former students at Woodbridge Elementary—stay focused, I love you all. Thanks for making it cool to have been Mr. Coleman and giving me material for an upcoming book!

To all the women I have loved on any level—friendship or otherwise—I am grateful for the experience and support. Stay in my corner, Robin Knox-Love, Taffy Dobbins, Keisha Harvey, Donise Thomas, Jeannine Graham, Jessica Berger, Erica Lane, Kim Lee, Cia Torrance, Nina West, Tammy Clark, Krystal Parker, Shawn Chase, Tanisha Ashford, and Shakeema Abdullah.

To all my surrogate sisters, Lisa Lamar, Rolawnda Chase, Lakisha Thompson, Erica Thompson, Tahisha Cunningham, Andrea Alston-Roberts, Lenore Worthy, Angela Oates, and Lisa Richardson.

Monica Allen, 143. What a journey this has been! You are such a special friend and I am glad to be your favorite author. Will you be in the audience when I make it to *Jeopardy*?

I would like to acknowledge the booksellers, stores, and vendors. Thank you for making *Before I Let Go* a hit. Kevon, Larry, Gail, and the entire Culture Plus Family. Thanks to Eric, and Karen at A&B. Natti at Afrikan World Books. My man Richard at Sephia Sand & Sable.

A heartfelt appreciation goes to Brothers Yao and Simba at Karibu Books. The name *Karibu* means "Welcome" in Swahili, and the entire staff at Karibu exemplify that. Thank you for the support.

Thanks also to my sensational editor at HarperCollins, Kelli Martin. You are a dream to work with. Believe me when I tell you that we are going to make history as a team. Thanks also to Rockelle Henderson at Harper. You all have made me feel very welcome and appreciated. I won't let you down.

Jimmy Vines, thanks for being the coolest agent and for all the outstanding advice. It has been a pleasure working with you. Show me the money, Jimmy!

I want to thank all of the authors whom I have met over the past year. It is truly an honor to share the stage with you. Eric Jerome Dickey, Zane, K'wan, Nikki Turner, B. Lawson, Zachary Tate, Azarel, Tiffany Womble, and all of the others whom I've had the pleasure. Best wishes to you all.

Last, I want to thank all of the artists who inspire. Writers, musicians, actors, and directors. Keep doing what you do. Remember that energy is neither created nor destroyed, only transferred, so keep the flow positive.

BEFORE
I LET GO

Chapter 1

SURVIVING THE GAME

My whole life changed when Shelly said those three little words to me: "Cory, it's over."

We were in the throes of a discussion about how to keep our soon-to-be long-distance relationship alive and well when I left home to go to Atlanta for graduate school. At the time, getting a good job and making plenty of cash were my main concerns. I'd never been rich, but I wasn't prepared to struggle due to bad decisions either. I believed wholeheartedly that an MBA from Georgia Tech in project management was sure to open a few doors for me in the future.

I'd done well in undergrad, but it wasn't as if schools were beating down the doors to get me to choose them. I had attended Morgan State University, a small black school thirty miles from my home in the suburbs of Washington, D.C. It was no secret that the prominent graduate schools held that against you. Their unspoken mantra seemed to shout "Sure, you may have performed well against your peers, but that doesn't mean that you can make it here with the privileged." That's why when I was accepted to grad school at Tech, I chose to go there instead of even *thinking* about applying to Temple, where Shelly was headed to work on her master's.

The fact that I was leaving the D.C. area and heading down south meant that we wouldn't be within driving distance, but I was convinced we could make it work. I knew it would be difficult missing her. Through my years at Morgan State it had always been easy to find me. If I wasn't hanging out downtown in the clubs with Brendan and

Nate, then it had been a safe bet that Shelly and I were together. Adjustments would have to be made. I'd assured her there would be long weekends and holidays for us to see one another. Hard as it is to believe now, I had had no idea that I was tearing Shelly's heart apart in ways that I couldn't have figured out at the time.

After she'd rocked my world with her statement, Shelly didn't look me in the eyes. I was speechless, trying to figure out where she was coming from. She went on to say, "A boyfriend 750 miles away can't meet my needs, Cory."

Her words and attitude made her seem like a different person. During the three years we had been together she had never given me any drama other than an occasional lovers' quarrel, and at first I expected this spat to be no different. But somehow Shelly had turned as cold as ice. I'd thought that I'd picked up on her fears, and maybe she was just feeling unsure of our being able to maintain the relationship over the long distance. When I questioned her about it she told me that she definitely had concerns, but not just about me remaining faithful. When I asked her what she'd meant by that, she flatly said, "When the cat is away the mouse will play."

"So what are you saying?" I asked her apprehensively.

"C'mon, Cory. Do I need to spell it out for you? Be realistic. I . . . I . . . just don't think we can expect to make it. There'll be so many women down there."

"And there'll be so many men up in Philly."

She'd stood up from the couch and said, "Yeah, that too."

I lost my temper at that point. I remember saying some nasty things and hearing her cursing me back in a combination of English and Spanish. Shelly was Puerto Rican and always spoke in Spanish, her native tongue, when she got mad or emotional. She didn't stop until I walked out her front door. Like any young couple we'd had a few major fights, but somehow we'd managed to make up each time. The only difference was that this time, in two days, she'd be leaving for Philly, and I was heading to Atlanta.

She didn't ring my phone during those two days, and when I finally called her to apologize, her younger sister Nina made it a point to tell me that Shelly had gone out on a movie date to see *He Got Game*. If she was trying to make me jealous, it had worked.

It worked so well, in fact, that my mind began to race with doubts about whether or not I should have ever trusted her.

At that moment I cut her off from my love and me as far as I was concerned. I hung up and began packing for my trip and my life in Atlanta. I was leaving early. I knew she would probably be calling back later, but I wanted to make sure that it was too late. I called my boys, Brendan and Nate, to see if either of them wanted to ride with me on the ten-hour drive to Atlanta. They both were willing to roll down to keep me company but neither was ready, and my anger wouldn't let me wait around.

It turned out to be better that I was alone. I'm not ashamed to admit that I shed a few tears on my ride down 85. I don't know why I tortured myself by listening to all of that damned slow music. K-Ci and JoJo's "All My Life," Brian McKnight's *Anytime*, and don't get me started on R. Kelly. By the time I reached Charlotte my rage had given way to paranoia. I had envisioned R. Kelly going half on a baby with my girl simply because she reminded him of his jeep.

My shattered ego coupled with my confusion and suddenly everything was all starting to make sense. I reasoned that Shelly must have been cheating all along. That was why she hadn't made a fuss about my decision to not go to school up North with her.

"That bitch." I said that to myself over and over again with each stretch of passing highway. I made up my mind somewhere on that interstate that when I got to Atlanta I was going to be the one keeping it on the down low with someone else's lady. Nate had always beaten the chicks to the punch with the trickery, and he had never endured half the problems with his women that most men faced in relationships. Instead of dealing with drama, he did dirty then cut things off before the women could do dirty back to him.

He'd told me that all women are capable of cheating, but not every woman is capable of loving you right. Which meant that you're more likely to get a cheater than a good woman. With that in mind a brother had to look out for himself first. And I knew that if anyone knew women, it was Nate. He said that you had to think crazy like a woman if you wanted to survive the game. He did more than survive the game; he seemed to have mastered it. Brendan, on the other hand, had had major problems not getting steamrolled by every woman he dealt with. I was determined not to be like him.

As far as I was concerned, from that point on, Shelly had ruined it for the women crossing my path in the future. I hadn't planned to become an all-out dog or anything, but I definitely wasn't taking any more shit off women. Above all, I was looking out for number one.

Though it was hard getting over Shelly, the distance helped. The next two years went by quickly, and I barely remember everything or everyone that I did. Atlanta was the bomb. I finished school and landed a job in the sales and acquisitions department of Pavillion Satellite Corporation that started me off with $86,000 a year. I also made a few good friends in Atlanta, mostly buddies I played ball with at Run and Shoot and occasionally hit the clubs with. However, they could never replace my right and left arms. Nate and Brendan were an impossible act to follow. They kept my spirits up through any rough times. I never told them that thoughts of Shelly still haunted me, but I think they knew. It seemed as though they always knew just when to call or set up a trip down.

They came down to visit almost every other month, and when they did it was always a wild weekend. Nate would tell me that with all the honeys in Atlanta I should have been screwing more. Brendan was always letting me know that I had changed a lot. He would say that, although I seemed more mature, I didn't seem to be as righteous as I once was. On one trip he stated that he couldn't believe I hadn't gotten into a serious relationship since Shelly and I had broken up.

What I had neglected to explain to him was that I *was* in a serious relationship. The only thing was that my girlfriend was married. She also happened to be one of my former professors at Georgia Tech and about ten years older than me. I kept that one to myself for a while.

Chapter 2

WHAT YOU WON'T DO FOR LOVE

I had never imagined that I would get involved with another man's wife. It wasn't as though I didn't have any single women to choose from while I was in Atlanta. The ratio had to be somewhere around 10 to 1. I think that getting involved with Paula stemmed from the emptiness that I felt after Shelly and I had broken up. I was trying to fill a hole in my heart that was more like a bottomless pit. Even with all of the lovely sisters in Atlanta, Paula was the first woman I met who had truly fascinated me by stimulating my mind as well as my body.

On top of that, it didn't hurt that Paula was fine. I had even fantasized about her many times while I was taking her course, International Business 405, but I had just chalked it up as a crush. That was, until one night when a couple of my coworkers and I met up with one another at a club in downtown Atlanta called Churchill Grounds.

Churchill Grounds was located on Peachtree Street near the Fox Theatre. Thankfully, it was less than twenty minutes from the job. At six o'clock, when we arrived, the place was just starting to become packed. I was glad that we wouldn't have to wait for a table, or worse, stand in line to get into the place, like those who arrived after seven.

We enjoyed the atmosphere that the Grounds was famous for during its Friday night happy hour. We all gobbled down appetizers while we listened to a local jazz band play in the background.

I made my way through the club and found a comfortable seat at the bar. I could see the stage clearly from where I was sitting. The band was grooving. They were featuring a female vocalist, who was dressed in a shiny, snake-skinned dress. She was doing a rendition of "The Sweetest Taboo" and was belting out the notes just like Sade herself. I was slowly bobbing my head to the beat, almost in a trance from the music and the Remy Martin I had been sipping, when I felt a soft hand gently grab my shoulder. And in the same motion, before I could turn to see who had this delicate touch, she brought her lips close enough to my ears to whisper, "Young man, are you sure that you're old enough to be in this club?"

I turned around to see the object of my biggest crush since leaving elementary school. She was standing there smiling, wearing a tight-fitting dress that made me do a double take. I felt as though I was the star in the opening scene of a jazzy urban love story. The ambience, atmosphere, and chemistry were almost too perfect for a love scene. She was as beautiful as I remembered, if not more.

Luckily, I was enjoying a nice buzz from the two hours of drinking. It helped keep me calm and cool, because even though it was out of character for me, I had to admit I felt a little intimidated by Paula. I know I shouldn't have, because things were different now. I was no longer a student sneaking glances at her. I had graduated from Tech and was probably making as much money as she was. I was confident in my appearance, because I was sure that with one look at the four-buttoned Armani suit and Prada loafers I was wearing, it would be clear to her that I had arrived.

With dredged-up confidence and a cool summoned from within, I returned her comment, "Well, fancy meeting my favorite professor and *dream* girl here." I shot her a smile that let her know how happy I was to have run into her.

She placed her hands on her hips. "Dream girl, come on now," she said. she rolled her eyes up into her pretty head. "Cory, you're not in school anymore. There's no need for you to be trying to butter me up, sweetheart. You already got the A from me and long since graduated, I presume." She broke into a quick laughter and showed her pearly white teeth. Then she looked over her shoulder as if she was looking for someone.

"Actually, I just graduated last year," I corrected her, then in an unsolicited response to her action, I asked, "Are you looking for your husband?"

"Oh no, I'm here with some girlfriends of mine. I thought that one of them was standing behind me. She must've walked off."

When she turned back around to face me I looked into her beautiful face, smiled again, and asked, "So, can I buy you a drink, Dr. Cooke?"

She replied sternly, "Didn't I just remind you that you are not in school anymore? Call me Paula, please. And while you're getting used to the idea of that, you can get me an apple martini, thanks."

We talked for a few moments while I ordered her drink. She then informed me that she and her girlfriends had a table on the other side of the bar, near the pool tables. I was all too pleased when she invited me back to her table to sit with them. I introduced her to my co-workers then I told them I was going with Paula and would be back. I doubted I would but I had to at least say so.

I was in heaven as I followed her around the bar and past the pool tables. It was hard to believe how great her body looked at thirty-something. She was unbelievable, and as we walked toward the table where she was seated, my mind filled with lustful thoughts as I watched her hips sway back and forth in front of me. I couldn't see any panty lines, and I imagined her wearing nothing underneath her dress. By the time I reached the table there was a shameful bulge in my pants. I was thankful that my jacket was buttoned.

"Here, sit next to me, Cory." Paula pointed toward an empty chair with a blazer draped over it. She then introduced me to the two women seated at the table.

I was thrilled to be joining the group. I sat down and inched my chair a little closer to Paula's so she could hear me talking over the band's funky rendition of "Love No Limit" by Mary J. We talked like two old friends. She even laughed at all of my jokes as time flew by. When the last call for alcohol came, her girlfriends announced that they were ready to go.

As the ladies gathered their jackets and purses, Paula told me how much she'd enjoyed talking to me and that she hoped to run into me again. That was all the invitation I needed to give her my phone number.

I, of course, gave her a business card, and then came across a little anxious I'm sure when I wrote my home and cellphone numbers on the back of it. I didn't even care. It had all happened so fast. I wasn't even thinking that she had been my teacher or that she was a married woman probably ten years my senior. All I could think about was that beautiful face and lovely ass. I wanted her so badly but doubted that anything would materialize from our chance encounter. That was until my phone rang at 3:00 A.M.

I had been asleep for only about an hour or so. "Hello," I whispered in a groggy voice.

"Cory?" the voice on the other end asked.

"This is Cory."

"Hi, handsome man," came the sexy voice on the other end.

"Who is . . ."

She cut me off. "This is Paula. I'm really sorry for calling you so late. I was just having trouble getting off to sleep."

"Paula", I replied. "Oh no, it's fine. I'm up." There was a break in the conversation, and as my consciousness came rushing back to me I continued with, "Aren't you married? Where's your husband?" I asked only because I was curious how she could call me at this hour.

She retorted in a matter-of-fact tone, "My husband is out of town at a conference in Houston. . . . Look, I'm sorry for disturbing you." It sounded as though I had blown it. "I didn't want to give you the wrong impression. I just wanted to talk. I'll talk to you some other time, okay?"

I sat straight up in the bed and wiped the corners of my mouth as I spoke. "No, no. I want to talk to you now. I was just a little surprised that you called. That's all. There is no wrong impression taken." I began to realize that this was my chance, no matter how tired I was. I went on. "Let's talk. Shit, let's go get some breakfast or coffee. Let's go watch the sunrise."

"Are you serious?"

"Extremely! Are you game?"

"I've got a better idea." Paula paused. "Why don't I come over there and fix you breakfast?"

At that moment I believed that the gods were working overtime for me. I quickly accepted her offer. As soon as I had given her directions and hung up the phone, I jumped out of bed to do the quick cleanup job that men do in situations like these. I changed the sheets, put pictures of a girl I'd been dating away, and hid the toothbrush she'd purposely left behind. I thought about trashing all her odds and ends as I removed her shower cap, hairpins, and contact lens cases, emptied the trash cans, and ran the vacuum cleaner. By the time Paula arrived at my place at a little after four in the morning, with a grocery bag filled with eggs, bacon, croissants, and orange juice, my apartment looked like it hadn't had a woman inside of it in months.

I still couldn't believe that she was in my apartment as I sat on one of the kitchen bar stools and watched her cook. I imagined that she was *my* wife as she made her way around my kitchen as if she'd been here before.

The food was delicious. We ate slowly as we shared background information and small talk. After clearing the dishes I walked into the living room, dimmed the lights, and lit a scented candle. As I started the CD player Paula came from the bathroom and joined me on the couch. Her body language communicated that she was unsure of what to do next. So she sat on the far end of the couch. I tapped the couch next to me to let her know I wanted her to slide closer to me. Then I said, "That is, of course, if you don't mind." She smiled as she moved closer and casually pushed me back onto the couch. As we talked with her back on my chest the body heat that we generated started to create sexual tension that could not be ignored. It seemed as though we began to melt into one another.

First, my hands began to massage her neck and shoulders as we talked. Then, almost instinctively my lips began to softly massage the back of her neck. I could smell and taste the Victoria's Secret peach fragrance that had been absorbed into her soft, brown skin. We began to lose ourselves to the passion, her soft moans began to excite me. Even though I had an agenda, the moves I made didn't feel forced or overly programmed. I was thinking that she had to have already decided that she wanted the sex as much as I did. She had to know the deal, coming to my crib at four in the morning. But still, she was a married woman. She may have just wanted the company, I thought for a second, then pinched myself mentally for being stupid.

Her movements were so subtle and delicate, the way she leaned her head back and to the side so that I could slide my lips across her neck. I slid out from behind her and she gracefully lay back onto the couch. I reached down to her feet and pulled her black sandals off. As I stood over her with her foot in my hands, watching her staring up at me, I began to massage the sole of her foot with both hands. My mouth made its way to her toes. This wasn't a practice performed for just anyone, but when a man is fortunate enough to be treated to an angel, he had best show his appreciation in a manner that is not easily forgotten.

I knew that she was enjoying what I was doing, because her eyes were closed and her hands were raking slowly through her hair. As Brian McKnight crooned softly in the background I positioned myself on top of her so that I could kiss her without placing the weight of my body on hers. I worked her lips gently from the corners of her mouth at first, and then I began hungrily kissing her. Our tongues danced a short, slow dance before I left her mouth to venture to her neck again. I had realized when kissing her neck moments before that it was one of her sensitive spots. I also figured that by working that one I would soon get to the sensitive spot between her thighs.

As her breathing went from soft to heavy, my hands began to unbutton her linen top, my lips never breaking contact with her skin. In a matter of seconds the cups of her cream-colored lace bra were flipped up over the top of her beautiful breasts, exposing her perfect nipples. As my tongue softly kissed all over her breasts, her body began to writhe underneath me. Still, I took my time. I rubbed her neck and sucked her shoulders and cupped her breasts before touching the nipples, which were noticeably standing up off her chest. When my lips gently clamped down on them while my tongue flickered over them, I heard her call out my name. "Oh, Cory," she crooned. "C'mon, baby."

Before she had time to change her mind about the impending acts of passion, I was on my knees in front of her with her skirt up above her waist. I swiftly pulled her panties far enough to the side so that my tongue could easily reach her wetness.

As my face found its new home between her magnificent thighs, the temperature in the room seemed to escalate. The sounds and smells we were generating took both of us on a ride. Her hands were on the back of my head, pulling me closer and my tongue deeper. She seemed to forget that I might need to breathe. But it was worth the work of trying to find air. The way she yelled out my name and her body shook when she reached orgasm, made my temporary deprivation of air worth it. We both stripped right there in the living room, with the moonlight shining in from the balcony as our backdrop. There was no time for thinking about what we were doing. No time for guilt, or for reasonable thoughts about what we were doing. There was only passion and lust.

Once when she pushed me back onto the couch, I was half hoping that she was going to return the favor, but she straddled me instead. Within, I was no longer thinking about anything except for how good it felt inside of her, and that this had to be the best sex in the world. I'd enjoyed my share of women, and only once before had I ever felt the insides of a woman who felt like this. For a moment I didn't know if I was inside of a woman or if someone had greased my manhood with the finest oils on earth and was now stroking it with the world's finest silk. Maybe I was caught up in the moment and the fascination of being with this woman whom I'd spent many nights fantasizing about, but I was positive that this was the best sex since Shelly. I would like to be able to say that I worked her long and hard that first round, but that's not how it went. Her grinding and moaning excited me so much that I had exploded in six or seven very intense minutes. Fortunately for me we were not through, and I would be given another chance to show her what I was capable of.

Moving from the couch to the bed was a blur, but I do know that we made some serious love all over my apartment. At one point we were on the balcony with me standing behind her, causing her to release unbridled moans of pleasure as the sun rose over Atlanta.

We were both exhausted by the time we hit the sheets to actually sleep. It was late the next afternoon before she left my apartment to beat her husband home.

There was every indication that, in the beginning, our relationship was based mainly on sex. But so was every relationship that I had ever heard of.

Gradually, though, things changed over the following couple of years. Somehow the sexual attraction gave way to an emotional bond. We grew extremely close, and at times we both seemed to forget the little fact that she was married. Eventually I had to hide that I dated other women. She couldn't handle the fact that I might get into a serious relationship with someone else. Even if I had I doubted that I would have ended things with Paula. If nothing else, I had become seriously attached to her and I often professed that I loved her, though not as intensely as I had her believe.

She often confided in me that she thought her husband was cheating on her but that she didn't care because she had me. She, of course, stayed married, but claimed that she didn't love her husband anymore. Paula admitted that she didn't think she would ever leave him, and I never griped. She had gotten so used to sneaking around with me behind his back, it seemed like there was no need. I knew that she was in love with me, as evidenced by the way that she would do anything for me. No request was too freaky, and no gift was too expensive.

She showered me with gifts, attention, and sex. It never bothered me that she was so dependent on me in her day-to-day life. It was as though she lived for my conversation, romance, and our lovemaking. I treated her as well as I could. I often sent her the white roses and violets that she loved so much but no longer received from her husband. I took her to Hawks basketball games and outlet shopping in Tennessee. We enjoyed the theater, ski trips, and horseback riding. I even took up tennis for her, because she was a Venus and Serena wannabe.

The thing that kept us closest, though, was the fact that more than anything we both enjoyed just being together, laughing, and loving each other. Those moments came mostly at night in my apartment. She would tell her husband that she was doing research and correspondence work with a professor in California for a textbook, and because of the time difference she was required to work into the wee hours of the night at least twice a week. He never questioned this.

I believe that it's safe for women to assume that the only reason why men don't question lies like the ones she told him is because we're too busy being up to no good ourselves. Paula and I never knew when his ignorance would end and perhaps bring a conclusion to our affair, but we both knew it was a day we dreaded.

When I took time to think about what I was doing—getting caught in a situation with a married woman—I felt bad. Not only because I was an adulterer, but also because I enjoyed it so much. It felt safe, believe it or not. I knew that Paula couldn't truly hurt me. The fact of the matter was that she didn't belong to me. The only problem was that she didn't fully understand that I wasn't truly hers either. It wasn't spoken, but it was clear to me that we used each other to get what we needed. She needed somewhere to run from her unfulfilling marriage, and I needed to run from that empty space in my heart that would make itself known to me every time I heard Joe or Maxwell crooning on the radio.

Chapter 3

FRIENDS TILL THE END

Brendan and Renee had been friends since junior high school, when she was one of the smartest girls in class and Brendan was one of the laziest boys. In fact, whenever one of them needed a favor from the other, the first thing that would come out of their mouths was "C'mon now . . . you know how far we go back. At least to the Bush and the Bump." But their friendship was much deeper than convenience. Unlike so many people who call themselves friends today, they shared a genuine love and respect for each other.

They made each other's acquaintance by more than chance. The two of them sat next to each other in three classes because his last name was Shue and hers was Shoreham, and when teachers sat students alphabetically, seldom was there a last name in between. Renee saw those seating arrangements as an opportunity to get to know one of the cutest guys in the eighth grade, and Brendan saw it as an opportunity to copy her homework and cheat off of her tests all year. They both accomplished their goals, and out of their newfound union grew a lasting friendship.

They had been there for each other in the darkest of times. During their junior year in high school Renee gave her virginity to a twenty-five-year-old married man, who told her the next day that he didn't think it would be a good idea for her to call him anymore. Without hesitation or reservation, it was Brendan who called the guy's wife and told her about the situation—before breaking the windshield of the guy's car.

Brendan also took half the money he had been saving for a car during his freshman year of college and wired it to Renee to pay for her last-minute airline ticket home from Boston when her father was in a near-fatal car accident. Renee long regarded that act as the nicest thing anyone had ever done for her.

For her part, Renee was the one Brendan counted on when he needed help doing almost anything. Whether it was a ride when his wheels were down or typing his term papers, Renee accommodated Brendan. When Brendan and Trina's breakup left him so heartbroken he could barely get out of bed, let alone go to work, it was Renee who refused to let him out of her sight for nearly two weeks. Nor did she ever tell him "I told you so," even though she had warned him about Trina several times.

Renee's suspicions had been based mostly on the fact that she had heard rumors about Trina in the hair salon, and from mutual acquaintances. Even though Renee couldn't stand Trina, she never thought much would materialize from her indiscretions. She definitely had no idea that Trina eventually would crush her best friend.

The moment of truth had come when Brendan left work early on a hot August afternoon and went to pick up a couple of tickets for a Jill Scott concert at Pier Six in nearby Baltimore Harbor that was to take place that evening. Brendan knew how much Trina loved Jill Scott, and since the Roots were performing with her, he was hyped up about seeing the show himself.

Brendan pulled into Trina's parking lot and was about to park in her reserved parking space when he noticed a forest green Toyota Sequoia parked in her spot. He expected her spot to be empty because she'd dropped her car at the dealer's for service that morning. He parked his Corvette next to the truck in the spot that was plainly marked with the word "visitors" stenciled on the curb and headed off toward her apartment building.

As he walked up the steps to her building he laughed to himself about how he had better be prepared to hear Trina cussing about her inconsiderate parking place intruder once he delivered the news that someone had parked in her fifty-dollar-a-month spot again. Brendan's heart was filled with anticipation to see his sweetheart of almost two years as he reached her door. He was looking forward to surprising her with the tickets. Just as he was about to grab the knocker, the door eased open. In an instant Brendan's heart fell into his stomach; he saw a brother standing in front of him in wrinkled linen slacks and a white dress shirt that had only one side tucked in. Under the stranger's arm he held a blazer and an attaché case with a tie hanging out of it.

He looked at Brendan's face and saw the shock and anger and realized that he should depart as quickly as possible. The stranger nervously called to Trina and informed her that she had company, and hastily sped out the door past the still stunned Brendan without even an "excuse me."

Brendan was still standing at the door as he watched the guy disappear down the steps and out of the building. He stood there partly in disbelief and partly in preparation for what he feared he had stumbled upon. Before the door could swing shut Brendan managed to snap out of his semicomatose state and catch it. Trina was calling out to her guest, not realizing that he'd already left the apartment. She was asking if it was the paperboy, all the while walking toward the living room. Her eyes nearly popped out of her head when Brendan greeted her with a searing look on his face that scared Trina to her soul. There was not much that she could say, since she was standing there in only a sexy silk robe, with her hair all over her head.

A vicious argument ensued. For most of it Trina tried to deny that any actual intercourse had taken place. Finally she tried to explain that he was an old friend who had stopped by and that things had gotten out of hand and eventually . . . one thing had led to another. All the while she insisted that he had not penetrated her. Brendan was not buying it for one minute. He began tuning her out while she was explaining herself. Somewhere during their argument he sat down on the arm of her love seat and placed his hands on his forehead.

His mind began to fill with thoughts ranging from choking her right then and there to wondering who was the dark-skinned brother who obviously had just finished body slamming his girl. Suddenly the image of the stranger's face popped into Brendan's mind, and it was the same face of the car salesman who had sold Trina her brand new Toyota Avalon just three weeks before. Then, all of a sudden, in the middle of the argument, Brendan jumped up and sped off toward the bed-room. Trina quickly caught onto the idea that he was going in for some concrete evidence. She gave chase, but it was too late. Before she could catch him he was inside her bedroom with the door locked. She began banging on the door. Brendan was oblivious to her screams and de-mands to be let into the bedroom. He looked into the trash can ex-pecting to see a condom wrapper. When there wasn't one he felt slightly relieved and thought for a second that she might be telling the truth. Then he moved to the bed. He stared for a second taking a quick inventory of it. He pulled back the sheets. Immediately his heart sank and his stomach felt as if it had shot up through his chest and was now lodged in his throat. She was busted. There was a wet spot on that bed that was the unmistakable result of some funky sex.

Brendan's blood began to boil as he walked to the window and slid it open and punched the screen out. Then he moved to the closet, which was already open. He could make out Trina's muffled cries and banging on the other side of the door: "What are you doing, Brendan? What are you doing? Open the door."

Brendan began grabbing everything on a hanger that his money had paid for and began tossing it out of the window—and inadvertently a few things that he hadn't paid for. By the time he had finished throw-ing a good two thousand dollars worth of clothes out of the window, Trina had gotten a butter knife and pried open the door. She came in crying and cursing. Brendan's face showed a picture of hate as he pulled the plug of the twenty-seven-inch Sony flat-screen television from the wall and yanked the cable wires from the back of the set. He was so hot at that point that if it had been 20 degrees colder in the room steam would have risen from his head. She read his body lan-guage loud and clear, which is why she didn't try to keep him from hauling the television set that he had bought her a month earlier out of the bedroom and through the front door.

He loaded the television in the passenger seat of his car and walked around to the back of her building, retrieved the clothes that he had thrown out of the window, and tossed them through the open roof of his car. By that time, Trina had thrown something on but was barefoot as she ran down the walkway toward Brendan's moving car. She was begging him, "Please don't take all of my clothes. . . . What am I going to wear to work?"

Brendan rolled down his window and attempted to throw the remains of a Slurpee on Trina, but he missed and hit the Hyundai behind her. As he pulled off and left Trina standing in the middle of the parking lot, there was the deafening sound of Brendan's Pirellis squealing as he peeled out of the complex.

Trina hadn't realized that they had created a scene. She stood there in her cutoff jeans shorts and a Washington Mystics T-shirt that was turned inside out; her hair was a mess, and tears were still running down her cheeks. Several people took notice of her and shook their heads in disbelief. Finally, the fly-assed sister in 2C who seldom spoke had been busted. She hung her head down low, as if doing that would make her invisible to the onlookers as she walked back into the house.

That was one day and one relationship that Brendan had tried desperately to forget about. But Trina had made it hard for him. She called him continuously for three months after their breakup, trying to get back together with him. As bad as he missed caressing that cocoa brown skin of hers and seeing that curvaceous five-feet-four-inch naked frame, there was no way he'd ever give her another chance to rip his heart apart.

There was no denying that he missed her. She was the most well-rounded sister he had ever had the pleasure of being involved with intimately. They would talk about everything, from politics, to sports, to home interior decorations. All of the kinky things that she used to do in bed with him crossed his mind from time to time as well. Especially when he was enduring one of his dry spells, as he liked to call the periods when he wasn't getting much good sex, if any sex at all.

He chalked up this disastrous relationship as one to grow on, and did his best to keep on keeping on. It was hard because, as nice a guy as Brendan was, he wasn't the kind of guy who met a lot of women. Even in a city like Washington, D.C., where the female-to-male ratio is rumored to be as high as 8 to 1, a fairly handsome brother, with a nice personality and a decent-paying job, can find it hard to meet a nice young woman, let alone one who isn't into playing games, like Trina.

In addition, Brendan had grown a little apprehensive about approaching women due to the little bit of weight he'd picked up over the previous few years. It was nothing that he could not have gotten under control with a few months of serious exercise and a strict diet, but his devotion to working out was weak, to say the least. Besides, he had bigger problems to worry about than being a few pounds overweight.

Chapter 4

SATURDAY NITE LIVE

Brendan walked into the house and dropped his keys on the counter of the breakfast bar. He didn't bother turning on any lights on the first floor because, even though he had only moved into Renee's townhouse two weeks earlier, he knew his way around in the dark as if he had lived there for years. He turned the corner and ran up the stairs. As he entered his bedroom he saw light coming from under Renee's door. He didn't bother to announce his presence, because if she had company he didn't want to disturb her. Before Brendan had moved in, he and Renee had sat down at T.G.I. Friday's over lunch and made a list of rules that would allow two old and dear friends to become roommates and still remain friends. Respecting the other's privacy was somewhere near the top.

As Brendan was showering he heard a knock on the door. "Yeah. What's up?" He knew it was Renee. She spoke loudly through the door, but Brendan couldn't hear her, so he told her to open the door.

She turned the knob and stuck her head in the door. Greeted with a burst of steam she asked, "Whew, is it hot enough for you in here, B?" She laughed at herself, and continued, "Your phone was ringing and the machine didn't pick up, so I answered it. It was your silly-ass cousin. I told him you were in the shower getting pretty and that I would have you call him back in a few, okay?"

Brendan wanted to be sure he knew whom Renee was talking about. "It was Shue, right?"

She replied, "Yeah. Who else is going to be calling at prime time on a Saturday night tryin' to find a party partner other than his crazy butt?" She was about to close the door but then opened it and asked, "So, are you all hanging out tonight?"

"Yep."

"Where?"

Brendan exaggerated his tone, "Daaaamn, Mom, if it's all right I'm going to a little get-together at one of Shue's friend's house up on Sixteenth Street."

"Shue's *friend?*" Her tone was curious and accusing at the same time. Shue, who was actually named Everson Shue, Jr., was Brendan's first cousin, and he described himself as "bisexual in a transitional phase" to becoming completely gay. He said he loved men but was having trouble getting over his urge for women from time to time. Renee continued. "Is it one of thooose parties?" She giggled out her words.

"Actually, it will probably be a mixed crowd up in that camp. Why, would you like to come?"

"No, thanks," she muttered. "Once I get Barry's boring ass up out of here I'm going to get some rest so I can get up and go to church in the morning, where you should . . ."

He cut her off midsentence. "Don't start, Mrs. Holy Roller, getting laid at midnight and in church by nine."

"Ooohh, you are so trifling, Brendan. You didn't even have to go there. But since you did . . . don't you drink too much tonight and end up bringing home a nigga." Renee burst into laughter and told Brendan to have a good time as she walked out of the door.

Brendan put on some navy blue wool slacks, a gray Donna Karan sweater, and a brand-new pair of black Ferragamos that he had spent a third of his weekly paycheck on earlier in the day, before leaving the store. As he looked for his keys on the bed and in his coat pocket, he called Shue to let him know he was on the way to pick him up. Before he hung up, Brendan asked if he thought the host would mind if he brought Nate along. Shue assured him that it would be no problem.

Brendan looked around the room for a second, and then remembered that his keys were on the breakfast bar. He slipped on his jacket and ran down the steps like a kid on Christmas morning, grabbed his keys, and was about to head out when his cell began to vibrate. He didn't recognize the number, so he chose not to answer. He thought about not calling back, but feared that it might be Jaqueline Allen, the general manager at Nordstrom where he was the manager of the women's shoe department. He decided to return the call from the car.

Brendan scanned the radio in the car as he exited the parking lot of the townhouse development and turned onto Central Avenue. He heard Michelle Wright on WPGC advertising a party that they were hosting tonight at the VIP club downtown. He figured that if the party at Shue's friend's house wasn't jumping, he might leave and go check out the party downtown. He turned the music down low enough to hear his cell clearly as he dialed.

"Hello," the voice on the other line blurted. The voice repeated itself. "Hello." Brendan replied, "Sorry, I'm on a cellphone and you blinked out momentarily. Did someone there call Brendan?"

"Yeah. Don't be funny, motherfucker, you know who this is." He recognized the voice on the other end. It was Trina.

"Trina?"

"Yeah, you know it." She was as sassy as ever. She went on. "Look, negro, we have a couple of things to discuss. And I think you know what they are." He started to hang up on her, but he knew that she would just keep calling him all night.

"Look . . . ," Brendan said, not wanting to get into it with Trina and ruin the good mood he was in. "I'll give you a ring tomorrow and . . ."

She cut him off. "No, I want you to come over here tonight. This is important."

"I don't even know where you are," he shot back.

"I'm at home. I had the number changed last week. This is my new number. I suggest that you write it down and use it." She added, "And don't think that I'm scheming by asking you to come over here. What we need to talk about really is important."

"Well, I'm on the way out now. It'll be late when I finish . . . maybe two or three. I'll call you when I'm on the way . . . that is, if I decide to come."

Trina sucked her teeth. "Just call me when you get here so I can get up to answer the door."

Brendan already had guessed that she was up to something. What could she possibly want him to come over so late for? Part of him was hoping that he might get laid if he went over there, but he feared going over and wasting his time arguing with her about the past.

Brendan had a feeling that all she wanted to do was ask him about his moving in with Renee, which he had intended to keep silent about. He had lied and told her that he was moving in with a coworker whom she didn't know in order to avoid the drama.

He definitely didn't want to listen to Trina tripping off his new living arrangements tonight. He had managed to keep it from her for three months, but Nate had slipped up one evening earlier in the week and mentioned to Trina's best friend, Kim, that he'd be busy helping Brendan move his new bed into Renee's house. Nate dated Kim from time to time, but usually only when he had absolutely nothing else to do. He had only volunteered the info on Brendan's move in order to get out of a date he had promised Kim.

Kim, of course, immediately relayed the information to Trina, and here was the drama. Brendan's only wonder was why it took Trina nearly a week to bring it to him. He was unsure of what other business Trina needed to discuss that was so important, but he was in no particular hurry to hear it.

As Brendan sped around the Beltway, he listened to Usher singing "You Got It Bad" and wondered if stars actually went through the things they sang about. If they didn't, then how come the lyrics to the songs they recorded always seemed to be so true to life? He made a note to ask a singer the next time he bumped into one.

As he neared the College Park exit, Brendan reached into his dashboard compartment to get a stick of Trident. He passed Home Depot, whipped into the Seven Springs apartment complex, and double-parked in front of Shue's building. He jumped out and walked to the front-door buzzer. He knew the gray-haired security guard seated just inside of the lobby could see him standing there, but he didn't bother to come and open the door. He pushed in the code to ring Shue's apartment.

"Hello." The muffled voice came through the speaker.

"Yo, it's me. Come on down. I don't feel like parking, and hurry up."

"All right already, B, hold your horses, I'm coming." Shue hung up the phone.

Brendan mumbled to himself as he walked back to the car, "I know this fool ain't ready."

Brendan turned around to see the security guard coming out of the door. "Hey there, son. You can't park there."

"I'm not gonna park here. My cousin is on the way down."

"Well, I'm just warning you, son. Deez summabitches is quick to give out a ticket. Two hundred bucks at a time, too."

Brendan replied, "Well, I definitely don't want to get one of those bad boys. I just buzzed up, though, and my cousin is on the way down." Brendan had no idea how long that would take.

The security guard walked a little closer, as if he was investigating. "With a nice ride like this, I'm sure you can afford a ticket. Heh, heh." When he laughed he showed his raggedy set of gold teeth. They were only gold because of the amount of plaque on them. The guard continued, "It sho' is a pretty one. What is it? One of them Japanese models?" Brendan laughed to himself as he noticed that the guard looked like the character Otis from Martin Lawrence's show.

Brendan replied, "No, it's a Chevrolet, sir," and cleared his throat, wishing Shue would hurry down so that he could leave before Otis asked to take it for a spin.

After a few more moments of chitchat with the old rent-a-cop, Shue finally came through the lobby door.

"What's up, cuz? Hey, Mr. Ennis." He patted the old man on the shoulder as he headed out of the building.

"Hey there, son," Mr. Ennis shot back.

"Man, get in the car so we can go before it starts to rain."

"Is it supposed to rain? Lord, I didn't see anything about rain," Shue said, looking up toward the sky. "I might need to change."

"Man, whatever. I will pull off and leave your ass right here." Brendan checked out Shue's attire. Shue had on some snug-fitting Versace jeans, a maroon V-neck sweater, and a pair of V2 boots. He was carrying a suede jacket in his hand.

"B, don't act like that. I cannot ruin this jacket in the rain." He held it out. "It's brand-new, baby boy, and of course you know it is brand name. Shoot, on top of that I might have to take it back tomorrow." He snapped his fingers as he laughed at himself, and he slid into the passenger seat of the car.

"Look, I don't know if it's gonna rain for sure. What you wanna do?" Brendan was on the verge of cursing Shue out, and they hadn't even left the parking lot.

Shue smacked his lips together. "Just drive."

As they got back onto the Beltway Brendan asked Shue to call Nate to make sure he would be at the meeting spot up on the Avenue.

"Nobody answered at his house."

"Hit him on the cell."

"What's the num . . ."

Brendan cut him off. "777-1848, that's 301."

Nate answered, "What's up?"

"Yo, B, where y'all at."

Brendan turned the radio down. "I'm at New Hampshire Avenue. Where are you?"

"I'm here at the Amoco waitin' on y'all niggas."

"All right. I'll be there in a minute."

"Later." Nate hung up and reclined the seat back in his brand-new Lexus SC 430.

Chapter 5

PLAYER EXTRAORDINAIRE

Nate was becoming a little impatient. He had only been waiting at the Amoco gas station for about five minutes, but he hated to wait for anything or anyone longer than *he* deemed necessary. He was tapping his finger on the bottom of the steering wheel and bobbing his freshly shaved bald head to the sounds of Jay-Z that were pumping loudly through the ten speakers in his car. He was beginning to feel a slight buzz from the weed he was smoking as he leaned back in the slightly reclined seat of his car watching the smoke drift out of his windows. He sat up, flipped down the visor, and opened the vanity mirror on it so that he could stare at himself while he lip-synched to the song "Girls." He thought about how sexy the women in the video were and hoped he would run up on something like that tonight.

Nate could stare at himself all night, especially when he was looking as good as he knew he was tonight. "Pretty chocolate nigga, you are. Mmmph," he whispered.

Nathan Montgomery was indeed his own biggest fan. He had to be, though. Who else would have been devoted enough to run "Big Nate's Fan Club," as he liked to call the ever-changing group of nine to ten women who comprised his social group of special friends. He called himself "Big Nate" in recognition of the reputation that he'd earned for being such an extraordinary player. He also figured that the size of his penis warranted some special recognition, since it obviously did its share of the work keeping him on top (literally and figuratively speaking).

There was no denying that the brother had big game. Though he was only six feet one and 190 pounds, well defined but by no means a bodybuilder, his slightly bowed legs, slender frame, and dark Hershey's chocolate brown complexion were all hot attributes after the dark-skinned brothers made a comeback in the nineties. It had become "in" to be a dark-skinned brother again. Women had long grown tired of giving all the play to pretty, light-skinned niggas who dogged them. Now they wanted to give it to pretty, dark-skinned niggas who dogged them instead. Nate didn't buy into the philosophy of color preference among women, though. He believed that women will go for any man they find attractive, and on top of that, he deduced that what makes a man attractive to a woman had to be much more complex than his skin complexion. A handsome brother was a handsome brother—point-blank.

As Nate checked the time on the clock on his radio, his radar began to go off. Nate's eyes zoomed in toward the cashier's island as he saw a well-filled, short, black skirt standing at the window paying for gas. As he saw the skirt turn around and strut toward the pump where the black Honda Prelude was parked, the preliminary verdict was in. The face didn't look too bad from this distance, but he definitely needed to get a closer look. Nate started the engine of his car and slowly pulled up to the rear of her car. He wanted to make sure she was unaccompanied by man or child.

He pulled up closer. It wasn't that he discriminated against kids, but the less distractions a woman had in her life, the better for Nate to work his magic. He could almost see inside her car. No man in the car. Closer. No kids. Closer. No car seat. Bingo. It was on.

Nate's window rolled down and he looked clearly into the woman's face. He was able to get a perfect glimpse before she looked his way. He saw a head of freshly done light-brown hair with blonde highlights, full lips, and a clear cinnamon-colored complexion. Nate backed his car up to the island behind hers and got out of the car. He pretended to need something from the cashier's booth so he would have an excuse to walk past her car.

"Damn. This bitch is tight," Nate thought, as he breezed past her.

As the numbers on the gas pump began to race, she looked up and noticed Nate staring in her face. Nate smiled at her, and his expression yelled to her that she was about to come under the attack of his uninvited advances. She looked back toward the pump and acted as though she was really interested in watching the numbers move.

"Excuse me, sweetheart, you got a second?" Nate delivered the serve.

Her eyebrows showed a hint of annoyance, as if to say, "Nigga, puhleeze. I don't feel like it." Her mouth said nothing, but her thoughts were clear: *Here comes another weak-assed brother who thinks he's gonna work his mack routine.*

"I know you must've been rushing: you didn't give a brother a chance to pump your gas for you." He paused and waited a second, and then saw she was about to comment.

As she moved the strands of hair away from her mouth with her finger she returned. "First of all, you didn't offer. Second of all, I can pump my own gas, thank you." The gas stopped pumping. She turned as she was putting the nozzle back.

"Well, Miss Lady, I appreciate your independence, but chivalry does still exist occasionally. You ought to take advantage of it when you see it." He was still grinning.

"Oh yeah, that's what you are, chivalrous? Am I correct?" She looked annoyed as she opened the door to her car.

Nate knew he was about to lose this one.

"Yeah, that's me. Something like the Black Knight in the Martin Lawrence flick. This is my chariot right here. So why don't you let me come pick you up one evening soon so that I can take you out and make you feel like the queen that you are." He saw her crack a half smile as she slid into her car. He was still alive. He walked over to her window and motioned for her to roll it down.

She obliged him.

"Look here, I . . ." Nate was cut off by the sound of a honking horn behind him. They both looked to the rear of her car. It was Brendan.

He waved Brendan off and held up a finger to say, hold up a minute. "Look, I'm not going to waste your time at this gas station, but you look damn good. If you are even half as beautiful on the inside as you are on the outside, then I *need* to get to know you. I'm not going to go into the whole spiel about whether or not you got a man, but let me get your number and we'll get into the details tomorrow."

She smiled and said, "What's your name?"

"Nathan, but you can call me Nate. All my friends do."

"Well, Nate, why don't you give me your number, and I'll call you."

Nate giggled to himself. Why the hell did women always say that same thing? They knew good and well if they liked you or not. Who did they think they were to decide when and if they would call? Nate never went for that. As far as he was concerned, plenty of women had shot him that same dumb-ass line, and he in turn had called their bluff. If they weren't giving up their digits, he damned sure wasn't giving up his. Sometimes when women tried that he'd shoot them a blank. It served them right for playing themselves. Nate figured that any honey in D.C. should be glad to have a nigga on his level trying to make their acquaintance, anyway.

Nate shot back, "What's your name, sweetheart?"

"India," she said, not sounding if she was sure she wanted to give it to him.

"Andy?"

"No. I said, 'India,' like India. Arie."

"Oh." Nate nodded. "That's a pretty name for a pretty girl," Nate offered. "Well, India, a fair exchange ain't no robbery. I value my number, and I'm sure you value yours, too. So go ahead and write yours down right quick for me, and here's mine."

It was as if he had used the Jedi mind trick on her. She scrambled for a pen and wrote the number down. Confidence will get you there when nothing else will.

As Nate leaned on the door of her passenger seat, he caught her eyes scanning his finger for a wedding ring. But then again, he thought she may have been admiring the diamond-encrusted Rolex he had dangling loosely on his wrist. Eye candy is what he called the flashy material things he owned, such as the watch, the cars, and even the expensive Italian furniture in his crib. Nate reached out to take the number from her hand, and as he removed the card he gently stroked her hand.

She had a puzzled look on her face. "What was that for?" she asked.

"I just wanted to make sure that I got underneath your skin before you left." He paused. "It's an old trick my uncle taught me when I was young. Watch, you'll be thinking about me until we talk."

"All of that from you brushing my hand. What are you supposed to have, some magical touch or something?" she chuckled as she spoke. "You might change my mind about this."

"You just wait and see," Nate said, as he reentered his still open car.

"I hope I don't regret this," India said, as she rolled her car window up.

"The pleasure will be all yours, baby. All yours," Nate mumbled once she pulled off.

He waved for Brendan to pull up beside him. Shue's window went down as Brendan's car paralleled Nate's.

"What's up, baby boy?" Shue chimed.

"What's up, nigga?" Brendan added.

Nate huffed. "What's up is, it took y'all fools forever to get here."

Shue smacked his lips. "Mmmph, it looks like you kept yourself busy with that girlie, though."

"Yeah, what was up with that? You just got those digits, huh," Brendan asked.

"Oh man, shit yeah. She was vicious, too," Nate answered.

"Vicious? Why in the world would you want to call her if she was vicious?" Shue asked, with a hand on his chest as if he was choking.

"Vicious just means she was all of it, Shue. Do I have to explain everything to you, fool? Since you decided to be gay, you are sooo late." Nate laughed.

"Excuse the hell out of me, smart-ass. And I did not decide to be gay. Gay is a state of being for me, okay. I've just decided not to fight it anymore. I always have been gay."

Nate cut Shue off. "Please shut this nigga up, B."

Brendan nudged Shue. "Yeah, be quiet man. I'm sure you'll have a big chance to express your gayness at this party. You ready, Nate?"

"I'm following you, dog." Brendan pulled off, and Nate whipped out onto Georgia Avenue right behind him.

As Nate followed closely behind, his mind raced with thoughts about the type of scene he would encounter when they arrived at the party. Would everyone there be gay except for him and Brendan? If it turned out to be like that, he would just have to jet out. He had faith that Shue wouldn't set him and Brendan up like that. Shue had mentioned to Nate on a couple of occasions that there were always freaky women who showed up at Amir's parties. It wasn't like Nate was homophobic or anything. He had no problems with gays as long as they didn't come on to him. As for tonight's action, though, Shue had Brendan and Nate convinced that the party would be full of lesbian and bisexual women who would be down for all types of wild adventures. That was good enough for Nate to at least give it a try.

Brendan had suspected that his cousin was gay from the age of thirteen, because Shue would never play any rough sports or sneak into the triple-X movie theaters down on Fourteenth Street on Saturday afternoons with him and Cory when they were kids. His sexual preference stayed up for debate, however, because Shue was always in the company of the prettiest and flyest honeys at H.D. Woodson High. But when Shue announced that he was going to the Rhode Island Avenue Beauty Academy right after graduation, it all but let the cat out of the bag.

Chapter 6

OFF THE HOOK

The party was in full swing by the time the three of them arrived. Shue knew that Amir, the host of the party, had plenty of cash, but Brendan and Nate were impressed by the amount of money that obviously had been spent on this party. There was a forty-foot, plush, red carpet that came out of the double doors that led to the foyer of the huge brick colonial. There were two young men dressed in dark gray suits and leather gloves standing on the curb. They were offering to provide valet service to the guests if they wanted it. There were at least three hundred peach-colored balloons tied to the railing in front of the doorway and the gate running up into the driveway. Amir had an American flag made out of Christmas lights in the front yard to show his patriotism. Small white lights decorated the bushes and lined the insides of the twin fifteen-foot bay windows of the living room. As they moved toward the house, Brendan could see couples dancing and flashing lights coming from the inside. Just inside the door there was a study that was closed off by a desk in front of its door. A perky little white girl in a full-length dress stood behind the desk checking invitations and taking coats.

As the trio made their way through the foyer Nate looked to the left and noticed an ice sculpture depicting the statue of David in the dining room.

"Yo, B, check that shit out," Nate said, as he nudged Brendan.

"Daaamn, that's top flight, huh?" Brendan replied, as he turned back toward Nate.

"You ain't lyin'. And look at all that champagne on that table." Nate motioned his head for Brendan to look at the bottles of Moët and Cristal champagne in ice buckets lined up in rows of at least ten on the table behind the ice sculpture. "That's where I'm about to be."

Nate tapped Shue on the shoulder when he returned from checking his jacket. Shue had been reading the coat-check girl her rights and made her promise to take special care of it because it was a Dolce & Gabbana jacket that he claimed had to be ordered four months ago. "Yo, Shue baby, what's up with the cupid ice figure? What is that, some type of gay symbol or something?"

"Negro, please. It's a statue of David," Shue replied.

"Oh, yeah. I knew that."

Shue gave the room a quick glance, and then with his wrist suddenly limp stated to Nate and Brendan, "Look here, fellas, I'm going to find Amir and let him know I'm here. I believe he's probably got something for me." Shue continued, "You two go blend with the others and have some fun." Shue grabbed Nate's shoulder. "Nate, look at all of these scandalous women in here. Half of them probably aren't gay or bi. They're just scheming, trying to get all the B boys to switch-hit, for at least a night. And Brendan, he's got two pool tables downstairs and another DJ down there if you're not with this Top 40 stuff playing up here." Shue leaned over and in a semiwhisper said, "Oh and Nate, please don't let cuz drink too much champagne. You know he can't handle his liquor."

"That's a bet. What's up with the drinks?" Nate asked.

"Look around."

Nate looked and saw people standing around with champagne bottles in their hands. He couldn't believe that this guy had bought enough liquor for folks to be going out like that. Nearly every other person was taking a bottle of high-priced bubbly, or wine, straight to the head.

Shue waved his hands, directing Nate and Brendan toward the dining room, and said, "Grab a bottle of what you like, and do your thing. That's how Amir carries things when he throws a shindig. Glasses and flutes are optional."

Shue nudged Nate's shoulder as if to say "go on," and then spoke into Brendan's ear, probably telling him the same thing, and then slithered off into the crowd.

"Shue said that Amir's got pool tables in the basement." Brendan spoke loudly.

The DJ had seemingly turned the volume up as he started playing some dancehall reggae.

"Yeah, he told me. But I'm going to get a drink and chill up here for a few," Nate answered. "I need to check things out up inside of this camp and see if any of these honeys are down for the swerve. You know what I'm sayin'?"

"Yeah, okay," Brendan replied. However, Brendan's body language showed that he didn't feel like staying upstairs, where it appeared to be the most crowded. After a few moments Nate handed him a half-empty bottle of bubbly and shot him a suggestion.

"Yo B, why don't you go see what's up downstairs. Try and get on one of the pool tables or something." Brendan nodded his head approvingly and took a big swig of the champagne. Nate continued, "I'll be down there in a few."

"Bet," Brendan belted out, before he made his way across the hardwood living room floors that had been turned into a busy dance floor by the couples who were getting their swerve on. They were made up of all sorts of combinations. Men with women, men with men, and much to Brendan and Nate's sexually aroused curiosity, women with women.

Nate was, of course, in his usual party mode. He was playing it cool, leaning up against the wall near the heavily padded white leather couch that had been pushed aside from the middle of the living room. He was watching the other guests walk past him into the kitchen as he eyeballed their outfits to see how they were dressed compared to him. Nate had said he was dressing down this evening. He sported a black shirt with bronze Moschino emblems all over it. He had the tails of the shirt hanging out of his tailored slacks, making his Mont Blanc belt barely visible, except for where his two-way pager and cellphone were clipped, with the shirt hung behind the antenna. He would have been both fly and comfortable, except that his boots fit a little too snug and made his corns hurt. He was going to have to do something about those damned corns.

Nate was noticing that the party had a nice selection of well-dressed people who included both women and gay men. Nate knew that gays as a rule were some of the best-dressed brothers around, and if he could hold his own with them in fashion, he was definitely making some noise.

"Excuse me, honey," the voice said, as her body brushed up against Nate's.

"No problem." Nate grinned as he held his bottle and glass up over his head to prevent the little lady from hitting his fresh bottle of Cristal.

The night was looking oh so good, Nate thought to himself. He would have tested the waters with the chick who had walked by moments earlier, but he figured he would hold off a little longer and make sure he didn't play himself out too soon. He knew that once he approached a honey and started hitting her with his rap, they usually tried to latch onto him and keep him tied up all night. He wasn't having it tonight. He already had his eye on a couple of potential victims. He never really thought of the women he dealt with as victims. But judging by the trademark chant that he had memorized from a rap song, which also described how he treated the ladies—:

> *I meet 'em, greet 'em,*
> *If they lucky I might feed 'em,*
> *Then I hit 'em, split 'em,*
> *Spend their money and forget 'em.*

—they were indeed victims.

Nate spotted the woman he wanted across the room sipping a glass of wine and laughing with a girlfriend. He had made his choice for the night. She was tall, about five-feet-ten-inches or so, and was beautiful, to say the least. He would later find out that she was of Nigerian and French descent. She looked like something out of a magazine, with a short leather skirt and calf-high boots. She was giving up just enough cleavage in the fitted, low-cut blouse she was wearing. Nate had taken one look at her and knew that he was going to try his hand with that.

Whenever Nate saw a woman he was interested in come into a club, party, or bar where the atmosphere was predetermined for mingling, he had a strategy that he almost never wavered from. He would wait for at least one guy to make an approach. His purpose for this was twofold. First, Nate knew that women liked to be approached a couple of times when they go out. It was simple to Nate. He knew that they did not go through the trouble of making themselves look so gorgeous so that they could be ignored all night. Nate also reasoned that just as a good batter doesn't swing at his first pitch, even if it is a good one, any woman worth anything rejects the first offer for a drink, dance, or romance. It just sends the wrong signal, Nate would say "Desperate broads always take the first offer, and then wonder why they get dogged out," Nate's mentor, Uncle Miles, used to say.

Second, Nate would make an assessment of what kind of mood a woman was in by checking out the body language that she used while rejecting her first offer. Most women sent signals on purpose, he believed. The problem was that most men weren't paying attention. Men hardly ever pay attention to the obvious, and that blows women's minds. Nate always said that if you really pay attention to a woman whom you have just met, and ask the right questions, you would have all the necessary information you need for success. As far as Nate was concerned the only things he needed to know was, first off, how long would it take to get into the panties; second, whether or not it was going to be worth it; third, and most important, did the woman show any signs of being a psycho or just more trouble than she was worth.

The woman who'd become the object of Nate's interest had just shaken her head "no," and smiled graciously, as she sent some muscle-bound cat with a tight shirt on packing. She had resumed laughing with her girlfriend when Nate walked up and joined their conversation without being invited. It didn't phase the ladies one bit, as they both eyeballed Nate and kept right on talking about people, what they had on, and laughing at two brothers who were dancing together in the corner to their own music. Nate, trying his best to be charming, had added a nice male perspective and a few comedic observations of his own.

"By the way, ladies, my name is Nathan Montgomery. I would prefer you both call me Nate, as all my friends do."

"I'm Sahleen," she said, extending her hand and smiling widely. Nate was pleased that she seemed welcoming. "This is Trish." Trish simply nodded.

Nate couldn't have cared less about Trish's reaction; he couldn't take his eyes off Sahleen. He was on a mission to exude just the perfect amount of charm and wit. He was fitting into their circle nicely when he brought the flow of the conversation to a screeching halt by asking, "So are you ladies gay or what?"

"Excuse me," Sahleen replied. "That's absolutely none of your damn business, if we are or not. But for the record, no, I'm not. Why? Are you?" Her counterpart just stood there in disbelief at Nate's arrogance.

"Hell, no," Nate shot back.

He stood there for a minute and gave her the low down on how he'd ended up at Amir's party. However, he failed to mention that he had been hoping to roll up on a bisexual honey before the night was through. Sahleen was so sexy, though, Nate didn't mind that she was straight. He was willing to put his hopes for a ménage à trois on the back burner for a dish like her. Nate had rolled up on a lot of fine ladies in his day, but during the conversation with his two new acquaintances, he wondered to himself if he was indeed looking at the finest ever. This was no joke. Sahleen was flawless. As a matter of fact, you could put Sahleen in a room with Halle, J. Lo, or Beyoncé and smart money says that she could turn the three of them into world-class "player haters." Nate didn't even want to ask her what she did for a living. He knew she was going to tell him she was a model, an actress, or something in that field. Ideally, he wanted to get those panties off her shapely ass before she began expecting him to treat her special simply because she had the status to go with that beauty.

Nate had been talking to Sahleen for about twenty minutes about nothing much. He was sensing that she was digging him, because when her girlfriend walked off to go to the bathroom, she elected to stay and continue her conversation with him. And when Trish hadn't returned in fifteen minutes, she never mentioned going to look for her.

It had not taken Nate long to secure at least a future conversation. Sahleen had seemed all to eager to write her number down and give it to Nate as soon as Trish walked off. She also seemed to be flirting a little more openly with him. Nate wondered to himself if Sahleen was lying about her sexuality, and that in fact she and Trish were lovers. He secretly hoped that maybe the three of them could hook up. Trish was nowhere in the same league as Sahleen, but she was still attractive. With her hair all over the place, she looked something like a young Chaka Khan.

Nate decided that he probably wouldn't risk getting anymore phone numbers. He had no idea who was acquainted with who inside of the party, and since he was already set with the tightest thing in there, he figured he could only do worse. He decided to find a spot to chill out and see if Sahleen wanted to sit down with him.

Nate looked over toward a couple of folding chairs that were empty. "Sahleen, would you like to have a seat?"

"If you dance with me first," she said. Then she continued, "That is, if you have any moves other than your playa-playa routine."

Nate's mouth dropped open as if he were shocked. "My dear, sweet lady . . . I have no idea what you are talking about."

Sahleen placed her hands on her hips, which were perfect, then took one off to poke her index finger into Nate's chest and say, "Boy, I can see right through you. I've seen the best of the best, and I know a playa when I see one." She grabbed his arm and said, "Now, let's dance."

Nate was grooving, and Sahleen was getting down. The DJ was playing Jagged Edge's "Where the Party At" and the crowd was getting pumped up. Sahleen turned her back to him, and Nate took it upon himself to get up on her behind. He placed his arms around her from

behind and she clasped the two of his hands with hers. Then, as the
beat got funkier, Nate began to gyrate his crotch up against her behind. She could feel him getting hard, as he held her closer. Normally
she would have been offended, but for some reason she was feeling
herself getting slightly aroused by his aggressive behavior.

The music switched, and as "A Woman's Worth" by Alicia Keys
played in the background, the two of them seemed to be forgetting
themselves. Nate spun Sahleen around so that he could talk to her and
look into her face at the same time. Nate wondered what Sahleen was
thinking. He was glad that she couldn't read his mind. She would have
known that he was scheming about how to get her home with him
that night.

Brendan had only been on the pool table for about twenty minutes,
and had already swept some bald-headed guy wearing a pair of huge
Alan Mikli eyeglasses off the table. The guy was demanding a rematch,
offering to bet Brendan twenty dollars for it. "C'mon, my man. Come
on," he kept taunting. "Twenty, what, you want fifty? Huh, c'mon. I bet
you can't do that again."

Brendan had only given the guy, who looked just like Planter's Mr.
Peanut, two shots before he ran the table. Brendan wasn't a pool
shark, but his experiences on the pool tables in the student union at
Bowie State had made him a campus legend back in his college days.
He could honestly say, though, that he had never suckered anyone
into a bet. He'd learned his lessons about trying to hustle brothers on
the rags long ago. One night at Guys and Dolls pool hall on Branch Avenue back in the day, he beat some pimps for close to nine hundred
bucks one night. He was laughing and slapping five with them one
minute; the next thing he knew he woke up wondering how he had
gotten blood and curl activator all over his T-shirt.

"Look, man, other people are waiting for a chance to play. I would,
but I ain't really trying to gamble," *Did he say fifty dollars?* he thought.
"I mean, if they don't mind, I might have fifty on me. Let me see."
Brendan counted up his ducats and turned to the people standing on
the side. "Do y'all mind?"

"Nah, take that fool's money," one bystander said.

Another joined in, "Yeah, buddy, go on ahead and get that money."

Finally, a woman dressed in a tight red dress sitting on a stool in the corner by the pool sticks on the wall added, "As long as the winner plays me next, it's fine." Brendan took one look at the woman and thought, *I got to win just so I can play her sexy ass.*

"Alright then, my man, let's do it. Let's do it," Mr. Peanut said, as he racked the balls up. Then he continued, "You break, my man. Here's my fifty." He sat the fifty-dollar bill on the side of the marble table in the built-in cup holder.

It was a tad bit ironic to Brendan that just as he lined up to break, one of his all-time favorite songs, Maxwell's "Ascension," started to blare through the speakers. This only pumped him up more. This and the fact that he knew that he was about to make an easy fifty dollars. Just as he leaned over the table to unleash a killer break, he felt a hand grab him firmly on the ass, and then heard a voice say, "If you win it, I'll help you spend it."

Brendan was startled, but not too startled to look around coolly at the freak in the red dress standing behind him.

In a matter of minutes Mr. Peanut was yelling double or nothing. Since there were two tables, no one minded that the two of them seemed destined to monopolize the one they were using. As a matter of fact, the people waiting for a game were enjoying the whipping that Brendan was putting on the annoying, peanut-headed nerd. They went at it for three more games, and three more times Brendan took his money, until finally the stranger grew tired of getting whipped—or ran out of money.

Brendan turned to watch his opponent storm off. He hoped the guy was not a sore loser and wouldn't want to try anything stupid. As he was stuffing the money in his pocket, he turned around to see the sexy chick who had approached him earlier heading back toward him.

"I thought you were going to play with Franco all night," she stated, as she walked right up to him and placed her hand on his forearm.

"Oh no, I guess taking his money just started getting good to me," Brendan stated, with a proud grin.

"What's your name?" she asked.

"I'm Brendan. And what's yours?"

She paused for a moment. "My name is Candice, but my friends call me Candy, and, you know, for a while there I was starting to think that you didn't want to talk to me," she said, pouring on heavy doses of sex appeal.

"C'mon now, I know you weren't thinking that. Let's go sit over there and talk," Brendan said, pointing to the leather couch up against the wall.

"It's so loud out here. Why don't you follow me, handsome? I know where we can *talk*," she said, taking his hand.

"Sahleen," The peanut-headed stranger yelled out, as he approached Nate and Sahleen while they were dancing. "Sahleen. I need some cash, baby."

"What?" she responded. She and Nate stopped dancing. "What do you need money for, Franco? You came in here with over six hundred dollars."

Nate stood adjacent to the two of them, trying to make sense of their debate. The puzzled look on his face that he was trying to disguise prompted Sahleen to explain.

"Nate, this is my photographer and good friend, Franco. And I don't have any idea why he's tripping. Franco, can't you see that I'm busy right now?"

"Look, Sahleen, I don't have time to argue with you. I'll give it right back to you. I just need a couple hundred," Franco retorted. "I just lost six hundred bucks to some clown on the pool table. I want to go back and play him before he leaves the party."

Sahleen's face blasted a look of disapproval. She was about to rip into Franco when Nate interrupted. "Say, my man. Did the guy you lost to have on a gray sweater, caramel complexion, and curly hair?"

Franco's nostrils flared as he nodded his head yes. "Yeah, that's him. How did you know?"

Nate paused momentarily. He didn't want to blurt out that it was his partner who had just schooled him and taken his money. Nate said, "I played him a little earlier. He was pretty good."

"He took your money, too, huh?" Franco smiled. Though Nate

didn't answer, it appeared that Franco felt better believing he wasn't the only sucker of the night.

Sahleen chimed in, "Well, that settles it. I'm not giving you any money to throw away." Then, she added, "I hope that you've both learned a lesson. You should have known better than to gamble with a stranger, especially at one of Amir's parties. You never know who he's going to have in here."

"What's that's supposed to mean?" Franco asked.

"It means that for all you know that guy could be a pool shark working the party and splitting the money with Amir." She pointed toward a fellow in the corner with a bright red blazer on and dreadlocks pulled into a ponytail. "Take that fool, for instance. A girlfriend of mine told me that he makes a fortune at all of the top-flight parties selling coke and Extacy to all of the hosts' friends and gives a cut to the host for the invite. You can just imagine how much he's made up in here. Half the folks in here are higher than a kite."

"Sahleen, get a grip. You believe everything you hear."

"Yeah, well, you're the one out six bills while your counterpart is enjoying your money—and calling you a sucker."

Franco grimaced. "Oh no, my dear. He's the sucker. He won't have the money very long."

Nate wondered what he was insinuating, and asked, "What makes you say that?"

"Well . . . ," Franco stated, "when I came upstairs . . . some transvestite was getting him all worked up down by the table."

"Say what!" Nate shouted.

"You know, a chick with a dick." Franco laughed at the thought of the guy leaving the party with the transvestite. "She looked good, though. I almost couldn't tell myself. By the time she, or should I say he, finishes with him, he'll be sucked dry, in more ways than one. If you get my drift."

Nate knew that his buddy could be gullible at times, but he hoped that Brendan wasn't that gullible. Nate didn't wait for a comfortable break in the conversation before he shouted out over the music, "Excuse me, Sahleen, I'll be right back," while walking hurriedly toward the steps leading to the basement. He sped off before she could even reply.

As soon as he reached the bottom of the stairs, he approached the first person he saw.

"Excuse me, brother." Nate tapped a gentlemen sitting on a bar stool watching a white guy teaching his boyfriend how to play eight ball.

"Yeess," the stranger replied, hoping that the chocolate dream standing before him was going to ask him to dance.

"Did you see a guy down here playing pool about five or ten minutes ago? He has on a gray sweater and dark slacks?" Nate asked, sounding a little worried.

The stranger rolled his eyes and sucked his teeth. "You walk up to *me* and ask me about some other man who I don't even know? I mean, really. How tacky is that?"

Nate took a deep breath. Trying to remain calm, he stated, "Nah, my man, it's not even like that. I'm just looking for a friend."

"Aren't *we* all?"

"Did you see him or not?"

"Not." The stranger said, and returned his focus to the pool table.

"Hey." The voice from behind the bar came. "You talking about the black guy with the curly hair?"

Nate turned around and looked at the bartender. He was muscular with a thick mustache. He was wiping a glass container out as he told Nate, "I saw him, but I don't think he's going to want to be disturbed right about now."

Nate swallowed hard, because if this guy's innuendo proved to be accurate that would mean Brendan could be getting turned out like a two-dollar ho right about now.

"Believe me, he'll want me to interrupt," Nate replied. "Which way did he go?"

"Check the laundry room around the corner," the bartender said, smiling.

"Thanks, man."

Nate headed across the basement floor and walked in front of the big-screen television, which was showing *MTV Cribs* without any volume. He turned the corner to see two doors, the first of which had light coming from under it. He knocked on it. There was no answer, so he turned the knob. It was locked. As he pulled his hand away from the knob the door swung open.

Smoke surged out of the door, and a voice that was not Brendan's yelled out, "Hey nordenus, don't you know what a locked door means." Then the door slammed shut.

Under normal circumstances the person in that bathroom would've received a beat down, but right now Nate didn't have the time, plus he had no idea who or what a nordenus was. He had to find Brendan. Nate walked to the end of the hallway and approached the other door. He placed his head, which was now glistening with sweat, against it. He listened for a moment, but heard nothing at first. Then there was an "mmmm" immediately followed by an "ooooohhh."

As his adrenaline reached its peak, Nate rushed into the laundry room and hit the light switch on the wall. Brendan was leaning back up against the dryer on the far side of the room, his pants down to his ankles, and his mouth now dropped wide open. He couldn't believe that Nate had barged in on him. Candy was on both knees in front of Brendan, clothing still in tact, dick still in hand when she turned around.

"Who the hell told you to come in here? Get out, you pervert," Candy said, looking angrily at Nate.

Brendan chimed in, "Come on, man, what's up? I'm a little busy right now, bro. I'll see you in a few."

Nate observed that Brendan was a little tipsy and that there were two empty glasses on the washing machine next to them. He also noticed that the transvestite had a very attractive face. Nate saw how Brendan could have been fooled by his good looks. Nate was staring at his gullible friend, who was still leaning against the dryer and still on cloud nine. Nate felt both bad and ashamed for his partner, and he was mad as hell at the freak who had taken advantage of his boy. On top of it all, Nate was feeling guilty for suggesting that Brendan go downstairs alone, anyway. Nate knew the only reason he wanted Brendan to go downstairs was so that he could work the party alone. Looking at this pitiful sight, Nate wondered if Brendan would ever get on the ball with the ladies or would he always be a seal among sharks.

Nate walked right up on the two of them and stated, "B, pull your pants up. This isn't what you think it is. Let's go."

"Man, what are you talking about?" Brendan asked. "Are you drunk or something?"

"Obviously, not as drunk as you. Now get your shit together and let's go." Nate was fuming at Brendan's ignorance.

"Man, you're tripping," he looked down at Candy, who was still holding his dick through all of this. "Look baby, I'm sorry about this. My partner here gets a little drunk sometimes."

Nate roughly grabbed Brendan's arm. "Hey man, don't be explaining shit to this freak."

Candy shouted out, "You go to hell, you black bastard." She released Brendan and attempted to stand up. She had just said the wrong thing to Nate. He was hoping to pull Brendan out of this situation, get him out of the party, and maybe make up some story about his new friend that would explain his actions. Maybe he was going to say her boyfriend was upstairs looking for her. Hopefully, something that would make sense. Whatever he was going to come up with before she decided to disrespect him didn't matter anymore. "What did you just call me?" Nate asked, with a piercing glance.

Brendan sensed the impending doom and was paralyzed at the thought of what was about to happen.

"You heard me," Candy yelled out, as she jumped up into Nate's face. "I called you a black . . ." were the words that made it out of her mouth before Nate landed a right cross on her cheek.

Her eyes closed as she fell back onto the laundry room floor. She lay there with her arms spread out, looking like a kid in the snow who is about to make an angel, except she wasn't moving. She was out cold.

Brendan knew why Nate had punched her. But what he didn't know was why he had come in there and screwed up his play in the first place. He looked at Nate, who was rubbing his knuckles, and burst out laughing.

"What the hell is so funny?" Nate asked.

"I can't believe you just hit a woman like that. You are absolutely bananas. I just can't believe it. One minute I'm in here getting my jimmy blown, quite skillfully I might add. The next minute, you're in here knocking her out like you're Ike Turner or somebody."

"Damn, B. You *still* don't get it, do you?"

Brendan just stood there and shrugged his shoulders.

"That ain't a woman right there. That's a nigga," Nate said, pointing at the still body.

"Whatever."

"I'm telling you. The guy you beat for the money came upstairs and told the chick I was talking to that you had just whipped him for some dough on the pool tables. Then he said that you were getting all worked up by a transvestite who was going to suck you off and hit you for your money."

"And you believed that I couldn't tell a woman from a man? You believed that bull?"

"Watch this." Nate said, as he bent down and pulled Candy's dress up to reveal a pair of snug-fitting panties. Nate grabbed her underwear and pulled it to the side and revealed nothing but bush and booty. "Oh, snap," he screamed out loud, as he staggered backward. "B, this is a woman. Oh, damn, damn, damn." Nate shouted and clenched his fist while doing his best imitation of Florida Evans on the episode of *Good Times* when James died. "That fool didn't know what the hell he was talking about. I ought to go back upstairs and kick his ass." Nate paused and looked down at Candy sleeping like a baby. "She still ain't moving . . . damn."

Brendan stood there waiting to see what the champ was going to do next. After a few seconds of watching the expression of perplexed anguish put a stranglehold on Nate's face, Brendan broke the short silence. "Look, man, let's get up out of here before somebody comes in here and accuses us of trying to rape this chick or something."

The idea was more than a little appealing to Nate, who replied, "Yeah, c'mon, let's roll."

The two of them sped out of the room and up the steps. When Nate and Brendan reentered the living room, Shue was in the corner talking to a couple of guys. One of them looked strangely familiar to Brendan for some reason. Shue saw them and signaled for them come over. Brendan was about to walk over there when Nate grabbed his arm. "Nigga, what you gonna do? You know we've got to leave up outta here."

"Well, man, I can't just leave Shue up in here without telling him I'm leaving first."

"Look, hurry the hell up. I'm headed toward the car. Give him your keys if you got to. I'll drop you off at your crib. But don't stay up here until we get an assault charge."

"Okay, alright already."

"Dude, I'm not playing with you. I'll knock your ass out, too."

Brendan laughed, "Who are you supposed to be, Debo or somebody?"

"Just hurry up. Oh, and ask Shue if he knows what a nordenus is."

"A what?"

"Never mind, just do what you got to do so we can bounce."

Shue nodded at Brendan and asked, "Where's Nate going? I wanted to introduce both of you to my friends here." Then he turned back to the group he was standing with. "Anyway, guys, this here is my cousin, Brendan." Shue then placed his hand on the shoulder of the guy who was standing closest to him. "Brendan, this is Stuart Hall, and this here is his partner, Glenn."

It dawned on Brendan who Stuart Hall was. He was the sportscaster from Channel 6 news. Brendan thought, *What was the world coming to? A sportscaster packing fudge. Who would've thought?* Brendan exchanged pleasantries with Stuart and his partner. What was a trip to Brendan was that Stuart Hall seemed pretty comfortable with people knowing he was gay, judging from the way his friend was all up under him.

After less than a minute Brendan pulled Shue to the side and told him what had happened in the basement. Shue had responded with an "Oh dear, that's ugly." And quickly told Brendan to go ahead, and that he'd catch a ride with someone else or catch a cab if need be.

Brendan started to turn away, then grabbed Shue's arm. "Hey, cuz."

"Yeah, what is it?"

"Nate said to ask you what a nordenus was." Brendan asked with a puzzled looked, wondering if he had pronounced it correctly.

Shue burst out laughing. "Why, did someone call him that?" He was still laughing.

"I don't know. Why? What is it?"

Still grinning, Shue leaned over to his cousin and said, "It's a cocksucker that has no lips." Shue tapped Brendan as if to say "get on" and walked back to his friends.

The visual image of that brought a smile to Brendan's face, but he figured he'd keep it to himself and maybe use it on Nate one day down the road.

Brendan saw Nate sitting out in front of the house waiting impatiently with a gorgeous woman sitting next to him in the car.

"Ain't this a bitch?" Brendan said to Nate as he walked around to Nate's side of the car and looked inside the window.

"Don't act like that, B. You know I was only looking out for you. I would hope that you would do the same for me." Nate smiled at Brendan. He knew Brendan was pissed off about Nate screwing up his action and now getting himself a prize for the night. Nate knew it wasn't fair, but the sooner people learned that life wasn't always fair the better, he believed. "B, hop in. I'll give you a ride up the street to your car."

Just as Brendan opened the door to get in, a voice yelled out from the steps in front of the house, "There he is. That's one of them right there." There were two very big men standing next to Candy at the top of the steps as she pointed toward Brendan, who was at least forty yards away. In an instant, Brendan was in the back seat of the car, and Nate's foot had slammed on the gas pedal. They were up the block, lights turned off so that no tag number could be seen, and around the corner before Candy and her rescuers could make it to the street.

Nate barely came to a complete stop at Brendan's car. Brendan wondered if he was expected to jump out of a rolling vehicle. The two said their good-byes as Brendan quickly climbed out of the back seat.

"You gonna be alright."

"I'm straight."

"I'm out, then."

"Me, too."

Nate sped off again. Brendan did the same.

Chapter 7

THE WAY LOVE GOES

could hear my phone ringing as I struggled to get my keys into the door of my apartment.

"Hello, you have reached Cory Dandridge. Please leave a brief . . ." the answering machine had started before I could pick it up. After racing through the door and to the phone, I dropped my luggage and shopping bags on the couch as I picked up the phone, cutting the machine off simultaneously.

"This is Cory," I announced.

"Hey, baby," she said.

I recognized the soft, raspy voice on the other end of the line and responded, "What's goin' on, baby girl?"

She started in an apologetic tone, "Did I catch you at a bad time?"

"No, not at all. I was just walking through the door, but actually I'm glad you called. I should have been home an hour ago, but my flight was delayed coming out of La Guardia. The airport security will delay a flight at the drop of a hat right about now." My tone changed when I remembered the news from my trip that I wanted to tell Paula. I began with, "Baby, guess what. I have some news that I'm really anxious to share with you," and asked, "Do you think that you'll be busy in about an hour or so?"

"Well, Marvin is out with a client playing golf, and I'd like to get out of here before he comes home. So if you want to see me I need to leave out now." Paula continued in a humble manner, "You know, so I don't have to go through any changes getting out of the house."

I understood perfectly. So, after exchanging a few minutes of small talk I told her to come on over, even though I had wanted the hour to shower and maybe straighten the place up a little. I said, "Okay. I'll see you shortly, then." I hung up the phone and plopped back onto the couch. I wasn't feeling so tired I needed sleep. It was more that my mind and body just needed a break from the nonstop motion I had endured during the past few days.

I'd just gotten back into town after three days in New York meeting with a relatively new digital security corporation that my company was attempting to buy out. In the relatively short time that I had been working for Pavillion I had grown accustomed to the aggressive manner in which we attempted to buy out smaller companies. After 9/11 most of the security companies were trying to expand to meet record demands for high-tech security. Our unspoken mission seemed to be to take over small companies that were doing something right before they became tomorrow's competition. Our researchers, or spies as most people called them, had alerted us to a new company, Hakito Electronics, that was on the rise. PSC research had informed the board of directors that this company was on the brink of introducing a variety of cutting-edge software that made innovative use of wireless technology. PSC knew that this software would allow them to put a virtual stranglehold on the digital security industry.

I was sent to New York because, not only was I the assistant director of the sales and acquisitions department, I was the top salesman for eighteen months running as well. At worst, I would sign a contract for them to use our satellites for all of their business, but George Bell, my glory-stealing supervisor, was positive that I could convince Hakito Electronics to sell us controlling interest in their company. I did exactly what was asked and made my pitch very aggressively, to convince them they needed PSC. To my surprise, though, it turned out that the only thing they were convinced of was that they needed me to join their company as soon as possible.

The meetings were extremely tense and heated. I actually believed that their board had decided collectively to hate me before I had even started my presentation. After the second day of meetings, I became quite frustrated with their stubborn refusals. I was quite indignant, I'm sure, when I expressed PSC's plans to delve into their market, which would cause a divide in the available profit margin for the next few years, until the supply for the cutting-edge software and digital programming chips that they produced increased. PSC, I'd explained, could afford to lose money, if need be, for a few years on this venture, but under those circumstances, a smaller corporation like Hakito could end up going bankrupt.

They wouldn't budge from their stance, more than likely because they knew that when they began heavy production the previous year in their new digital technology division they had virtually cornered the market. Their extensive research and knowledge of the future of the industry enabled them to recognize the idleness of the threats I delivered. They had the patent rights on their side. It would be at least two years before they would have to share their superior design secrets. By that time they would surely grow in worth from a multimillion-dollar company to a possible billion-dollar one.

I was truly surprised that, after the meeting hadn't gone as well as I'd hoped, instead of throwing me out of their boardroom, the entire clan of management heads invited me to lunch. I admired their good sportsmanship and agreed to join them. As we dined at Benihana on East Fifty-sixth Street, the surprises kept coming. Jamison Hakito, the nephew of the company's founder, told me that both he and his uncle found my no-nonsense, borderline rude approach to business to be just what their company needed.

As lunch went on, Jamison continued complimenting me. He admitted to me that he had spoken with a headhunter I'd used back in Atlanta and was impressed with my background and credentials. I was impressed that he had been thorough enough to research me before I'd come up. Before I finished my pepper steak, he flat-out offered me a job.

Although they nearly sold me then and there when they told me all of the ways I would benefit from joining them—generous stock options, executive privileges, and the like—I told them I needed some time to think it over. They told me to take a week or two to get back to them, but they had two positions to fill immediately, and if I wanted either I should let them know as soon as possible.

I hated to imagine what Mr. Bell would think about me leaving PSC when I told him of their offer, if I decided to take it. He would probably assume that I had gone there and seen an opportunity to sell myself and run with it. Nothing would have been further from the truth.

I basically made up my mind when, on the ride back to my hotel, Jamison told me that one of the positions available was as head of the sales and production team in their Washington-Baltimore offices.

It was like fate was calling me home. I had thought about moving home for the past few months, since my mom had suffered a mild stroke. She wasn't sickly, but it was just that Mom, even at fifty-five, had a tendency to overdo it. My older sister, Brenda, was there to check in on her, but she had enough pressure just trying to raise her children, Tory and Kyle. With this job offer and the chance for me to move back home to the metropolitan area, suddenly it seemed things were falling into place.

As I sat on the coffee-colored love seat, I looked out the balcony door. I was enjoying the feel of the cool leather on my naked back as I noticed the beautiful November day that Atlanta had been blessed with. I began to think about how much I would miss the city and the people if I elected to take the job with Hakito Electronics. It was so pleasant in the area near Phipps Plaza, where I had made my home. The thought of actually leaving made me feel a bit nostalgic. Since coming to Atlanta to get my master's degree at Georgia Tech I'd made so many good friends, and none greater than Paula. I guess that's why I was more than a little anxious how she would receive the news of the job offered to me while I was in the Big Apple.

It was getting close to when Paula should have been arriving at my apartment, if she had left her house immediately, as she'd said. My mouth was getting a little dry, so I rose from the sofa to get myself a glass of Welch's white grape juice. While up and moving around, I opened the balcony window. On the way to the balcony I stopped and turned on the stereo. I reached into my packages and pulled out the new music I'd scooped up from Best Buy. I emptied the CDs out and ripped off the plastic covering. I loaded them all into the player and started the Glenn Lewis disc first. I read the cover to see which song I had seen the video for on BET in the hotel. That song first, then I figured I'd check out Mary J.'s joint. Ja Rule and Ludacris would have to wait until later.

The breeze blowing into my living room felt so inviting that I stepped out onto the balcony and decided to sit out there until Paula arrived. I turned the music up loud enough so that I could hear it on the balcony.

It was at least 65 degrees and unbelievably comfortable on the balcony. While resting one leg up on the rail, I lay my neck down on the plastic back of my lawn chair. I closed my eyes, but I could see the rays of bright sun turning the inside of my eyelids to orange covers. With the perfect amount of wind blowing across my face, I was beginning to drift into deep relaxation mode. I almost didn't hear Paula at my door, but rose quickly when the second series of knocks came.

I opened my door and saw Paula standing there smiling. She was as beautiful as usual. She had her hair down instead of in the usual pulled-back style she sported to go along with her classroom image. She stepped into the foyer and greeted me with a hug and a soft kiss that made me feel warm inside.

"Hey, handsome, I've missed you." She kissed me again.

"It's only been four days, baby," I replied, as I gently squeezed her hands and pulled her to the couch.

"I know, but it always seems so much longer when one of us is out of town." She went on, "Answer me this: How come when we sneak off for a couple of days, time always goes so quickly?"

I scratched my head and acted like I was deep in thought. "I don't know. Maybe time just flies when you're getting done." I smiled, and she offered a frowning, disapproving look before walking off.

Paula went into the kitchen to fix herself a glass of spring water. I heard a package opening and she reentered with a handful of Girl Scout cookies.

"I know you don't mind, these being your favorite and all."

I replied, "Just don't get too crazy with 'em. Even though you did buy them."

She ignored me as she made her way back into the kitchen for a second handful. While she was in the kitchen I walked into the bedroom to retrieve the Manolo Blahnik boots I had brought Paula back from Manhattan. As I was pulling them out of the bag, she walked into the doorway of the bedroom.

"Watcha doing?" she asked.

"I'm looking for a little something I picked up for you." I pulled the Bergdorf's shopping bag out.

"Oh, wow, thanks, baby." She opened the box so she could take a good look at the boots. "One thousand dollars. You paid one thousand dollars for these boots?"

"Oh damn, how did you know? I pulled the receipt out of the bag, didn't I?"

"There's another one right here on the side of the box."

"Oh, sorry. I told them it was a gift and to remove all of the tags."

She shook her head, smiling in disbelief at my generosity, and walked into the bathroom. As I finished putting away the rest of the clothes in the garment bag, Paula walked out of the bathroom clad only in a black lace bra that made her breasts stand straight up and a pair of matching thong panties.

I knew what time it was and welcomed the advance. I pulled the covers back and she slid seductively into the satin sheets and lay on her stomach directly in front of me. My view was superb as I undressed quickly and joined her.

We spent the next couple of hours enjoying each other by giving each other massages between bouts of making love. When eight o'clock rolled around, she got up to get dressed. As she slid her shoes on she turned to me and woke me with a kiss on the forehead. Then she asked me whose music had been on the CD player earlier.

"This cat named Glenn Lewis. He just came out, but he is blowing up."

"That CD is nice. I think I'll take it with me." She grinned. I shook my head no. "I promise I'll bring it back."

"Just like you brought back Jill Scott?" I swiped.

"Now, you knew you weren't getting that back. That was the CD of the year. Plus, I gave you the fifteen dollars for it."

"Did not."

"Did too."

We went back and forth until I grabbed her and pinned her down on the bed and kissed her for a while. As our clothes began to fall off again Paula placed her hands on my chest to push me back.

Then in a curious tone came . . . "Oh, Cory, I almost forgot. . . . What's the news that you wanted to share with me?"

Chapter 8

HANDLIN' YOUR BUSINESS

I had never imagined in my worst dreams that things would get as ugly as they did with Paula when I delivered the news of my upcoming move. I had decided to accept the job with Hakito Electronics. If anything, I expected her to congratulate me on the power move I was about to make. Job offers like this one were usually unheard of for young black men. It's the kind of thing that's read about in fiction or seen in movies. But in real life big-time salary increases don't just fall into the laps of brothers like myself, no matter how hard you worked to prove yourself.

Paula definitely showed her true colors when I delivered the news. Maybe I shouldn't have slept with her right before telling her I was leaving, but there's still no way in hell that she could rationalize acting like that. The cursing, crying, and other theatrics were a bit much. During her tantrum she even threw the boots I'd bought her on the floor and told me to keep them. What took the cake, though, was that she even had the nerve to insinuate that I had used her.

So what if I was leaving Atlanta? It's not as though I couldn't come back to visit, and she could always find a way to sneak up to Washington for a weekend. But after the big blowup we had I wasn't sure if her visiting was something that I would consider.

I even gave her the reasons at the top of my list for moving home. I explained to her that I had been contemplating moving home in order to keep an eye on my moms and to become an active and positive influence in the life of my nephew, Kyle.

Her response to that had been "Your mother is grown. She's not going to slow down unless she really wants to." She then added, "Kyle is your nephew, not your responsibility. His father should be taking care of that. You will just perpetuate his absentee behavioral pattern. If he knows someone is there to take up the slack of his duties, he'll just continue to be a typical black man—avoiding his responsibilities."

After we argued for at least an hour, she left, only to return ten minutes later and issue me an ultimatum. When I opened the door for her, she said, "Listen here, Cory, I'm only going to say this one time. If you leave Atlanta without me, be it next week, next year, or five years from now, you had best forget that you know me. It will be over. And when you regain your senses and call trying to come back, it will be too late." She turned and stormed down the stairs, stopping midway to add yet another threat. "Oh, and Cory," she said. "If you've just been using me till something better came along, I swear you will regret the day that you even smelled this pussy."

Her verbal thrashing had me standing there with the dumbest of looks on my face. I had never imagined that Paula could get foul and come out of her mouth like that, which only goes to show you that you never really know a woman until you've pissed her off. It took me a while to cool off after that whole scene, and I have to admit I wondered what she meant by that last statement. If I ever decided to speak with her again, we'd have to clear up that matter. I've never been one to play that game. She could bust a windshield and slash a tire if she wanted to, but she had a car, too. I haven't ever understood why men let women do that and then sit around with a dumb look, saying, "Man, she's crazy." It should be more like, "Man, I must be weak."

It was nearly half past noon and time for me to get ready for a Sunday afternoon filled with nothing but football. As comfortable as I was in the bedroom, I was forced to go into the living room to watch the games, because I had installed the DirecTV only in the living room. Satellite TV is the shit. I get every single Dallas Cowboys game, even if it's a regionally covered game. The Atlanta Falcons were cool. I even had a Michael Vick jersey, but I had to see my Cowboys every week. When I first got to Atlanta the only thing I liked about the Falcons was Darlene, who was a Falcons cheerleader. We met at Club 112 and had been screwing ever since. Every single man needs a woman who doesn't mind if he calls at two in the afternoon or two in the morning. Darlene was that kind of woman for me. I didn't know if it was a sex thing or if she just truly liked me that much. If she was emotionally attached, she never let it become a problem by becoming demanding and needy. I wasn't sure if she had a man, and although I was fond of her as a friend and sex partner, I didn't care enough beyond that to ask.

While I flipped through the channels I thought about inviting Darlene over after the game, since the Dirty Birds were playing at home against the Saints. There were so many games on that I couldn't find the Cowboys game. The satellite dish was definitely coming with me back to D.C. I might've even been able to get my subscription into my negotiable benefits package from the Hakitos, though I seriously doubted it. It had nothing to do with work. It didn't matter, anyway. There was no way that I was going to be forced to watch the Redskins every week.

I was looking forward to going to Mike's Barbershop back home, walking in there with my Cowboys leather jacket, baseball cap, and my number 22 jersey. I always got a kick out of the friendly arguments that Mike, myself, and anyone who happened to be in the shop had about our favorite teams. That's one thing that women never will understand or appreciate: the way men get legitimately worked up about football, as if it were really *their* team.

I opened the front door to get my Sunday edition of the *Atlanta Constitution*. After I shuffled through the paper to get the sports section, I sat on the couch and grabbed the remote. As I flipped the channel to Fox to prepare myself for the NFL pregame show I began to wonder what I was going to eat. I was planning to stay in my apartment all day with the phone unplugged. Maybe I'd order carryout from Mick's. A nice juicy steak, a few ice cold Coronas, and a Sunday with plenty of football action was all a man could ask for in life. Who needed women?

My pager interrupted my pregame activities. I was hoping desperately that it would not be Paula. It wasn't so much that I was against having a discussion with her again, so long as she was willing to rein in her emotional outbursts. I just wasn't up to it at that moment, not while I was getting into my official NFL 'couch potato' mode. I simply preferred not to be disturbed, at least not with anything as trivial as relationship problems, with someone else's wife on top of that.

I picked up the two way from the coffee table and immediately recognized the number. It was Nate. I had called him the previous night, and here he was getting back to me in a stunning seventeen-plus hours.

I dialed his number as I watched Terry Bradshaw and James Brown taking jabs at Chris Collinsworth, their cohost, about the pitiful Bengals, on the Fox pregame show.

The phone rang one time before he answered. "What's up, my nigga?" Nate shouted through the line.

"That's how you answer the phone, boy? What if I was your grandmother, fool?" I replied to his greeting.

"I know it ain't Nana; I got caller ID. Plus, you know she's in church till at least two o'clock every Sunday," he retorted. "So, what's up witcha?"

"Oh, thanks for calling back so quickly, black boy. It wasn't anything major. I got shot in the abdomen while I was grocery shopping at Kroger's last night, and I wanted to know if you could help me out by donating a kidney. Don't sweat it, though. I called someone else."

"Stop playing, man. You know you simple as shit." Nate laughed, then continued. "For real, though, wasn't nothing up?"

"Well, actually, a lot is up. I got into some real drama last night with Paula." I began to explain.

"Come on, Cory. I don't even know why you stressing over no married chick. How many times have I told you about how to handle them married hoes? You got to straight handle your business with them. If you let them get the upper hand, you in for some shit. I'm telling you, dog, that's for real. Married broads get crazy when they mess around. They start thinking they own a nigga and whatnot."

"Yeah, I know, I know, but this was something different. I shared some news with her that I thought would make her happy for me, at least, but she ended up turning it into some how-it-was-bad-news-for-her type shit."

"What, you finally found out that Shelly's daughter is yours, and not that 'bama ass nigga Eric's," Nate joked.

"That ain't even funny. Why you gonna even play about something like that?" I replied to his joke about my first love and the child she had by a guy she started dating a month after we broke up. Back when things first went down, rumors flew in our circle of mutual friends. Everyone found it hard to swallow that we had broken up in August and by October she was pregnant by her new boyfriend. My sister, Brenda, swears to this day that Shelly's daughter, Amani, is mine.

"Cory, don't be getting all sensitive, but you know that's your kid. You know you Shelly's baby's daddy. Haaa haaah." Nate was cracking up laughing at himself.

I interrupted him. "Yo, you finished being an ass? Do you want to know what Paula flipped out on me for?"

"Yeah, man," Nate said, in a now semiserious tone. "What did you tell her that got her tripping?"

I had kind of wanted to surprise Nate with my news, and not in the context of a story about Paula. But since I needed to unload on somebody, I started in. "Man, do you remember when I told you I was headed up to New York for a few days last week?"

"Yeah. How was it?" he asked, interrupting again.

"Well, you know the city ain't the same since 9–11. The mood is nothing like it usually is."

"That's to be expected, though."

"True. But still, I had these power meetings. Man, let me tell you things got heated after that."

"What you mean by that?" he asked, finally letting me know he was interested. He probably thought I was going to tell him about some exploits that I had had with a woman up there. He was way off, though.

"I went up there to secure a buyout for my company. I was supposed to scare the owners and boardmembers of this smaller company into selling a division of their company to us. But they weren't scared at all. As a matter of fact, they didn't like the proposal I made to them at the meeting we had. They did, however, like the way I presented it to them."

"And . . . ?"

"They made me a job offer. A sweet one, too."

Nate was silent for a second. Then asked. "So you took it?"

I replied, "Not yet. But I'm going to."

"So that's why she went ballistic . . . because you're moving to New York?"

"Something like that." I left out the detail that I was moving to D.C. and not New York.

"You see, Cory," Nate said. "Bitches are so jealous. They don't want to see a nigga get ahead for real. But they talk all that crap about how black men don't have any ambition or goals. That's the shit that pisses me off. I hope you put her ass in her place. What can she do for you, anyway? She's married and been screwing around on her husband for the last two years. It isn't like you could ever trust her ass. Did she think that you were supposed to sit around and wait for her ass to leave her husband?"

"That's what I'm saying."

"I don't know what these broads be thinking about. But hey, you must like that shit. You love all your women. You are a playa with sensitivity. Couldn't be me, bro," Nate said, sarcastically.

"Yeah, that's me. Call it what you want, but you need to learn to show a little respect for these sisters out here. You keep it up and you are gonna wind up a dirty old man, sitting outside the high schools chasing young girls while everyone else is home with a family."

Nate roared with laughter. "Fuck you," he bellowed. Then he went on to ask, "Did you tell your moms that you are going to take a job in New York? I can hear Mrs. Dandridge now. She's going to be mad worried about you living up there after the terrorist attack." He switched his voice into a Mother Jefferson–style impersonation, imitating my mother: "Cory, baby, you know New York is so dangerous, honey bunch." He laughed more, and loudly. I had to move the receiver slightly away from my ear.

I broke his laughter to answer his question. "As a matter of fact, I didn't tell Moms that I was moving to New York because the job isn't in New York."

"Oh, yeah. Well, where is it?" he asked, suspiciously.

I paused, then asked. "Do you know how to keep a sucker in suspense?"

He replied. "No, how?"

I just paused, and there was silence on the line.

"Nigga, forget you. Where is the job?"

"It's there," I stated.

"Straight up? In D.C.?"

"Yeah, not downtown, though. It's right off of Rockville Pike."

"Aww, shit." I heard excitement in his voice. "That's good, man. That is real good. So when you moving back?"

"Probably the day before Thanksgiving. Let's see. Today is the twelfth, and I'm giving my notice tomorrow. We're off for Thanksgiving anyway, so I'll just let that Tuesday be my last day. My boss is going to be pissed anyway, but hey, what can you do. He knows that I've been throwing the idea of transferring back up north for a few months."

"Yeah, but he probably thought you'd be working for him, not the competition. But like you said, what can you do? Is the money the same?" Nate asked, getting all up in my business.

"Nope, it's better. Much better," I said, in a harmless brag.

"Good. Now you can trade that old-assed Maxima in."

"My car still runs good. I don't have to show how much money I have by buying a big old fancy ride. That's what's wrong with brothers today. Instead of putting some money in the bank, or even buying a house, the first thing a nigga does is go out and buy a BMW, a Benz, or a Lexus. Why? Just so he can get a piece of ass."

"What's wrong with that? Money won't get in the bed with you, and it damned sure can't make you come. You need a woman for that. And I don't know how much ass you getting now with that hooptie you driving now, but I will guarantee you one thing." He paused.

"What's that?" I asked.

"You'd be getting more if you were pushing a tight ride." He laughed out. Then he went on, "Man, you getting a fresh start. You need to treat yourself. If you're waiting to be debt-free, it won't ever happen. You're always gonna owe somebody. It's the American way. And if you owe money, it might as well be for a damn Mercedes. Even Brendan knows that shit. You still haven't seen his 'vette, have you?"

"Yeah, I saw it when I was home in August. I don't know why he bought that, anyway. He only got it to impress Trina, and they aren't even together now."

Nate added, "Oh, I don't even want to talk about their ill relationship."

"Don't tell me he's still fooling with her," I asked.

"Man, he says he not, but Shue told me that he thinks Brendan's still got the jones for the chick. I can't figure it out."

"When did you talk to Shue? He's speaking to you again since the incident at Houston's?" I laughed. Shue had been pissed off because Nate saw his ex-girlfriend waiting in the lobby for a table, and then invited her and her girlfriend to share their table one night, just so he could meet her girlfriend. She didn't know that Shue was now into boys, and she kept grabbing his crotch underneath the table.

"Oh, he's been over that. But check it out. Brendan and me were hanging out with Shue at this party last night. The party was off the hook. The dude who had the party was some rich fag who lives up in a big-ass house on Sixteenth Street not too far from the zoo. I think he owns a few stores in Georgetown. We had a crazy wild time up in there. But I think Brendan is a little mad at me right now."

I asked him why. He told me the whole story about him punching the chick out. I was almost on the floor in laughter. I had him call Brendan on a three-way, so that I could mess with him about what had happened.

Nate told me to hold on while he clicked over to dial Brendan's number.

"Don't say anything. I'm not going to say you're on the line yet," I commanded Nate.

"Alright, I'm going to hit the mute," Nate responded.

"Hello," Brendan answered.

"Good morning, my brother."

"Cory?" He asked.

"You know it. What's happening?"

"Ah, man not too much. No, I take that back. I've had more drama than *The Young and the Restless* lately."

"For real. Well, shit, I've had some, too. What's up with Nate? You talked to him?" I almost broke out in laughter as I set him up.

"Oh man, don't get me started on that crazy nigga. Man, we went to this party last night, and this fool ended up turning the party out. You won't believe what this fool did, Cory. You are not going to believe it."

"What'd he do?" I asked.

"Yo, Cory, I had the finest honey in the party on her knees in the laundry room. It was a house party, right. But listen up. I'm getting my shit sucked. She's hitting me off like Heather Hunter or somebody, a real pro."

"You lying," I said, acting as if I didn't know what he was going to say about what happened next.

"If I'm lying, I'm flying, bro. You know this kind of thing never ever happens to me, but it was happening last night. Then, all of a sudden this fool bust through the door, flips on the lights, and then comes over and hits the girl with a right cross and knocks her slam out!" He paused, then said, "Do you believe that shit?"

I started cracking up laughing, and Nate took the mute off his phone and was laughing on the line as loudly as I was.

"Is that sucka on the line?" Brendan asked.

"Yeah, it's me, and you didn't even tell the whole story. It's a good thing I already told him the story behind the story. You know it was an honest mistake, B. You know I was only trying to look out for you"

"Whatever, man."

"Cory, see how this little chump be acting? That's why I'm glad you're movin' back up here," Nate said.

"What?" Brendan said. "You moving back, homeboy? Is everything alright with your moms?" Brendan asked, concerned.

"Yeah. I just got a sweet little job offer up in Rockville. Thanks, Nate, for telling my news. Between you and my mother I may as well put it on the Internet."

"Telephone, telegram, or tell Big Mouth Nate," Brendan added.

"That's Mr. Big Mouth to you, chump," Nate shot back.

"Hey, don't neither one of y'all go around telling everybody I'm moving home. I'd like to surprise a few folks when I get back."

"Cool," they said in unison.

We went on talking and joking. Brendan told us that he had gone over to Trina's after he left the party the previous night, and it had turned out to be a disaster. He said she confronted him about his moving in with Renee. She accused the two them of being romantically involved.

Everyone who knows Brendan and Renee always believed she would've been the best choice in the world for Brendan, but they'd always been platonic.

When Nate asked him if he at least had gotten some tail for all of his frustration, Brendan let out a disparaging sigh, and then told us the details behind that. After Trina argued with him for about an hour, he told us, she walked into the bedroom and came out in nothing but a T-shirt and panties. Brendan said he was beginning to think that it was all going to be worth it.

A man can endure just about any hardship at any time, just so long as at the end of it he ends up getting the sex. Brendan told us how she got him all worked up by kissing all over him and rubbing his dick through his pants. Then, when they both finally had stripped down to nothing but the drawers, and the time had come to lose those, she told him she couldn't do it because she was on her period.

We laughed, and Brendan told us how she had said he should just be happy to lay there and hold her.

Nate commented, "Well, did you at least get some head, baby boy?"

"Nah. She said that since I wasn't her man anymore, she couldn't be doing that. Then she was like, 'if you want me to do that, then you've got to come correct.' "

"I hope you didn't fall for that and tell her you'd give her another chance," Nate asked, condescendingly.

"Did you, Brendan?" I asked.

"Hell, no," Brendan lied . . . sort of. To get her to suck it, he'd told her that he would seriously think about giving their relationship another try. She was so happy she'd gone at it like never before. After she'd finished Brendan had realized that all he'd missed was the sex. And while that was a valid reason to maintain a relationship in his eyes, he knew that it would never work between the two of them. She liked to argue too much. She wasn't trustworthy, and Brendan knew that even if she tried to be faithful to him it would be a challenge for her. Trina was a real freak in bed. Brendan reasoned that of all the men Trina had ever slept with, at least half would occasionally get the urge to come back for a piece. Brendan knew he had to face it. The thought of it would always have him wondering what she was doing when they weren't together. No matter how much she said she loved him, or that he was the only man she wanted, Brendan knew that women like Trina never changed.

As halftime approached for the first game, I realized that we had been on the phone for almost two hours. My hunger alarm had been going off for the last hour, so I mentioned that it was time for us to end our long-distance male-bonding session.

We informed each other of our plans for the remainder of the day. Nate said he was going to run a few errands for his grandmother and then shampoo her carpets. He would have preferred to just pay his buddy Chauncey at Carpet Masters to come in and do it profession-ally, but she said she preferred him. She said that a personal touch is always best. Nate was never one to argue with his grandmother. What she said always went. No questions asked.

He had more love for his grandmother than for anyone else in the world. She had raised him from the time he was eight years old, and she appeared to be the only female he could muster any real love or functional respect for.

Brendan was going to work at five to close the store. He said that since he was up for a raise, Jaqueline, the head honcho at Nordstrom's, was watching him closely.

We said our good-byes, and I told my partners I'd call them later on in the week with the details of my move. I hung up and called Mick's to place my order.

I washed my face, brushed my teeth, threw on some sweats, and was out.

Chapter 9

TRINA-FREE

Brendan had just come in from closing the store when he realized that he'd left his cell in the car. He considered leaving it there overnight but knew the battery would run down in the chilly November night air. Just as he was about to go back out to the car to retrieve it, he heard his phone ringing upstairs. Brendan threw his keys and jacket on the couch and headed upstairs toward his bedroom. On the third ring he reached the cordless and picked it up.

"Hello," Brendan answered.

"Hey, baby." Trina's voice bubbled through the line.

"What's up?" Brendan returned. His tone didn't hide his lack of enthusiasm.

"Hold up, nigga. Why are you coming off like that? It wasn't like that last night."

"Look, Trina. I just got in from work. I'm really tired, and I don't really feel like talking. How about if I call you back in a couple of hours, after I eat? I have a long day ahead of me tomorrow. I'm filling in for a manager at another store, so I've got to leave out extra early. So, if you don't mind, I'll give you a call back, okay?"

Trina sucked her teeth and began to ramble. "I really would like to see you today, Brendan. I cooked your favorite dinner for you, shrimp Alfredo, and I even made some of that garlic cheese bread that you like so much. You know, like the kind you get at Red Lobster. I really went through a lot of trouble, so could you come over for just a little while and eat, or you could pick up a plate and take it with you." Her pitiful homemaker routine was a bit of a laugh to Brendan. When did she start cooking for him? It was really a case of too little, too late.

"Trina, you obviously didn't hear what I said. It's nearly eight o'clock now. I have to get up at six in the morning to be out to Mon . . ." He cut himself off when he realized that he had almost slipped up and told her that he'd be working at Montgomery Mall tomorrow. She worked at the National Institutes of Health, which was only ten minutes away from the mall. The last thing he wanted was for her to come out to his job on her lunch hour to try to talk him to death about the sad state of things between them. He ended with, "I'll call you back once I get myself prepared for tomorrow."

"So you ain't coming over?" She asked angrily.

"No," he responded.

"Son of a bitch. I bet if you thought that you was getting some ass or your dick sucked again, you'd be on your way," she yelled. "I cooked all of this damn food. What am I supposed to do with it?"

"I don't know. Give it to that nigga from the car dealer, or that personal trainer your ass is always going to see. I don't really give a damn, Trina." Brendan had let her exhaust his patience and was now arguing loudly. As they began to trade hurtful remarks about their sordid history, he looked over to see Renee standing in the doorway with a pained look on her face.

"Brendan, that's all you do. Just bring up shit from the past. You really need to grow up. You need to be a little more mature. You act just like a little boy sometimes," Trina said. Her voice seemed to be calming, almost as if she was satisfied to have pissed him off.

Renee was still in the doorway, and as she turned to walk back into her room, she made a comment to Brendan that was something of the nature of his being silly even to let Trina get to him. Brendan agreed and caught himself.

"Yeah, Trina, you're right. This whole conversation is pointless," Brendan said.

"I'm glad you realize how childish all this arguing is. We could really have something wonderful again if you would just let bygones be bygones."

It dawned on Brendan at that moment that it was time for him to enact the hard-line stance with Trina that he should have taken weeks before. He had been reading a book that Renee had left on the kitchen table called *Acts of Faith* by Iyanla Vanzant. He actually hadn't been reading it, more skimming through the pages. He was reading the catchy quotes at the top of each page; there were quotes for every day of the year. The quotes were spiritual affirmations to be meditated on by the reader. Brendan had found his eyes glued to the pages. One page, however, had particularly captured his attention.

The quote was for August 28, and stated, "Anything dead coming back hurts." It was a quote taken from Toni Morrison's novel *Beloved*. The quote didn't mean much to Brendan because he had never read *Beloved*. In fact, he didn't know much about Toni Morrison other than seeing her on *Oprah* from time to time and remembering that her books rested on the shelves at his mother's house.

The explanation of the quote given by Vanzant was what had reached out and grabbed him. It was as if the words were written for him and his apparent inability to cut off his ties with Trina.

As Brendan sat back onto the bed he wondered if Trina would ever get the point: She'd ruined their relationship. She had demolished any hint of faith in her that Brendan had ever held; all hope of trusting her had faded long ago. He paused as he looked at the nightstand and reached for the purple paperback that had been resting next to his alarm clock for two weeks. He was still annoyed at Trina's pushiness, and her nerve, for insinuating that he was the one who somehow needed to straighten up. Then he began speaking to Trina in a calmer voice. "Trina, sometimes I don't think you understand what kind of pain you've put me through. I mean, it seems sometimes that you don't realize how bad you hurt me."

Trina interrupted him. She hated to discuss what she had done wrong. "Brendan, how about all the things you've done to me? The lies, giving rides home to women from your job, and look at you now, living with another woman."

"Trina, there you go again. This isn't a trade-off about who's done what. If it were, though, it would be quite apparent who had been guilty of throwing the most shit in the game. That is not the point. I just want you to understand where I'm coming from now."

"Brendan, all you're trying to do is pay me back for what I did last summer. You have barely spoke to me for the past three months. We have finally started to put it behind us, but you seem bent on getting me back. You avoid me, and you only halfway return my phone calls."

Brendan still was holding the book in his hands, wondering if he should read the passage to Trina. "Look, Trina, I'm not trying to pay you back. I will admit, though, that I have not fully forgiven you. But I have forgiven you enough to be friends with you. That doesn't seem to be enough for you, though. I know now from last night's experience that I can't expect to just be able to sleep with you and not have you think that everything is fine between us. I apologize for coming over there with those selfish intentions."

"Brendan." She tried to break into his conversation, but he kept talking.

"No, it was wrong. If we keep it up, we're going to wind up right back in the relationship without ever having worked out our issues."

"I don't have any issues. You are the one with issues. Those things are in the past as far as I'm concerned," Trina said.

"No, that's where you're wrong. If we're together, and one of us has issues, then we both have them. You probably can't comprehend that right now. Furthermore, you don't seem to understand that I don't trust you anymore. And without trust we're standing on shaky ground. On top of that, sometimes I think about what you did, and I get so angry with you that I almost feel like I hate you. I don't want to feel like that about anyone. It would be better for me to just walk away from you totally. And that's what I have decided to do."

Trina's voice suddenly became shaky. "So this is it? It's over, just like that? You haven't even thought about this. You didn't even talk it over with me, I mean . . ."

Brendan cut her off before she started rambling again. "I have thought it over. It's not about you anymore, Trina. I do still care for you, but you hurt me, and that was your doing and your choice. You didn't have to fuck around on me, but you did what you wanted. You did what made you feel good for the moment. Now I've got to do what's going to make me feel good for a lifetime."

"Brendan, I have changed. I know that was wrong, but how long are you going to torture me and hold it over my head? Please, just give it one more chance."

"Trina, listen to something. It may help you understand why this is the right thing for me to do." He flipped to his page of divine inspiration. "Check this out." He began reading into the phone, " 'Anything dead coming back hurts.' That's a quote from Toni Morrison. I know you know who she is, as much as you watch *Oprah*. Anyway, I read that in this book, and it has deep meaning. You see, our relationship is dead, Trina. When our trust died, when my faith in you died, our relationship died." Trina tried to start talking, but Brendan kept reading. "Listen, there's more. It says: 'If you keep going in and out of the same relationship, chances are you are going to get hurt. People come together in a relationship to learn. Once you learn your lesson it is time to move on. Take your lesson from the last time and move on to something new. If you insist on drinking from the same used cup, you will eventually get sick. You can do the same old things in just so many ways until you lose track of what you are doing. How many ways can you cry? How many ways can you hurt? How many ways can you convince yourself that you can make this work? When a relationship is over, you must learn to let go. No matter how much you love the other person, or how afraid you are that you will never love again, you cannot squeeze juice from a piece of dried fruit, so don't bother to try.' " Brendan paused. Trina was quiet on the other end of the line. Then he asked, "So do you understand why I have to let this go?"

Brendan asked again, "Trina, I know you understand, right?

After more uncomfortable silence, Brendan could hear breathing coming through the line. Trina sounded as though she were about to burst into tears. She was hurt, but she knew that everything he had said and read was true. She knew it was her fault that Brendan didn't want her anymore. She'd played one too many games. She knew that when Brendan had caught her messing around on him that she was lucky he hadn't caught her sooner. Now that the time had come for her to face the music, she wasn't ready. Brendan was the best man she had ever had. He had respected her even when she hadn't respected herself, and now he was truly leaving her. He didn't have a lot of money, but he was generous with what he had. He was kind and caring. He was handsome and a good dresser. He was everything that Trina could have asked for. Why hadn't she learned sooner? Why had it taken losing him before she realized how much he meant to her?

She wanted to beg him to change his mind, and ask him to forgive her over and over again. As soon as she opened her mouth to try to speak, she felt the tears that she could no longer hold back welling up in her eyes. She could only force out, "Alright then, Brendan. If that's how you want it then, okay. Good-bye. But I know . . . you'll be back." She spoke out before she hung up the phone, and buried her crying face into her pillow.

Brendan couldn't believe that she had hung up the phone like that. He chalked it up as typical Trina behavior. He wasn't about to let her undignified reaction ruin the afterglow of what he had just done. Breaking off a relationship is hard to do. And when you love someone the way Brendan had loved Trina, it was nearly impossible to be the one to shut the door, even if the relationship had gone sour. But now that he had provided that closure to the great romance of his life, it was time for him to bask in the glory that comes with taking a stand for oneself. Brendan felt a sense of relief at having stood his ground. The puffed-up feeling in his chest made it hard to hide the fact that he was proud of himself. He felt like calling someone to tell them about it, but there was no one to call. He had already lied to Cory and Nate about the state of things. They were under the impression that he'd laid things on the line to Trina the night before. He knew Renee was tired of hearing about Trina. She had told him to curse her out and be done a long time ago. Renee had little patience for stupidity, and dragging out a breakup over three and a half months was beyond stupid in her book. Brendan decided to take a shower and get into bed. He felt as though it would be a short night's rest before getting ready to enjoy the start of his new life. He was young, black, and Trina-free.

As Brendan pulled the down-filled comforter up to his shoulders, he thought about the eventful weekend that he had endured. He lay there listening to *Love Talk and Slow Jams* on WPGC, trying to get his feet to warm up. His body made full use of the bed. He was stretched out because there was no one there to block his usage of both sides. There had been no one else other than him in the bed since he'd purchased it and brought it into Renee's townhouse a month earlier. He wondered for a moment when he would get a chance to break it in. When the time came, or the opportunity finally presented itself, Brendan wondered how he would feel screwing some chick thirty feet from where Renee was sleeping. They'd discussed his having company, and she had assured him that she had no problem with his entertaining in any fashion that he chose. But for the life of him, Brendan couldn't figure out why he had the inkling that it would be awkward for him to get his groove on with her so close by. He didn't bother to give it much thought because he knew it was something that he was going to get over eventually. He wasn't about to go wasting money that he didn't have on hotel rooms. And he figured that it would be at least a year before he had saved up enough money for the down payment on a condo or townhouse of his own. On his salary, if he didn't cut back on his shopping, he wasn't going to have enough money to pay his credit card bills, let alone a down payment.

An Angie Stone cut played all the way through, and Earth, Wind & Fire got halfway through "That's the Way of the World", before Brendan was sound asleep.

Chapter 10

GOT 'EM OPEN

A s Nate walked through the Safeway he was thinking that he couldn't believe he was about to go home and cook dinner for Sahleen. When she had called him earlier that morning and told him she was headed out of town the next day for a photo shoot, but that she wanted to see him, he was eager to set up a date. He had suggested Sequoia's, an elegant seafood restaurant located at the Georgetown Harbor. Sahleen had shot that idea down when she told him she wasn't in the mood for going out. She said that she had made a routine of getting to bed early on the nights leading up to her photo shoots so that she could look fresh and rested.

It took Nate by surprise when she suggested that he pick up something from the store and cook for her. It surprised him even more when he agreed. She gave no suggestions or requests other than saying, "Nothing special or spectacular, as long as it's hot and tasty, just like I like my lovers." Nate still couldn't believe that he was cooking for a woman after he had already gotten the sex. Cooking, sending flowers, and all of the other sweet stuff were for suckers as far as Nate was concerned. He only considered it fine to give and do the sweet things in order to get them into bed.

Of course, he knew that women appreciated things like that, but for Nate it wasn't all about what women liked, especially not after he had already gotten the panties. Nate didn't mind a dinner date and maybe a movie for ladies who he considered to be "dime pieces," meaning perfect "tens." He sometimes even extended himself beyond that mark, if a honey was truly "all of it." Once Nate had dropped a couple of hundred bucks, which was usually two dates, the lady had best be prepared to set that ass out on a silver platter. He would tell his boys that he didn't mind feeding them and letting them be seen out with him.

Nate's philosophy was summed up by one of his trademark bits of knowledge: "If you take a woman out and show her a nice time, she'll always want to go out with you. Sure, you'll spend a couple of dollars in the short run, but it should be worth it in the long run, depending upon how much ass you get out of it."

With Nate everything was a methodical step in a patented program to either get the sex from a honey or weed out the women who were looking for a relationship. Nate used all of his cunning to figure out, as quickly as possible, just how badly a woman wanted to get with him. He always claimed that if a woman is attracted and interested in a man, she will give it up after a few dates. That is, unless she wants to make a "good impression." Women never seemed to learn that men don't give a damn about a "good impression." They much prefer the "first impression," simply meaning, if the sex is good, it doesn't matter when they give it up, on the first date or the tenth—the brother will be back.

"So why make a brother wait, just for appearances sake?" Nate would ask a honey in a minute. If a brother has any game whatsoever, he should have the chick at his crib or in a hotel by the third date. Getting her to his crib is essential, because home field advantage is a factor. Women tend to be more vulnerable when in a man's home. In her own apartment or home, she tends to feel more empowered, basically because she's in her domain, and she can kick a brother out anytime she gets ready. At his spot, there's the ever so slight intimidation of not having complete balance. If a brother uses that slight intimidation to his advantage without making her feel threatened, he's in every time, Nate would say.

Ask ten women where they were the first time that they made love to the guy that they are dating now. It's a safe bet that only two or three of them were at their place. It's easy logic. Even if they don't plan it, that's just the way it usually happens. If she doesn't like the sex, she can make up an excuse to leave. Likewise, in his own castle a man can pull just about anything he wants to in order to get rid of a date should the need arise.

There are endless rules and laws of the game called love and romance, and Nathan Montgomery came about as close to being an expert on them as anyone. His areas of genius just happened to be on dog mentality and covert missions of deceit. Rule number one for Nate was to never get caught at his game. Nate emphatically believed that the quickest way for a man to play himself out is to get busted a few times. Women talk, and a bad reputation spreads quickly. In addition to getting a bad name, it's rough on the ladies when they find out the man of their dreams doesn't really give a damn about them. So letting them down easy if possible was a good way to avoid key scratches on the Lexus and supersized guilt trips.

Nate headed toward the cashier with all of the ingredients to prepare his specialty, turkey spaghetti and French bread. There was no denying that he could feel excitement about the evening ahead. It wasn't all that strange for Nate to be feeling excited about a woman, because women were one of the things in life that thrilled him most. Actually, his love for a new romantic conquest was right up there with money, cars, music, and parties. But what was a rarity was that he was so excited about a second date.

It was only Wednesday and he hadn't stopped thinking about her since dropping her off on Sunday morning. They had enjoyed what could have been a one-night stand after she'd left the party with him.

He had gotten her to leave the party with him that night by promising her breakfast. When they reached the Georgetown Café it was packed, so he offered to cook for her at his house. Once they reached his exclusive apartment building on Vermont Avenue, neither one of them so much as mentioned food. This, of course, was fine with Nate.

Once in his apartment Sahleen complimented him on his art collection, which mostly was made up of box-framed black-and-white photos. Most were Tim Hinton originals from his upscale art gallery in Upper Marlboro. There were a couple of pieces from an up-and-coming artist, Anthony Carr, but Nate's favorite was a huge lacquer-framed color photo of Muhammad Ali standing over a knocked-out Sonny Liston, daring him to get up and fight.

Nate had led Sahleen straight through the living room and into the bedroom, where they lay staring up at the ceiling and talking for nearly an hour about their lives.

Then, out of the blue, Sahleen requested that Nate light some candles and put on some music. He obliged her with an ocean-scented and relaxation aromatherapy candle from Pier 1 Imports. He searched his living room for a CD that would set the desirable mood. When he couldn't decide between Gerald Levert and Carl Thomas, he decided to put the radio on. When he heard the Isley Brothers singing "Choosey Lover" on Magic 102.3, he pumped up the volume and headed toward the bedroom.

By the time he returned Sahleen was standing by the window completely naked. Once he saw her naked silhouette in front of him, he almost passed out, as the blood went rushing from his head and straight to his penis. Nate casually pulled his shirt off and his pants fell to the floor just as quickly. He walked up behind her and kissed her shoulders until she turned around to offer him her lips. They kissed passionately, like two old lovers rather than two strangers, and Nate enjoyed sweeping his new friend away in a frenzy of passion and lust. Once they stood face-to-face Nate looked into her eyes, trying to read her.

She looked so innocent to him, but life had shown him that looks mean nothing. Just because she owned the most beautiful face did not mean she wasn't still a typical woman. To Nate this meant that she eventually would want something from him. The fact of the matter was that Sahleen simply liked what she saw. He was dressed extremely well, brimming with confidence, drove a fancy car, and had a laid-out apartment. Nate had already rationalized that she knew she wanted to be a part of his scene, even if the price was what she possessed between her legs.

Nothing new, Nate thought, as he placed the palms of his hands on top of Sahleen's head while pushing it down to his groin. She obliged him for a short while before pulling him to the bed. Nate wanted to give Sahleen all the foreplay she could handle. He had pulled out the baby oil and was rubbing the small of her back, all the while fingering her gently. Then he began sliding his tongue down the back of her thighs, while she made futile attempts to keep from squirming. It had been a while since she had had her toes sucked and the balls of her feet kissed, but she enjoying every minute of it. There was a river forming between her thighs before Nate buried his tongue inside of them. Her eyes were closed while Nate made music with the slurping sounds of his lips and tongue. In her mind she was singing Aaliya's "Rock the Boat" as she came all over Nate's face.

Sahleen had Nate sweating as his lean, chocolate body worked on top of her. He was gently squeezing her behind and pulling her up to meet his grinding thrust. She rubbed and sucked his glistening chest while digging gently into the middle of his back. They kissed some more, and then all of a sudden Nate pulled his body from on top of hers. Her mouth fell open with displeasure, and she begged him not to stop. Nate wanted to get behind her, though, and he did. As he pounded her she tried to muffle her screams by biting the pillows, but she could still be heard. He could feel her body beginning to go limp from pleasure, so he allowed her to lie flat on her stomach. As he was doing push-ups in and out of her, Sahleen's body began to lift off the mattress. He grabbed her by her hair and yanked her head back. She screamed out to let him know that she liked it rough, too. Her moans became screams of passion as she began to climax. She called out Nate's name and told him in plain terms, "Oh, baby, this big black dick is driving me crazy." With each stroke Nate could feel the tingling start to get stronger. He was looking down, watching each in and out motion. He wanted to stay there forever, but he couldn't take anymore. Sahleen's wetness squeezed him and Nate exploded inside of her.

Mama had it going on, Nate thought. He even wondered why in the world she had given it up so easily. It didn't matter. Nate's ego and body were caught up in the rapture of having a model in its midst, and Sahleen was overwhelmed with the excitement of being with one of the smoothest and most confident black men she had ever encountered.

Though they would describe it as casual sex to anyone they told about the incident, in both of their minds they had "made love" to the other person. This was out of character for Nate. He usually tried to fuck the cowboy shit out of women the first time he lay down with them.

When Sahleen gave her body to a man it was usually after she had pulled emotions out of him he sometimes didn't even know he had—and had spent several thousand of his dollars proving he was worthy. Sahleen had captured the hearts and minds of many powerful men in her twenty-six years. And she was wise beyond her age. She had grown up fast in Miami, Florida, living with her older sister, Iris, after the death of her mother. (Their father had long since moved back to France.) Iris modeled for the Ford Agency and was seldom home; by the time Sahleen was in the ninth grade she basically had her own apartment. Iris made very good money, and was able to take good financial care of Sahleen. She and her sister moved to New York City's Lower East Side for Iris's job.

Though Iris was on location for nearly seven months a year, she didn't have the heart to send her baby sister to Ohio to live with their only aunt; Sahleen stayed and went to private schools. She learned how to be sneaky, so it wasn't unusual for her to have her boyfriend spend every night of the week without her sister ever catching on. It was strictly for the company. Sahleen learned that with money she didn't need anything from a man except company and sex—and sometimes not even for those. Iris made sure the bills were always paid in advance, and that Sahleen had a credit card for clothing and plenty of cash in the house for food and entertainment.

Sahleen graduated from Sisters of Trinity School with decent grades and headed off to the Fashion Institute at San Francisco. She stayed for one semester before calling Iris and asking for help getting into modeling. She told Iris quite matter-of-factly that she was too beautiful to be designing clothes to put on women who weren't half as attractive as she. It was true. Iris made some calls and had Sahleen back in Manhattan preparing her portfolio within two weeks.

It just so happened that on the plane back across the country Sahleen met a man. That man was Franco Berra, a renowned photographer. Franco had been one of the most sought after freelance photographers in the country, but he had grown tired of all of the traveling. Franco told her he was relocating to work for an agency in Washington, D.C., and that they were looking for "older" models, which meant over twenty-three. Sahleen had explained that she was just getting started, but that she'd love to work in D.C. He promised to call if he could find a use for her. They exchanged numbers and kept in contact for the next four years while Sahleen steadily made a name for herself.

Franco invested heavily in the agency and became part owner of Mobley Models Agency. Finally, two days after her twenty-second birthday, Franco called Sahleen and offered her a contract. Mobley had gained the Nordstrom and M.A.C. Makeup accounts and needed some new faces for the five years' worth of ads they were now guaranteed. Sahleen was on her way to Washington, and to prominence. Before long Franco had made Sahleen his pet project, and that meant getting her face everywhere. Sahleen had a chameleonlike ability to change faces, so she was seldom recognized. The face in the Nordstrom's catalog looked different than the one on the back of *Essence* magazine. The face in the Cash Money video looked different than the one in the Jaheim video. Sahleen did in fact have it going on. And now she suspected she had Nate going, too.

"Twenty-four seventy-nine. Paper or plastic?" the smiling cashier asked.

"Plastic is fine, sweetheart," Nate returned, as he handed the cashier a crisp fifty. Nate collected his bags and headed out, making eye contact with a cute cashier on the way. He reached his car and threw the groceries into the passenger seat.

As Nate jumped into the car he felt his phone vibrating. He looked down to see who it was, hoping that it wasn't Sahleen calling to say she was on her way already, or even worse to say that she couldn't make it. He didn't recognize the number.

The voice on the other end answered, "Well, hello."

"Who is this?" Nate asked.

There was quick laughter as she spoke. "You mean to tell me that you're so popular that you can't even remember who you have given your number to? This is India. I met you at the gas station last Saturday evening."

Oh damn, I almost forgot all about you, Nate thought but didn't dare say. Instead, he offered, "Oh damn, girl, I've been thinking about you since we met. I'm glad you finally called."

"Yeah, right. Well, why didn't you call me? Don't start off lying."

Nate started in on her anyway. "No, really, I have been thinking about you. I would've called, but I've been out of town since Monday." He sounded so convincing that he figured, why stop there. "I just got back in town today. I was going to call you tonight."

"Is that so?" India asked sarcastically.

"Yeah," Nate answered. Then he went on, "So what's going on this weekend? I wouldn't mind hooking up with you on Friday or Saturday if you're free."

"As a matter of fact I am free. So, where are you taking me?" India asked.

"Oh, I'm sure I'll come up with something that you will enjoy."

"Now Nate, I'm not sure if that sounds proper," she said.

"You, bastard!" Nate shouted.

"Pardon me?" India asked, taken aback.

"No, not you, this jerk just cut me off as I was trying to pull out of this parking lot." Nate added, "Excuse me. I suffer from an occasional bout of road rage."

"Yeah, okay. Maybe you should talk to a professional about that." She laughed. "Would you like to call me later?" she continued.

"Well, actually, I might be tied up later, but if it's not too late when I get in I could call you," Nate replied. He turned the radio down as he reached into one of the plastic grocery bags to pull out the Pringle's potato chips.

"I should be up pretty late. If you want to call me later that will be fine."

Her voice was soft, and sexy. Nate thought she sounded like Nia Long, which was a definite turn-on for Nate.

"Well, don't rush a nigga off the phone. I have a minute now, miss," Nate said, trying to sound cool. "So, has a brother been on your mind or what?"

"Pardon me?"

"Is that your favorite line? Pardon me?" Nate asked.

"It is when people make wild remarks out of the clear blue sky," she said.

"Well, Miss India, what I really want to know is, what is a fine sister like yourself doing unattached. You did say that you were unattached when we met, right?"

"Well, actually, I just got out of a two-year relationship this past September."

"Oh, well, you're probably just playing the field right now, huh?"

"No, to be honest I've only dated one person since then, and it was nothing serious."

"Is that by choice or just the way the cookies are crumbling right now?"

"I guess you could say it is by choice, Nate. I just want to make sure that the next time I get serious I have the right man for the job."

Nate paused, then changed the subject. "So, where do you live, if you don't mind my asking?"

"I actually live in Landover with my mother right now. I moved home after my relationship ended," India explained.

"Oh, you were living with your friend, huh? So who got the Sony when you two split?" Nate asked in a joking tone.

"I paid for everything, so I took everything. It's in storage right now while I'm looking for a new place. I'm thinking Mitchellville or Forestville, maybe. But either way I'm out of here by December one. Moms is driving me crazy."

Nate figured that she was trying to justify living at home, but he didn't care where she lived, as long as she had a car and someplace to go when he finished with her at his house. Nate continued to chitchat with her until he reached his complex. He waved at the man in the security booth as he waited for the gate to open. He quickly said his goodnights to India and promised to call her the next day to set up their date for the weekend.

Nate strolled up to his building and looked back over his shoulder when he heard a horn beep behind him. He looked back and saw a silver Acura coupé pulling up. The window went down. It was Kim. She shouted, "What's up, negro? You got a problem with your cell or something? I have called you at least six times today."

Nate was both shocked and stunned at this surprise visit. "What the hell?" he asked himself.

Nate couldn't believe that, for one, she had made it through the gate, and two, that she had the audacity to show up at his spot unannounced. As he approached her car she could see how tight his face was. Kim didn't care, though. She was tired of being used by Nate. She started to get out of the car, but Nate pushed her back in.

He said, "Look here, Kim. I don't know what in the hell possessed you to come over here uninvited, but whatever it is you were smoking, you had better flush the rest. You know I don't play this shit. You are seriously violating." Nate pointed toward the gate, as if to say "get the hell out of here" without opening his mouth.

"I don't want to hear that shit, Nate. I am tired of this. You call me when you are bored, or when none of your other bitches want to be bothered. You expect me to come over here and screw you at one o'clock in the morning, and leave at seven. You want me to drive over here in the rain, go to the damn grocery store, or clean your damn apartment up, but you don't want me to show up over here when I want to see you." Her voice was shrill and biting. "Trina told me everything, Nate. I know about the other bitches. She told me that I should leave your ass alone and that you are just using me, but that's alright, you haven't heard the last of me," she said, as she began to cry. She slammed her car into reverse before Nate had a chance to respond.

"The nerve of that chick," Nate mumbled as he walked into the building, not wanting to admit that she had put him a little on edge. A pissed-off, psycho stalker is just what Nate needed in his life right now. He figured that he would have to smooth things over with Kim tomorrow, maybe even take her out for lunch.

As he was putting groceries away it dawned on him that he was feeling a little guilty about the way he'd been treating Kim lately. She was a nice girl. She was definitely attractive, and had a body that was tight with a capital T. She always kept a few dollars in her pocket, unlike so many of the gold diggers running around town. She was a top stylist up at The True You Hair Salon in Wheaton. To be honest, she had it going on. Plenty of brothers tried to kick it with Kim, but she was stuck on Nate. She wasn't loose like Trina: Kim was a real lady, but Nate treated them all the same. It didn't matter to him.

It was almost seven, and Sahleen had phoned to say she was on the way over from her Crystal City apartment. Nate had finished cooking, the salad was on the table, and the candles were lit. He had showered and groomed. He had lathered up extra good with his Bath & Body Works peach-scented soap. His cologne was blending with it perfectly. The apartment smelled like the inside of a scented candle shop. He was ready. He had on a pair of Diesel jeans and a Calvin Klein undershirt. His platinum necklace was tucked inside his shirt; the boxing glove charm with the 6-karat diamonds usually brought questions that Nate wasn't up to answering just yet. He found himself in a mood to just lie back and chill with Sahleen. He wanted to ask her questions. He wanted to hear everything about her life and her career. He found his sudden interest in her surprising. For the first time in a long time he was curious about more than just the physical.

Sahleen arrived and was pleasantly surprised by the aroma of gourmet cooking coming from the kitchen. She noticed how clean his apartment was, and with the mention of his obvious skills in the kitchen another plus, she joked with Nate that he would make someone a good husband someday. He had definitely put his best foot forward for Sahleen. Nate pulled out her chair, fixed her plate, and then cleared it when she was finished. He'd poured her wine and convinced her to lay on the couch with her feet up while he washed the dishes. He was a perfect gentleman, and had done everything right. Sahleen relaxed and tried to remember the last time she had been treated in such a manner by someone she found truly appealing.

When Nate finished in the kitchen he joined Sahleen in the living room.

"I really enjoyed the dinner, Nate. You impressed me, I have to admit."

Nate, feeling full of himself, just smiled and sipped his glass of wine.

"I'm going to have to go soon, Nate. My plane leaves at seven in the morning."

Nate looked at the clock and said, "It's only eight-thirty. How much beauty rest does a woman of your beauty require?" Nate asked sarcastically, then added, "You can sleep here and get up in time to go grab your bags."

"Well, I don't have much to pack, but I haven't even gathered the things that I do need to take, and Mobley will send a car to pick me up at six-fifteen." Sahleen was still lying back on the couch as she went on about how she was not looking forward to the long day she was guaranteed to have to work the next day. She explained that the fashion show she was doing in Manhattan was going to be videotaped and would be shown on the Style Channel. She was especially proud that the proceeds from the event were going to the victims of the terrorist attacks and the Red Cross. Everyone in the industry would be there, and it would be closed to the general public. Only those who knew somebody on the inside could get tickets.

Nate realized that if he didn't make a move soon Sahleen would be ready to leave without breaking him off a piece. He decided to move their party of two to the bedroom. Nate walked into the bedroom and pretended to look for something, and then he yelled out for Sahleen to come in. When she came to the room she found Nate in nothing but his underwear and baby oil.

Sahleen laughed out loud, and said, "Man, you are tripping. What happened to your clothes?"

Nate laughed also and lit a candle. After he started the CD player and walked toward her, he said, "Isn't this how you did it the other night? What's wrong?" I hope you don't have a problem with a man making the first move. Do you?" His voice dropped a few octaves, and he was now in his bedroom form. "You're not one of those types of women, are you?" Before she could answer the lights were flipped off, his body was pressing up against hers, and his lips and tongue were sliding across her neck.

"N . . . n . . . no," Sahleen muttered, as she slowly leaned her head back and allowed her body to answer Nate's advances. Then she whispered, "No problem at all."

Chapter 11

WEIGHTLESS

There's a certain excitement you feel when you're traveling on the interstate and you realize the next exit is your destination. This time it was a one-way trip. I was actually moving back home to D.C., so the feelings were multiplied. Inside I had a swirl of emotions, nearly all good, as I exited I-95 in Laurel and headed toward my mother's house. I would be spending my first three nights there until I got some furniture and moved into my apartment. The next day was Thanksgiving, after all, and as good an excuse as any to be under my mom's roof for a couple of days. Not that I ever needed an excuse to stay with my moms. If she had her way, I would be there even longer.

The first thing I noticed as I pulled into the driveway was the large amount of leaves scattered all over the yard and walkway. It looked as though no one in the entire neighborhood had decided to rake theirs, either. The section of Laurel Mom lived in was tidy and quiet. The lawns were neat but not in the obsessive kind of way that other truly upscale neighborhoods tend to demand. If every house had leaves on the grass it was probably safe to assume that recent winds had put them there. Mr. Fields from across the street usually came over and raked Mom's leaves so he could bag them up and make fertilizer with them.

The air was crisp and far easier to breathe than it had been when I had been home in the summer. I knew it was just a matter of time before I would be dealing with the unpredictable D.C. winter weather. I hadn't had to deal with any real snow in five years, but I knew that that would soon change. The winter weather in Washington, D.C., is no joke. Now, of course, it's nothing compared to Chicago or Boston, but the average person will freeze their buns off dealing with D.C. weather from December, and sometimes November, right on through March. I was going to have to do some serious winter shopping on Friday. There were bound to be sales galore, since it was the official start of the Christmas shopping season. I needed plenty of winter gear, because the thickest coat I owned was a medium-weight ski jacket that Paula had bought me the previous year, and I didn't own a pair of thermals.

As I was pulling my garment bag out of the trunk, the front door of the house swung open. "Hey, Grandma," a voice yelled out, "Uncle Cory is here." Kyle came running out the door and straight to me.

"Hey, what's happening, l'il man?" I said, as I embraced my nephew. "It looks like you grown an inch since I've seen you last."

"No, not quite a whole inch, but my feet have grown to a size seven and a half."

"Is that big for the sixth grade?" I asked, not having a clue.

"Kind of. But there's this kid named Leonard who wears a ten and a half. He has the biggest feet in the school."

I closed the door to my car, and with the garment bag slung over my shoulder and my overnight bag in my hand, I headed toward the door. Mom was waiting in the doorway for us.

"Hey, baby." My mother greeted me with a big hug and a kiss on the cheek. "How was your trip?" she asked. Without waiting for my answer she looked at Kyle and said, "I thought I told you about running outdoors without your coat. Your momma can't afford to take off from work to run you to the doctor's for something you can prevent. Do you understand me, Kyle Dandridge?"

"Yeah," he answered, in a slightly dejected manner.

"Kyle," I said, "that is not how you respond to your grandmother, or any adult, for that matter. What do you say?"

"I mean, yes ma'am, Grandma."

"Okay, then. You boys have a seat in the family room. I'll bring down some food for you. Kyle has been waiting for you to get here to eat. I told him it was going to be close to eight when you got here, but he didn't care. So wash up, and I'll be there in a bit."

I went upstairs to put my bags down, and took a seat on the bed while I removed my Timberlands. As I looked around my room my eyes glanced at my high school diploma. Instantly I thought of how Moms had switched to the night shift at the hospital so that she could be available to drive me to private school and pick me up until I turned sixteen and could get my driver's license. She had said that my father had always planned for me to go to Dematha, which is one of the top private high schools in both academics and sports in the country. Pops had saved for years so that there would be no cutbacks around the house. He had said, "If we always live within our means, then when it is time for you to go to high school and for Brenda to go to college, there won't be any big savings crunches."

It turned out that that money would not be needed to pay for me to go to a private school. Pops passed away from colon cancer during the spring of my eighth-grade year. Being the responsible man he had always set out to be, he had nearly two hundred thousand dollars worth of life insurance policies for Moms and us. My mother never even had to touch the money my father had saved. With the insurance money, Mom had been able to pay off the house and send me to private school, and had I not gotten an academic scholarship to Morgan State University in Baltimore, she could easily have paid for me to go there. Brenda had gone to Howard University and commuted. Howard had been far more expensive than Morgan State. Looking back, I was glad to have been able to save my mother the cost of the tuition.

Losing my father was the saddest experience of my life. I remember it was a cold February day when I was called down to the office at school. Brenda was sitting there waiting for me, and my uncle Freddie was in the car. I knew something was wrong the minute I saw Brenda's face. Usually, nothing much fazed her. She was sixteen and deep into her own adolescent world of makeup, boys, and going to go-gos, where live bands such as Chuck Brown & the Soul Searchers, Rare Essence, or Experience Unlimited were playing.

Her face in the office that day, though, was shaken and scared, and the way Uncle Freddie drove to the hospital I didn't need to ask if my father was in bad shape or not. When we reached his room on the sixth floor my mother was sitting on a chair beside the bed and Earline, Freddie's wife, was standing beside her holding her hand.

I remember Mom asking Freddie and Earline to excuse us so that we could be alone with our father. I still didn't expect that those would be the last four minutes of his life. It seemed as though he had waited for Brenda and me to get there to be by our mother's side and for him to see us. I noticed that the tubes in his nose that had been there on my previous visit on Sunday afternoon were gone. I remember my mother being strong while Brenda and I cried like babies watching his every strained breath. When he stopped breathing, his mouth slightly ajar, his face shocked and lifeless but his body still surprisingly warm, my mother didn't call a nurse for five minutes. She just stood over him and stroked his hair and kissed his face. She asked us to get on our knees and give thanks to the Almighty God that we had been fortunate enough to have our father's presence as long as we had, that he had been a good man, husband, and father. We did, but I remember being mad at God, although I would never say it out loud. My mother had explained weeks before that there would be no prolonged use of life-support systems. She later would tell us that she and my father had always agreed that whoever reached that path first, the other would not allow any machines or technology to keep them alive. "When my maker is ready for me, I will meet him gladly and without reservation," she said. She also made us promise that day that when her time came we do the same thing. We did.

I could hear Kyle exiting the bathroom and running back down the stairs, the same way that I used to. I got up from the bed and looked in the mirror. Although I knew I wasn't going to be living here in this house with my mother, I knew that I was home. I knew that this is where I belong, eating my mother's cooking and raking her leaves for her, and teaching Kyle how to cut the grass and wash a car. Suddenly I felt relieved. I wasn't exactly sure what it was I was relieved about, but I felt as though a big weight had been lifted from my shoulders. I could have floated right up to the ceiling. Where I had always been bogged down in Atlanta with thoughts of home without actually being homesick, I was now feeling quite weightless. If anything went wrong, or if anyone needed me, I would be here to fix it. I could be responsible like Pops had been. If Mom didn't want to take money from me for things, I could just go out and spend it on her if I chose to do so.

I had my feet up on the ottoman and a TV tray in front of me. CNN was showing continued coverage from Ground Zero and footage from the battle being waged in Afghanistan. I switched to *Comic View*.

I was washing down my second helping of chicken and dumplings with a huge cup of cherry Kool-Aid. I was feeling fat.

"Ma, I am going to have to join a gym quickly. I can see right now what I am in for up here."

Kyle was looking at me, smiling and agreeing without talking. He was sitting over in my father's reclining seat with his feet up, revealing the brown bottoms of his dirt-riddled tube socks. He had eaten a healthy portion as well.

"Are you ready for dessert, fellas?" Mom asked.

"No, thanks," I answered. "Tomorrow is Thanksgiving. I'll need to save some room for that, right?"

"What about you, Kyle?" she asked, as she took both of our plates and headed to the kitchen.

"No, I'm full. But can I have some later?" he asked.

"Later you can get it yourself. I'll be asleep. You know I am bushed, Kyle. I have been cleaning up since seven o'clock this morning. Cory, I'm going to get into bed. If you need any extra blankets . . ."

"I know where they are, Ma."

"No, I was going to tell you that I washed them all today. They are in the laundry room on the table. Oh, I am so sorry. I almost forgot to tell you that Nate called you just before you got in. He wanted you to hurry and get back to him, something about a big party downtown."

"I think that's where my mother is going," Kyle added.

"Who knows?" Mom replied.

"Well, I'll call him back. I'm kind of tired, though."

"Son, you should get out and see your friends. You can sleep in tomorrow. Kyle is probably going to keep you up all night playing video games if you stay in tonight, anyway."

"Yeah, Uncle Cory. I just got an Xbox."

"How'd you manage that? I heard those things were hard to get."

"Yeah, they are. But my mom gave Nate the money and he got it for me. He must have stood in line all night," Kyle stated, gratefully.

"I'll bet he did," I answered, knowing better. Nate had more hookups than Hustle Man.

"So, you want to play *Madden 2002?*"

"That sounds great, Kyle, but let me call Nate back and see what he is talking about."

"Yeah, I might crush you too bad anyway. We can play tomorrow before the Cowboys come on. Do you know who they play?"

"They play the Broncos," I answered. "Who are you rooting for? And hand me the cordless phone, please."

"You know I like the Cowboys just like you. Even though we're not doing too hot this year."

"And it won't be easy trying to stop Denver."

I dialed Nate's number and heard my mother yell down from the top of the steps for Kyle to turn the television down. He was playing video games and had become oblivious to everything that was going on around him.

"Turn it down. Didn't you hear your grandmother?" I barked, while trying to listen to Nate at the same time. I was beginning to notice that Kyle had become a little hardheaded. Nothing major. He just wasn't as focused on authority as I felt he should be. It was a problem I welcomed the challenge of helping him overcome.

"So you said you already have me a ticket, huh?" I replied, getting my attention back to Nate.

"Yeah, man, and they are sold out. These brothers that call themselves the Positive Black Man's Coalition are throwing the party. They throw this party every year. It's going to be packed. But the place is huge."

"So where is it at?"

"The Grand Hyatt, downtown. But don't worry, I'll come and

scoop you up. Be dressed in an hour. And I hope you have some tight gear with you. Because they do dress to impress up in that piece."

"Yeah, okay, I'll be ready in an hour. Brendan is going too, right?" I was thinking I wanted to hang out with my boys, but I could have just as easily gone out to a restaurant or a bar.

"Yeah, he's picking up the tickets from my man, and he's going to meet us out in front of the hotel at eleven o'clock. So, later."

"Later."

I was in the kitchen eating a piece of Mom's famous lemon cake when I saw Nate's headlights; I washed my hands and headed toward the door. I looked down into the family room and saw that Kyle was still playing his Xbox. I yelled down to him to pause the game long enough to come up and lock the door behind me.

I gave Nate a strong soul brother handshake when I slid into his Lexus. It was nice. It was only three weeks old and had the strong scent of leather and that unmistakable new-car scent that I hadn't smelled since I'd bought my Maxima six years ago.

Looking at my attire, Nate said excitedly, "Damn boy, I didn't know you had it like that. I figured you would have turned into a country 'bama down there in Georgia. I didn't know you were down there going out like a Fashion Fair model." I was looking pretty dapper. I had on a dark gray suit by Christian Dior and a spanking-brand-new pair of thick-soled Coach loafers.

"And that's a tight watch, my man," he added.

"You like?"

"Most definitely. Who makes it?"

"Esquire."

"Yeah? I'm digging that. Is that a new brand? How long have they been out?"

"A good while. Man, don't you know Atlanta is one of the hottest spots for fashion in the country? Right behind New York and Los Angeles. You better ask somebody."

"Yeah, I hear you. So what else is up? How was your ride up?"

"It was cool, but you know I'm not big on driving. If I hadn't needed to bring the car up I would have flown."

Nate changed the CD from Ludacris to Nas, and asked, "So when is all of your stuff going to be here?"

"Actually, I sold most of my furniture to a friend of mine. I gave it to her pretty cheap since it was short notice; I only had a week or so to get it packed up. So I just hooked her up. She's real cool people. You remember the honey I told you about who is a cheerleader for the Falcons, who gave me tickets to all the games, don't you?"

"Yeah, Donna, right?"

"No, Darlene. But anyway, I figured it would help me out as well. My clothes and some other stuff like pictures, kitchen stuff, stereos, and televisions will be here on Saturday. I pick up the keys to my apartment on Friday morning."

"Yeah, you did say that they got you an apartment up in Rockville, right?"

"Uh, huh. It's right up the street from White Flint Mall."

"So when do you start work?"

"Not until the fifth of December. So I have a couple weeks to get some things together. I need to go shopping Friday to get some winter gear, and I'll probably go pick out some furniture on Saturday if I don't have time Friday evening. That's really about all I have to do. This company gave me five grand to cover my moving expenses. I got the check last week. I couldn't believe they kicked me that much dough just for dragging a few boxes."

Nate laughed. "How much of it have you spent moving so far?"

"Maybe a grand," I said, laughing. "And that was mostly for shipping the stuff I wanted."

"Yo, you got over big time."

"You know how we do it. I'll probably spend the rest on furniture."

"You won't get much furniture with that. Nigga, my couch was five grand by itself."

"That's your nonpriority-having ass. I'm going right around the corner to Marlo's and maybe Ikea. I saw a sale paper at Mom's crib tonight. I can get a leather couch and love seat for fifteen hundred, a cherry oak bedroom set for about another twelve hundred, and I'll probably just eat in the kitchen or on the sofa for the time being, unless I see a dinette set I really want."

"I hear you. I can hook you up with a key to my spot if you need to crash in the city from time to time. You know the spare bedroom is yours whenever you need it, or the den for that matter."

"That'll be cool. I'd do the same for you, but I doubt you will be out my end all that much."

Nate nodded his head in agreement. After a short pause he said, "We are going to have to hook up with some bunnies and throw you a little welcome home shindig. I got a nice little honey that I want you to meet. I told her about you. I know you'll like her. At the very least you can hit that ass. She's going to be down here tonight. Her name is Jay. Yo, she is phat as hell. She has her own business. She does some consulting work with computers or something of that nature. I'm not sure, but she's got it going on. She has a nice little townhouse out in Capitol Hill."

"So why aren't you tapping it? You know I don't want any of your leftovers," I said emphatically.

"Nah, man. It ain't like that at all. She a cousin of this honey I see from time to time," Nate mentioned, trying to reassure me.

"You still seeing the hairdresser, what's her name?" He talked about so many women I couldn't keep up.

"You mean Kim? Well, since she flipped out a couple of weeks ago and showed up at my crib unannounced, she's been on punishment." He laughed, but deep inside he still felt a little uneasy about the way he'd dogged her out. When Nate offered to take Kim out to lunch the next day to talk about some things, she declined. She stunned Nate a little when she told him not to call her until he made up his mind about what he wanted to do and was ready to treat her with the respect she deserved.

Under normal circumstances, Nate would have made sure that he had her in his hip pocket. But for the last couple of weeks he had been spending all of his time with Sahleen when she was in town, and if he wasn't with her then he was chilling with his other new friend, India.

"So how are you and the supermodel doing?" I asked.

"Man, I don't even want to get started, Cory. She is so fine, and man, can she fuck. Plus, she's a stone-cold freak on top of that. On the real, kid, we be getting down."

"So could this be the one?"

"The one what?" Nate boomed back.

"You know what I'm saying. You have been spending a lot of time with her."

"Yeah, true. As a matter of fact, every day that she has been in town since we met we've been hanging, which has only been six or seven days . . ."

"But still, that's a lot of QT for *you*, bro."

"What do you really know in six or seven days?" Nate said, but inside he knew that he could fully admit how he was feeling about Sahleen. It was uncharted territory for him. The sex definitely had him going. The fact that he found her so damned intriguing was a whole other ballpark.

"What about the other one?" I asked, remembering him telling me briefly about meeting another chick the same night.

"India. She's fine, too. Not fine like Sahleen, but she's still *all of it*, for real, though. She reminds me of Nia Long, only with bigger titties. She kind of sounds like her, too. We've been out twice, and she's been to the crib once."

Waiting for the details that didn't come, I had to ask, "So did you sleep with her yet?"

"Nah. I just kissed her and sucked on those pretty-assed titties. The next time, though, dog. The next time."

"What does she do?"

"She's an accountant for Verizon. And she is fly as shit. I think she's really into the church. She has invited me to church with her like twice already. Somebody needs to tell her she is going to up and run a nigga like me away with that nonsense."

"She's into the church, but you're sucking her titties on what, the third date?" I burst out laughing. "These fake church people crack me up. If you are going to be about it, then be about it. Hypocrites, I swear, are the worst."

We talked and laughed about old times the rest of the way. I watched the homeless people sleeping on the steam ducts as we rolled past the Convention Center.

Nate smoked a blunt, and even though he cracked the moon roof, I think I caught a small contact. I hoped that it didn't piss me before I started work.

We pulled up in front of the hotel. It was crazy. It looked even more packed than Atlanta's Club 112 on a Saturday night. There were wall-to-wall ladies, and they were indeed dressed to impress. There had to be at least five hundred ladies and a few hundred fellas lined up outside trying to get in.

We found Brendan double-parked across the street talking to a fat guy in a Coogi sweater. Nate waved for Brendan to follow him, and we rolled past the crowd of people, around the corner, and into the hotel parking garage.

"We are full," the attendant said with attitude.

"Not for me and the car behind me. VIP. Here." Nate showed him a Central Parking card with a stamp on it and slid him a twenty. His man Chris was the GM, so Nate always had downtown parking covered.

"Two spots on level three," the attendant said, as he waved us by, backed into his box, and said something on his walkie-talkie.

We had been inside for almost two hours and people were still coming in. I couldn't believe some of the dresses that the sisters were wearing. I may have just been used to the Atlanta version of cold, but these sisters had backs out and sleeveless dresses in 45-degree weather. Don't get me wrong, I was glad to see the sisters out in all of their splendor.

Women from the D.C. metropolitan area seem to keep themselves up better than any other women in the country. Traveling east and west I'd found the only women who are as into hair and nails as the ladies here are the Detroit sisters, even if they are a few years behind the styles of the East Coast women. The bad thing about it is that Washingtonian sisters know it. They've all got plenty of attitude. Every chick, even the ones who aren't fine, believe that they are, and don't try to tell them that they aren't it-on-a-stick. Hell, I was used to women approaching me in Atlanta. All of the games that these D.C. honeys like to play would take some getting used to—all over again.

Nate had gone to the bar while Brendan and I stood profiling near the entrance of one of the ballrooms. I was definitely impressed with the magnitude of the party, if you can call a gathering this size a party.

The Positive Black Man's Coalition had rented out the entire hotel, which had ballrooms on two levels. The floor above had three: one had a jazz band called L!ssen; another had a DJ spinning reggae; and the third had the Marcus Johnson Project performing live. On the floor I was on there were two ballrooms, each with a DJ. They were the largest of the five. There had to be at least four thousand people at this function.

I looked up to see Nate making his way back through the crowd with two bottles of Moët in his hands and two ladies. The ladies were also carrying glasses. He turned into the ballroom in front of us and motioned for us to follow him to a table that was occupied by a lone woman.

As we sat down Nate said, "You know I had to get some champagne to celebrate my man Cory coming home. And by the way, ladies, these are my boys. This chump here is Brendan, and that's Cory," he said, pointing in my direction. Then he went on, "Fellas, these three ladies here are Chelsea, with the pretty silver dress on; that's my sweetheart Erika right here; and this is the pretty lady I was telling you about Cory, Jay." He paused and turned his conversation toward Jay, who was seated right next to me. "Jay, I was telling Cory about you on the way over here."

Jay was fine. She was short but very attractive. She was slightly bow-legged and had a cute haircut and the whitest teeth I had seen in a long time.

"Nice to meet you, Cory. Nate has told me an awful lot about you. All good things."

"Nice to meet you also. You look really nice this evening." She was rocking an olive-colored skirt and matching blazer. The diamond studs in her ears made her look elegant and expensive.

"You look nice, too. I like that suit. Nothing like a brother in a nice-fitting suit. More brothers should put one on from time to time, you know?" she asked rhetorically, as we made small talk about our careers and alma maters. She asked about my move back to the nation's capital, although she seemed to have been informed by Nate of most of the details. She wasted no time asking about my love life, which I thought was a bit forward but typical. After all, no sense wasting time talking to me if I had a woman—or one that meant enough for me to claim. A lot of women figure, if a man lies about having someone, then obviously that someone can't be all that important, and therefore she has a green light to work her magic.

We all talked at the table, and I even danced with Jay for a while, until she needed a bathroom break. When she headed there I made my way back the table. On the way I thought that I couldn't remember seeing so many fine women in one place. I made some serious eye contact with more than one or two lovely ladies, and when I reached the edge of the dance floor my eyes became fixed on a sister who was at least six feet two. She was wearing a black cat suit and was dancing very seductively without a partner among a group of women.

She had the face of a baby doll, and her body was all curves. All my instincts were telling me to roll up on her and get her on the dance floor, but I didn't want to take a chance on blowing what I had going with Jay if she came looking for me. I painfully decided to pass on this one and grudgingly walked right past the sexy Amazon. As I purposely walked right in front of her so that I could check her out one last time, I saw her glance fixed on me as well. I kept walking and staring in her face. Then she smiled at me. With her smile, I immediately changed my mind and decided to go back and approach her. Even if we didn't dance, I was going to have to at least ask for her number. As I approached her someone grabbed my arm. I was startled slightly and turned to see who it was.

"Oh, my God. I thought that was you," the voice said excitedly, as my heart dropped into my stomach cavity, I thought this stunning vision before me was someone else for a moment. Instinctively, we embraced like the two old friends that we were. "Cory, what are you doing here? Are you home for the Thanksgiving holiday?"

As my senses came rushing back to me, the Amazon that I had sought less than a minute ago was now an afterthought as I stood looking in disbelief at the young lady in front of me. It was Nina Sanchez, and damn, she was grown up. I took in all of the changes since I had last seen her. There were hips where there had been none before. Her breasts, though they had not become huge, had filled out, to say the least. And although her face had matured, she still had the same little girl features and flawless skin. I answered, "You won't believe it, but I just moved back home for good today."

"Really, Cory. That's great."

"Baby girl, you are looking good," I said with a smile. Nina was a dime, and she probably knew it. I couldn't help saying it, though.

"Thanks, Cory. You ain't looking too bad yourself. I mean, look at you, all cut up. I see you got a little bling-bling going on too." She said, grabbing my earlobe and pointing to the flawless karat there.

I explained my job thing to her while she nodded politely. Then I asked, "So, how old are you now, Nina? I haven't seen you in, what . . . five or six years?"

"I'm twenty-four, be twenty-five on New Year's Eve."

"Damn, time flies," I said, really and truly meaning it.

We kicked it for a few more minutes before she asked, "Hey, let's dance, Cory. You do still dance, don't you?"

I took her question as a challenge. I took her out to the middle of the floor and completely got my groove on with Nina. She was quite the dancer herself. We danced to Ja Rule, Nelly, and Mystical's "Shake It Fast" before the DJ put on a slow cut, Jaheim's "Anything." I waited to try to read her body language. When she moved closer and continued dancing, I followed suit. I was a little thrown off balance by both of our actions. Though I truly knew, I still wondered, "What is going on here?" As I realized that I had been all too willing to keep the dance going, I found Nina's head on my shoulder. As the song wound down, I was sure she had questioned my willingness to hold her that close while we danced. I chalked it up as simply missing someone who used to be part of your life.

We headed for the bar, and when we got there she told me that I had caught her just as she was getting ready to leave, and would be sure to let her sister know she had seen me. She wrote her number down on a piece of paper and told me to keep in touch. I gave her my cell number, and told her that my home phone wouldn't be on for a couple of days. We embraced again, and as my nose once again filled with the smell of her Miracle perfume, I assured her I would call her, and told her to wish her sister well for me. I watched her walk off. Her ass jiggled like J.Lo's as she headed toward the exit. I felt a little funny about the way I was looking at this girl, who I had first met when she was fourteen. Then she was just the annoying little sister of the love of my life, Shelly.

Back at the table everyone was laughing, except for Brendan. Nate later told me that he was in a bit of a huff because he had seen Trina and her sisters, and of course they had exchanged words. Other than that, all was well as we prepared to leave. The lights had come on and it was after three in the morning.

As we exited the hotel lobby, Brendan went over to talk to a young lady he recognized from the store. He told us to go on and said that if he didn't catch up with me then, he would stop by the house the next day.

When we reached the car Nate told me that we were going back to his crib, and that Jay and Erika were going to meet us there in a half an hour. I thought for sure he was bullshitting me, and I told him so.

"Nah, kid. Jay is on your shit hard," he assured me, then added, "The night is young, my man. The night is young."

I reclined my seat back a little and smiled. "Just like we used to do, back in the old Mirage and come-as-you-are nights at the Classics, huh man?" I asked my partner, referring to our early days on the club scene.

He responded, "Exactly."

He had done all of the work for me tonight, though. He had entertained the ladies while I was off kicking it with Nina, and paid for their drinks all night. In other words, he had gotten them ready. I told him that I had seen Nina and how I had felt crazy as hell when I first saw her, because I had thought she was Shelly at first.

"What was that all about, cuz? Do you think that you still have feelings for Shelly deep down inside?" he asked me.

"I don't even know, but I guess you wouldn't know anything about that now, would you, bro?" I shot at him sarcastically.

He paused for a second, and with Sahleen on his mind he said, "Maybe not much in the past, but who knows what the future holds. I could see myself having feelings for somebody."

I was shocked, and chuckled involuntarily. He tried to explain how intrigued he was with Sahleen and how he wasn't sure about India's potential. I went on to tell him how fine Nina was and how we had danced to the slow cut.

"Man, I know you aren't thinking about trying to get with her, Cory. You know how those Puerto Rican chicks are. Shelly will cut you deep if she ever finds out some crap like that. Hell, she'd probably cut the both of you."

"No, no, man. It's not even like that. It was just nice seeing her again. She was my little sweetheart back in the day. She used to have a little crush on me, but I was like a big brother to her."

"Well, I'm warning you. If she fantasized about you a little bit back then . . . just watch your step, especially if you still could have feelings for Shelly."

I assured him that I had everything under control, but I wasn't sure he was convinced. He ended up changing the subject to the ladies on the way to meet us at his apartment. They were parked at the gate waiting for us because the security guard would not let them in. Nate gave the guard permission, and they drove in right behind us. As we got out of the car we both watched the ladies' behinds as they moved past us on the walkway. They were both very blessed.

Nate looked over at me and winked as he whispered, "Handle your business my brother, handle your business." I nodded and smiled, because I knew I would do just that.

Chapter 12

THANKSGIVING

Brendan woke up to the noise of his growling stomach. When he felt the urge to run to the bathroom, he knew it wasn't because he was hungry, and that the growl was actually a grumble. He had obviously eaten something that didn't agree with him. His daily diet, which almost always consisted of at least one meal from the eatery at the mall, was probably the cause of this morning's pain. Brendan only hoped that his thirty-minute bout in the bathroom would put him back on track.

He would have to take some Maalox or Pepto-Bismol, because the way he was feeling right now, he wouldn't be up for eating anything, even though his aunt Helen was cooking this year. When it came to holiday dinners it was no secret that Aunt Helen was the best cook in the family. Among larger black families this is a title that is coveted among sisters. It had gotten pretty heated in the past when it was time to decide where dinners would be served for the holidays. Brendan could remember arguments from past family reunions about whose cooking was preferred at those monumental Shue family get-togethers. In fact, at the reunion of '84 Brendan remembered his uncle Ryan getting into a fistfight with his uncle Lawrence because Ryan, after a few drinks, had insulted Lawrence's wife Judy's homemade biscuits. Uncle Ryan hadn't lied when he told Judy that instead of bringing any more of those biscuits to the family gatherings, she should get a contract with the National Hockey League to use them as hockey pucks. As everybody laughed at Uncle Ryan's joke, Uncle Lawrence had been rolling up his sleeves as he prepared to pounce on his older brother. The two rolled around in the grass for fifteen minutes before anyone even bothered to break it up. Aunt Judy never brought those biscuits again after that, and the cooking issue remained a big one with the Shue family.

Once Brendan had gotten his stomach back together, he showered and got dressed. It was almost one o'clock in the afternoon when he was finally ready to head out the door. Renee's door was still closed, and he thought about knocking to see what she was up to. He knew she was eating with her family. It was a big deal this year at Renee's mom's house, because her sister had flown in from Chicago and brought her husband and their new baby, Chandler. Renee had gone shopping and purchased half of the clothes in Nordstrom's baby department for Chandler, using Brendan's discount, of course. He was her only nephew, and also the first baby to be born into her family since her older brother's twins nearly ten years ago. Her mother often asked Renee when she was going to settle down and make a family. Renee was the middle child of three and often felt the pressure of being the only one yet to marry and bear children.

She was fast approaching thirty, and she had made it a personal running joke that her biological clock was ticking so loud it kept her up at night. She had said that if she hadn't found the right man by thirty-five she was going to solicit a sperm donor of the very best stock. And she was serious.

As Brendan put his coat on and turned the television off, the phone rang. He didn't recognize the number on his caller ID. It read D and S Ali. He knew no one with the last name Ali, he thought, as he answered the phone.

"Hello," he said calmly.

"Brendan, whatcha' doing?" It was Shue sounding as if he was in need of a favor.

"I'm headed to Aunt Helen's, which is where you need to be on your way to as well."

"I know, I know, but I'm stranded at a friend's house in Glendale," Shue said, and then he paused. "Why don't you come pick me up? I don't feel like driving today. Plus, my car has been acting really weird lately."

"Man, hell no. That is completely out of the way, in the opposite direction. So I suggest . . ." Brendan's phone beeped. "Hold on." He clicked over. "Hello."

"Hello, may I please speak to Brendan?" the soft voice on the other end asked.

"This is Brendan," he said, trying to sound equally polite.

"Hey, Brendan, this is Laney. I met you last night at the party."

Brendan, pleased that his new acquaintance had called so soon, instantly perked up. "What's going on with you? I didn't think that you were really going to call."

"I don't know why you felt like that. You're very nice, and handsome, too."

"Thanks, but you know how everyone is so jive, not just men, you know?"

"Yeah, I know. But I'm not like that. If I say I am going to do something, then I'm going to do it," Laney said convincingly. "I told you that I would call. And I did, right? Look at you, doubting a sister already."

"Yeah, that's right. I'll have to give you a check for that one." He was smiling. "So, what are you doing today, big plans for dinner I'm sure?"

"Well, I don't have a lot of family here, so I'll more than likely be heading over to my girlfriend's mother's house for dinner."

"So you're not from here?" Brendan asked.

"Nope. I was raised in South Philly."

"So what made you move down this way, your job?" Brendan heard his line click. It was obviously Shue, who he had completely forgotten about, finally hanging up.

"It's a long story. Maybe we'll get together one day and talk about it."

"Well, I hope so. I would love see you again and get to know you. You seem really nice."

"Thanks."

Brendan talked to Laney longer than he should have. He knew that his aunt would have his head if he didn't show up with the ice that she'd called and requested. Laney gave Brendan her cell number and asked him to use it to contact her, because she was staying with some friends and didn't want a lot of people calling her on someone else's line. He asked if she would be busy later on, and about the chances of the two of them catching a movie. When Laney said she would like that, Brendan was ecstatic. He thought that maybe he had found a woman who wasn't into playing games.

They said their good-byes for the time being, and Brendan hit the road.

Nate rolled over and saw that Erika was still sleeping next to him. It was getting late, and he could hear movement out in front. Nate slipped on his underwear and headed into the bathroom to relieve himself. When he came out, he went to the door of the second bedroom. It was slightly cracked, and Nate opened it.

"Damn, Nate," Jay's sleepy voice said. "You don't know how to knock, brother?"

"Girl, this is my house. I don't have to knock. Where's Cory?"

"He got up about an hour ago. He said he had a lot of things to do. He gave me his number and told me to call him later."

"Hmm," Nate said, as he nodded his head.

"What the hell are you looking at me like that for, boy?" Jay noticed that Nate was staring at her exposed right breast and immediately pulled up the covers. "You ain't nothing but a freak; you need to stop."

"Look, you need to stop faking on me like that, Jay. Erika is knocked out in my bed, and she ain't going to wake up no time soon, so why don't you let a nigga slide up in there with you for a minute. Don't act like you didn't enjoy it the last time." Nate gave her a piercing stare.

Jay just looked at Nate. She was thinking to herself that she couldn't believe how bold he was. She also knew that she had enjoyed herself with Nate the night she had come home with him from Jokes On Us in Laurel, where she had bumped into Nate at a Tony Woods show. She had been with a few of her girlfriends, none of whom knew Erika or Nate. He had ridden to the show with a friend of his and used the old "Can I get a ride home with you?" routine. Jay, wanting to help him out in what seemed to be a jam, agreed to give him one. After she dropped off the friend who was riding with her, she found herself at Nate's apartment, and eventually in his bed. She had felt like crap afterward. Jay knew Erika was not hung up on Nate, and in fact had a boyfriend in the Air Force. Jay still knew that she was stepping on her cousin's toes by sneaking behind her back. Nate was the only man Erika had been sleeping with since her boyfriend had been stationed in San Diego, and Jay could easily predict how pissed she would be if she found out.

For some reason, at that point Erika's feelings didn't seem to matter. Jay sat in the bed with a blank stare on her face as she watched the bulge in Nate's underwear grow before her eyes. While he waited for a strong refusal from her that never came, Nate went into his room, where Erika was still sound asleep. He reappeared within a few seconds with a condom. Jay had made a weak attempt to regain her composure and some control of the situation. But before Jay could pull herself from underneath the covers to get her clothes on, Nate was on top of her, getting her worked up again. Within a few moments, Jay had given in, and her legs were wrapped around Nate's back.

As Nate began hitting it harder and harder the bedpost began to hit the wall. Nate was in seventh heaven, as he could truly compare and assess how much better Jay was than Erika. Nate had wondered why he hadn't dropped Erika from the picture all together. But just as quickly as he wondered, it came to him. He figured, why cut one back when he could screw them both. Jay was obviously out of control. She had fucked him last summer, fucked his boy a few hours ago, and was now letting him hit it again with her cousin in the next room. He laughed to himself as he turned her over. *Somebody is going to take this little freak home to their mother one day. That brother is going to be so proud that he has his self such a pretty little mamma with her own business and a bright future. All the while, he won't know that she is a little whore with no self respect*, Nate thought, while he pulled Jay by her hair.

Unexpectedly, as Jay began to climax, she screamed.

"Shhhhhh, girl," Nate said, covering her mouth with his hand. She bit down on his fingers. Nate kept hitting it. Jay's sex was good. He knew Cory had enjoyed this last night. "Did my man tear it up for you last night?" Nate asked. "Huh, Jay? Did you take care of Cory last night like this?"

"Oh yeah, baby, I took care of him."

"Was it good?" Nate moaned.

"Oh hell, yes, he was so good. You both are gooood."

"You bitch!" Nate and Jay both Jumped away from each other as they heard Erika's voice behind them. Jay scrambled for the sheets. "Jay, how could you do this? What the hell is your problem?"

Nate interjected, "Look E, don't get all bent . . ." His words were cut off when Erika threw one of Jay's shoes at him.

"Oh, and you motherfucker!" Erika shouted, "You have lost your damned mind. How are you going to screw me and my cousin, too? Okay, okay, you are messing with the wrong bitch now, you black bastard." Tears began to run down her face as she continued. "It's on now, Jay. I can't believe you. I ought to beat your ass. You are a fucking slut. I heard you in here last night screaming. You sounded like you had a good enough time with Cory. But you still had to go and do my man, too."

"First of all, that wasn't me screaming in here. It was Cory. And second of all, Erika, you seem to be forgetting that you have a boyfriend, or a fiancé, whatever the hell Carlos is to you," Jay said, as though she was hurt that Erika had cursed her out.

"You know something?" Nate asked. "I think it's time that both of you leave." Their mouths dropped open. "It's Thanksgiving, and I don't have time for all of this negativity, and if you two get to fighting up in my spot I will have to whip both of your asses."

After Nate reemphasized his demand that they leave, they both cursed at him as they gathered their belongings. Nate, unfazed by their wailing, stood over them and watched them dress. Jay called a cab, because she knew there was no way that she was getting into Erika's car. Within twenty minutes both ladies were gone, and Nate was shoving soiled sheets into the washing machine and lighting incense. He jumped into the shower and was looking forward to dinner at India's.

She had insisted that he accept her invitation when he told her that his grandmother would be eating at the church with the pastor and a few select members. Each year the deacons and the sisters who had given their time and effort to church community-empowerment opportunities, such as minding the babies in the nursery and helping serve food to the homeless, were at a Thanksgiving feast catered by the Florida Avenue Grill. The meal was unmatched, and Nate's grandmother wouldn't miss it for all the tea in China. Nate didn't mind. In fact, he was used to dropping his grandmother off each year, even though she could drive. It made it necessary for him to see her on Thanksgiving and had become a sort of yearly ritual, just like shampooing her carpets.

India was excited to have a date coming to dinner, and Nate was up for a good meal, since India had promised that her mother was a spectacular cook. If she was wrong, Nate's pager would surely go off with an emergency that required his immediate attention. In addition, he had told Cory that he would come past his mother's house later.

As Nate prepared to leave the house, he wondered what Sahleen was up to. She and her sister were visiting their aunt in Cincinnati. He didn't have a number to reach her, and he was a little irritated that she hadn't called him since he had dropped her at Dulles Airport the previous morning.

I had come back to my mother's house and crawled right back into my bed. I had no idea that I had slept until nearly two o'clock. I finally woke to Kyle telling me that the Detroit game was already on, and that I needed to get up because people were on the way over. My mother had poked her head into the room long enough to issue me a command to shower and get dressed before Uncle Freddie and his family arrived.

"See, I told you, Uncle Cory. It's time for you to get up," Kyle said, while fiddling with a Nintendo GameBoy in his hand.

"Alright, okay, I'm up. You happy now?" I asked.

"Yeah, now get dressed. My mom and Tory are downstairs."

"Really, and neither of them came up here to wake me up. That's a shock."

"Grandma told them not to. She said that you drove all day yesterday and that you stayed out all night doing God knows what with Nate last night, and whose truck is that in front of your car?"

"It's Nate's truck. I borrowed it because . . . never mind, get out of here so I can get dressed. I'll see you in a few." I rolled over and called Nate to ask him if he was still stopping by and to ask how he was going to get his truck back. He told me India was picking him up for dinner and that he would have India bring him out here after he ate at her mother's house. He asked me to page him sometime between four-thirty and six o'clock just in case he needed to get away from India's family. He'd added that, if things were cool, he might not call back. I promised him I would. He said he had to go because Sahleen had just called him. He seemed a little too anxious to talk to her. He said that she was in Ohio or something, and then he rushed me off the phone to talk to her. It was unusual behavior for the Nate I knew.

Uncle Freddie said the grace. It was one of his usual graces, as long as ever. He gave thanks for everything from the turkey to the napkin holders. He prayed for the victims of the Twin Towers and the Pentagon, the homeless, and the hungry children in Africa and the inner cities. I mean, he went on and on. But we knew that it was vintage Uncle Freddie. Then he ended it by giving thanks that I, his only nephew, was home for good. I was touched, but I was glad he was finished. Kyle sat to my left and my beautiful niece, Tory, sat to my right.

"Pass the bread. Pass the gravy. Can I have some more turkey?" That was all that could be heard for the next thirty minutes, along with the clanging of Mom's best silver and china. As plates were scraped clean there was only sporadic conversation, at best. However, as everyone started on second helpings, the conversation picked up. At first it was geared mostly at me, and of course, my big move home. Aunt Earline seemed to be fascinated with my stories about Atlanta. She couldn't believe how greatly things had changed in the South. She told us her stories of the South, from when she worked in a sewing factory in South Carolina during her summer vacations from college, back in the sixties.

As dessert was served Brenda told me how proud she was of the grades Tory had brought home so far this year. Tory was an honor roll student and captain of the junior varsity cheerleaders. When I asked about Kyle's grades, she told me he was improving but still had a ways to go. Not that my nephew wasn't intelligent. Truth be told, he was a gifted child. He simply suffered from a poor attention span. The experts called it ADD. I called it, simply needing to get his butt spanked if he didn't calm down and do what his teachers said to do from here on out. I looked over at him when my sister spoke about Kyle's misadventures in the classroom. He was looking in every direction other than where my eyes were focused: at him, and glaring.

After the plates were cleared the ladies, minus Tory, went inside to do the dishes. She came into the family room with Uncle Freddie, Kyle, and myself. Mr. Williams and his wife, who were dear friends of the family, had arrived late and were at the table still enjoying the delicious, ten-course dinner my mother had prepared. She cleared the empty plates from the table but left some foil and food out, knowing that everyone would be sure to take at least one plate of food home. If they didn't, Moms would be eating leftovers for a month with all of the grub she had prepared.

Just as the Lions game reached the fourth quarter I remembered to page Nate. I felt so full that I was considering taking a nap when I heard the doorbell ring. I heard my mother telling Brenda to answer it. Within seconds I could hear my sister giving one of her "big sister" greetings to Brendan.

"Boyyyyyy. Where's you been hiding? You looking good!" I heard her say. Then she went on. "You know, Cory doesn't have to be here for you to come past to say hello."

I heard him upstairs talking to my mother in the kitchen, and she then reintroduced him to people he had met at least ten times. I finally heard Moms excuse Brendan to join us. He walked down the five steps into the family room where we were.

"Hey, what's going on everybody?" I heard him say.

"Hey there, youngblood. What do you know good?" Uncle Freddie returned.

"Not much," Brendan replied. "Who won the first game, Cory?"

"It's almost over now," Uncle Freddy answered. "Detroit may lose the rest of their games this season."

"You finished up sort of early at your aunt's house, huh?" I asked, looking at the clock. "What's going on tonight?"

"Not a heck of a whole lot. I may check out a movie with this chick I met last night."

"Come with me for a second, I want to show you something." I got up off the couch and headed toward the steps. Brendan followed.

"We don't want to hear your conversation. You don't have to leave, Uncle Cory," Tory said, giggling.

"I'm sure you don't, and stop being grown," I said sarcastically, as I headed up the steps and into my room.

Once I entered the room I pulled out a photo album of some of my friends from Atlanta and tossed it to Brendan.

He thumbed through the pics enthusiastically for a minute before he came out, "Hey, that cutie I met last night just before you all left the party last night is sweet, Cory. I told her that I would call her today . . . as a matter of fact, I'm going to hit her up on the cell right now."

As soon as Brendan called Laney, the phone rang. I answered, "Dandridge residence."

"Cory?" I heard Nate say.

"Yeah, it's me. What's up? You told me to page you, right?"

"Oh, yeah. But everything is straight. India's family is cool. Her mother threw down with this meal, and this gravy she made is like a secret weapon." He said with a slight laugh. Then he added, "Yo, everybody over here is suffering from 'niggaritis.' It's pitiful, Cory. It's like ten out the fifteen people who ate are asleep, even the little kids, man."

"What the hell is 'niggaritis?' " I was puzzled.

"You know, when you eat and fall asleep right after dinner. Like these niggas did."

"Well, shit then, I guess if that's the case, then I'm suffering from a bout of niggaritis my damned self, because I'm definitely thinking about laying down."

"Nah, hold tight. I'll be through there within the hour. India is going to bring me out there to pick up the truck. Where's Brendan?" he asked.

"He's right here on his cellphone talking to some little honey he met last night. He said something about taking her to a movie."

"Yeah, that doesn't sound like a bad idea. Tell him that me and India might roll with them."

I turned to Brendan and gave him Nate's message. He nodded to confirm that it was on, and I relayed the response back to Nate.

He responded with, "Why don't you come along, Cory? Call up a honey and see if you can get a date." He cut himself off. "Yo, I forgot. You just got back and don't have too many selections to choose from."

"Exactly. As a matter fact, I'm starting off with a clean slate. I told Jay that I might call her later on."

"No, no. You can't call her," he explained. "She will run her mouth to Erika if she sees me with another honey. Why don't you call Nina? You got her number last night, right?"

"I thought last night you said that I should stay away from her, and today you're saying I should take her out on Thanksgiving Day, after she finishes dinner with her family and her sister, probably. Make up *my* mind, will you?" I said sarcastically.

"I'm just saying, Cory, it's nothing but a friendly movie date. Not even a date for real . . . it's just hanging out as friends, like a buddy thang, you know what I'm saying?" Nate shot back, trying to draw my attention as far away from Jay as possible.

"I don't know, man. I'll think about it, though, and let you know when you get here." As I hung up the phone with Nate, Brendan walked back into my room with the movie section of the *Washington Post*. He browsed the section while coming to a verdict on what movie, what time, and finally, what theater. Decisions, decisions.

The idea of catching a movie seemed like a good one. I thought about calling Nina for a minute, but then just as quickly began to think of all of the reasons I should not. And there were quite a few that came to mind. What if someone saw us? How would I act on a *date* with Nina, and what if she was as beautiful as she was when I saw her last night? That last thought made me a little nervous as I battled the urge to call her.

Brendan had gone to pick up Laney and would meet Nate and India at the Sony Theaters in Calverton. Nate came into the house long

enough to introduce India to my family, as he had introduced probably a hundred or so others in the past ten years. India was everything
he had said. She was sexy, and when she spoke her voice was one that
could probably drive a man crazy. I thought she should be on the
radio. She seemed like a really nice sister, as well. That was as far as I
could venture with her, though. I no longer bothered to put any real
persona with the women in Nate's life. If I took the time to actually
realize that they were real people with real feelings, I would find myself feeling sorry for them. That had happened once before and had
been a big mistake. It had nearly caused a rift in the friendship between Nate and me, and I had learned my lesson. What he did was
strictly his business.

They both tried to convince me to go to the movies as a third leg,
since I didn't have a date, but I declined. I told Nate to call me in the
morning if he was going to go shopping with me. He nearly forgot the
plate of food my sister had made for him to take. But he gladly took it
when she reminded him.

I told India that it was nice to meet her and she assured me of the
same as they headed out the door. It was seven o'clock when they left.
At seven-fifteen I left the house, headed for the AMC Movie Theater
at City Place in Silver Spring, where I was meeting Nina.

Chapter 13

ALL I WANTED FOR CHRISTMAS

I t was the Friday before Christmas and I had completed my first three weeks at Hakito Electronics. Each day had gone as smoothly as the first. Jamison Hakito had come into the office from New York to personally introduce me to everyone at HE. He was the coolest Japanese man I had ever met, and I had met quite a few working in the tech world. Every day that Jamison was in town he wore custom-tailored suits and expensive loafers. Even his assistants, who were Japanese as well, were dressed to the nines. They followed him around everywhere he went, writing down whatever he said and remembering anything that he forgot. He walked through the building with an air of confidence and control that I hadn't seen when we first met in NYC. It made me wonder how in the world my bosses at Pavillion had ever thought that we would be able to bluff or bully him and his company into a buyout of its digital programming division.

On my first day Jamison had taken me out to lunch at the Montgomery Grill in Bethesda, and then to an art gallery that he knew up on the Pike that was located not far from my apartment. He told me to pick out five pieces of artwork that I liked, as they would be framed and go into my office the next day. It dawned on me at that moment that the walls of my office, which was a top-floor, corner spot overlooking a man-made lake, had seemed a little bare that morning when I arrived. I had probably overlooked it, though, because of how stunning the cherry oak desk, conference table, and bookshelves were. There was also a couch, a small wet bar, and a private bathroom. I had been prepared to purchase my own artwork, but since Jamison and HE were springing for it, I figured, why not? They were surely writing it off anyway, so when the four pieces and the two statues I chose came up to thirty-seven hundred dollars, I felt no reservations at all.

It was a hell of a welcome aboard, and it didn't stop there. As we drove back toward Gaithersburg, Jamison explained to me in greater detail what my position entailed. Essentially I would be responsible for cracking a whip and ensuring that sales and production levels stayed at a comfortable match. This meant that if sales were up, I was responsible for ensuring that the people in production kept up, and if they didn't keep up, I was responsible for rolling heads. Dealing with the sales division, however, was going to be a bit more complex. When problems arose with sales, I was first to report the problem to Jamison, who was my direct boss. I was then to advise him of my planned actions, be it with marketing, the sales team, or customer service. When it came down to it I was the "man" next to the "man," and that was alright with me because it paid so well.

After our lunchtime conversation, which lasted back in my office and through the remainder of the afternoon, Jamison and I reviewed some of the details of my contract. It stipulated my six-figure salary and bonuses galore that could easily add another forty grand if I met some very reasonable incentives.

There was four weeks of paid vacation, of course, five days of personal leave, unlimited sick leave, and HE had even thrown in three days for family emergencies. I had never seen such a thing, and when I asked him to explain it, he said that HE was family friendly, with a lot of single mothers employed there. If I chose to leave before that time, I could not work for one of their competitors for two years. It also stated that should I be released for my performance or conduct, HE would pay the remainder of the salary left on my contract. It seemed pretty sweet to me.

Later that afternoon a Fed Ex package arrived at my office. I opened it to find a box of fancy linen-stock business cards with all of my contact information on them. In the box, I also found a Dell laptop computer, a Palm Pilot, and a top-of-the-line Nextel cellular phone.

Jamison had taken the liberty of hiring an administrative assistant for me from a temp agency but said I could hire a permanent one as soon as I wanted. He told me I would need a good one, and the sooner the better. He had someone e-mail me the listings of all the secretaries inside the company who wanted an interview for the position. Jamison explained that since I was part of the executive management team, my assistant would be paid a starting salary of forty-five thousand dollars, which would be a significant raise for anyone I hired from within. He suggested that it would be nice if I hired someone who was already familiar with the company, but assured me that it was my choice.

I fumbled through the papers on my desk and pulled out a folder. It contained information on the last two candidates I would be interviewing for my still vacant administrative position. I was trying to familiarize myself with some of the information about the ladies before they arrived. I was becoming a little irritated with my second temp. Had the first one made it to work on time once, I may have offered her the job. She was certainly proficient enough in every other category, but punctuality was a must. I had interviewed at least twelve women from inside the company, but only one seemed to have the kind of personality I was looking for.

I was seeing one of my two candidates before lunch and the second afterward. Mrs. Vance, the first, arrived. She was a somewhat stocky woman who looked to be in her late thirties. She was average-looking at best, and wore very thick glasses. She knew her stuff, though. Looking at her résumé I could see that she was extremely experienced in all aspects of running an office and knew the software as well. She had even worked in the corporate offices of Panasonic in Corpus Christi, Texas. She had only left her last job because her husband, who was in the Navy, had been transferred to Bethesda Naval Hospital. She took the liberty of explaining to me how perfect she would be for the job. She was right, and I even let her know how impressed I was with her qualifications. The interview lasted the better part of half an hour. I told her I still had to interview one other person, and that she would be notified Wednesday at the earliest, since Tuesday was Christmas.

I watched her try to swish her blocky hips as she swaggered out of the office with the same confidence she had come in with. I just shook my head as I went to grab my coat for lunch. Before I left I remembered to have my acting assistant forward my calls to voice mail. I didn't trust her to take messages for me, since she was liable to take fifteen-minute breaks any time I left the office.

When I returned twenty minutes later with a turkey sandwich from Subway and a newspaper under my arm, there was no sign of my worthless temp. As I made my way back to the receptionist's desk I saw a young white girl in a gray pinstriped business suit seated in the reception area. Our eyes met briefly, and I smiled and nodded as she moved her lips to say "hi" without any sound coming out. I asked the receptionist where my assistant had gone. When she informed me that my sorry assistant had told her she was going to the mall, I nearly went off right there. I had several reports that needed to get done before I left for the four-day weekend. As I began to complain to the receptionist, Carol, whom I had become somewhat familiar with during the past few weeks, she informed me that the seated young lady was my afternoon interviewee. I looked at my watch and realized that she was half an hour early for her one o'clock appointment. After introducing myself, I invited her back to my office.

I offered her a seat at the assistant's desk while I went back into my office and wolfed down a few bites of my sandwich. I checked my mouth for crumbs, washed my hands, and went back out. I told her to come back into my office and have a seat at the conference table. As I grabbed the folder with her résumé, I opened the door to my office that she had allowed to swing shut behind her. I didn't want to make her uncomfortable by being in a closed office with a man she didn't know. In addition, I was curious as to what time my temporary assistant would stroll back in. I grabbed two twelve-ounce bottles of spring water from my refrigerator and handed her one before I sat down. She thanked me, promptly took the top off the bottle, and reached for one of the Styrofoam cups that were in the middle of the table.

I took a seat directly across the table from her and opened the folder. Heather Primrose, I read.

"Good afternoon Miss, or is it Mrs., Primrose?"

"It's Miss Primrose, for the time being. I am engaged, though." She gave me a phony, laughing smile.

"Oh, really. Congratulations. That's great," I said. "So when is the big day?" I said, trying to sound as if I really cared.

"In August of this coming year."

"That's really great." She asked if I was married, and we made some small talk before I got down to the interview. She had attended Montgomery Community College but had studied nursing. She explained that she had worked as an administrative assistant briefly in a law firm the previous year year but had left the job to go back to school. She then went on to tell me that the bills were coming, and she simply would have to attend school in the evenings instead. When I asked her why she had applied for this job, she explained that a friend of hers who works in accounting had seen the job listing and had encouraged her to apply. As she talked about all of the wonderful things she had heard and read about HE, I noticed that, other than a small overbite, she was actually rather attractive. She had dyed blonde hair, green eyes, and at least a pair of 36DDs being restrained under her blazer. Maybe 38s.

None of this fazed me much because I wasn't into white women at all. I had gone out with a white girl only once in my life, and it wasn't supposed to have been a date. I had been paired with a fellow student for a project in grad school. We had been working closely for two months, so when the project was complete we decided to go out and celebrate the A that we received at a bar. We ended up meeting at Fat Tuesday's in Atlanta's underground mall. We had a pretty good time drinking frozen daiquiris with double shots, and eventually ended up back at her place fooling around. We had mediocre sex that night but never spoke much after that semester. I saw her from time to time with her boyfriend, and she always looked scared of speaking to me, in front of him, as if he then would know what had happened. Although I had gotten a few offers from other white women, at PSC, I had shied away, thinking that they were all as silly as the first one I had screwed.

Heather was very personable and took every break in the conversation as an opportunity to ask me about the company and about me. It felt as though I was the one being interviewed and she was merely deciding if she wanted to take the job. Heather was nice, but nowhere near as qualified for this position as Mrs. Vance. While sitting there I had all but decided to call Mrs. Vance before I left for the weekend and offer her the job. God only knew what time I'd be leaving, since I had to finish reports for the New York office and send them out by midnight. I brought the interview to a close by telling Heather how nice it was to have met her and that she would be hearing from me sometime before the New Year.

As I extended my hand to her, she looked me in the eye and said bluntly, "Mr. Dandridge, I really want this job." I was sure that the look on my face made her aware that I was completely puzzled by her statement, or request. I wasn't quite sure which one it was. Then she said, "I overheard you mention to the receptionist that you had reports to get done. It doesn't look like your assistant is coming back any time soon. If you give me the job, I will start right now on those reports. I swear to you that I will do a great job. I won't leave until they're finished, and if you hire me you can do it on a thirty-day probation." She continued, rambling, "If you evaluate me in a month and my performance is not rated top-notch, I will resign with no questions asked."

I listened to her go on for another minute. I finally cut her off. I was thinking as I listened to her talk. She had surprised me with her aggressiveness, and I really did need help right then and there. I was feeling a little leery about being in a position to help one of my own by hiring Mrs. Vance, and choosing not to. By hiring little "Ms. White Bread" I would be letting my entire race down, now wouldn't I? I thought it over in my mind quickly as I pictured Mrs. Vance at that desk with her block hips and snatch-back hairdo, then I looked at Heather and those 36DDs again. I said, "Okay, your first assignment is to put that probation agreement in writing. I am going back into my office to finish my lunch. If the temp comes in send her back to me. Oh, and to log onto the computer type 'Dandridge AA.' "

"Oh, thank you so much, Mr. Dandridge. You won't regret it." She took my hand really fast. "You won't regret this," she said again.

I went back into my office and ate. Within ten minutes she was in my office with the agreement. I told her I would have the receptionist come back to witness the signing a little later. Then I showed her around the office. I showed her how to work the phone system, and the copier. I explained to her that I arrived between eight-thirty and nine, but that I wanted her there at eight to answer the lines. I told her that she could usually leave by five and that she would have an hour for lunch, starting at twelve-fifteen. There would be some travel required, maybe once every three or four months, and occasionally she would have to work late. She just nodded her head happily, agreeing to everything I said.

My temp had the nerve to come back into the office at two o'clock and catch an attitude because Heather was seated behind the desk. I explained to her that she was finished with her assignment. To get rid of her I lied and said that I would tell her temp agency I had given her the rest of the day off. She lost the attitude and left happily. She also had the nerve to insinuate that I should have offered her the position but perhaps hadn't because she wasn't as attractive as Heather.

Heather worked hard, and we finished the reports by seven-thirty that evening. As we prepared to leave I assured Heather that I had every confidence that she would work out. I wrote her a personal check for two hundred dollars for helping me out in a jam. I told her to consider it a Christmas bonus.

"Wow, this is unbelievable," she said.

I asked her if I had discussed a salary with her yet. When she said no, I told her it would be about forty-five thousand dollars.

"That is so awesome," she said, growing more delighted, if that was possible.

As we rode the elevator I asked her if she would like a ride to her car, since it was dark out, and I was sure she had parked a fair distance away. She accepted my offer and rode the elevator down to the parking garage with me. As we approached my car I activated the remote to the alarm, then opened her door.

"Thanks," she said.

"It's freezing out here tonight," I said, as I got in on my side.

"Oh, it's not that bad," she said. "I'm from Maine originally, and this is nothing to me."

"Well, I'm from here originally, but I just moved back from Atlanta last month, and I am nowhere near used to this weather yet."

As we pulled out of the garage, she complimented me on the smooth ride of my car.

"This is a BMW right?" she asked.

"Yes, it is," I said, trying not to sound too impressed with myself. I had broken down after my first day at work at HE. I had taken a look at all the cars parked in the reserved spots next to the one given to me. My poor Maxima looked so out of place next to the Jaguars, Mercedes, Range Rovers, and Lexus's that populated the executive row. I had headed straight to Passport BMW in Marlow Heights and leased a brand-new X5, silver with black interior. Nate had been so thrilled that I had gotten a new ride. All he could say was, "Watch how much pussy these bitches are gonna start throwing at you now."

I had given the Maxima to my niece, Tory, who had just gotten her learner's permit. She was going to need a car now that I had convinced my sister to let me pay to send her to private school for her last two years of high school. The Maxima was parked in my mother's garage for the time being, and Tory brought all of her friends by just to sit in it with her and make big plans now that she and her crew would have wheels the following summer.

I pulled up to Heather's car and she got out and thanked me again. She told me that she would see me bright and early on Wednesday morning. Then she smiled and told me how wonderful I had made her Christmas. I was sure that I had. As I pulled off I hoped that I wouldn't ruin Mrs. Vance's New Year's celebration when I told her I had given the job that she deserved to someone else.

Chapter 14

THINKING OF YOU

I was tired as hell, and the last thing I felt like doing was going into anyone's mall, but the Christmas lights and decorations that I saw as I exited the Beltway onto Rockville Pike reminded me that I had to. Since the malls were open until eleven, I decided to get the last few gifts that I needed to complete my shopping. I had done well getting the majority of it over with during the two weeks I was off when I moved. I had, however, forgotten to pick up gifts for Brendan's little brother, and for some reason I was feeling compelled to buy something for Nina.

Though I hadn't spoken to her for almost two weeks, she was on my mind. I had only seen her once since we went to the movies. We'd met for a Sunday brunch at Hogate's Restaurant on the waterfront. During that brunch we had had a chance to really get to talk and catch up. Without my asking she had told me everything that Shelly had been up to since we had parted ways.

Shelly was doing well for herself, according to Nina. She was a guidance counselor at a middle school in Takoma Park, Maryland, a largely Hispanic community in Maryland that is located just outside the D.C. line, and was preparing to work on her Ph.D. Shelly's relationship with her daughter's father, Eric, was up and down, as Nina put it. Eric didn't seem to have the goals and motivation to match Shelly's drive, she said, and it had become a constant source of friction between them. They had been dating for five years now and hadn't gotten married yet. Shelly had her own townhouse in Wheaton and

Eric was living at home with his mother. Knowing Shelly the way I did, I found that a little odd. When we were together all she ever talked about was being married. It was her dream to have a husband, three kids, and a nice home, she would always tell me. Now it seemed as if most of her dreams were centered around her career.

I had told Nina all about my relationship with Paula and how it had ended with my move. I didn't bother to mention Darlene, who I had also been seeing pretty regularly on the side. She had been a great friend and a reliable sex partner. We had the kind of "no strings attached" relationship that most men long for. When I had told Darlene about my move she showed up at my house with three brand-new white dress shirts and three silk ties as a congratulatory and going away present. She had shown the kind of support that Paula hadn't, and I had been really impressed. That was precisely the reason why Darlene would be coming up to spend a few days with me after the football season ended.

As for Nina's situation, it appeared she was in a strained relationship that sounded like it was in trouble. The guy she was dating was separated from his wife and trying desperately to remain close to his children. His wife had become very adept at holding the children over his head as leverage, and Nina felt that his actions were indicating that he wouldn't be able to handle a divorce, a custody battle, and a relationship with her as well.

Once she told me about her situation I had decided to back off a bit. I wasn't sure where I would, or whether I should, fit into her life, anyway. Too much time had passed for me to try to come back and play the big brother routine. To be totally honest, though, Nina was just too damned fine. She reminded me of everything that Shelly had been, and then some. Brendan had told me in a long-distance conversation in the fall that he had bumped into Nina at the Taste of DC on Columbus Day weekend downtown, and that she was finer than Shelly had ever been at that age. I hadn't believed him then, but now I'd seen for myself. After seeing her, I had to be honest with myself. I knew full well that if I spent much time with her, the physical attraction would surface, and who knew what kind of uncomfortable feelings might come from that scenario. I couldn't bear the thought of hearing that she didn't see me that way. I wasn't quite sure of the proper way to bring up something that was basically improper: "Hey Nina, I know that I was nearly engaged to your sister back in the day, but I was wondering if maybe now you and I could . . ." I don't think so. That was some Jerry Springer–type drama.

At any rate, I had planned to call her on Christmas Day to wish her a merry one and invite her to stop by and pick up the gift I had gotten for her. As I exited the car and walked hurriedly toward the mall entrance, I laughed at myself for the changes that I was going through just to have an excuse to see Nina again.

Christmas Morning

Merry Christmas, Paula," I said, as I answered the phone. I'd paged her just fifteen minutes earlier. We hadn't spoken in more than a month, and I was curious how I would be received. Getting established at work had kept me really busy, and I had also been caught up in the excitement of being home. In the previous month I had done a lot. I knew that none of this would be legitimate justifications to Paula for not contacting her, and I was prepared for a tongue lashing, and maybe even a little cursing. Paula was in Atlanta, but she was from Chicago's South Side and had never lost that edge, which was available for show to anyone who got her wrong. I figured that I had most definitely fallen into that category, so I was shocked when she replied softly.

"Merry Christmas to you too, stranger." There was a pause, then she went on. "So how has everything been going for you and your family?"

"Well, very well thanks, and what about you?" I replied, still a little off balance.

"Cory, do you need to know how things are with me? Do you even need to ask?" Her tone was beginning to change a little, into more of what I had expected. She breathed deeply, and then added, "Cory, you hurt me when you left, and also by your lack of remorse for hurting me, but like I said before, I knew that you'd leave me someday . . . I always knew. But if you want to know the truth, I don't regret loving you one bit. As a matter of fact, your leaving helped me realize something that I wouldn't have had you never left."

"What's that?" I asked, bracing myself for a sharp answer.

"I realized that only because I had you in my life was I able to stay with Marvin as long as I did. I know now that my happiness has to come first, and having all of the material things like this house, these cars, and the clothes, none of them have been able to make me truly happy. They do take your attention off being unhappy for the moment, but in no way are they the answer. That's why I'm leaving Marvin. Not for you, but for me."

"You're leaving him?"

"Yes. After the holidays I'll be out of here."

"So you've told him?" I asked.

"No, not yet. I didn't want to ruin the holiday season. His mother is staying at the house through New Year's Eve, but I've already gotten my divorce papers drawn up. They will be served on the third of January."

"I'm stunned, Paula. I don't know what to say."

"You don't have to say anything, Cory. You can tell me that you still love me, though."

"Of course I do."

"Then say it, Cory. I need to hear you say it."

Her tone had me feeling extremely pressured, but I pushed the words effortlessly out of my mouth: "I do still love you, Paula." What was strange, though, was that when the words came out of my mouth, the image of Nina's face popped into my mind.

"Well, seeing is believing, Cory, but I gotta run. We can talk later. Now, where can I reach you?"

I gave her my numbers, and she quickly wrote them down. After quick good-byes she blew a kiss through the line, and we hung up.

Things had gone better than I had imagined. There had been no hysterical ranting, and I was off the line, having been allowed to enjoy the rest of my Christmas Day without guilt.

I hung up the phone and immediately dialed Nina's apartment.

The phone rang once and a male voice answered it. "Hello, I mean, Merry Christmas."

"Merry Christmas. Is Nina available?" I asked, hoping I wouldn't be causing a big fuss if this was her friend. If it was, he needed to be home with his kids, not babysitting Nina on Christmas morning.

"Nina just ran to the store to get some batteries. She'll be back soon. Can I tell her who called?"

"Yeah, tell her that Cory called."

"Cory? Okay. I'll have her call you as soon as she gets back. Does she have your number? Well, it's on the caller ID if she doesn't have it," he said, being as polite as possible. Then I heard someone in the background saying, "C. Dandridge? Is that Cory Dandridge? Let me see that telephone." I heard a voice in the background ask, "Cory, is this Cory Dandridge?"

I knew the voice. It was Shelly. My heart dropped completely into my stomach this time. "Yeah, this is me. Shelly?" I said, trying to sound unsure if it was her voice, but I was sure she knew I had recognized it. She was my first love, the one that was supposed to last a lifetime, and everyone knows you don't forget that voice—ever.

"Cory, what are you doing calling Nina to wish her Merry Christmas? She hasn't heard from you in years, and neither have I, for that matter? And the caller ID has you listed with a Maryland phone number. Have you moved back to the area?" she asked, in a voice that indicated a lot of wonder. Nina obviously hadn't mentioned that she'd seen me, let alone been out with me twice. I was glad she had kept our secret, but now I had to think on my toes and come up with something.

"Actually, Shelly, I have moved back to the area. Nina must have forgotten that she gave me her number. I told her I was going to call some time ago. I saw her probably . . . let me see, it must have been sometime around Thanksgiving or sometime close to then." I closed my little cover-up with, "I told her that I would catch up with her sooner or later to see how you guys were doing, and what better day than Christmas, ya know what I'm saying?" It was the best I could do.

She just said, "Oh, uh huh. Well, that's nice of you to think of *us*, Cory." She was suspicious. I smelled disaster, and I knew why. Shelly knew me well. She knew that when I'm nervous or lying I always say "Ya know what I'm saying?" Then she said, "It has been a long time,

Cory. Many Christmases have gone past, but it's nice to hear from you. You and your family are doing well, I hope."

"Most definitely, everyone is wonderful, and I am doing well. I can't complain." I wanted to say "Does a hundred grand–plus a year sound like I'm doing well? I'm pushing a Beemer with TVs in it. I'm in better shape than you would ever remember. I'm doing damn good, and when you see me you will know that you made the biggest mistake of your life by walking out on me. Now look at that broke nigga you got." But of course I couldn't say that. "So, you came to visit Nina this morning. That's nice."

"No, actually she transferred her calls to my house. When she got here I wasn't dressed and Amani needed some batteries for her Roller Baby doll's RollerBlades, wouldn't you know. She also needed some for Amani's V-Tech laptop, so she ran to the 7–11 for us."

"Did you say laptop, as in computer?"

"Yes. It is for kids, though. It has spelling and math drills on it. It even has a mouse to go with it. It's really cute." Shelly laughed. Then I heard someone in the background talking to her. Shelly said, "Hey, I need to run now. Duty calls, but I'll tell Nina that you called us. We're all doing fine as well, so take care of yourself and tell your mom and sister that I wished them a Merry Christmas, okay?"

"Okay, sure thing. You take care, too." After we hung up, I thought about how Shelly had basically said that there was no need for me to call back now that I had spoken to her. At least, that's what I got out of it. It's not that she had to come right out and say it. It was just the attitude I had detected when she said that I had called *them*, and that *they* were doing fine. Shelly still had enough nerve for two women, and the reasons why we eventually fell out began to come back to me.

Two hours passed, and I was just about to get dressed to go to my sister's house and take all of their gifts to them, when Nina called back from her cellphone. She sounded really upset.

"What's wrong? Did I mess up by calling you?" I asked, feeling as though I had made a big mistake.

"It's not your fault, Cory." She was upset, and just like her sister it made her accent more pronounced.

"What happened? Did she accuse you of something?"

I heard her sniffle before she spoke, and I didn't want to believe that I had caused her a bunch of strife. "Cory, when I came back from the store she pulled me back into the kitchen and started talking casually. She was setting me up. She started asking me about my ex-boyfriends. She was saying shit like 'Don't the holidays make you kind of remember old times, like when you dated Jonathan or Manuel?' "

"I was like, yeah, sort of. Then she asked me if I ever wondered how any of them were doing. I told her that I talk to Manuel's aunt sometimes when I go to the dentist's office. She's, like, the receptionist at my dentist's office." Nina was talking so fast, I had to tell her to slow down. She did, and kept talking. "Cory, the bitch is so slick. She was setting me up, because after I talked about Manuel for a few moments, she came out of the blue and made a comment about wondering what you were up to. I had no idea that you'd just called or even would call today. I had transferred my calls to her house, and I never would have done that. Shit, Cory, I haven't heard from you in two weeks, and when I left messages, you didn't call back. I figured that after we went to brunch and you didn't give me your home number then, that you obviously didn't want me to call. So anyway, when she said that she wondered what you were up to, I slipped up and said, 'Me, too.' "

"No, you didn't."

"Yeah, I did." Nina went on to describe how Shelly had just nailed her by announcing that she had heard that I was back in the area. Nina said that when her response was "Really?" as if she had no idea, Shelly's expression had turned ice cold. Then she had led Nina to the caller ID and told her I had called. She had played her little sister like a drum. Shelly drilled Nina for ten minutes straight. She wanted to know why she had lied and acted as if she didn't know anything about my being back, and about seeing me. When Nina had produced no answers, Shelly accused her of always having had a crush on me, and lit into her about her motives. When Eric came up the stairs and heard the two of them arguing, he'd asked why they were arguing. Nina, in her rage and defensive stance, told him that she and Shelley were arguing over my call.

Then Eric flew into a rage himself. He wanted to know why in the hell Shelly was so concerned, and said that after five years it shouldn't matter to her one way or the other. He told Shelly that if Nina and I were getting married tomorrow, it would be absolutely none of her business. He added that if Nina and I were comfortable being friends on any level, then all Shelly can do is stay out of it. Shelly, never one to go easy, wasn't having it. She proceeded to curse out Nina and Eric. As soon as Amani lay down for a nap, more than an hour after things had died down, Shelly started again. She eventually threw both Eric and Nina out. Before she asked Nina to leave she turned to her baby sister and said, "I don't know why you would keep something from me, Nina, for any reason other than you're fucking Cory. If you are you'd better be careful, because he is a dog, just like Nate. I won't mention it again, though, and I just hope that you have more class than to be hanging around with my leftover."

Nina expressed to me how hurt she had been by Shelly's words. She'd been especially stung by her hope that Nina possessed enough class not to date me. She said that she, like Eric, didn't think that there was anything wrong with us hanging out together. She added, "It's not like we're fucking or anything, right Cory?" she asked.

I didn't answer that, but I did convey to Nina my dismay at being referred to by Shelly as her "leftover." If anything, she was my leftover. I had taught that girl everything about life and relationships that she needed to know. And shit, as far as sex went, there had been no uncharted territory left for her to discover by the time we had split up.

I had forgotten that Nina was on her cellphone until I heard a horn honk. I asked where she was headed. When she replied that she didn't know and that she was just driving, I gave her my address and convinced her to stop by, even if it was just for a little while. She agreed to come after I assured her it would be no inconvenience. *If she only knew*, I thought. When she arrived less than fifteen minutes later, I greeted her at the door with a hug.

When she entered my apartment, she nodded her head in approval. "This is a nice apartment, Cory," she said.

"Thanks," I said.

"It must cost a fortune to live here. Rockville is so expensive, anyway. I didn't think they were recruiting our kind up in this neck of the woods." She smiled. Then she added, "But I guess if you're making enough papers to afford a spot out here, then you must be okay, huh."

"Maybe," I answered, smiling back. "Or maybe I just know somebody who is somebody."

She walked around the love seat and sat down on the couch with her coat still on. "Let me take your coat," I said. I put it on the back of one of the dining room chairs. As I walked back into the living room I turned the TV volume down and cranked up the CD player.

"So Cory, what's up?" She said, as she looked right into my face.

"Nothing much. I just wanted to make sure you were okay, and I have a little something for you. Hold tight," I said, as I walked over to my dining room table, reached into a shopping bag, pulled out two boxes that were wrapped identically, and walked back over to Nina and sat down next to her.

"Cory, I can't take a gift from you. I wouldn't feel right, not having anything for you." She paused, and went on. "I didn't get to do much shopping for anyone this year, except for my mother and Amani. I was so broke, Cory. Why in the world would you buy me a gift? You haven't even called me, and . . ."

I cut her off midsentence. "Look here, Nina. It's not about what you have for me. I bought you something because I wanted to, because I knew that you deserved something nice. I don't know what your man got you, but I knew that you deserved more."

"I don't have a man anymore, Cory," she said, in a tone that didn't reveal whether or not she was happy about it.

"Whatever. It doesn't make a bit of difference to my giving you something. I just wanted you to have these things. Now open them up and stop talking," I commanded.

She just looked at me as she began to open them. I stopped her, and said, "No here, this one first." She obliged me. When she opened it, her eyes showed her pleasure as she pulled the last piece of wrapping paper off a bottle of Bvlgari perfume.

"Oh man, Cory, this is wonderful." She was smiling. "I have been wanting some of this for a while, but it is very expensive. You shouldn't have, but I am glad you did." She laughed and said, "Thank you so much."

"Go ahead and open that one," I said, pointing to the bigger box.

She quickly pulled the wrapping off to reveal a purse. She just shook her head and said, "Cory, I can't believe you did this for me. It's a Coach. It's gorgeous. Thank you so much. This is the sweetest thing that anyone has done for me in a really long time."

As I looked at her surveying the bag, I stared at her pretty lips. She had on nothing but lip gloss, and that was all the makeup she needed. She was so naturally beautiful. I still didn't know what I was doing with her. While I was still looking at her she jumped up and walked to the balcony door. "Look, Cory, it's starting to snow. Can you believe that?"

"Yeah, the weatherman has been calling for snow the past two days. It's coming down pretty thick, too."

"Do you think it will stick?" she asked.

"I don't know. It's definitely cold enough. I probably should try and get out of here. I need to run to my sister's house to drop off the gifts for the kids, and afterward my mother is making Christmas dinner." I looked back outside, and there was no way I was going to do a bunch of running around in this weather. I figured that I could call Brenda to meet me at Mom's, and that way I could kill two birds with one stone. She walked back over to where I was still standing, in front of the glass door.

"Cory, do you want some company with you while you ride? I'm not going to my mother's. I already called her from the car and told her that I wouldn't be coming over for dinner."

"Sure, I'd like that a lot as a matter of fact, and I know my mom would love to see you again. But did you tell your mother why you wouldn't be coming?"

"Somewhat. I didn't go into the full details, but I just don't feel like going another round with Shelly right now."

"I understand," I said.

After a short pause Nina took hold of my arm and asked, "Cory, why if you hadn't bothered to call me, did you go through the hassle of buying me those gifts? Or did you buy them for someone else?"

I was a little shocked, and quickly answered. "Of course I bought them for you. If I had gotten them for someone else would I be handing them to you? They were for you. I saw them and I just wanted to give you something. Don't make such a big deal out of it and spoil it for me, okay. As long as you like them, that is all that matters, right?"

Nina nodded her head, I think in response to me—and in time to the music. She was still holding my arm. "Cory."

"Yes."

"I have something for you, too. But I don't want you to think I'm giving it to you because you bought me the gifts. If you had called me in the past couple of weeks, I'm sure I would have given it to you already. But since you didn't call me or return my pages . . ."

"Nina, I had gotten a new pager from my job . . ."

"Shhhhhh." She said, now holding my hand with one of hers. With the other hand, she placed a finger on my lips. "Now close your eyes," she added.

I obeyed her request, and my eyes shut immediately. Her hand went behind my head and onto the back of my neck as she pulled my mouth to hers. Her lips melted onto mine, and they were a perfect fit. *I can't believe I'm kissing Shelly's little sister,* I thought. I could remember when she was a skinny little teenager with nubs on her chest and the skinniest little legs. Now she was kissing me, and I was kissing her back just as passionately. My hands were on her waist and both of hers were around my neck.

We stayed locked together for at least ten minutes, kissing like two teenagers in the back seat of a car. When we finally pulled away I asked her if she was sure about what she had done. When she kissed me again and began to unbutton my shirt I knew that she was. Clothing dropped to the floor, and before I knew it I was sitting on my couch with Nina on my lap facing me. She stared into my eyes while she started to grind and slide on top of me. She hadn't bothered to take her panties off. With one hand I slid them to the side and entered her. I could feel the wet material of her underwear between our bodies. I took both of her breasts in my mouth at the same time. She threw her head backward and gave me a loud moan to let me know that she liked the feeling. Our bodies moved fast, then slow, for the next ten minutes, until her breaths became rapid. I knew she was ready to

come, and she started crying out in Spanish the same way Shelly used
to. I felt her hands reaching down between my legs caressing me as she
jerked and came. When her muscles clamped down and squeezed me
I couldn't take any more, and I came inside of her.

The connection between Nina and me made my Christmas in ways
that no material gift could have. I thought it was a little strange that
afterward we both seemed to feel fine about having sex—for the most
part. I did feel a twinge of guilt at having been with the younger sister
of my ex-fiancée. At the same time I had to admit that something so
taboo was a bit of a turn-on. It was one of those things that might cross
the mind of a man, though he would never intend to act on it. I had
found out something about myself, since I had seized the opportunity.
I obviously had a problem with respecting boundaries, but was hoping
I could put my emotions and libido in check before the situation got
out of hand. The lovemaking was good—but not "mind blowing" good.
When a girl blows your mind the first time she has sex with you, she's
trouble. At least, that was my personal belief. Either she's too experienced or you're too inexperienced for her, was my philosophy on that
matter. With Nina there seemed to be comfortable room for improve-
ment. I knew she had held back a little, and I liked that. She was going
to make me work to get her all.

She went with me to dinner at my mother's house. We had a great
time, as the snow continued to fall. Brenda was the only one who
seemed puzzled about Nina being there with me. I saw that she repeatedly shot looks at me as if to say "What the hell is going on?" I ignored her, because I was feeling good, and so was Nina. At that point,
that was all that mattered to me.

Brendan and Laney showed up for dessert, and he brought his little
brother, Kenny, to play with Kyle. Brendan's parents lived two streets
over, and he made it over easily, though the weather seemed to be getting worse. He was riding with Laney because he said that he didn't
trust his Corvette in the snow. I couldn't blame him one bit, as I
wasn't used to driving in the slushy streets anymore myself. When it
was almost nine o'clock, Brenda announced that she was spending the
night rather than driving home. I decided that it was getting late and

was time for me to head home; plus, I was hoping to see if Nina would be in the mood to repeat our earlier escapade.

As I drove slowly around the Beltway, Nina fell asleep. I took the opportunity to call Nate, who was spending the day with Sahleen and his grandmother. I told him who I was with, and he had a million and one questions about Nina and me. I tried to speak in code, just in case Nina woke up. Nate finally gave up the hope of getting the entire story right then and there. He told me about his day's events. He had spent the morning with India, and then told her he was headed out of town to have dinner with family so that he could have an undisturbed evening with Sahleen. It had worked for him as usual, and he and Sahleen were headed to Crystal City to Sahleen's apartment to do a little "stocking stuffing," he said. I hung up with Nate and saw that Nina was still sleeping. I had questions about where this was headed, but I wasn't afraid of the possibilities.

For a second, Paula popped into my head, and I hoped that she was doing well. I wondered if she had gotten the gift that I'd sent to her office. I also thought about Darlene and wondered who she was spending the holiday with. I hoped that they both were doing fine, but they were six hundred miles away and by no means my primary concern. Nina was there next to me, and that meant a lot. As a matter of fact, I kept thinking over and over that her being there was all that mattered. She had been on my mind ever since I saw her that first night. I had been curious about Shelly, true enough, but the satisfaction that I felt looking over at Nina made me realize she was definitely who I wanted. I had tried not to admit it to myself during the previous month, but I was now prepared to admit it to Nina as soon as she woke up. I only hoped that now, since her curiosity had been satisfied, she wouldn't be through with me, because if I had my way, I definitely wasn't through with her.

Chapter 15

RUDE AWAKENINGS

Nate could hear the audience booing as the ladies told their stories onstage. He was standing just behind the stage and he could see the ladies on the small TV monitor in front of him. He didn't want to be here, and he couldn't figure out why he had even allowed himself to be talked into coming. He knew that the whole idea had been Kim's. It was late March, and he figured that she should have gotten over him by now. Ever since she had come to his house unannounced, only to be dissed, she had promised Nate that he would get his. Now it seemed as though her prophecy had come true. Nate could feel beads of sweat on his brow and moisture building under his shirt collar. It wasn't like Nathan Montgomery to get nervous. He was fearless, a soldier's soldier, and he couldn't remember the last time he had felt so uptight. Just as he was thinking about bolting right out of the studio, the stagehand came back and began to lead him onto the stage.

As he saw the bright lights blasting him in the face he heard Jerry Springer say, "Let's meet Nate!" While he walked onto the stage he could see the faces of India and Sahleen there, his current loves. Kim and Erika, who were seated onstage as well, were the most recent victims of his trappings. Both had received their walking papers in an improper fashion, within twenty-four hours of one another. Kim hadn't received a decent apology for Nate's treatment of her since being sent away from his apartment in tears. Erika and her cousin Jay still weren't speaking to each other after the episode in Nate's apartment. Reluctantly, he took the empty chair. Kim and Erika were seated to his left;

Sahleen and India were on his right. He was thinking, *How in the world did my shit get blown out of the water like this?*

His gut tightened when he glanced over at the face of Sahleen and India. They were both scowling, and India looked as though she had already cried buckets. A sinking feeling was suffocating him as he came to the realization that Sahleen and India knew everything. Then Jerry walked over to him.

"So, Nate, you have been a very busy young man," Jerry stated, acting as if he were deeply bothered by the accounts of Nate's behavior.

Kim had come out and told of how she'd met Nate at a birthday get-together for his friend Brendan one Friday night the previous year. He had been so sweet. He had taken her to Atlantic City for the weekend the day after they met. She had decided to accept his invitation to go only because she thought that he was a gentleman like Brendan. She had admitted that she'd made an extremely poor decision. At the time, though, he had just seemed so exciting and classy. He had told her that he was interested in investing in a hair salon. Since she was a top-flight hair stylist with a large clientele, he told her that she would probably make a great partner.

Kim had said that she had been "gassed up." Jerry had asked for an explanation, and Kim had told him that she had been "gung-ho," or really excited about everything that Nate had promised. Jerry had asked her to continue. She had told the audience about how she had sexed Nate that weekend, and she had admitted it had been really spectacular. Then she had given a sad account of the treatment that she had received during the following seven months. She had receipts for all of the presents that she had showered him with. She had said she was still paying for the televisions in his Lexus. He had run up her Discover card bill to twelve hundred bucks on the Internet, buying throwback jerseys from Mitchell & Ness. To make things worse, some chick who he had been screwing from Southeast D.C. had slashed her tires. She had known because the girl finally had come to her job and made a scene, swearing that she was carrying Nate's baby. She had been lying, but had thoroughly embarrassed Kim in front of everyone at her job on a Saturday, when the shop had been packed.

Jerry had grimaced as the crowd oohed and aahed. She had summed up her story by telling of how she had spent Thanksgiving, Christmas, and Valentine's Day home alone, pining away after Nate had dumped her. All of her friends at the salon had sworn that Nate had timed the break-up so that he wouldn't have to be bothered with her during the holiday season, and that as soon as Valentine's Day had passed, he would come calling. Nate had never come calling, but what had caused Kim to call the show was that she had seen Nate with India one night, and then three days later had seen Sahleen driving his car down Georgia Avenue. After a little investigation, Kim had found out that Nate was going out with both of the women she had seen, and she had made it her personal goal to inform both of the women about what kind of person they were dealing with. She had become determined to wreck Nate's game, and to keep him from causing more heartbreak for her sisters. Now, here she was, spilling her guts on national TV just to get revenge on Nate.

Nate merely nodded his head as Jerry quickly gave him the condensed version of the accusations.

Jerry asked him to respond to the women.

Nate looked over at Kim and Erika, and paused. Then he looked back at Jerry and simply said, "Jerry . . . that bitch is lying."

The crowd roared, and Kim flew from her seat, accompanied by Erika. They both pounced on top of Nate as he and his chair flipped backward. His legs went up into the air as he rolled to the floor behind the stage. India was screaming, while Sahleen sat motionless with her legs crossed. The camera panned in for a close-up to show the two women whaling away at Nate. He was cursing, and yelling for security to get the crazed women off him.

The show broke for a commercial, and order was restored. When they came back from the break, Nate was back in his seat. Kim and Erika had been removed from the stage. His shirt had been ripped to shreds and his face was scratched up. He was now seated between Sahleen and India. He was trying to catch his breath, and then Jerry walked up to the stage.

"Nate," Jerry said, "naturally you understand why those ladies were so upset. We found out about you and Erika and, I should say, Erika's cousin as well." Jerry turned and worked the audience. He said, "Nate, these ladies each have something to say to you, and I think that now is as good a time as any for you to be honest with them. Do you think that you can do that?"

"Yeah, Jerry, I can do that," Nate muttered.

"Well, I'm going to let the two ladies take over." Jerry folded his arms and said, "Sahleen, you go first." Then he stepped off to the side of the stage.

Sahleen turned to position her body toward Nate while still sitting with her legs crossed. "Nate," she said, "I just want to know why you have been playing these games with me."

Nate tried to start explaining, but no words came out. Sahleen went on. "Nate, we've been seeing each other for four months now. Every day that I am in town I spend with you. Don't I?"

Nate nodded yes.

"Don't I make you happy? Don't I please you good enough, Nate?"

Nate nodded yes again, but his eyes were facing the ground. He looked as ashamed as a little boy who had just peed his pants in front of the class.

"Have I spent all of your money, Nate?" He shook his head no. Sahleen rambled on. "Do you have any idea of the caliber of men that would do anything, including forsaking all other women, just to be with me, Nate?" She paused, gritted her teeth, and continued. "And it's not just because I'm beautiful, either. It's because I am a decent human being, Nate, and worthy of the same respect and devotion that I give . . . you selfish son of a bitch."

She looked as though she was preparing to swing at Nate as well, and Jerry moved back to the stage. "Nate. What do you have to say? From what it sounds like to me, you obviously have to be a smooth talker. So where is all of that right now? You have to give some explanation . . . I mean, for cryin' out loud, Nate, how do you explain this infantile, selfish behavior?"

"Wait a minute, Jerry," India interrupted. "I have something to say before he says anything." She stood up. "Nate, I trusted you, and apparently all you have given me are lies. I have been available to you night and day. Obviously, I am nothing to you but a backup for when Mrs. Fly Thang isn't available." Sahleen looked up as if to say, I know that you aren't talking about me. India saw Sahleen's body language, and her voice dropped a few octaves as if she were possessed, and she said to Sahleen, "Oh bitch, believe me, you would want to stay in your seat unless you want some of what Nate is going to get."

"Hold up! Why you gonna stand up here and threaten me like that? It ain't even like that, India. I didn't mean to hurt anybody. I mean, I just . . . I really do care, but . . ." Nate was fumbling his sentences as if they were burning hot French fries on his tongue.

"Shut up!" India yelled. She was standing over Nate now. "You have done it this time, fool. I was willing to be there for you. I tried to take you to church, to give your sorry ass a chance at redemption, but nooooo. You just had to stay stuck in your own ways. I even gave myself to you. I had taken a vow of celibacy, damn you. You with your seductive hands and long tongue. Oooohh, you make me so sick. I made a vow that the next man I gave my body to would be my husband, but you have made a liar out of me. But this is the last time you make a fool out of me or anyone else," India shouted as she stepped back. She then reached into her purse, which was on the floor next to her seat. Nate watched stunned as she pulled out a chrome revolver. Nate leaned back in his seat and Sahleen screamed. "Now Nate, before I do this I want you to take a look in that audience. Look real closely."

Nate was panting, and said, "India, c'mon now, don't do anything crazy and get yourself into trouble. Really . . . I'm not worth it." His eyes showed pure fear.

"Oh, I know you're not worth it, but I'll tell you what. I'll let the audience decide. How 'bout that, Nate?"

"Jerry, Jerrrrry!" Nate yelled out.

Jerry Springer was running up the steps and out of the studio, followed by his security guards.

India pointed the gun straight at Nate's face. The tip was less than three feet away from his nose. Then she turned to the audience with the gun still pointed at Nate. "Ladies, what do you think I should do? Should this bastard live or die? I'm going to let you all decide."

Nate looked around the barrel of the gun and into the audience.

Suddenly the lights that were so bright, that they had kept him from making out the faces in the crowd, began to dim. He could make out face after face. He began to shiver when he realized that the audience was filled with all of the women that he had dogged out in his illustrious past. There was Nadiya, the girl who stood up her fiancée at the altar thinking that she and Nate were going to be together, only to find out that he really wanted to sleep with her friend Jennifer. Next to her he made out the face of Frances, the waitress he had promised to introduce to a friend in the recording industry but had never called after he'd gotten the sex. Next there was Julianne, the personal trainer. She had her back to Nate. She had claimed that Nate only recognized her from the backside. He had promised her it would only hurt a little. He had lied. Even Brenda was in the audience. It had been their little secret, but Nate had had the nerve to videotape her to prove to Brendan that he'd hit it. If Cory ever found out, he would kill Nate. He eventually gave Brenda the tape after she'd found out from Brendan what he'd done.

The audience began to chant, "Shoot him. Shoot him. Shoot him." As the audience grew louder and louder Nate squirmed and sweated.

India said to Nate, "Sorry, Nate. The verdict is in . . . and unfortunately you lose."

"Please," Nate begged. "Please don't shoot me, India." Nate wanted to get up and run but he couldn't move. He turned to Sahleen and said, "Sahleen, I am so sorry, baby. I never meant to hurt you. I love you, baby." Nate couldn't believe he was saying those words, but he knew he was about to die. So he said it again and again as he covered his face. "I do love you, Sahleen. I do."

Sahleen smiled and pulled Nate's hands from his face. He fought the force of her pulling and tried to resist. Then she spoke loudly as she grabbed his hands, "Nate. Nate. Wake up. You're having a bad dream."

Nate's hands finally gave in as he woke up. His body was drenched with sweat. He had fallen asleep with the thermostat set at 80 degrees. Sahleen, thinking that Nate was cold, didn't bother to change it. As he came to his senses, he felt a sense of relief. *It was just a dream*, he thought. *No more of that damned Domino's Pizza after eleven.*

"What were you dreaming about, baby? You started moving really wild, and talking in your sleep," Sahleen asked, trying to hold back a grin.

"What the hell are you smiling for?" Nate snapped. He was still on edge from his *Springer* nightmare. He jumped out of the bed and headed for the bathroom. He had never told Sahleen that he loved her. It had only been four months, but now she had reason to believe that Nate was more smitten than he would ever let on. Nate came back from the bathroom, after turning the heat down and cracking the window slightly. He crawled back into the bed and attempted to go back to sleep. It was only eight-fifteen. Much too early to rise on a Saturday morning. Sahleen, on the other hand, was an early riser, and she had been up for almost an hour. She didn't bother Nate, though, as he lay still in the bed drifting back to sleep. Instead, she just sat up watching him and trying to make sense of the words he had spoken in his dream. He had definitely said that he loved her. Of course, it was in his sleep, and Sahleen was left wondering how much credibility to lend to a subconscious "I love you."

It still was nice to hear, she thought, as she pulled the comforter over her feet. There was a draft blowing into the room through the window. Sahleen was just about to close it when Nate turned over. She saw that he was still sweating a little. She wiped the moisture from his forehead with her robe, which was on top of the covers. She then slid down under the covers and pressed her body close to his. Even though he had been sweating quite a bit, he still smelled like the Dove body wash he scrubbed with twice a day. Sahleen felt herself warming up from Nate's body heat, and she hoped that he wasn't coming down with something. If he were, she would be there to take care of him, if he allowed her to.

When Nate had come down with the flu in January, he went straight to his grandmother's house, where she nursed him back to health. Sahleen didn't make a big deal out of the rejection that she felt when he refused her attempts to make soup or go to the pharmacy for him. Nate made it clear that it was his nana, and only his nana, who could provide the necessary care that he needed when he was sick.

Sahleen was rubbing Nate's freshly shaved head and just appreciating his presence. She moved her arms down so that she could hold him while he slept. Then she wondered, *How in the world did I make him fall in love with me so quickly?* She just giggled and hugged him tighter. Then she made herself a mental note to ask a question a little later on. Maybe during breakfast she would have an opportunity to ask him who this India person in his dream was, and what in God's name had Nate done to make her want to shoot him?

Brendan and Laney were headed around the track for their twelfth and final lap. Brendan was winded and was using every ounce of willpower he had left to turn the last corner. Laney began sprinting full speed, and pulled away early on the last lap. She always sprinted the entire last lap, sometimes the last two. Since she had been running with Brendan, she had slowed her pace down to accommodate him. Laney was encouraging Brendan to change to a more healthy diet as part of his New Year's resolutions. The exercise program was just an add-on to his new state of health consciousness.

Brendan and Laney had spent New Year's Eve at Baltimore Harbor eating seafood at Phillip's Restaurant. Laney had treated Brendan to a dinner, which consisted of lobster tails, Alaskan crab legs, Maryland crab cakes, and steamed shrimp. It had been her suggestion that the two of them enjoy a nice high-calorie and cholesterol-loaded meal as long as Brendan agreed that they wouldn't do it again until the Fourth of July. She also had convinced him to name at least five things that he could promise to do in order to become healthier. She had promised him that if he kept at least three of the five promises, she would make him very happy that he did. She also had surprised him after dinner with a key to a room at the Downtown Renaissance Hotel, which was located just across the street from Phillip's. Laney called it the "fireworks" agreement: If he went along with her diet and exercise suggestions she would ensure that he saw plenty of fireworks all year round.

Spring was only a few days away, and Brendan had kept up his end of the bargain, and so had Laney. Brendan had lost seventeen pounds since the new year began, and he was feeling better about himself than he had in years. When the couple first started working out, Brendan could barely do a mile. Now, just a month later, he was running up to three miles a day, four days a week.

Laney had turned out to be good for him. He was happy with her in just about every respect, except that she worked late on weekends. Not this weekend, though. She had taken off from work because it was Brendan's birthday. Cory, Nina, Nate, and one of his girlfriends, either Sahleen or India, were going to meet them for dinner at the Cheesecake Factory. They never knew which girlfriend Nate was going to show up with, but it didn't matter. Both of Nate's honeys were easy to look at, and both were nice. India was a little more down-to-earth as far as he was concerned, but Sahleen was cool, too. Shit, when you are that fine it's kind of hard to be totally down-to-earth, Brendan often thought.

After their early jog at PG Community College, Brendan and Laney went back to the house to shower. Renee was in the kitchen drinking coffee while she scanned the *Washington Post* to see who had a sale going on.

Renee offered Laney a cup of coffee.

"No thanks, but I could use a glass of water," Laney said, while pulling her hair back into a neater ponytail.

Renee was handing Laney the cup of water when Brendan asked, "What about me?"

"You," Renee said, pointing to the cupboard, "can get it yourself. You know where everything is, I believe."

"How are you going to treat a brother like that on his birthday? Man, I can't get no respect," Brendan said, doing a poor impersonation of Rodney Dangerfield.

"Brother, I have your gift in the car, and I told you that you get dinner on Sunday wherever you want to go. Now, don't press your luck." Renee meant it.

"So why can't you go out with us tonight?" Laney asked. She asked in a humble tone. She really wanted Renee to like her. She could tell how close Renee and Brendan were, and she wanted to gain Renee's respect, if not her admiration. Laney was smart enough to catch on to the fact that Renee's opinion meant a lot to Brendan, and without it she would face an uphill battle trying to get any closer to him.

"I told Brendan that my book club has its monthly meeting tonight. I might have skipped it except that tonight it is my turn to host it.

Plus, I chose the novel, *Let That Be the Reason* by Vickie Stringer. . . . The book was all of it, girl." She paused to take a sip of water. "Brendan will do fine tonight, though. He has you and his boys to contend with. I'll make it up to him tomorrow, I'm sure, if he has any energy left." Renee kept flipping through the pages of the paper.

Laney didn't particularly like Renee's statement about "making it up" to Brendan. Her eyes narrowed with cattiness when that comment slipped out of Renee's mouth. She decided at that minute to make sure that Brendan wouldn't have any energy left when the morning came. Laney knew she was being silly, but she didn't care. She wanted everyone to know that she was the current owner when it came to Brendan Shue. She could care less how long or how great a friendship he had with Renee. He was her man now, even if he didn't know it yet.

When Laney went up the steps to Brendan's bedroom he was already out of his sweats and clad only in his underwear. She quickly pulled up her hooded sweatshirt and kicked off her Nike Air Max running shoes. Once her tights came down she caught Brendan staring at her firmly shaped butt when she turned around.

"Birthday boy, what is that shit-eating grin for?" she asked.

"You know, girl." Brendan smiled, while grabbing Laney and pulling her to the bed.

"Boy, please. Let me take a shower or something first." She tried to protest.

Brendan started to kiss her. "Nope. It's my birthday, and I get whatever I want. And I want you now, sweat and all."

Even though Laney found his request a little gross, she remembered her mission to leave the man drained by morning. "Okay, baby. Whatever you want."

Brendan grinned widely as he slung his underwear on top of the TV. Then he said simply, "Fireworks, right?"

Laney closed her eyes as her sports bra came off. "Yeah, baby. Fireworks."

Chapter 16

CHOKING ON IT

Nina and I arrived first at the Cheesecake Factory in White Flint Mall. We went in to get a table, only to find that the place was packed. I had never eaten there before, but Nina had been there a few times and told me it was always like that on the weekends. It was only a few blocks from my apartment, so I volunteered to get our names on the list for a table. We sat in the waiting area watching all the people walking by the restaurant into the mall. Nina was looking really nice, as usual. She had on a skirt and a suede shirt. I had gotten used to Nina crying broke all the time, but at least I knew where all of her money was going. Obviously it went into clothes, because the car note on her Civic and her rent were her only major bills, and the two combined weren't a thousand dollars. She made decent money, somewhere close to fifty grand, as a bookkeeper for Remax Realty, one of the leading real estate companies in the country. She was taking courses at Trinity College at night and on weekends trying to earn her bachelor's degree in accounting. She was only thirty hours away and seemed pretty focused.

She sat quietly next to me, holding my hand as we waited, while I took notice of two brothers laughing loudly by the payphones. They were acting as if they were intoxicated, but I could tell that they weren't. They were just loud. One of them was sort of tall and looked familiar for some reason, but I couldn't figure out why. I knew that I didn't know him, and the way they were acting I was glad that I didn't, so that they wouldn't come over and do the whole handshake thing.

Nina began talking to me about a restaurant down on Wisconsin Avenue that we should have gone to and perhaps avoided the crowd. As she went on, I was thinking about how lucky I had been to stumble onto her at that party that night. We were becoming an item, although we still had yet to put any titles on our relationship. Nina was spending at least three nights a week at my place, and I was spending one at hers occasionally as well. My mother had wondered out loud if I was doing the right thing by dating Shelly's baby sister. She'd said, "Cory, with all of the single women in this area, why would you pick one that you had to stir up trouble with? You need to think of the rift that you're going to cause in that family, and really ask yourself if you're going to be worth the damage that you cause between sisters. How would you feel if you were in Shelly's shoes?"

It had been a good point, but the only thing my mother was unaware of was that Shelly didn't know what was going on. Within a couple of weeks after Christmas, Shelly had apologized to Nina and never asked her about it again. Nina believed that Shelly had assumed there was nothing going on between us because Shelly would assume that if something were Nina would have told her about it. Shelly couldn't have been more wrong, because Nina and I were enjoying each other immensely and were basically fucking like a couple of jackrabbits. We had gone skiing in the Pocono Mountains with Nate and India, and she had accompanied me to Manhattan on a business trip. She had shopped at Burberry's, Saks, and Bloomingdale's, my treat, while I went to meetings. One night she even got me to see *The Lion King.*

"We were obviously destined to meet up again," she'd told me. "It seems as though we would never have bumped into each other otherwise."

There was no denying that I hadn't had a chance to go out much at all since I had moved back. The job had been extremely demanding. Each department head had come to realize that I was becoming Jamison Hakito's right-hand man. I'd even felt some jealousy from those who had been at the company longer than I, especially from a

coworker named Roy Wells, who ran the accounting department. He
was the only other black in management, but was not considered an
executive, which meant the poor fellow did not have a parking space.
I had only become aware of his disdain for my manner of doing things
when my assistant, Heather, who was working out beautifully, told me
that he'd questioned her about my spring reports, which were due by
April 15, tax day. He had had the nerve to ask her if my projections
were going to be as unrealistic as my winter reports had been, which I
had compiled after only a month at HE.

There had been a companywide roar with the projections I had
made. When I assured Jamison that the figures in my projections were
reasonable, he came down to give me his personal approval. In order
to meet my projections, nearly every department had to pull overtime, and for management that meant late nights and weekends.

Of course, my actions didn't win me any friends around the office.
However, Jamison had been pleased when only a month after I had released my projections, the company was ahead of schedule, and we
were able to cut back on the overtime for those who didn't want it.
The grumbling among the employees quickly wound down, and I
came away looking like a genius. I'd increased the sales and production
in my department within my first two months at HE, and increased
the revenue of the company for the month of January by 40 percent.
If I kept this up, HE would be able to count on nearly an additional
four million dollars for the quarter.

I looked up and saw Brendan and Laney walk through the revolving
doors, followed by Nate and India.

"What's up, Cory? Hey, Nina, you two been here long?" Brendan
asked, as he slapped me a soft five that went into a handshake and
then a manly hug. The ladies exchanged hellos.

"Oh, I guess about twenty minutes. Our table should be ready
about now. Let's go in and check." I turned and led the way. "So, how's
everything going, birthday boy?"

"Cool, my brother. Real cool. Laney got me some nice gear and Renee bought me the new Jordans."

As Nate and India walked up behind us, Nate said, "Wait 'til you see what I got you. You are going to love it."

"Yeah, right," Brendan said. "Probably some more X-rated DVDs." He laughed as he gave India a hug and shook Nate's hand.

Nate had gotten Brendan tickets to see Allen Iverson and the Sixers. They were coming to town to play the Wizards in two weeks, and the tickets were sold out and damn near impossible to come by. Nate had two tickets behind the Sixers bench, and he was going to give Brendan both tickets, because he figured he would want to take Laney.

The hostess seated the six of us in a comfortable wrap around booth. Brendan and Laney were seated in the middle. Nate took one end, and I took the other. I told Brendan that I hoped that he and Laney wouldn't need a bathroom break, because I wasn't getting back up. We joked around for a hot second before our waitress came to our table.

"Hello, I'm Helen. Welcome to the Cheesecake Factory. Can I get you all a drink while you look over the menu?"

India suggested that we all share a bottle of wine rather than champagne, since we would be drinking on an empty stomach. It sounded like a good idea to everyone, but we gave the final word to Brendan. He said, "Sounds good to me."

"Alright then," Nate said. "Helen, bring us two bottles of your finest. Whatever it is."

Helen held a perplexed look on her face for a second. Then stated humbly, "Sir, our finest would be a French zinfandel . . . and its $163 per bottle, sir. We do have Moët & Chandon which is about $75, if you prefer."

Nate gritted his teeth, but kept his cool. It was Brendan's birthday, and he wanted everything to go well. He forced a smile as he reached into his pocket. He pulled out a fifty-dollar bill. "Helen, right?" She nodded her head. "Look here, Helen. Take this. This is the tip for the zinfandel. Now get it, and make sure it's chilled just right. Today is this guy's birthday." He pointed at Brendan. "He gets whatever he wants. We'll worry about the price. You just worry about getting it to us, okay sweetheart?"

She smiled a cheesy grin and said, "No, I didn't mean anything by it." She was still grinning as she reached to accept the fifty. "I just wanted you to know that it was a little pricey. Not many people come in here and order it. That's all. I'll go and make sure that they have two chilled bottles." She sped off before Nate could change his mind about the tip.

"I'm feeling you, big dog," Brendan said, to compliment Nate on his manner of dealing with the waitress. Within two minutes someone from the bar was at the table with a cart containing the wine and two fancy ice buckets. He popped both bottles and poured for everyone. People at nearby tables took notice, obviously wondering what we had done to receive such attention. As we sipped the wine, I noticed a look of contentment on Brendan's face that I hadn't seen in a long time. Laney, meanwhile, looked as though she was simply thrilled to be there. Her demeanor showed that she was surprised at the level of love our clique had for one another. She did her best to fit not only because she wanted Brendan as her man; she wanted to stay a part of our scene. Occasionally she said something to reveal that the somewhat polished presentation she put on was new for her. I understood how it could have been hard for someone to fit in with us. We were all such a combination of street and class at the same time. Sort of like Whitney Houston. One minute we were showing the best of our intellect and grooming; in the next we were keeping it ghetto. We had all been out together many times, and occasionally she seemed to be trying too hard to fit in with Nina and India. It wasn't necessary, though, because both of them had already accepted her as Brendan's girl. I was also beginning to see that India, as much as Nina, admired Laney's "semi-fly, semi-homegirl" approach to life. Half of the time Laney came off like someone whose only concern was an aspiration to rise above humble beginnings. Other times she seemed to care less about fitting into the standards of uppity black folks, almost snubbing her nose at others who appeared to be status seekers.

Laney had a good sense of humor and had us all laughing when she joked about her trip to the hair salon that morning. When the food came, everyone dug in, and it was so good that we all struggled to keep our faces out of our plates long enough to keep the conversation going. We all were enjoying our food immensely, but none of us more than Brendan. He had decided to forgo his diet for the night, and was working on a platter of grilled pork chops, mashed potatoes, and mixed vegetables. He was wondering out loud how he was going to have any room for the marble fudge cheesecake he was already planning to order, when one of the men I had noticed outside of the restaurant by the payphones walked up to the table.

Again, I wondered why he looked so familiar. When Nate looked away from India and spotted him, he gave a slight grin and extended his hand to the guy.

"What's up, Donny?" Nate said enthusiastically.

"Ain't too much, man. I'm just out with the fellas getting a bite to eat. What's going on with you, Nate?"

"We're just out celebrating my partner's birthday."

"I heard that," he said, as he nodded his head to the rest of us and said, "What's up?" We acknowledged him. Then he continued, "Joe is over there paying the bill." Donny pointed over toward some other tables. "I'll tell him that I saw you." As he walked away, he looked back and took another glance in our direction.

"Who was that clown?" India asked.

"That was Donny Clark. He plays reserve point guard for the Wizards," Nate answered.

"Yeah, okay. I thought I recognized him. He doesn't get much time, though, does he?"

"Nah. He's like the third string or something. But hell, he's still getting a couple hundred grand a year for that," Nate said, while squeezing a lemon slice into his ice water.

"Nina and I saw him standing outside while we were waiting for our table. He was with some other tall guy."

"It was probably Joe Simpson. That's who he said he was here with," Nate added.

Brendan seemed surprised. "I wonder why Joe Simpson is hanging out with a third-string bum like Clark."

"Donny is like a flunky to Joe. Joe is pressed to have people around him who ride his dick. To be honest, he gets on my nerves."

"Who is Joe?" India asked.

"He's the starting forward for the Wizards," Nina answered. "You know, the one with the gray eyes."

"Oh yeah, I know who you talking about now. He does that Nike commercial where he's playing basketball and a thunderstorm starts, and when everyone else leaves because it's lightning, he keeps playing, right?" India asked.

"Yeah, girl." Nina laughed.

"What the hell is so damned funny," I asked. "I know you ain't sweating that nigga."

"Cory, stop being so jealous," Nina said. "You know I don't trip off of nobody but you." Then she squeezed my hand and kissed my cheek.

Brendan asked Nate to call for the waitress, and when she came Brendan asked her to wrap the rest of his food, but to bring him the fudge cheesecake he had been craving ever since he had been on a diet. No one else wanted dessert, but Nina ordered a slice of cheesecake to go.

Laney had been particularly quiet ever since Donny had come over to the table, and Nina took enough notice to ask her if everything was all right. She assured Nina and Brendan, who now had seemed to notice her uneasiness, that she was fine.

"I think I may have eaten too much. I might just need to go to the ladies room, if you will excuse me, Cory," Laney said, sounding a little more nervous than sick.

"I think I'll join you, as a matter of fact," India added. "Could you let me out, sweetheart?" she said, as she gently nudged Nate's shoulder.

Before either Nate or I stood to let the two ladies out, Donny was back at our table with Joe Simpson and another guy, who was too short to be an NBA player.

"Hey hey, what's happening player?" Joe said to Nate as he shook his hand. All eyes were on Nate and Joe. The ladies looked as though they were wondering how Nate knew Joe well enough for him to come up to our table. I wasn't surprised anymore. Nate knew everybody and everybody knew Nate. One night while we were hanging out together in Atlanta, Toni Braxton walked up and kissed him on the lips. I also witnessed Marion Barry giving him a pound and a hug at the

Million Man March, but when George Foreman sent a bottle of champagne over to our table one night at the Mirage in Las Vegas, I totally flipped out. After that nothing would ever surprise me.

"Not much. We're just finishing up with our birthday celebration for my man Brendan right here."

"Oh yeah, happy birthday, my man," he said, as he reached across the table to shake Brendan's hand. As soon as he did that, his eyes locked with Laney's. There was a pause, then Joe exclaimed, "I'll be damned, I can't believe this shit. It's you."

"Who are you talking to?" Brendan asked, then realized Joe was staring straight at Laney.

Joe ignored Brendan and kept talking. "I bet you never thought I'd see your ass again." There was an evil scowl on his face.

Brendan looked at Laney's face. She had the same look that Trina had had when she was busted.

"I don't know you, and you don't know me." Laney ushered out the words. She wasn't convincing, though.

"Don't even try it, bitch." Joe took a deep breath, and then said, "If you weren't here with these people I . . . I swear I would whup your ass."

"Hold up, man. What the fuck is your problem?" Nate stood up. It seemed for a second that some serious shit was about to pop off right then and there.

"Hey man this . . . this whore robbed my ass last year."

"C'mon, man. Get the fuck out of here," Nate said.

"Let me out of this booth, Cory," Brendan said.

"Shit, nigga, get out. But I know you aren't trying to fight over no stripper. Man, I know that ain't your lady, is it?" Joe asked indignantly.

"Joe." Nate placed his hand on his chest, indicating he wanted Joe to back up. "You are making a scene at my table. I'm only going to say this one time. My lady is at this table and this is a birthday celebration. You are going to have to move on with all of that bullshit." I got up and stood next to Nate.

"Man, who the fuck are you supposed to be?" asked the shorter guy, whose presence Nate had never acknowledged.

"What, nigga? You say something?" Nate said, as he glared at the stranger. Nate noticed that the man had taken a defensive stance and clenched his fist, as if to get ready for action. When he didn't reply, Nate stated emphatically, "And dog, you better unclench your fist." I noticed people beginning to stare in our direction. I wasn't sure if it was because Joe Simpson was standing there or if they could actually hear what was going on. Nate continued glaring icily at the shorter guy.

As the stranger's bottom lip quivered his hands loosened up. Joe's tone lightened up. "Nate, man, I ain't tripping. I'm not trying to disrespect your folks either, but really, that chick . . . she straight robbed me." He started talking to Nate while we listened. Laney's face showed no expression as she sat helplessly pinned in her seat. "Last year, the night after I got traded down here from Philly, I had a little going away party at my crib. One of the players brought four strippers over, and your friend here was one of them. After just about everyone had left the crib, me and three of the other guys paid her and her girl-friend to stay and do a little private afterparty for us. Well, she stayed, and I gave them at least six or seven hundred dollars apiece for doing it. She and her friend fucked me and my boys all night long." He paused and looked Laney right in the face. "We had been drinking all night, and when we passed out at like five or six in the morning, those bitches stole a bunch of shit. They emptied everyone's pockets and took my Rolex and a chain that my father had given me on draft day."

Everyone at the table was silent and just looked at Laney in disbelief. We figured he had to be lying. Then Joe added, "But they forgot to take the tape we made of them dancing and fucking all of us. I gave the police a portion of the tape so that they would have a picture of them. If you want to see the tape of your little porno star friend here anytime, just let me know. Nate, you got my number." Joe just shook his head, then said, "I'll call the police in Philly and let them know I saw you. I hope you got some good money for the watch." He glanced down at Nate's wrist and added, "Nice watch, Nate . . . watch your back." Then they walked off and left our table silent. I looked over at Brendan, and if I didn't know better I would have sworn he was choking on his food. I think he was just trying hard to swallow the worst birthday surprise that anyone could have imagined.

Chapter 17

NO ANGEL IN DISGUISE

There was silence in the car as Brendan sped around the Beltway. He was in a complete funk while his mind raced with images of Laney turning tricks with the Sixers's starting lineup. The thought of it was making him sick. There was a churning in his stomach that didn't come from eating bad food. It was from getting burned and lied to by someone he had been starting to care about and believe in for the second time in less than a year. He felt like such a complete idiot. He had been going on and on for the past four months to Cory and Nate about how special Laney was. Only to find out that she was special to a lot of people for the wrong reasons.

A damned stripper! Brendan thought. *And she'll sell that ass if the price is right. I can't believe this. How could she do this shit to me? Shit, she helped me get into shape, and everything. Maybe that's why she is in such good shape. All that dirty dancing, I bet. That must have been why she always has plenty of money. How else could she move into her apartment in December and have it completely furnished within two weeks? I know she must still be stripping. Probably every nigga I know has seen her naked ass. Man, why does this always happen to me?* Brendan glanced over at Laney. She was looking straight ahead. *Look at her. She hasn't said a word. No apologies, no nothing. I should stop the car and kick her ass out on the Beltway.* Brendan knew he wouldn't, though. It wasn't his style. His mind was racing. *I never dogged anyone, and still I get this shit every time. Maybe I should be like Nate. That way, if one of my women messes up, I'll already have another one.* He tried to break his train of thought as the anger and pain began to force a lump in his throat. He swallowed hard again, and before he knew it, tears had welled up in his eyes. He didn't want to wipe them and let Laney know how badly she'd crushed him. The car was zooming toward the Kenilworth Avenue exit before Laney attempted to break the silence.

"Brendan," Laney said, in a voice that was so low it was almost a whisper. Brendan didn't answer. Laney looked at him and saw the tears on his cheeks. She felt terrible guilt on top of the humiliation and shame she was already feeling from the episode. "Brendan," she called again.

Brendan grumbled out a pitiful, "Yeah."

"Brendan, I'm sorry I ruined your birthday. I'm sorry for everything."

"Why the hell did you have to turn out to be a liar? Huh? I trusted you, Laney. This is so fucked up. What did I do to deserve all of your lies?" Brendan blasted her.

"Brendan, listen to me. All of the things that he said weren't true. I don't want you to think . . ." She paused. "All of the things he said weren't true, Brendan."

"Well damn, Laney, the whole scenario is so damned foul that it doesn't matter what parts aren't true," Brendan snapped. "So what's not true? You slept with three guys, not four, or did you only get three hundred dollars for doing it?"

"No, Brendan. Just listen." Laney's voice began to crack.

"Listen to more of your lies, Laney? I don't think so." The car pulled into Laney's apartment complex. "Don't you think I have heard enough for one night?"

"Brendan, I just want you to know something. I know that you are really upset right now, but maybe if I just explain . . ."

He cut her off. "Explain shit, Laney. Laney, you can't just explain shit like this away. You can't explain lying to someone for four months. You can't explain withholding the little fact that you were working as stripper last year in your hometown. And you sure as hell can't explain letting four guys run a train on you for loot. God, I can't believe you." The car stopped in front of her building. "Just get the fuck out." Brendan couldn't believe he had said that to her. It felt good, though, and the second time it came instinctively. "Just get the fuck out of my car."

Laney looked at Brendan. She looked straight into his eyes. She knew that it was his wounded pride and hurt feelings talking and not him. She knew at that minute that Brendan seriously cared for her. She also knew that he would probably never give her a chance to explain. They stared at each other for a second, and as Laney turned to get out of the car she spoke with a sincerity that she knew Brendan would recognize. "I know now that I should have told you everything about my past, but you would probably never have treated me the way that you did." A tear began to slide from her left eye. "And I deserve to be treated like this. But you know that if I had told you everything up front, there's no way you would have given me half a chance. I understand that you probably hate me now, but I know that I almost made you love me." Laney burst into tears, and Brendan's heart dropped into his lap. Laney went on with tears rolling down her yellow cheeks and snot running out of her nose. "But know this, Brendan. I'm not a bad person. And if you ever change your mind, and you want to listen to what I have to say, call me, okay?" She sniffled, then to Brendan's surprise she said, "I love you." Then she was gone up the walkway.

Brendan walked into the house, and there was music blasting from the basement. He almost forgot to turn the alarm on, but then turned back toward the door to arm it. As soon as he pushed the last button two hands were over his eyes.

"Guess who, birthday boy."

"I don't know. I give up," Brendan said, sounding completely uninterested.

The hands came off, and he turned around. It was Gladys. Gladys was one of Renee's closest girlfriends.

"Hey, Gladys. What's going on? I haven't seen you in a while." Brendan's tone of voice lightened up. Gladys would never be mistaken for being the cutest girl in the world, but she had a body on her. Brendan loved watching her. Back in the day, before Gladys had gotten married, Brendan used to accompany Gladys and Renee to the

Classics nightclub. He never got to first base with her, but she did entertain his flirting from time to time. "So, are you ladies having a good
time?"

"Boy, you know we are doing the damn thing." She laughed out.
"You know a *Waiting to Exhale* kind of thing."

"I get it. Doing a little male bashing and sipping some wine, right?"

"Not necessarily in that order, but you get the picture. Hey, come
help me take this stuff downstairs. Renee is already tipsy, so I came up
to get some more wine. Why don't you just take the whole thing
downstairs?" She was referring to the two-gallon box of white zinfandel. "I'll take the rest of these Tostitos and salsa down. We might even
let you stay downstairs and talk with us and give us a male point of
view."

"I don't know if I should set myself up like that, Gladys." Brendan
laughed.

"Don't be silly, Brendan. Grab another wine glass and come on."

Brendan did as he was told and got a move on. When he walked into
the basement he saw the other four ladies scattered all over the sitting
room like throw pillows. Shoes were off, and the drinks were flowing.
It was just like a scene from the movie. Renee was sitting on the floor
in front of the couch playing Angela Bassett. Evelyn, her cousin, was lying in front of the fireplace being Whitney Houston. Tanya was doing
Loretta Devine on the love seat, with her feet hanging over the edge,
and Andrea was on the other couch sitting Indian-style chilling like
Lela Rochon. Brendan headed for the empty leather chair as he was
greeted with "hellos" from everyone. Gladys announced that she had
asked him to join as a representative of the lesser sex. Tanya was the
only one who protested his crashing their party. Everyone else thought
it was a good idea.

When Renee asked him why he was home so early from dinner, he
made up something about Laney getting sick.

"That's too bad," Renee said.

"Yeah, but don't worry. We'll take care of you, Brendan," Evelyn
said.

"Yeah, I wish," Brendan said, in a tone that left no doubt what he
meant by it.

"Now, you see," Tanya shouted. Brendan came to the quick deduction that Tanya had drunk the most wine. "That is just what we're talking about. The only thing on a man's mind is sex."

"No," said Brendan. "It is the prominent thing, but not the only thing."

"Whatever. That is all a man can think about," Tanya stated.

"Brendan, is that true?" Gladys asked. "It can't be. Because my husband thinks about every damned thing but sex."

"No, some men have much more on their mind than sex," Renee answered. "I know for a fact that Brendan isn't like that. We have been close for . . . for forever, and he has never ever tried to make a move. Isn't that right, Brendan?"

She was actually wrong. Brendan had in fact tried to put a move on Renee. It was the night of their senior prom. His parents had paid for a hotel room for him, and when Renee's parents told them that they wouldn't wait up, they eventually found themselves at the Holiday Inn. Naturally, Brendan tried his luck, unsuccessfully though, and they both had erased it from their memories. After that night the two never found themselves in a compromising position again.

Brendan immediately remembered his prom night attempt, but mentally swept it under the rug and replied, "Yep, you know it."

Evelyn, who was now standing and refilling her wine glass said, "I don't care if a man wants sex. Hell, I want sex, too. But he's not getting it for free."

"Now you know that sounds a bit like a hooker," responded Andrea. "I don't care about how much a man spends. I have to connect with him on a deeper level. If he spends thousands on gifts and trips, or if he spends ten dollars in Blockbuster and on some KFC, it doesn't matter. If I'm not feeling him, I'm just not."

Gladys smacked her lips. "Bitch, you know good and well that you haven't ever had a brother spend nowhere near a thousand dollars on you and you refused to drop your drawers." Everyone laughed, including Brendan.

Trying to save face, Andrea asked Renee, "Renee, tell her about Weldon Jackson. Just tell her."

"You mean the guy who owned the mattress company?" Renee asked.

"Yeah. But actually, his father owned the company. The mattress kings, they called themselves."

"You did tell me he spent quite a bit of money trying to win you over." Renee cosigned for Andrea.

Andrea, regaining her confidence since Gladys's remark, went on. "Yeah. That fool spent so much money trying to impress me it turned me off. Fancy restaurants and shows are nice. Sometimes, though, a sistah just wants a brother to keep it real."

"What you mean, keep it *real* girl?" Tanya asked. "I know you aren't saying keep it cheap."

"No, not at all," Andrea said. "Let me break it down for ya. All I am saying is, I just don't need a brother trying to floss all the time or trying to buy my affections. I know I told you about the time this fool Weldon calls me from out of town. He was at some convention in Illinois, and he tells me to stay home this particular Saturday morning because he had a surprise coming for me." She paused long enough to sip her wine, all the while remaining seated Indian-style. "I have to say, I was shocked."

"Why is that?" Renee asked.

"Well, by this time I had sent him enough signals to let the nigga know that I wasn't really interested in him, but he wouldn't give up. So I tell him I don't want anymore gifts, but he insisted that it hadn't cost him a thing and to please accept it. Well, about an hour after we get off the phone, a knock comes at my door. When I get it, I see that Weldon has had a king-sized bed with a canopy frame delivered."

"Are you serious, Andrea?" Tanya asked.

"Hell, yeah. Ask Renee. She's seen it."

"Did you keep it?" Brendan asked.

Everyone looked at Brendan as if he had just gotten off the short yellow school bus.

Without answering Brendan, Andrea laughed out, "The trip part about it was that one of the guys who delivered the bed was a fine-looking brother. He was slim, but had muscles, and the cutest baby face and dimples. Turned out that he was working his way through college. He was so polite. He even offered to come back after he got off work to help me put the frame together. When he came back he was showered, clean, and in a pair of jeans and a wife-beater that made him look so sexy. You see, I was *feeling* him."

"Let me guess," Brendan said. "It was him who got to christen the mattress with you and not the guy who sent it to you."

"Yes, but not that night. I made him wait, of course, but the point is that the money isn't the major factor. Weldon is probably a millionaire, and here is a guy who is delivering mattresses for him. Rashad, the delivery guy, is able to have a woman that Weldon couldn't get no matter how much money he spent or had."

Brendan nodded his head, and said, "That still sucks. You still played games. To hell with your signals. You should have just come right out and told him that you weren't interested in him. He could have spent his time and money on someone who would have panned out for him." Brendan was now sipping his second glass of wine.

Tanya joined in. "He got to enjoy her company on quite a few occasions. Why isn't that enough? How come if a man doesn't get sex from a woman, it's a waste of time for him to spend time with her?"

Brendan shot back with a finger pointing to emphasize how strongly he felt. "How come women think that men just want to spend time with them for no reason at all? It's like women think that we have nothing else that we could be doing." He paused. "I don't mean *doing* like that. I mean, shit, what do I mean?" Brendan said out loud. "I mean, women should realize that men don't take women out and spend time with them if they aren't interested in them or attracted to them. We're not after company or to just be buddies. Chances are, if a man is over twenty-three, twenty-four, he already has enough platonic female friends to last a lifetime. A new telephone buddy is probably the last thing he's after. The fact of the matter is that he's probably looking for someone special to share his life with, maybe even to marry, and at the very least have a physical encounter with. But it always seems that sisters are always to go out with anyone as long as he's treating."

"Brendan, what's wrong with that?" Gladys asked.

"Yeah, why shouldn't a sister accept a meal? It's not like it's diamonds or something," Evelyn added.

"The same reason that women don't like when men want or expect something in return for that meal."

"Well, Brendan, I see your point. If a woman repeatedly accepts things from a man whom she has no real interest in, or sees no potential for growth in the relationship. But what about when two people are just getting to know each other?" Renee asked.

"Well, that is a little different. A man should be a gentleman, of course, and I would think that most men wouldn't mind taking a woman out a few times, his treat. But if she isn't showing interst then he should ask her what's up. If things don't seem to be going in the direction he wants, then he should move on. I mean really, it shouldn't be too much to expect a sister to be up front with him." Brendan put his feet up on the coffee table and finished his statement before anyone had a chance to interrupt. "After all, if she isn't interested in him, it's not like she's not going to all of a sudden start calling him up, and paying his way to dinner and movies. So why should she let him keep trying and wasting his time and money?"

"Well, you know, Brendan, I really never thought about it quite like that. I do let a lot of guys take me out even though they really aren't my type," Evelyn said.

"Yeah, sometimes I do, too. But I think it's because I'm just giving them a chance to grow on me," Renee said, laughing.

The system was pumping the new Tweet CD. Everyone's eyes were showing the effects of sipping wine. Even Andrea, who was supposedly the designated driver, was beyond tipsy. As the clock moved toward 1:00 A.M., the conversation wound down. Tanya had dozed off right in the chair and started snoring, Evelyn was on her cell making a booty call, and the conversation was now among Gladys, Brendan, and Andrea. Renee had gone upstairs to clean the dishes, and was making a pot of coffee. By the time she had come back downstairs, Gladys had come right out and admitted that after only three years of marriage, she was having an affair. She had told them it was because her husband was boring and didn't have the fire that he used to have. She also said he didn't pay her the same attention that he had before they were married.

When Brendan asked her if she had ever tried talking to her husband and letting him know how serious things had gotten, she replied, "Kind of."

"What do you mean, kind of?" Brendan asked. Andrea's eyebrows were raised, as she was totally shocked.

"Well, I've tried to talk to him before, but he's always too tired or too busy working," Gladys said.

Andrea smirked, "Well, isn't he working two jobs, girl?"

"Yeah, to pay off Gladys's student loans, credit cards, and for that house that she couldn't wait to have," Renee added, as she reappeared with the coffee.

"You see," Brendan said. "If you let the ladies tell it, the men are the dogs. Now if that isn't the coldest shit I've heard. This brother is working at the Navy yard and at UPS, breaking his back so that you don't have to stress over money. Look at how you repay him. Instead of letting him come home to a hot bath and dinner on the table, you've got him coming home to a piece of used you-know-what."

"Brendan," Renee said loudly.

Gladys just sat there with a stupid look on her face. At that moment she was wishing she hadn't dragged Brendan down the stairs to join them. But she knew he was right.

"Hey, Gladys, I don't mean to sound judgmental, but I just think that's wrong. But it's your life." Trying to smooth things over, he added, "I probably don't know the whole story."

It didn't work. Gladys couldn't believe that sweet old Brendan had come down on her like that. She sat there and rolled her eyes. Brendan said goodnight to the ladies and made a quick exit while they sipped coffee.

As he made his way up the steps, Evelyn commented on how good Brendan was looking these days. Andrea added that she hadn't remembered Brendan being so outspoken and sure of himself. She said, "It's kind of sexy, a man who you can talk to like that. You know . . . about real things. A handsome brother like Brendan, too. He looks like he's been in the gym." She turned to Renee as she placed her empty mug on the table. "You got it good, girl. You have a good one living right under your roof."

"C'mon. You all know it's not like that with us."

"Whatever, child. Then you need to be seriously considering making it like that," Evelyn said, as she slapped Andrea five.

"You two are a damned trip." Renee was a little embarrassed. She didn't want to admit it, but she had always recognized that Brendan was attractive, even before he had lost the weight. But the thought of anything ever sparking a fire between the two of them seemed such a far-off possibility that she had definitely brushed off the notion.

The ladies headed out the door into the night air. If the coffee hadn't gotten their heads straight, then the cool March air would have. Renee locked the storm door and headed up the stairs.

Chapter 18

IF THE SHOE FITS

Brendan got out of the shower and felt relieved. The steam had relaxed him. No one could tell that his birthday dinner had been ruined from looking at him now. He was definitely cool, even though he had broken up with Laney a few hours earlier. In addition to that breakup, he would no longer be rooting for the Washington Wizards, not as long as they had that asshole Joe Simpson playing for them. Even though Brendan was a Michael Jordan fan, he hoped that they lost every game for the rest of the season.

He was in his room drying off when the phone rang. It was two in the morning, and who in the world would be calling? "Hello."

"Yo, boy, I'm just checking on you. Just wanted to make sure you were okay."

"Yeah, man. I'm cool."

"I called you earlier," Cory said.

"Yeah. I was down in the basement with Renee and her girlfriends. They were having their little book club thingy."

"Was Evelyn over there with her fine ass?"

"Yeah, and so was Gladys."

"Damn."

"You wouldn't believe that Gladys is cheating on her husband."

"How do you know?"

"She came right out and told me. You know, we were just rapping, and the next thing you know she just came out with it."

"Maybe she wants you to be next," Cory laughed.

"If she did, I doubt it now. I kind of bombed her out about it. I think she was a little pissed with me when she left."

"Oh, well. But you seem straight, though. What happened in the car on the way home?" Cory asked.

"Man, I told her what I thought about her. And I told her to get the hell out."

"You put her out of the car?"

"I mean, we were in front of her building."

"Oh."

"She had the nerve to tell me that she loved me."

"There's a lot of that going around," Cory laughed.

"Say what?"

"We'll get into that later. I just wanted to make sure you didn't give Laney the beat down."

"Never that. I'm fine . . . I mean, for someone who just broke up with their lady on their birthday." Brendan managed a slight chuckle.

"Well, hit me tomorrow," Cory ended.

"Nina over there?" Brendan asked.

"Yeah, she's in the bed, though."

"Okay then, bro, peace out."

"Later." They hung up. Brendan reached into his dresser for a T-shirt. When he turned around, Renee was standing in the doorway.

"Girl, you scared the shit out of me. What are you doing?"

"I came in here to ask if you wanted some." Renee extended a bag of microwaved popcorn. "And to ask why you really came home so early, but I don't have to ask anymore, since I heard you say you broke up with Laney."

Brendan had a funny look on his face. Renee saw it and thought he was peeved because she had overheard him. She really hadn't intended to eavesdrop. But it wasn't that at all. The look was the result of a combination of things. It was the way that things had gone down at dinner. It was all of the wine that he had been drinking. It was because of the hot shower. But most of all it was because Renee was standing in front of him in a cotton chemise that was somewhat transparent. Brendan could see the outlines of her breasts, and her nipples looked like they were hard. And hadn't she just asked him if he *wanted some?*

Renee stood there waiting for a response. Instead, he just looked at her. Her jet-black hair was in big loose curls, which was his favorite style for her. She knew it because he had told her about a hundred times, and she had probably considered that when she had gotten it done earlier in the day, since she was taking him out for his birthday. Her face was kind, as usual, and she was ready at two o'clock in the morning to listen to him if he needed her. She was his best friend and almost like the sister he had never had. But damn, tonight she was looking good to him. Renee was far from chunky but could be considered voluptuous. Her frame carried her 140 pounds nicely. Her face was round, with a dimple in her chin, and she had deep, dark eyes. Most men's eyes never got past her nice hips and ample breasts, and therefore missed her subtle beauty.

She finally spoke. "Brendan, what is your problem? Are you okay?"

Brendan spoke. "Yeah, I'm fine. I'm still a little buzzed from the liquor, that's all." Renee looked down at his boxers. His dick was pointing straight at her. She tried to remove her eyes from his crotch and bring them back up to eye level, but he caught her staring. Now she had the silly look.

"So can I have some?" Brendan asked.

"What, some of my popcorn?" She breathed in deeply.

"Nah, I don't want your popcorn." Brendan moved toward her.

She instinctively moved backward. Her head must have been swimming a little, because she was ready to stop backing away. He reached for her shoulders to pull her back through the doorway. With one hand she held onto the popcorn and with the other she reached blindly for Brendan's crotch; he was still pointing thirty degrees north, and her hand found him easily. The popcorn fell to the floor as their lips, unfamiliar to each other, met for the first time since prom night.

They had both wondered often enough when and if this moment would come. How it would feel. Renee had wondered most about how their relationship would change and if it would grow into something more. Brendan had wondered most how it would feel to be inside of Renee. Would it be good? He, unlike Renee, had never given much thought as to what effect the two of them becoming intimate would have on their friendship.

Their lips stayed locked. Brendan's hand flipped the light switch on the wall before they slid onto the bed, still intertwined. Brendan's hands were all over Renee's brown body. He was more aggressive than he would have been normally. The chance to satisfy years of pent-up desire and curiosity was at stake. This was the thought on Brendan's mind as he attempted to get Renee all worked up before she had a chance to change her mind. It was working. Renee was losing herself to Brendan's touch and kisses. Every time she thought about stopping him, his lips would find a spot on her body that would send shivers throughout it.

Before Renee knew it, Brendan had her chemise up over her head, and was sliding her panties off. She had never imagined that Brendan would be so smooth and commanding in the bedroom. She always imagined him as the bumbling type. As a matter of fact, in her mind she often thought that he might still be the goofy young kid who couldn't get her bra unfastened on prom night. She had had no intention of giving Brendan any that night, but had he been half as smooth as he was at this moment, it would have been hard for her to say no.

Brendan managed to slyly squirm out of his underwear without breaking the action, and he placed his naked body on top of hers. There was no talking, only heavy breathing as his lips and tongue danced across her nipples. His other hand disappeared between her legs. Renee's heavy breathing became low moans as her bottom began to wiggle in response to his gentle touch. His mouth slid down to her belly button, and his tongue darted in and out of it just as quickly. He only stopped at her belly momentarily. Renee was a little shocked that she was lying in Brendan's bed. *This is Brendan*, she thought, as her mind began to race. *We can't be doing this. This is like my brother. Why am I letting him kiss me like this? I know I am going to regret this in the morning, but damn it feels good.* "Oooohhh, shit, Brendan," Renee yelled out, as his tongue found its mark. *I am wet as a waterfall. I hope that he's not drowning down there. I can't believe Brendan is working his shit like that . . . I hope he doesn't think that because he's doing that . . .* "Oh damn, Brendan . . . I'm gonna come . . . Baby, I'm coming," she yelled out, as she grabbed the back of his head. Her body shook for what seemed like minutes.

Brendan was feeling like "the man." He couldn't believe that he had finally showed Renee what he was capable of doing. He wasn't finished, yet. He wiped the wetness from around his mouth with the towel that he had thrown on the bed earlier and climbed back on top of her. As her senses came back to her, she wondered if she should continue. It was too late to stop now, she thought, and after he had made her feel so good, she wanted nothing more than to please him. And she did. She played the passive role a little while longer, while Brendan continued amazing her with his passionate and gentle love-making. He wasn't startled when she placed her hands on his chest and pushed him until he was on his back. Brendan could make out the sincerity in Renee's face as she rode him with all the expertise of a working girl. The outlines of her body in the dark looked sexy on top of him and were turning him on even more. It didn't take much more of Renee throwing it at him before she drove him completely over the edge. He called out her name as he let go. There was deep breathing as the two tried to regain their wind. There was no time to discuss whether it had been right or wrong, because within five minutes they were both asleep in each other's arms.

Morning came with a clarity that hadn't been available at night. When Brendan turned and saw Renee lying there next to him instead of Laney, he knew that things had definitely taken on a twist that he had no idea how to make sense of. Things had happened fast. He hadn't even had a chance to tell Renee what really had happened between him and Laney. He probably wouldn't. The whole thing was a little embarrassing to him. Just dealing with the fact that yet another woman had duped him after Trina was a task in itself. He could already hear Nate's jokes coming, and if he ever mentioned it to Shue, he surely would never hear the end of it.

Now he had complicated things in a way he had never imagined. He tried to figure out what had finally made he and Renee fall into bed together. There had been no signs of it coming. Brendan had not taken Renee's usually sweet self, nor her occasional sexy nightclothes, as any indication that something was brewing. As adults, though, the two of them could have predicted that something would happen eventually. They both should have known, and probably did, that living together would sooner or later cause a spark to ignite between them. Maybe deep down they both wanted the other but had never admitted it. Now the deed was done, and there was no taking it back.

Brendan stared at Renee's sleeping face and noticed that her eyebrows were going every which way, and that the corners of her mouth were white. "So this is what it's like to wake up to her," he thought. For a second he thought about Trina's face in the morning and how she had looked, as though she hadn't really slept, the way most people do. She would wake up with no crust in her eyes, no bags under them, and her hair always seemed to be in place. He remembered thinking that he was going to marry her because it would be like looking at an angel every morning. He had found out, though, that how a woman looks in the morning isn't the most important thing when looking for a wife. It was a good thing, because Laney definitely didn't have that angelic morning glow, nor did Renee. He couldn't remember anyone before Trina having it either, which prompted him to the conclusion that it was a rare quality he had better be able to live without.

It was nearly eleven o'clock, and Brendan was sitting on the bed tying up the laces of his Adidas when Renee woke up.

"Good morning," Renee said her voice still scratchy. "Going running?" It had been his routine on Sundays, and at least four other days during the week.

"Yeah. I have a little hangover, but I still gotta do what I gotta do," Brendan said.

Renee looked at the clock. "Damn, it's late."

"Yeah. I started to wake you, but you were sleeping so soundly," he said, as he stood and zipped up the jacket to his Gore-Tex jogging suit.

"I guess I needed it." She smiled.

They exchanged a little more conversation about their plans for the day merely to avoid what needed to be said. As Brendan headed for the steps, Renee called him back.

He poked his head inside the doorway, and she said, "So, will you be around later? I guess we should talk."

Brendan didn't know whether it sounded more like a question or a statement, and he replied, "Yeah, I'll be around. We're still going to dinner tonight, right?"

Renee was relieved; he was still acting normal. "Yes. You just have to let me know where. I'm headed to the mall with my mother, but I'll be back here by five or so."

"Cool, I'll see you then." Then he walked over to his bed and kissed her on the forehead. "Everything is going to be fine, so don't trip at all. Okay?"

She nodded and smiled. Brendan had reassured her that things would be fine. She believed him, because he wouldn't lie to her. Her mind was still racing with emotions and thoughts brought on by their lovemaking. On top of that, things had happened so quickly that she hadn't had the chance to ask him what had happened between him and Laney.

Brendan was finishing his third lap when he noticed a woman seated in the bleachers. He had finished his fourth when he realized it was Laney. She'd taken a small chance that she would find him there because she wanted to talk to him in person. There would be no wasted phone calls in which he would have the chance to brush her off or hang up on her. When Brendan ignored her on his fifth lap, she questioned whether or not he had seen her. When he looked right at her as he came past on his sixth, Laney stood up. She began stretching right next to the fence. He passed her once more before she began running.

His pager went off as he finished up his twelfth lap. He pulled it from his waistband as he wiped the beads of sweat off his forehead. He was sweating the alcohol out of his system, he thought. His hangover was gone, but his mouth was as dry as a desert. He knew that he would have to quit soon. Laney had been jogging behind him for the last mile. When he first saw her, he thought that she had come there to confront him, but now he wasn't sure. He wasn't sure if he wanted to talk to her, anyway.

That was bullshit, actually, because deep down Brendan knew he wanted her to beg him to forgive her. He wanted her begging to be strong enough to equalize the shame and pain she had caused him. As his pace dropped from a rapid run to a light jog for his cool-down phase, he knew it would be impossible. No matter what she said, it wouldn't be enough. He would be letting himself down if he gave her another chance. Besides, he had more to worry about now. He had to tend to the issue of Renee. He wasn't sure where that was headed, but he knew that he would have to put her feelings first. He couldn't bear the thought of ever making Renee feel cheap or used by him. Laney's actions had caused her to stumble from number one to number two overnight.

Brendan was now walking, and Laney ran right past him. She was moving fast. So fast, in fact, Brendan hardly got a glimpse of her tight ghetto booty as it bounced from side to side with each stride. She was running in spandex tights and her usual sweatshirt. He did notice that she looked sexy, as usual. He always felt turned on when she ran, no matter what she wore. There was hardly a day that, after they had jogged, they didn't end it knocking boots. It wasn't happening today, though. Laney watched Brendan head for his car, and she lost her nerve. She figured that if there were even the slightest change in attitude on his part he would have waited for her to finish. But he had figured that when she kept jogging she had actually come to jog and not to talk. She had taken him there to run initially, and perhaps she was going to keep running there whether they were together or not.

I couldn't believe that Nina and I were arguing over something so silly. We stood in the video store, and she was insisting that we rent *The Brothers*. I had foolishly mentioned that I had seen it twice in the theater. When she asked me whom I had seen it with, I had told her that I had gone with a couple of friends back in Atlanta. Her next question was "With two different dates, huh?"

Now here we were in Blockbuster arguing about something that had happened last summer. "Well, forget it then, Cory. I don't want to see anything that you watched with another bitch, let alone two."

"That is beyond stupid, Nina," I said. "If you want to see the movie, then get it. What difference does it make who I saw it with?"

"So now I'm stupid," she said, nostrils flaring.

"I didn't say you were stupid. Look, if you are getting the movie, just get the doggone thing. I'm not going to stand here and argue with you about it."

Her eyes were squinted as she looked at me and then she rolled them in her head as she turned back toward the shelves. "How about this? Did you see this with one of your girlfriends, too?"

I didn't even look at the movie, and said, "No, I've never seen that. Get it. C'mon."

I heard her suck her teeth, then mumble something in Spanish.

"Don't start talking that shit either," I said.

"Oh, I'm sorry. I meant to say that in English," she said in a sarcastic tone. "Do you want to know what I said?"

"I don't know. Do I?"

"I said you are a dog just like your boy Nate."

I stopped walking and turned to her. "What the hell does my seeing a movie have to do with me being a dog like Nate? Huh, just tell me that."

She could tell that she had finally irritated me, which was apparently her goal. She then cracked a half-restrained smile and said, "If the shoe fits, wear it, nigga."

I saw a girl off to the side of us looking entertained, and I headed off to the check-out counter. Nina followed. We didn't say anything else until we got to the car. Nina stood by her door and waited for me to come to her side and open it. When I hit the alarm and jumped in on my side, her mouth dropped open. I laughed to myself when she got into the car. I said, "You know dogs don't open doors. At least, Nate doesn't."

"Yeah, okay. I got something for you when we get back home."

"I bet you do," I said, as I reached for her thigh.

"Stop it, dog," she laughed out, as my hand slid up her skirt. She pulled it back out from between her legs and looked directly into my face and called my name. When I answered she said, "You can't get enough of me, can you?"

I just smiled in response, and she asked again, but this time she poured on her accent: "Tell me, Popi. You can't, can you? You can't wait 'til I get you back to that apartment, can you, and show you how Nina trains dogs, can you?"

I wasn't sure if I was too fond of that dog business, but I definitely wanted to keep her in the mood that she seemed headed toward. I was starting to notice that she liked to start little arguments like the one we had just had so that we would have an excuse to make up. I wouldn't protest, because everyone knows how good make-up sex can be. It is so emotional. There's nothing like taking out hurt feelings, bruised egos, and anger on your lover in bed, especially when they are willing to let you do it. Especially when they love when you do it.

"You still didn't answer me. Can you wait?"

"No, baby, I can't. Do you want me to pull the car over?"

"Mmmm. That sounds like a good idea."

"We're almost home, girl. We might as well wait," I said, trying to sound practical.

She burst into laughter. "Boy, I know you didn't think that I was going to give you some after you called me stupid, walked off, and then didn't open my door. On top of that, I told you last night that I loved you, and all you produced was a dumb-assed grin. What's up with that? We have some talking to do when we get upstairs." She started with the jabbering again as the words flew out of her mouth like a machine gun. "I mean, Cory, it's not like you have to say the same thing, just because I did. At the very least, though, you could have acknowledged what I said. I mean, it's only fair that you let me know where things are going, and if you just . . ."

I cut her off. "Nina, Nina." The second time I said her name a little louder. I had her attention. Then I said it: "I love you, too." The words came out, and then there was silence.

I hadn't said it to her the previous night because I just needed some time to take in that she had said it to me. I knew that loving her would be the easy part. Dealing with her attitude might not be as easy. She was spoiled, bossy, and jealous. But I was starting to feel as though I needed her in my life for the long haul.

I probably would have taken a little more time to come out and tell her if she hadn't forced my hand; now we were going to have to deal with things a lot sooner. On top of the feelings that had grown so unexpectedly and so much faster than I had had time to comprehend, one of us would eventually have to tell her sister. It would have been hard enough coming to her if I felt totally right about what Nina and I had been doing. Deep down inside, I was hoping that love could never be wrong. Lately I had spent a lot of time comparing the romantic feelings that I had with Nina to the "out of control" love I had shared with Shelly.

Being a man, I found it uncomfortable going through so much emotional turmoil. Like most men I was more used to *doing* than actually feeling. I still had feelings swirling around in my head where Paula was concerned that were prompting me to call her; I still had some issues to resolve with her. I still needed some closure. Paula hadn't called me in a couple of months, but I knew that she still loved me. I still cared for her as well, and I had the feeling that one last weekend with Paula might be in order before I totally ended it by telling her that I had moved on.

I knew that it might be selfish of me, and possibly warrant Nina saying I was a dog. But no matter what I knew, I was trying really hard to fly straight with Nina. I'd resisted and turned down many advances from women at the company and old acquaintances, who had been coming out of the woodwork once they found out I was back in the area. Believe me when I say that it wasn't easy. Nate had warned me about the temptation that the spring weather would bring, with all of the short skirts that would hit the streets, clubs, and malls.

Nina still hadn't said a word since I'd said those three little words. I let her have her moment until I parked the car. She sat there and waited as I went around to get her door. She just smiled as I took her hand and helped her out of the car. I definitely had my honey. Nina was all that, and the shoe definitely fit.

Chapter 19

"THE TALK"

Nate was now nearly an hour and a half late. Sahleen's flight to Barbados had been delayed because of severe weather along the coast of North Carolina, and she had insisted that Nate wait with her. As they sat in the lobby of Gate C at BWI Airport, Sahleen sipped on some Starbucks. Meanwhile, Nate sat anxiously, trying hard not to act as though he had somewhere to go.

"Baby, is something wrong?" Sahleen asked.

"Nah," he answered. "What makes you ask that?"

Sahleen smacked her lips together and picked up her latté. "If you don't want to wait, then go. I'm sorry. I really didn't intend to hold you up."

Nate sensed her suspicion. It was so unlike him to get rattled, but something about Sahleen, probably her overpowering intuition and strong spirit, often made him uneasy.

He was beginning to doubt his own game. He kept feeling as if Sahleen had him figured out. It seemed that she would call at the oddest hours, right when he was about to get into something, and demand his company. Or if she was out of town, she always had thirty or forty minutes of intense conversation for him. By the time she was finished with him, he was usually too on edge to go through with his plans. Often India was the one left hanging, just like she was right now.

At this moment she was at home, dressed and waiting for Nate to arrive. He was supposed to have picked her up at five o'clock to go see

Maysa, who was performing live at Blues Alley in Georgetown. Sahleen's flight was supposed to have left at four-thirty. But here he was at a quarter after six, waiting in the airport. He had promised India dinner before the show, but the clock was ticking, and his two-way pager had been going off every ten minutes.

Sahleen reached into her attaché case and pulled out a large manila envelope. "I almost forgot," she said. "I need you to mail these bills off for me." She handed Nate the envelope. He nodded his head in agreement. "No later than Monday afternoon. I messed around with the cable bill, and I don't want to have to pay a reconnect fee."

"Okay, okay." Nate was glad that she had changed the subject and redirected their attention, away from his impatience. "So, when are you coming back?"

"I thought I told you already. Thursday, but I won't need you to pick me up. Franco's car is here at the airport. He left yesterday, but we're coming back together."

"Five days in sunny Barbados. Must be nice." Nate smiled. Everything was an effort. He was as nervous as a rapper who'd pissed off Suge Knight. His two-way had just gone off again. India was growing tired of his excuses.

"Yeah, baby, but you know it would be nicer if you were going to be there," Sahleen said, as she leaned closer to Nate and put her head on his shoulder.

"I wish I could come, but you have got business to conduct, and it's not like you'd have time to spend relaxing or . . ."

Sahleen cut him off unintentionally. "I know, I know, but still, I can wish, can't I?" She paused, then lifted her head off his shoulder. "Do you still want to come to New York with me for the Shawn Simmons video?"

"You know I want to. When is it?"

"They've pushed it up to the weekend after next. Her new single is going to be released Memorial Day weekend, and they want the video done by the first week in May."

"Baby, you know I can't wait for that. Next to you, of course, Shawn Simmons is the bomb."

"Next to me my ass. I saw how you and Brendan reacted when she sang at the *Soul Train Awards*. You would have thought she was naked, the way you two were howling and whatnot."

"Now, you know that was Brendan. I don't even trip like that. Plus, it was television," Nate laughed. "But you have to admit, that dress that she wore left nothing to the imagination."

"Just imagine what we'll have on for the video," Sahleen said.

"I'll wait and be surprised like everyone else."

"You won't have to do that. You'll be on the set when we shoot, of course. And if you behave, I'll make sure that you get to meet Shawn in person."

"Oh, yeah. Well, in that case, I'll have to be sure to behave for the next couple of weeks at least." They both laughed out loud.

"*Flight 312 now boarding to Barbados at gate C 12*," the announcer blared over the loudspeaker.

"That's me."

"I heard."

They stood and locked in a quick embrace and a quick dance of the tongues, and Sahleen walked off toward the terminal. Nate headed for India.

Brendan and Renee sat in the bed with their heads propped up on oversized pillows. They were naked and still sweating, watching the BET movie channel. This had been their routine for the last month, since they had first slept together. As a matter of fact, they had only slept apart one night. That had happened only because a late snow had surprised the nation's capital.

In D.C., by the end of March the threat of snow is almost nil. This was the snow that caught everyone off guard, particularly Brendan. That night some flurries had been predicted, but instead nearly four inches of snow and sleet had hit the ground, coating the streets and making driving home an unnecessary risk. Brendan had taken a night to hang out without Renee. He, Nate, and Sahleen had gathered at Nate's to watch the *Soul Train Awards* show; Laney ending up at Nate's apartment had been unexpected.

It had just been a coincidence that the snow came on the same day Brendan had reluctantly agreed to see Laney. She had come to his job and told him that she really wanted to talk to him. She had sounded convincing enough, when she assured him that she didn't expect anything but conversation. Though he was still angry with her from his birthday disaster, he was starting to miss her, and therefore he agreed to let her meet him at Nate's. Laney was reluctant to meet him where his friends would be gathered, but she realized it might be her only chance. Plus, she hoped to gain some support in her battle to win Brendan back.

Although she stayed with him for the night, Brendan didn't sleep with her. He wanted to, but his anger, coupled with his new situation with Renee, made him hold fast. But two weeks had passed since that night at Nate's, and Laney was slowly but surely melting Brendan's anger. Her approach had gained ground for her, even if it was only an inch at a time.

She wasn't pressing him the way Trina had after their breakup. Her approach was subtle, and more effective. She would leave sweet messages on his voice mail when she knew he wouldn't be at home. She had sent flowers to his job, and had even had a mobile car detailer come to his house to wax and buff his car in the parking lot early one Friday morning; he hadn't known it was being done until he came out of the house to go to work. Laney knew how much Brendan loved his car, and that had really gotten to him. Laney's onslaught was really beginning to wear him down, but it didn't change the fact that he was truly enjoying his fling with Renee. Even still, he found himself starting to return phone calls, even when the message said "Brendan, I don't want anything. Just wanted to hear your voice. Laney. Bye."

Renee wriggled her bottom and then lifted it off the bed. "Uhhh."

"What?" Brendan said, momentarily moving his eyes away from the screen.

"I was in the wet spot," Renee whined.

"It's all yours. Why are you tripping?" Brendan smiled at her.

"It is not. Hand me a towel."

Brendan hopped out of the bed, grabbed a towel, and tossed it to Renee. "You want anything to drink? I'm going to get a glass of Minute Maid."

"Yes, please. But hurry back before I miss you."

Brendan shook his head and headed down the steps. While he poured lemonade into the oversized cups, he thought that he had really gotten some shit started with her. He wondered when they would be having "the talk." The "where do we stand, and where is this headed?" talk.

Earlier in the week the three of us had eaten dinner at Ben's Chili Bowl after leaving happy hour at the Bar Nun. While we pigged out on Ben Ali's famous chili burgers and cheese fries, Nate had taken the opportunity to confide in Brendan and me the status of his relationships. He actually admitted that while he had been avoiding "the talk" with India, he was somewhat curious as to why Sahleen hadn't been trying to initiate one. Judging from the way he went on about it, apparently it troubled him. By the end of the conversation he had just chalked it up to her pride and decided that he would hold off as long as she could. Looking back on the conversation now, it should have been obvious to us that he actually *wanted* to have the talk with Sahleen for the first time in his life, though he would never actually admit it, even to himself.

Brendan had brought up the fact that Nate had been dating the two women pretty much exclusively since November. "Damn, you're right," Nate had replied. It was nearly May, and he knew he wouldn't be able to ward off India's request for a heart-to-heart too much longer.

I had asked him if he originally had intended to stick around with either of them for so long. His response had been, "Not really." But at this point in the game it was simply too late. Whether Nate wanted to admit it or not, he was in love with his situation. Both ladies were gorgeous. If she were taller and slimmer, India could have passed for a model herself. Both were independent go-getters and outgoing sistahs with great personalities, and both, it appeared, were crazy about him.

. . .

Brendan was headed back up the stairs and was almost at the top when the doorbell rang. He entered the room and set the glasses down. Renee was lying on her stomach looking really comfortable. "You expecting anybody?" he asked, as he put his underwear on.

"No. I thought I heard the doorbell. Put on a shirt; it might be my mother. She said she might be coming out this way to go to Target."

"Alright," Brendan shot out, as he grabbed his pajama bottoms.

Brendan pulled the door open and stood there, shocked. It was Laney.

"A little early for bedtime, isn't it? Why do you have pajamas on?" Laney continued, while Brendan's mind raced. "It was a rhetorical question."

"What are you doing popping up like this?" Brendan replied.

"Don't worry, I don't want to come in unless you invite me. I just wanted to drop something off. I'm about to go to Philly for a bit, and I wanted you to have this before I left." She handed Brendan a shopping bag.

There was a momentary silence that was broken when Renee made her way down the steps. "Who is it, Brendan? Is it my mother?"

"No, it's for me," he said, but he didn't have to say it loudly, because Renee was now standing beside him in a terry-cloth bathrobe.

"Well, hello Laney. Long time no see."

Laney's eyes showed Brendan her concern and curiosity about the picture. Why in the world were they both in their nightclothes at eight-thirty on a Saturday night? And why did it look as if every light in the house was off?

"Hi," was all Laney said to Renee. "Well, Brendan, I'm off. It looks like I caught you at a bad time, and I apologize for that."

"No need to apologize."

"Next time you might want to call first," Renee said, and she turned and walked toward the kitchen.

"What the hell is her problem?" Laney said, loud enough for Renee to hear.

"It doesn't matter, but you really shouldn't be buying me stuff. I mean, I just don't want to confuse matters, ya know what I'm saying?"

Laney was biting her bottom lip to keep it from quivering. Then she stated, "Look, I told you I don't expect anything from you. I know my keeping things from you hurt you, but you never gave me a chance to explain. Just open the package when you have time. Maybe it will help you understand." She started to back away. "Do it when you have some time to yourself, though. Just do that for me, at least." She turned and walked away without saying good-bye.

Brendan closed the door and headed upstairs with the shopping bag in his hand. He put it in his bedroom behind the door, and headed for Renee's room. Once he walked into her room he saw that Renee had turned the movie off and had the video channel on.

"Why did you cut off *Baby Boy*? You know I love that flick."

Renee just glared at Brendan, and then he knew at that very instant it was coming.

"I guess we need to talk? Huh?" he mumbled.

"Yeah. You guessed right," Renee said, arms folded.

Brendan walked into her bathroom to relieve himself. He looked into the mirror, stared into his reflection, and tried to come up with some answers to questions that hadn't even been asked yet.

"So, is now a good time?" Renee called from the bedroom.

Brendan made his way back to the bed. "What's wrong, Renee?"

"What's wrong is, I don't like her just popping up over here like that. And I don't know why you didn't bomb her out for showing up like that, anyway."

"C'mon now, why would I have . . ."

"And when did you start speaking to her again? What's going on with you two, anyway? I thought you weren't speaking."

"Look, she just said she had some things to get off of her chest. I never told you that I wasn't speaking to her. I told you that she had tried to initiate several conversations with me, but that I wasn't ready to talk to her at that point," Brendan said calmly.

Renee breathed deeply. "Oh, but now you're ready to resume talking with her?"

"I didn't say that. I didn't mean that all of a sudden I am going to forgive her for anything. She just wants to be my friend. That's all. She's not pressuring me, or even trying to talk about our relationship."

"I guess she doesn't know about us? I can tell from the way she looked at us that she didn't." Renee rolled her eyes and shook her head in disgust.

"Now, why would I call her and explain what I was doing with you? That's none of her business."

"Well, I think you had better make it her business."

"Hey, why are you getting all bent out of shape?" After a pause Brendan continued, "If this whole situation is making you uncomfortable, I understand."

"No, Brendan. The situation isn't making me uncomfortable. *You're* making me uncomfortable. But if you want to forget the whole thing ever happened, we can."

Renee was lying. At least about her ability to forget. There was no way she would ever be able to forget what had happened between them. She had foolishly allowed herself to get involved with her best friend. It was *When Harry Met Sally* ghetto style. She somehow knew, though, that in this version she would be the one hurt if the affair went too much longer. Brendan had been the victim too many times before, and Renee knew that sooner or later the law of averages would have to balance things out and give him one in his favor. "Brendan, did you hear me?"

Brendan was sitting down on the bed and had his hands clenched together between his legs. "Yeah, I heard you."

"Well, what do you think?"

"About what?"

"Brendan, don't play with me. What do you think about us just forgetting the whole thing and going back, if it's possible, to just being friends?" Renee managed to stumble out.

Brendan closed his eyes and thought for a few seconds before he spoke. His mind was filled with uncertainty. He didn't know what was coming next. While he still couldn't quite see himself in a relationship with a stripper, he still longed for Laney's company and her touch. And to make matters worse, even thoughts of Trina crept into his mind every now and again. If it were any heart other than Renee's that he was dealing with, he wouldn't have thought twice about continuing on until he sorted things out. "I guess if I am making you uncomfortable then maybe we should chill until I sort everything out."

Renee just nodded her head.

"And what about Barry?" Brendan said. "He still has clothes over here. He has been calling you nonstop. You never told him anything. We both need to get ourselves . . ."

"I told Barry about us last week," Renee mumbled out. "But hey, don't worry about it."

Brendan felt like crap. Now who would Renee turn to? Barry had been her Mr. Dependable. He had been the one she called for movie dates and dinners, and for Blockbuster nights in the house, always his treat. Renee used to brag that she only had to sleep with him every so often to keep him coming back. Renee had 'fessed up, and he was surely pissed off. But probably not half as pissed off as Renee was right about then.

Brendan picked up his belongings and headed toward his room. The room that he hadn't slept in for almost five weeks. The results of "the talk," Brendan thought. It seemed as though everyone always ended up worse off after it than they had been before they had it.

It was only nine o'clock on a Saturday night, and the lights were out in the house and on Brendan and Renee's relationship as well. When Brendan got back up to take a shower, he noticed Renee's door was shut. He wasn't tired, so he called Shue to see if he was home.

"Hello," Shue answered.

"Hey, it's me, cuz."

"What's going on, Brendan?" Shue sounded tired.

"Not much. I was just calling to see what you were getting into tonight."

"Me? I'm not doing anything tonight. I'm having company in a little bit, and that'll probably just be that."

Brendan was disappointed. He was hoping for a party or a movie or something with his older cousin. It was not meant to be this night. "Okay. Well then, I'll just give you a call tomorrow."

"Good deal. Talk to you tomorrow." They hung up.

Brendan finished putting on his underwear and headed down into the basement to watch some television and maybe do some thinking as to what he was going to do—about everything.

· · ·

As soon as the door opened, it started. India opened the door and looked at her watch. Nate stepped through the door of India's apartment and followed her to the bedroom.

"I'm not going, Nate. You may as well leave. I am tired of this shit."

"Come on now, baby. I told you earlier that I had to make a few runs. You know how time gets away from me sometimes, Indy baby."

India smacked her lips and huffed. "Whatever. Time always gets away from your ass. Excuse my language, but damn, Nate, this shit is ridiculous."

"Look, I told you I had to drop my cousin off at the airport. He missed his flight, and I didn't want to leave him until I was sure he had another one."

"Yeah, and you couldn't find a second to call and return my page. You are so full of shit. I'm sick and tired of this. I refuse to let you do this to me any longer. If you don't know what to do with me, then believe me, I will find a man who does." She walked back into the kitchen.

"What is that supposed to mean?" Nate asked as he watched her toss a birth control pill into her mouth and guzzle down half a glass of water.

"Exactly how it sounds." India slammed the glass down on the counter. "I figure that you don't have your priorities together. We've only been seeing each other for about six months. I met you in October, and it is April now . . . not even six full months, and how many times have you stood me up, called and canceled a date, or been two hours late? Just like you are now," India rattled off, with her hands on her hips.

Nate just stood there. He couldn't even count them himself.

"I didn't think you could recount them. But let me help. Christmas day. We were supposed to spend the day together. I saw you for what, twenty minutes? Same damn thing on Valentine's Day. The night we were supposed to see the OJays and Gerald Levert. What did we see, the last half-hour? How about the money I wasted on the play at the Warner Theater?"

"I gave you that back."

"That's not the point, and if you think it is, then there is nothing for us to talk about."

"Look, I know you are mad, but let's go and get some dinner and talk things over."

"No."

"No?"

"No."

"So what are we going to do? Sit around here and argue about it for the rest of the evening?" Nate asked.

"No. You can sit around here if you like. I have made other plans."

"You did what?"

"I made other plans." Nate's eyes showed disbelief. India reached into the refrigerator and pulled out a bowl with freshly cut watermelon slices. "You expect me to sit around and wait for you all night. Well, I got a news flash for you, partner. It ain't gonna happen no more."

Nate was stunned, to say the least, but what could he say? "So what kind of plans did you make?"

India answered him while chewing on the watermelon. "Um goin' ow wif a few of ma . . ."

"Swallow the food, child." Nate was letting on that he was upset.

She swallowed. "I'm going to the Soundstage and probably down to Dream with a group of my friends. And now . . ." There was a knock at the door. India answered with Nate looking over her shoulder as she let her friend inside.

"Hey girl, you ready?" The girl at the door asked.

"Just about. Gimme a quick second and let me grab my jacket. Oh, by the way, this is my friend, Nate. Nate, this is Regina. We work together."

"Hi, Nate."

"Hey."

"All right, I'm ready." Nate didn't have time to say much. He just stood there with his lips poked out. He was wishing that he were on that plane with Sahleen. "Nate, if you're not leaving now, please make sure you lock the door behind you." India turned and ushered Regina out of the door. "Girl, your hair looks good. You just got it done today?"

"No, child. I need it done bad," Regina said, patting her hair. Then she said, "Nice meeting you, Ned."

"Nate," India whispered. But they were in the hallway already and the door was closing shut behind them.

Nate sat on the couch, pissed off and not believing what had just happened. He had thought that India would never give him any problems. As fine as she was, though, she wouldn't sit around waiting for him forever. He wondered, *What am I tripping for?* The time was coming when he would have to let her go, anyway. What was he doing with two girlfriends any damned way? Sahleen was perfect. She was always flying in and out of town. He had time to do what he had to do, whatever that may be, and then be finished with his dirt by the time she was back in town. India was always around. Waiting usually, but now demanding. That was precisely the reason she was going to have to go soon. He just had to hit that ass a few more times, and he was out. Sahleen was the bomb, anyway, and she never sweated him.

Nate picked up the cordless phone and sat on the couch. He turned on the television and began scanning the channels while he contemplated calling another female from India's house because his cell was dead. It seemed a bit too risky, and he truly didn't feel like answering any questions about why he had dialed *67 before calling them. Before he realized it, two hours had passed and he had watched an entire NBA play-off game between the Nets and the Hornets. It was almost ten, and he was nowhere near tired yet, so he dialed Cory's number. After four rings, he heard a voice on the line. It was Nina.

"Hello," she said softly.

"Yo, girl. What's up?"

"Nate?" Nina asked.

"What's happening?" Nate asked, nearly repeating his first greeting. "Let me holler at Cory right fast."

"Cory is out of town. He didn't tell you?" Nina asked, sounding surprised that Cory hadn't touched base with his main man.

Nate recalled a conversation with Cory earlier in the week and said, "As a matter of fact, he did. But I thought he said he was going next weekend, not this weekend. Atlanta, right?"

"He said some place right outside of Atlanta."

"Why didn't you go?" Nate asked. He knew why. He was just curious about what story Cory had come up with.

"Well, he didn't leave until this morning, and he's coming right back tomorrow afternoon. He said one of his boys was getting married. It wasn't a big deal. Some white boy he used to work with. He said that the guy, Chad, was real cool, but that it wasn't a big deal. Plus, he had promised to watch Kyle and Tory for Brenda this weekend. That's why I'm over here at his place," Nina explained. "Brenda is working part-time now, trying to save up some money for Tory's college tuition."

"Yeah, Cory mentioned that to me." Nate thought, *The boy is pretty damn slick. He has his girl watching his niece and nephew while he is out of town boning his ex-girl, or mistress, sex partner—whatever he viewed Paula as.*

Nina blew her nose into the line. "Sorry, allergies." She sounded as if she was wiping. She went on. "Well, let me go check on them and see what they're watching. We rented some videos, none of which I wanted to see, so I'm in bed."

"You go ahead, and I'll catch up with Cory tomorrow night," Nate shot back.

"Alright. Take care, Nate," Nina said, still sniffling.

"You, too. Peace." He hung up and dialed Brendan.

On the first ring, Brendan answered, "Hello."

"What's up, dog?" Nate asked emphatically.

"Nuthin. I'm just in here chilling, watching some TV," Brendan answered listlessly.

"Damn, nigga, you sound like you asleep."

"Nah. I'm just chillin."

"Yeah, I'm sitting up over India's crib. She ain't here, though. I just finished watching the Hornets get that ass busted," Nate said.

"Me too," Brendan said. "Man, Jason Kidd was taking the Hornets's defenders off of the dribble every other play," Brendan added.

"Yeah, the Hornets played like some shit today. The Nets are going to bust that ass when they go back to New Jersey, too."

Nate nodded his head in agreement even though Brendan couldn't see him through the line, and said, "No doubt. This series is over. I think New Jersey is going all the way to the finals."

"Yeah, but it don't matter. Nobody from the east will beat the Lakers if they get past Sacramento."

"True dat."

Brendan, out of his own restlessness and desire to find a temporary escape from the discomfort he was feeling under the same roof as Renee, asked Nate, "So what are you, or should I say, *who* are you getting into tonight?"

"I'm not making too much noise tonight. To be honest, I'm going through some changes with these broads, man." He paused for thought while he flipped the channels again. "That's why I called you. I was thinking about getting into something."

"Like what?" Brendan asked.

"I was thinking about hitting the Platinum Club," Nate replied.

"I don't fool with the Platinum on the weekends. Wednesday night is the shit down there. I don't even think they get too many people on the weekends," Brendan said.

"Well, it's not like a Wednesday night for sure, but you can catch a couple of stragglers down there. Maybe bump into a strange piece down there, ya know," Nate offered as an incentive.

"Nah, the joint is weak. Too many niggas standing around fronting and acting like they somebody. I can't roll with that phony crowd tonight."

"Well, what about Dream? You know that's where all of the bitches are tonight," Nate said, as he flipped the top off a Corona he had found in India's fridge.

"Man, Dream is going to be crowded as all hell. Plus, I'm not really up to waiting in any lines tonight." Brendan had let out yet another excuse.

"C'mon now, B, when was the last time you ever waited in any line when you were with me?" Nate asked, sounding as if Brendan might have bumped his head. "All I have to is call Marc and let him know we're coming."

"Oh, excuse me. I must have forgot who I was talking to." Brendan did know better. Nate was as connected as a brother could be in the city. He didn't even wait in lines at movies. Brendan added, "Plus, my cheese is a little tight. I just got my ride serviced on Thursday, and that put a dent in my wallet for sure."

Nate laughed. "Look, don't worry about it, dog. I got you. Now stop making excuses." Nate thought about all the excuses that Brendan was giving him. "What's wrong with you, boy? You know you haven't hung out with me or Cory since that shit with Laney happened on your birthday."

Brendan flipped the channels. *Richard Pryor Live in Concert* was on BET Starz and he left it there briefly. "I know. I just haven't felt like going out lately."

"Well, it's no sense in you sitting in the house moping around and contemplating over that shit." Nate went on: "You got to keep on movin'. She's the one that's trying hard to win your ass back. You can't shed no tears or waste no time on some booty that you've already had."

"Believe me, I definitely haven't been moping at all," Brendan said, with a self-assured attitude that aroused Nate's curiosity.

"Oh yeah, what, you got yourself a new bunny?" Nate asked.

"Not really new, but I guess . . ." Brendan paused. "Nah, never mind. I ain't saying anything to your ass. You can't keep a damned thing to yourself." Brendan was right. Nate could do a lot of things, but keeping a secret, or rather someone else's secret, wasn't one of them.

"What, nigga? Who am I gonna tell?" Nate asked, trying to gain Brendan's confidence.

"For starters, Cory. Then you'll probably tell both India and Sahleen, maybe Kim if you bump into her, and of course she'll tell Trina whenever she does her hair. Let me see who else."

Nate huffed, "Aw man, cut that shit out. You know you are being petty, man." Nate wasn't finished. "C'mon now, what is it?"

"Okay, okay. Stop whining. But I'm telling you, Nate, if this shit comes back to me, that's your ass," Brendan shot out.

"All right, all right," Nate said, as if Brendan was killing him. He knew why, and he knew he deserved it. Nate had carelessly and some-times purposely let a few of Brendan's confidences slip down the drain.

"Well, just listen then," Brendan started off. "You remember that night when I was over your crib and Laney called me, and I told her to come over to your spot."

"Yeah, what about it?"

"Well, I knew that she was going to call me that night. We had spoken earlier in the day and I agreed to get together with her. I just didn't want to do it over here."

"Why not?"

"Because I couldn't," Brendan offered, waiting for Nate to figure it out.

"What the hell do you mean, you couldn't? Was Laney banned from over there or something?"

"Well." Brendan breathed in deep. "Let me just say that, due to changes in the situation over here it wouldn't have been cool for me to bring any other ladies to the house."

Nate paused, and so did Brendan. Then Nate blurted out, "What? Are you fucking Renee or something?"

"Why do you got to say it like that?" Brendan asked, sounding slightly offended.

"Are you for real, B? Say honest to God!" Nate burst into laughter. "My nigga. You finally hit that ass," Nate screamed. He kept saying it over and over, as if Brendan had hit the lottery. "You finally hit that ass. You finally hit that ass."

Brendan interrupted. "Man, chill with that shit."

"I'll be damned. You finally hit that ass."

"Bye, man."

"Nah, I'm straight. So what's up? How was it? Wasn't it like incest, though?" He added, "You two are super tight. I know that shit had to be weird."

"Kind of," Brendan said.

"Hell, I know. I fucked one of my cousins at a family reunion one time. That shit was wild. She was like a third or fourth cousin, though."

"You know, you got issues," Brendan said.

Nate changed the subject back. "So when did this thing with Renee go down?"

"On my birthday, that night after I left you all."

"So it just happened that one night?" Nate asked excitedly.

"Nah. It happened like every night for a few, and when she was on her period . . . but even on those nights . . . never mind." Brendan caught himself.

"She gave you some head? Damn. I know she broke you off some head."

"Anyway. *This* is going to be the first night that I'm going to be sleeping in my own bed."

"Why *tonight?*" Nate asked.

"We had a little falling-out. Laney messed around and popped up over here unannounced and brought me a package. We had just finished getting our groove on. Renee was mad because I didn't go off on Laney for coming over. Plus, she didn't know that me and Laney had started speaking again."

"So are you and Renee supposed to be *together* or what?"

"We haven't discussed all of that. But we've been spending a lot of time together lately. Much more than usual. Plus, like I said, we've been sleeping in her bed together every night. I guess she just assumed that we were doing something."

"Well, did you ever tell her that . . . you know . . . that she was your girl or something?"

"We never actually discussed it, but any decent woman will assume that if you are you coming home to their house and sleeping in their bed, you know, and having sex with them every night."

"Not necessarily," Nate checked him. "Not necessarily. Some women don't want the relationship. Did you have 'the talk'?"

"We had it today after Laney left," Brendan said, sounding dejected.

"And now your ass is sleeping in your own bed," Nate laughed out. "Enough said."

Nate laughed some more. "That's why you have to avoid 'the talk,' my man, at all cost. At all cost. Never discuss with them today what you can put off indefinitely. That's what my uncle Miles used to tell me."

"Your uncle has been married for a while now, right?" Brendan asked.

"Yeah. Ten years to his third wife." Nate laughed out. "But he says that the third is going to be the one that lasts." After a brief silence, Nate added, "You know how he says he knows for sure?"

"How?"

"He said that he used to have 'the talk' all of the time with his first two wives, but he said he ain't never having it with this one."

"So what does he do when shit hits the fan and she wants to talk things out?" Brendan asked.

"He said that he just tells her that actions speak louder than words, which is true. Then, he said, he taps that ass."

"Yeah, I guess that could be true." Brendan thought about how he had been acting lately. He wondered what his actions had been telling Renee, by having sex with her almost every night. Had he in fact stooped so low as to use his best friend? If so, were he becoming more like Nate than he would have ever suspected possible? "I guess it definitely is," Brendan repeated, referring to the actions-speaking-louder-than-words statement Nate had quoted from his uncle Miles.

Brendan tapped the remote in his hand and came to the heartfelt conclusion that he needed to go upstairs and have another talk with Renee and really set things straight. He needed to be honest with her about every feeling and emotion he'd been experiencing since they had first fallen into bed that night. He knew that if he approached Renee with honesty that the two of them would be able to work things out. They always had before. With that, he closed his conversation with Nate and headed upstairs. To talk.

Chapter 20

ONE MONKEY DON'T STOP NO SHOW

There was a band playing and about half of the three hundred people in attendance were on the dance floor. Everyone was dressed spectacularly and seemed to be enjoying themselves. Chad's first-year anniversary party was a big deal around PSC. They had rented out the West Ballroom of downtown Atlanta's Peachtree Plaza Hotel. His wife's family was from old Georgia money and had no doubt sprung for the affair. Her grandfather was in attendance, and he was the spitting image of the late Colonel Sanders of Kentucky Fried Chicken fame. I wondered how he felt to be in a room with such a mixed crowd. Not that the crowd was equally split, but it looked as if Chad and his wife, Gillian, had plenty of ethnic friends. Although he looked about eighty years old, he had a wife who looked to be in her late forties tending to his every whim. Most of the people there were coupled up, and I immediately thought about Nina and how she would have enjoyed the trip down. I felt a little guilty when I thought about how I had lied and told her I was in Atlanta for Chad's wedding, which actually had taken place the previous year. There was no way that I would ever get caught, though. I knew that as long as you base your lies loosely on the truth, you could usually pull them off. Even though I had told her more than my fair share, I didn't ever want to get into the habit of lying to Nina. The relationship that we were building was growing more important to me each day.

I sipped my glass of wine while I sat at a table with a few of my former coworkers. It had been more than five months since I had seen them all, and while I was enjoying their company, I still couldn't truly say that I missed too many of them. Not that they weren't good folks; it was just that the people I was currently working with were better folks, not to mention that when you're running things, people really treat you well. I never took much time to analyze motives at HE. As long as people did what I asked, I couldn't have cared less why they were attempting to kiss my butt. I did realize, though, that most of the people in my department knew I was responsible for doling out raises and bonuses.

I danced to a couple of songs with Stacey from customer service after finishing my third glass of wine. When I told her I was about to leave, she asked where I was staying. I lied and told her I was staying at the Omni. I was actually staying right upstairs. I knew Stacey was probably trying to get freaky, but if so she had lost her mind. I didn't want her when I was working there, so I don't know why she would have thought she had a chance now.

"Maybe I'll call you over there later," she said, as she hugged me good-bye. "Mmm. You smell nice, Cory."

"Okay, you do that." As I walked away I thought, *Did I say the Omni? I meant the Peachtree.*

I headed out of the ballroom after giving Chad and Gillian my congratulations. Chad thanked me for coming and said he was ready to leave as well. They were taking a second honeymoon to Rio de Janeiro, and he said that they both needed some rest. We laughed for a minute about the Braves and their chances of getting back to the World Series. He walked me to the entrance of the ballroom and asked me to consider him for any openings that HE might have that he would be qualified for. I told him, sure. I was surprised at his request, but then, everyone longs for a change from time to time, as long as it is for the better. We shook hands a final time, and I headed for the front desk.

"Any messages for Dandridge in 1718?" I asked the front-desk clerk.

"Yes sir, you have two messages." She pulled two pink "while you were out" slips out of a drawer. "And a lady dropped this off for you." She handed me an envelope. "You can ignore the message light on your phone now. The lady insisted that I make sure that you get this, so I left an urgent message flash on your phone."

"Thanks," I said, as I turned and walked toward the elevator.

I looked at the messages. "Call Nina if you get in before eleven. No emergency." And "Darlene, call me at 770-555-1329 when you get in," I read out loud. As I left the lobby my mind was filling with thoughts of the fun I had had with Darlene during the time I had lived in Atlanta. I thought back on the night she had picked me up from my apartment in her Falcons cheerleader uniform, ready to do some role playing in the back seat of my car. A man may not want to marry a freak, but he never forgets one.

I entered the room and instinctively turned on the TV and called Nina back. "Hey, baby," I said.

"This is Tory, not Nina." My niece laughed into the line.

"I know who it is. You're my baby too, right?" I asked.

She giggled some more. "I guess."

"You guess nothing. You won't be guessing when you want to hit those malls on your birthday next month," I said sarcastically. "Where's Nina?"

"She's asleep. She said to tell you she waited up as long as she could, but she took some medicine for her allergies, and it made her drowsy."

"Okay. What are you guys doing?"

"I'm watching *The Fast and the Furious*, and Kyle is in the other bedroom playing with his Xbox," she said.

"Well, tell Nina I called and that I'll call her tomorrow to let her know what time to pick me up from the airport."

"All right. Good night, Uncle Cory."

"Night, baby."

I kicked my shoes off and settled onto the bed. I started to call Darlene back, but I decided to open the envelope. I suspected that it was from Paula, but she had been supposed to meet me here at ten-thirty. It was almost eleven. Why in the world had she come all the way over here to bring a damned letter and not wait to see me? I was about to find out. I ripped open the envelope and began to read.

Dear Cory,

I know you were expecting to see me, but I thought it would better this way. Believe me when I tell you it wasn't easy (not to come and be with you tonight), knowing that you are here in town and waiting for me. I have missed you, and have thought about you often. However, the stinging reality of the situation that we have wrought forces me to follow my mind because the heart can be treacherous. I can't say for sure that I even know what your motives were for wanting to see me. It is impossible for me to deny that I was knocked off of my feet momentarily when you called me at the university yesterday. Luckily, I had enough time to think about it before you arrived here in town.

A lot has happened in my life since we last spoke. I realize that I should have called you and told you, but I have really been busy trying to pull things together. The divorce proceedings were canceled. Marvin and I decided to work things out. It was a tough decision to make, but I realized that I could never leave him. While I do admit to loving you, Marvin is the only man who I have ever needed. He has afforded me the opportunities to pursue my dreams, and I can't ignore it any longer. Though I no longer blame him for forcing me into your arms, I did find it necessary to ask him for a lot of renewed commitment toward making me happy, and I promised him the same in return. Things have begun to turn around for us and, remarkably, he has really changed. He told me that nearly losing me scared the life back into him. I don't think that he has been on a golf course three times without me this entire year. More amazing, though, is the fact that he has even agreed to cut back on his patients so that we can spend most of our time together traveling during the next year. His reason for doing this, believe it or not, is because he thinks that we should make a couple of additions to the family. He has convinced me that we should adopt children. We won't be doing this right away, though, because we are taking time to get to know each other again.

Cory, I don't want to bore you with details of my life when I know what you really want is my presence. At the same time, I don't think that you returned to Atlanta to ask me to run away with you, or walk away into the sunset with you for that matter. I really don't know, and I guess it's better that I don't. I don't think I could bear the thought of you delivering the news of your love for another woman, or even worse, that you only wanted to make love to me for old time's sake. At any rate, I am glad that I had the opportunity to leave this letter with you. I hope that you are happy for me, and I hope that all is well with you and your family, especially your mother.

I will be leaving Georgia Tech for a while, maybe for good, at the end of the semester. So if you have a pressing need to speak with me, then you can reach me there the same way that you did yesterday for the next two and a half weeks. After that you probably won't be able to contact me. I no longer have the pager, and my sister has a new number.

Cory, it is important to me that you know that I will always care for you. You were the biggest part of my life for the last few years. You did wonders for my self-esteem and confidence. You are a wonderful young man and a very capable lover. Sadly, though, on the flip side, you also tore my heart to pieces when you left without any consideration for what impact your departure would have on my life. You showed me that loving you is not safe, and I desperately need safety. I know that you didn't intend to be so volatile and toxic, but I don't think that you can help it. One day, though, you will learn to make better decisions, just as I finally have.

Things probably are working out for the best, and I will consider your invitation an opportunity and a test. An opportunity to close the door on the past that you and I shared, and a test to determine how badly I want to change and make my marriage work. It is also a test to see if I even deserve the love that my husband has once again offered me. It is a test that I badly need to pass, and for some reason I have the need to ask you if you've had any tests lately? If you haven't, they will come, because life is nothing but a test.

Like Erykah Badu says, "Maybe I'll see you next lifetime."
Love always,
Paula

"Well, I'll be damned," I said aloud. No one was listening except for Stuart Scott and Dan Patrick as they introduced the eleven o'clock edition of Sports Center on ESPN. "Ain't that a bitch?" My head was shaking in disgust. I felt like trashing the letter, but I felt compelled to read it once more. "After all the things that she had told me over the years, all of it bullshit." I walked to the thermostat because it was getting stuffy in the room.

She had gotten back with him. I know that I should have expected that she would. Paula never did seem to be the type to stand on her own two feet. She probably never really even knew what she wanted, just took whatever was convenient for the moment. "Stinking bitch," I said out loud. I wondered what would've happened if I had come down here to ask her to be with me or to tell her that I still loved her and wanted her back? I'd have been shit out of luck, that's what. Would she have been worried about my feelings? She sure didn't hesitate to tell me how great things are going for her and her limp-dick husband. I know that she's missing this sex, and I hope . . . I caught myself and spoke aloud. "Let me get ahold of myself. Why am I so pissed off? It's not like I don't have someone. And of course I did come down here only to be with her one last time." I began talking to myself inside of my head to calm down.

I reasoned that everything was fine when I had dumped her, but now that Paula had picked up the pieces and moved on, I was upset. *Cory*, I said to myself, *that isn't right*. I was right, as usual, and tried to change my entire train of thought. Good for her and her simple-assed husband. The hell with the both of them. I have something prettier, younger, and . . . I couldn't actually say smarter. Paula was damn near a genius. I couldn't say better in bed either. Paula was the bomb between the sheets, totally uninhibited. Nina was still learning, but then, she was only twenty-five. Why was I comparing my baby to some married chick, anyway? Nina had integrity, more than Paula probably ever would. Paula had probably decided to fuck around at the first hint of unhappiness. I doubt if I was the first, although I had never asked. She had never volunteered the information either. When I thought about all of the things I was feeling, I felt stupid. Why had I even allowed myself to get all worked up? Paula was back with Marvin. Fine. She wasn't coming tonight. Fine. I had someone better any damned way.

I usually wasn't one to use alcohol to calm my nerves, but I found myself craving a shot of something strong. I was still reeling a bit from the letter. I drank down the first of the miniatures I'd purchased on the plane in hopes of dulling the sting of my wounded pride. *I'm not in love with Paula; I'm in love with Nina,* I kept repeating, in hopes of putting my feelings into perspective. Then I prepared to do the only thing I imagined I could do in order to take my mind off Paula.

I picked up the phone and dialed Darlene's cell number. She didn't pick up, so I left a message. I flipped the channel to see what movies were on the hotel cable and got up to fix myself a drink. I reached into my garment bag and pulled out the rest of the whiskey and vodka miniatures I had purchased a on the plane. The four bucks a shot on the plane was still cheaper than what the hotel charged for the stuff they stocked in the cabinet. I hated popping the little plastic seal on the cabinet and paying two dollars for a bag of chips or three dollars for a bottle of Veryfine cranberry juice, but I did just that. I wasn't about to drink the shots of Absolut straight, though I could have. If I left the room to go find a vending machine (which they probably didn't have, so that they could force you to buy up everything in the cabinet during your stay), I might have missed Darlene returning my call.

I had just finished my first drink when the phone rang. "Hello," I answered.

"Cory. What's up, baby?" Darlene's voice crackled through the line. She was on a cellphone.

"Not much. Thinking about you," I offered, in my smoothest tone. "What are you getting into tonight?"

"Actually, I'm on my way to the club," she answered. "One of the guys from the Braves is having a party at Club 112 tonight. You want to come?"

"Oh, I don't know. I'm a little tired. Why don't you stop past here on the way? You knew I was in town. Why would you go and make plans?" I asked, sounding like her father.

She laughed. "Well, my situation is a little complicated. I'm sort of seeing someone, but I guess I could stop past there for a quick visit. I can call Tina and Connie to let them know I'll just meet them there in about an hour."

"Well, how far are you from here?" I figured she had to be close if she was going to stop by and be in Buckhead inside an hour.

"I'm pretty close to you now, right off of Lenox Avenue. I could be there in about fifteen minutes." Before we hung up, Darlene asked me for the room number.

Darlene arrived looking good as sin. She had on a tight-fitting pair of low-rise jeans and a snug-fitting BCBG top. Darlene was a real doll baby, and I wondered silently why I had never considered making her my lady. She had a body that most women would kill for, and she had a great personality, though she could be a little dizzy.

"Where's my hug, boy?" she said, extending her arms.

After we hugged we kissed a quick kiss on the lips, I said, "I see you cut all of your hair off."

She nodded in agreement. "I know. I just got so tired of sweating it out every other day."

I remembered that she was an aerobics instructor as well as a cheer-leader and student. "So you're still teaching the aerobics," I asked, even though I knew. One look at that body, and I knew.

"Hell, yeah. I gotta eat, don't I?" We laughed.

We made small talk as she sat down. I offered her a drink from my cabinet. She walked over and helped herself to a grapefruit juice. I remembered that she didn't drink alcohol. I kept my eye on the clock to make sure I didn't let too much time pass by before I made a move. I didn't want to seem too desperate, but I was feeling the sting of rejection after Paula's letter. I needed something to pick me up, and for some reason I was thinking that sex with Darlene could do the trick.

There was never any doubt in my mind that I would be able to get her to comply. Even though our relationship was based mainly on a sexual attraction, there was a certain connection between us that she had never been able to deny. The fact that I was no longer in town seemed to romanticize the whole notion of us falling into bed.

Knowing what I did about approaching her worked to my advan-tage as well. Darlene was no different than most women in that she hated an overly aggressive brother more than anything. At the same time, women wonder about men who are too passive. A complete man has the right combination of confidence and humility. That was me in a nutshell. I wasn't going to attack her as if she owed me the ass, but I wasn't going to just let her stop by my room without trying her.

After about twenty minutes, I asked her to fill me in on what was so complicated about her "situation." I was referring to her statement about why she had made plans.

Her complication turned out to be nothing more than a relationship she was entertaining in her mind. "Well, it's really not that big a deal," she said. "I'm kind of dating one of the guys on the Braves team. Antonio Gomez. You've heard of him? Right now things are in the early stages. We both are feeling like commitment is coming from this whole thing, but we're trying not to rush into it. I know that you and I have a history, but I just don't want to mess this up."

Of course I'd heard of him. He was the left fielder . . . well, he wasn't the starter, but he did see some action as a designated hitter. "Yeah," I answered.

"Like I said, it's not that serious yet, but he has really been after me. He invited me to this party, and it's, like, invitation-only. The thing is, Connie and Tina really wanted to go because there's going to be a whole bunch of celebrities there. You know how they are. Anyway, the only way they can get in is with me, so they have been begging me all week to make sure I go." Darlene finished her grapefruit juice.

"Well, where are they now?" I asked.

"I told them to me at Churchill Grounds up the street at twelve-thirty," she said matter-of-factly.

"Well, then," I said. "It's almost twelve. You had better come on over here and let me have a few kisses and hugs before you go." I patted the bed beside me.

"Cory, don't even try it. I just told you that I was dating Antonio." She shook her head no.

"Darlene, I know you know better than that. You don't date professional athletes, rappers, or movie stars." I laughed. "Either you're one of the chicks that they are screwing, or you're the one getting cheated on. You know better than to think that you're involved in some type of real courtship, at least, anything that would make you deny me."

I stood and walked toward her. "I'm shocked," I said, as I took her by the hands and pulled her up from the chair she was seated in. "I know you know better. Right?" She smiled as she stood with me. She said nothing as I put my arms around her waist.

"You smell good, Cory. What are you wearing?" I could tell that just that quickly her defenses were weakening. When it came to me Darlene always seemed to fit the category of "old faithful."

"Mmmm, you taste good," I whispered, as my lips brushed her cheeks and found her neck.

Darlene breathed deeply, while each of my hands gripped a cheek through the fabric of her jeans. To my surprise, Darlene backed away. She looked into my eyes and unzipped her pants. Then she pulled her shirt carefully over her head, so as not to mess up her short but meticulously styled hair. She unfastened her bra. I had expected more resistance but was fine with her cooperation.

"Just as I remembered them," I said to myself. Her breasts were small, but she had the prettiest and most perfectly shaped nipples I had ever seen. I joined in with her and began coming out of my clothes.

When we were both naked she flipped off the light and moved back toward me. She asked me for it. I pulled a condom out of my bag, and she slid it onto my dick with her mouth. She made wearing one not such a bad deal. Plus, I had to think of Nina. As she pushed me back onto the bed, the phone rang. I didn't answer it. I didn't return the favor by going down on her; she didn't give me a chance. Darlene had pulled me up to her face, showering me with kisses. Normally I hated a tongue in my ear, but the way she licked me it sent sensations straight to my penis. I started to penetrate her very slowly. I gave her an inch and several strokes at a time. I hadn't entered her completely, and she began to complain. "Stop teasing me, Cory."

"Be patient," I answered. I continued to stroke only the opening to her womanhood. Every ten or twenty strokes I went slightly deeper. By the time I had entered her completely she was soaking wet and breathing in frenzied short breaths. I was feeling the need to have my ego stroked, so I was doing my best to blow her mind. When I felt her about to reach her peak I plunged deep inside her.

"Ohhh, Gawwwd," she screamed. It seemed as though all the air had left her body. Instantly she locked her legs around mine, pulling me deeper. At the same time her hands were pushing at my chest.

"You like that?" I asked. I started pounding away at her. I repeated, "You like that?"

"You don't know howww . . . much." Her head began thrashing back and forth. There was a coat of sweat forming on her face and breasts. "I don't want to come yet. Oh, Cory, slow down, please," she begged.

I wanted to enjoy it. I also wanted to leave her drained. I stood her up and guided her to the wall and entered her from behind. She wrapped her hands around my neck, pushing her bottom against my pelvis. I remembered how she loved this position, so I ground her from the back until she started to shake. We went at it for about ten more minutes at a really furious pace. She asked me if I had missed her pussy.

"Of course I did, baby," I said, as I pushed her down on the bed. I entered her from behind again. She could tell I was ready to come so she began talking seductively. We told each other lies and made promises to always keep in touch. She even told me that she loved me. I wasn't willing to go that far, but when she came, I came with her. And during that orgasm I did go as far as telling her that she had the best pussy in the world. She loved to hear me tell her that. They all did. And I told them what they wanted to hear. But in reality, Darlene didn't even have the best pussy in *my* world, which was all I could really vouch for. That title belonged to someone who was in my past.

We lay there for only a moment before Darlene stood up and went to the bathroom with her clothes in hand. I heard water running and I knew she was washing up. The lights were back on, but I was still naked. I was feeling temporarily satisfied. My trip hadn't been a total waste. I laughed when I thought that. Why is it that if a man doesn't get laid when he's out of town, whether he's at a wedding, a conference, a vacation, or a funeral, he considers his trip incomplete? I didn't know the answer to that one, but it was a fact. I then told myself that this would be the last time I would ever venture out on Nina. Although I had had a few indiscretions during past relationships, I was far from a habitual cheater. It was one thing to run around as a single man, but I had taken responsibility for someone's feelings and I needed to own up to that.

"Cory, come give me some sugar. I'm about to leave." She kissed me on the cheek this time.

"You coming back after the party?" I asked, as I wrapped a towel around my waist.

"You want me to?" she asked. Her eyes said that she wouldn't be back. I nodded my head an affirmative "yes" anyway.

"Maybe. I'll see what I can do." She smiled at me and hugged me once more.

That meant good-bye. Darlene said that she would call me in a couple of hours if she were coming back and insisted that I promise to listen for the phone.

"Sure thing," I said, and waved her off.

She probably was going home with Gomez. I couldn't help thinking that he was probably already planning to take her home after the party to drill that cute little booty, just as I had moments before. *Enjoy the used twat, Antonio, you sucker,* I said in my head, as I let her out of the door. "I know he's paying for it, one way or the other," I said under my breath, as I watched her head toward the elevator.

As I climbed into my bed, I hoped that Darlene wasn't thinking that she had done me any favors by saying she might come back. I was satisfied for the moment. At the very least, I was relieved of the self-imposed stress from Paula's letter. If she came back, fine. If she didn't, that was cool too. I drifted off thinking of my plane ride home and Nina. I knew at that moment she was in my apartment at home, sleeping in my bed, and probably in one of my T-shirts. At that moment I felt secure and even more satisfied knowing that my lady's whereabouts could be accounted for. I even felt a twinge of regret for having come to Atlanta. Justifiably, though, it served me right. I should have left well enough alone. Paula had moved on, just as I had. If she had come over here tonight I would definitely have told her about Nina, and she would have been the one feeling dejected. It was supposed to have been my grand closure, though.

Oh well, I figured. She had moved on not knowing that I had also. I guess that was why I was feeling so ambivalent toward things. Ego, no doubt. As I slowly drifted off, an old saying found its way into my head: "One monkey don't stop no show." I heard it over and over in my head until I realized that after all that I had been through with Paula and Darlene, all I had been in their lives was one single, solitary monkey. I didn't dwell on it, though, because soon enough sleep took over, and it took my thoughts to a more peaceful place.

Chapter 21

DO YOU EVER REALLY LOVE?

Luckily for me the young brother on my flight noticed lipstick on my collar. We struck up a conversation while standing in the line waiting for our boarding passes. He was a young brother, probably no more than seventeen. His name was Kevaughn, but he told me to call him Key for short. The brother said that he was taking the college tour. He told me that he was going to visit Howard University in D.C. and my alma mater, Morgan State University, in Baltimore. He was undecided, but he knew that he was going to choose between the two. His mother and father had just separated and he had stayed in Atlanta with his father to finish his senior year in high school.

Anyway, we ended up sitting next to each other on the plane and we talked casually about sports and colleges. Eventually the subject turned to women, and I ended up mentioning that my girlfriend was picking me up from the airport. He took me by surprise when he responded with, "Then I sure hope that's her brand of lipstick on your collar, or you are going to get the third degree."

"Shit" is what I wanted to yell when I excused myself to go to the restroom to check the damage. Darlene had come back the previous night after all, and when she dropped me off at the airport an hour earlier she'd gotten a little sentimental. The previous night she had told me that I had been right about her baseball player. She told me that he had had at least three women at the party and made it obvious that he was screwing them as well. She said that she couldn't take it and had left to come straight back to my room.

When we got to the airport she couldn't keep her hands and lips off me. I didn't have the heart to tell her that it was probably the last time she would ever see me, and I just let her pour her affections out all over me. I guess that somewhere in the mix she had smudged her M.A.C lipstick on my collar.

"Thanks, Kevaughn." Then I remembered and corrected myself, "I mean, Key. You saved a brother's ass." I hated to use profanity around the young brother, but I was excited by his keen eye. Though I hadn't seen it, any woman would have caught it before the first blink.

"Don't mention it, Cory," he said. "Us men . . . we gotta stick together. Don't playa hate, but congratulate, ya know," he said, smiling as if he were proud of me. I guess he assumed that whatever business I had been in town for had not been a waste of time.

I immediately thought about what kind of example I was setting for this young fellow. Looking at him with his close haircut and dimpled face, looking like somebody's baby boy, it was hard to fathom that he had already considered himself a man who needed to be part of the collective society of players. Before he had made that comment I had considered introducing him to my niece. Tory was a sophomore in high school, and I knew she was interested in boys. However, she wasn't boy crazy like most of the girls I had known at that age, including her mother. My sister, Brenda, had kept a phone glued to her ear during most of her high school years. If she wasn't on the phone talking to a guy then she was talking to one of her girlfriends about one. Tory was more laid-back. She already seemed to know that there will be time for boys later on, thank goodness.

Key and I talked for almost the entire flight home. Though he didn't know me from Adam, he was talking and listening to me as though I was the big brother he had never had. He asked me questions such as, how much money should a man spend on a first date, and for my opinion on dating older women.

As the flight came to an end he asked, "So, Cory, do you think it's okay for a man to have a little something-something on the side as long as he takes care of home?"

I shuddered when I had to answer this question. Here I was, wanting to tell him that it wasn't right. Yet I knew I would be a complete hypocrite, so I told him, "Key, it truly depends on the situation. Most of the time, it's not right. Most women don't deserve that kind of treatment."

"So what did your girl do to deserve it?" he asked. He meant no offense but had smacked me in the face with my own behavior.

I was quiet. "Nothing," I answered, and he realized that my tone showed shame and he let me off the hook.

"Hey, man, I hope I can keep in touch with you. I can e-mail you or something."

After we got off the plane I gave Key one of my business cards. I told him to give me a call so that maybe I could hook him up with a summer internship with the company. I was sure that he could get into the mailroom, at least. If he was as sharp as he seemed, I might even offer him a clerical position. He didn't seem to want to leave my side. As he walked with me through the terminal he said that it was his first time in the Baltimore-Washington area. He called it that because that was the name of the airport. I explained to him that although the two cities were only forty miles apart, they were two completely separate areas. Neither city liked to have its identity fused with the other. The people acted differently, and they had different styles as well. In addition, there were separate football teams, separate harbors, museums, and so on. I assured him that he would see the difference when he visited them both.

As we walked toward the sliding doors that led to the outside, his mother called his name. "Kevaughn, over here, sweetheart." We both looked.

"Take care, Key, and have a good time," I said, as I extended my hand.

"Thanks. Nice meeting you, Cory. I'll call you." He shook my hand and readjusted his bag on his shoulder. "Oh yeah," he said. "Which college would you go to if you were me?" He was walking backward toward his mother, who had a "who is that you're talking to?" look on her face. His expression showed me that he wanted an answer and fully expected a good one.

I didn't want to influence his decision. I had already been a negative influence simply by showing up with lipstick on my collar that didn't belong to my lady. Hopefully our conversation would lend him a clearer view of what I felt was acceptable behavior for a man. But when it came to his decision on a school, I didn't want to tell him my preference, so I just stuck to the facts. "Both are great schools," I said. "Howard is just much larger; depends on what you like, I guess. Give me a buzz after you visit them both, and tell me what you think."

"Okay, I will," he said, as he turned to face his mother. No sooner had she hugged him than I could tell he was explaining to her who I was and why he had been talking to me. I headed toward the doors when I saw Nina pull up to the curb.

The cool spring air hit my face, and I noticed the difference in the temperature from Atlanta's. It had been in the high seventies when I had boarded the plane at one. Back home it had to be in the low sixties, and with the breeze it felt cooler. I knew that I looked silly with my shirt tied around my waist. I had on nothing but a plain white T-shirt. I opened the back door and threw my garment bag into the back. She had Ashanti blasting.

She leaned across the seat, and I met her with a kiss. It was a long one. I thought about what I'd done with Darlene and how I had just kissed her a couple of hours ago, and I pulled away.

"Wow. You missed a brotha last night, huh?" I said, smiling.

"You know I did, baby. I should have gone with you," she said, as she pulled off. "You didn't want to drive, did you?" she said, as she looked into the rearview mirror.

"No, I'm straight."

She slid the roof back nearly halfway. I felt the breeze come sliding in. It was too damned cold for the roof to be open like that, but I knew better than to say anything about being cold. She would have told me to put my shirt on, which I couldn't do, thanks to Darlene's lipstick. "That air feels good," I said, as I reached to close the roof a little.

"Then why are you closing it, Cory? It's stuffy in here. If you're cold then put your shirt on. And why do you have it tied like that anyway? You look like a fag."

"I'm not cold. I just didn't want it blowing on my head like that. It was warmer in Atlanta," I said, and I knew I needed to change the subject. "So, did you drop Tory and Kyle off or did Brenda come and pick them up?"

"Actually, I met her at your mom's house, since it was on the way to the airport anyway." She pointed toward the back seat, and I saw a paper bag on the floor. "Your mom cooked, and she fixed us plates. She made your favorite dessert."

"Lemon cake," I said excitedly.

Nina just smiled.

"Good. Now we don't have to go out to eat, because I have, like, no food in my house," I said, sounding both relieved and disgusted with myself.

"Negative. I went grocery shopping last night before we came in. So, actually, you do have plenty of food."

Nina was a good damned woman. You don't find one like that every day. I'm talking about a woman who will clean up, wash the clothes, and keep the refrigerator stocked. Even though she is there at least four days a week, she still doesn't owe me anything. I mean, it's not like she just cleans up after herself. She's cleaning ovens, scrubbing mildew out of the shower, wiping out the fridge and the microwave, wiping the dust out of the linen closet, and cleaning the balcony windows—on the outside. Crazy shit like that detailed cleaning might not ever get done if it were left up to me.

"Baby," I said, making sure I had her full attention. When she glanced over at me I said, "I love you. I really do."

"You better. 'Cause I love you, too," she said.

"Say it in Spanish, like you do when I'm inside of you."

She complied. "Papi, te amo." She sounded so sexy. She was so gorgeous and special. I don't know why I had cheated on her with Darlene. It was only the second time in four months I had done it, but I still knew it wasn't right. It wasn't as though I had no control over myself. I truly didn't know why I had done it. Nina was everything I had ever wanted in a woman, and then some. I had to get my priorities straight before I wound up walking around wondering how I had lost the best thing that had ever happened to me. Again.

• • •

Brendan sat on the edge of his bed. He held one of his new sneakers in his hand, debating whether or not he even wanted to run in them and mess them up. They were brand-new Nike Shox running shoes, which Laney had definitely put a couple of dollars into. His old pair of Adidas had begun to show the wear and tear of nearly four months of running. Laney had obviously taken notice and had sprung for a new pair. She had gone beyond the call of duty once more, and seemed intent on buying her way back into Brendan's good graces.

An envelope also lay on the bed next to the shoebox. When Brendan finally put the shoe down, he picked up the envelope and opened it to find a letter. Brendan nudged his door closed, because he had heard Renee up and moving around in the kitchen. He didn't want to be disturbed. He propped a pillow up underneath his back as he scooted closer to the wall.

Dear Brendan,

I hope that you enjoy the shoes and that you do a lot of running in them. I don't want you to ever forget that you deserve the best, even if you get a new running partner. I believe that you know it (that you deserve the best), and I am sorry that you don't think that I fit that category any longer. I have had time to do a lot of thinking in the last month, since we went our separate ways. I know that you are the man for me, but if you decide that I am not the woman for you, then I will understand. My only regret is that you have not given me a chance to explain. I hope that you take the time to read this letter with an open mind and heart. It is not easy for me to write about these things, but I will in order to make you understand why I did some of the things that I did.

Like you said, there is no explanation for having sex with those men that night, and I wish that I could say that they forced me, but I cannot. I was not in my right mind, though. I was really depressed. My sister had just died in a car accident, and my mother was strung out. I know that you can't relate to a parent who is an addict, but Brendan, I grew up with it every day, from the time that my father ran out on her when I was in the sixth grade and left me and my sister behind.

I wanted to go to college, Brendan, and better myself, but no one was offering me any scholarships, so I had to make money the best way that I could. I was tired of standing on my feet at IHOP twelve hours a day just to keep a roof over my head. So when a friend from high school came into the restaurant one day and told me how good I was looking and how much money I could make, I just did it. It was something I just planned to do long enough to save up money for school and a new start somewhere outside of Philly . . . somewhere away from my mother.

Brendan flipped the page. His hands were shaking, and he couldn't believe what he was reading.

Somehow, though, weeks turned into months, and before I knew it two years had passed. I had plenty of money in the bank, and I had been accepted into Delaware State. I was prepared to leave last year when the accident with my sister happened. I was still going to leave. My mother promised to get cleaned up so that she could care for my sister's little boy. She'd done well for the last year, at least I thought she had, until I got a call from the state saying that my nephew had been taken into custody. It turned out that my mother never got any better, and had in fact gotten worse. She had left my nephew, Tyler, who is five now, at home for three days by himself. He had missed school for two days. The school finally called the house, and he answered the phone. Eventually, his father's mother took him in, with my promise to support him. His father is in jail doing life. Things had been really rough on me, and life had cut me no breaks, until I met you. I never made it to Del State, but I did get a fresh start. But I guess the past has a way of coming back to haunt you.

I am sorry that I ever got you mixed up with me without telling you about my life, but I knew that you probably would never have treated me the way that you did if I had. I only told you the good things, the things that I wanted you to know. I have learned only to look at myself that way. In high school I was a state champion in track. I won at the Penn relays in my senior year. I felt good then. I had overcome some major odds. Everyone was proud of me. I could have gone to a couple of colleges then. I was offered partial scholarships, but my mother told me to wait and save some money. She couldn't afford it. Well, you see how that turned out. After that, I stayed out of trouble while everyone else kept making a mess out of my life. Before I knew it, I was babysitting for my sister all of the time. If I wasn't doing that then I was working to keep the lights on when my mother and her boyfriend smoked up the electric bill.

Eventually I ended up doing the wrong thing, not even that dancing is the wrong thing. I should have never started doing the private parties and getting greedy. I wasn't the one who stole from that party, though. Sheila did that, and I know I should have stopped her, but she would have never listened anyway.

As Brendan flipped the page, a tear welled up in the corner of his eye. He was beginning to feel like shit. Who had he been to judge Laney, he thought, as he read on?

Brendan there is more to tell, but nothing worse than these things. Just more about my family. I hope that this helps you understand, if that is possible. I am in Philly now checking on my nephew. He has been sick lately, and I am concerned. I don't know how long I will be gone. I just want you to know that I love you. I have never loved any man since my father, and he left. I guess that's why I can accept it if you must go, too. I am learning that leaving is just something that men do. I have decided that I will not contact you again. I won't make it hard for you. If you have a change of heart you can call me. If I don't hear from you, then I wish you all the best. Loving you now and forever,
Laney

Chapter 22

CAREFUL WHAT YOU PRAY FOR

Nate walked into the barbershop and greeted the owner, Mike, and his longtime barber, Dee. It was pretty tranquil in the shop for a Thursday. Although each of the barbers had a customer, except for the new one, who sat reading the sports page attempting to look busy, there were only a couple of customers waiting to be served. Even Dee, who usually had customers lined up four deep, was slow.

"Where's everybody at, Dee?" Nate asked jokingly.

"Shit, they ain't in my pocket. Check yours." Dee laughed back. "If I don't get some people in here quick, I might have to borrow a grand from you."

"Yeah, right." Nate stood and grabbed a magazine, then sat back down. "Is anybody in front of me?"

"Nope." He turned to the older gentleman seated next to Nate. "Mr. Johnny, are you going to me or Mike today?"

Mr. Johnny shrugged his shoulders. "It don't really matter. It looks like Mike is going to be finished sooner, so I'll check him out today."

"Okay, then," Dee said. "Nate, you're next."

"Bet."

Mr. Johnny looked at Nate and said, "That's a pretty ride you got out there." Nate had parked directly in front of the window. "What is that? A Lexus?"

"Thanks. Yeah, it's a LS 430."

Mr. Johnny pulled out a piece of peppermint. "I prefer American models myself. I'm looking at that new DeVille." Mr. Johnny's eyes lit up when he mentioned the Caddy.

"Yeah, those are nice."

"Yo, Nate, you should get you a Cadillac. Being as though you one of the last true pimps." Dee laughed out. He was always on joke time. If he wasn't talking about Mike's big aunt, then he was talking about Clarence's raggedy teeth. He kept everyone laughing. Mike was even more hilarious. He had to act more mature since he was the owner, but he was just as much a clown as Dee. Between the two of them, people came to the shop just as much to hear them crack on each other and argue as they did to get a haircut, it seemed.

"No, my brother. That's you. You know you're the Mack," Nate said. Dee had just as many women as Nate. When the two of them spoke, it was always to compare notes and share stories. Since Nate had been dating Sahleen and India, though, he hadn't been able to keep up with Dee, and Dee made a point of mentioning it every week.

Mr. Johnny stepped into Mike's chair. "Mr. Johnny, do you hear these jokers?" Mike asked, as he put the cape over him. "Like they know anything about women."

Dee smacked his lips and shook his head. "Maaannnn. Here he goes again, the king of the player haters."

"Hell, you have to be a player first before I can hate on you," Mike said, as he tapped Mr. Johnny's shoulder.

"Heh, heh." Mr. Johnny laughed.

"Mike, you know I got plenty of ladies. Nate might have slowed his roll, but I get more ass than you get air," Dee said.

"You're supposed to. I'm a married man now, but when I was out there kicking it . . ."

Dee cut him off. "You know that you weren't running the broads like I do. I saw some of those raggedy chicks you used to go out with."

"Who?" Mike said defensively.

"How about that one that you thought was so fine, you know that horse-head chick with the big feet." Everyone in the shop burst into laughter. Dee went on. "And don't ever forget about the one that pops by here now and then . . . that chick's butt is shaped like a VCR, with her wide-backed self."

"Oh man, I didn't ever mess with her," Mike stammered out. "She's an old friend. I'll tell you this, though . . . that horse-head bitch was fine back in the day."

"C'mon Dee, ya'll fools are crazy," Nate said, laughing. He knew just who Dee was talking about, and her butt *was* shaped like a VCR.

Dee finished up with his customer and collected his money. Nate got into the chair, and Dee put the cape on his favorite customer and cleaned off his clippers.

"Man, the dude I just cut gets on my nerves," Dee said. His tone had now dropped low enough so that he was talking loud enough for only Nate to hear.

"Why?"

"That fool always comes in here with a bunch of grease in his hair. I told his ass like twenty times to wash that shit out before he comes in here." The clippers went on, and Dee began to shave Nate's head. "So, what's been happening?"

"Nada. I'm about to roll up to the Rotten Apple in the morning."

"New York. What you going up there for?" Dee asked, hands moving back and forth.

"My chick, the one that models, is shooting a video with Shawn Simmons."

"Shawn Simmons. No shit?" Dee's voice perked up. "Yo, that bitch is tight. She is so phat."

"Yeah. I'm just gonna chill on the set of the shoot. Maybe I'll sneak into her trailer or something." Nate smiled.

"I know I would." Dee cut some more, and then asked, "So that's the chick Simone, right?"

"Sahleen."

"Yeah. So she's big into that modeling stuff, huh. I mean, like she's making money doing that?"

"Hell, yeah," Nate bragged. "She just directed her first shoot down in Barbados. She just got back last Thursday."

Dee nodded his head. "Oh, yeah. And she's going straight to NYC tomorrow."

"Yeah. She stays on the road at least half of the month," Nate said, as Dee pushed his head forward so that his chin was touching his chest.

Dee was getting the hair off Nate's neck. When he finished he spun the chair to shape up Nate's mustache. "Do you think she got any friends? I want me one of those damned models."

Nate sat quietly until his mustache was finished. "I don't know if she has any friends. She doesn't talk about any of them much. I can ask for you, though," Nate offered. He didn't really plan on hooking Dee up, though. Dee was cool, but aside from cutting hair he was into some risky business out in the streets. The last thing that he needed was for Sahleen to think he was hanging out with drug dealers. Dee wasn't hard core or anything. He only hustled enough to pay for his Dinali, his motorcycle, and to have money to spend on women and clothes.

Dee was a wild character. Nate enjoyed talking to him and hanging out with him from time to time. As a matter of fact, Dee was going to South Beach with Nate, Cory, Brendan, and a couple of other friends for the Soul Beach Music Festival at the end of the month. When neither Nate nor Dee had the change for Nate's fifty to pay for the haircut, they walked next door to the carryout.

Nate ordered a gyro and offered Dee lunch.

"Just get me some fries, thanks."

"You got it." Nate ordered the fries.

They sat in a booth while they waited.

"So, have you seen Cory this week?" Nate asked.

"Yeah, as a matter of fact he came through Tuesday. Brought his wife with him."

Nate nodded.

"Your boy is in love, ain't he?" Dee said, while chewing on a straw.

"Uhmm. I guess," Nate said.

"I don't blame him. She's fine as shit. What is she, mixed or something?" Dee asked.

"Puerto Rican."

"I knew she was something. She seems nice. He told me the other day that he's going to let her move in with him, probably before the summer is out."

Nate was shocked. Not about Cory letting Nina move in, but that he had confided in his barber before him. "He told you that for real?"

"Yeah. He said he's been looking at rings and shit. He's gone." Dee smiled.

Damn. Nate thought, *Cory is moving kind of fast. He's only been dating Nina for four full months. I knew he was digging Nina, but I had no idea that it was so serious.*

"Damn," was all Nate said aloud.

"You didn't know that?" Dee asked. Nate could tell that Dee was a little shocked, but as a barber he was used to hearing the life story of everyone who got in his chair. He sometimes felt more like a therapist than a barber. Dee kept on talking. "He told me that he used to go with her sister back in the day. What's up with that?"

"That's kind of wild, huh?" Nate offered.

"Yo, that shit is mad foul. What kind of sister does some shit like that?" Dee had a smile on his face.

"I guess they figured that it was a long time ago." Nate had no answers. He was the last to judge. "Plus, her sister moved on like five years ago or something. I doubt if she would trip."

"But I know most bitches wouldn't want a man that their girlfriends had fucked, let alone their sister." Dee thought about it, remembering that he had knocked off several women who traveled in the same circles. "At least he wouldn't get into a relationship with them. But hell, if a player can get away with it . . . more power to him."

The Korean lady behind the counter called the number on Nate's ticket, and he jumped up to grab it. Dee didn't move, so Nate assumed that he was going to sit there and eat his fries. Dee smothered them in ketchup and ripped open three packs of pepper and sprinkled them on what seemed to be one spot.

"So what's the deal with the other honey that you've been seeing?" Dee asked, referring to India. India had come to the shop with Nate a couple of times to get her eyebrows arched.

Nate was chewing a mouthful of his gyro. "Nuttin'. She was tripping on me last weekend, but we've been straight this week."

"She reminds me of my son's mom before she got all fat and shit."

Nate ignored his last comment, and added, "Last night I took her up to the Bombay Club. It's a real upscale spot on Connecticut Avenue.

You ought to take a honey up there one night. You have to wear a suit jacket up in that piece, though. The night before that we went to the Café Atlantico on Eighth Street. As long as I'm putting in major time and funds, she's happy."

"Man, you don't mind spending major dollars on those honeys, do ya?"

Nate leaned back and wiped the corners of his mouth. "As long as I get what I want, I'll spoil from time to time. But shit; I don't take them all out, though. Some of them don't get shit but Blockbuster and Domino's." Nate laughed.

"You got that right."

While they finished eating they rapped about Dee's love life, which was off the hook as usual. Between tying women up, using vibrators on them, and having them lick whipped cream off his body, he said that he had met a nice girl that he was spending a lot of time with. Nate confided in Dee the feelings he had been having lately about being ready to slow down a bit. Nate had just wanted a reaction from Dee. Nate had already slowed down. Between the two women in his life, Nate hadn't had time to run the streets like his old self. As a matter of fact, he hadn't spent time with another woman the entire year. It was getting harder for him to lie to himself every day. He was in love for the first time in a long time, if not ever, with Sahleen. Meanwhile, he really enjoyed India. He even cared about her, but she was more of an insurance policy. The feelings that he held for her served as a safety net in case Sahleen messed up. Plus, he enjoyed having sex with her as much as she did with him. Sahleen wasn't always available, and why should he be forced to jerk off, he rationalized.

Nate and Dee walked out of the carryout and gave each other a handshake, and Nate slipped Dee a twenty for the baldy.

"Thanks," Dee said, as he walked back into the shop. "Hit me when you get back from up top."

Nate nodded his head and said, "Alright then," as he slid into the seat of his car and drove off.

I tapped my steering wheel while I sat in traffic on I-270. I was in the slow lane, and it seemed to be moving the fastest of the four. Unfortunately, I had been forced to get used to the stop-and-go traffic whenever I drove this route. Today, though, it was especially bad. It had begun to rain around four-thirty, and the usual rush-hour gridlock had been compounded. You would think that people could drive in a little rain, but it seemed like everyone except for me had lost their minds.

Boney James's version of "Sweet Thing" was playing on 105.9, the all-jazz station, as I reached for a pack of Starburst that Kyle had left in my car the previous weekend. I thought about calling Nina to let her know I was running late, but I decided to just keep pushing on when I saw the flares up ahead. Realizing that there was an accident gave me hope that the pace would pick up as soon as I cleared it.

It was a quarter to six, and I was supposed to pick up Nina at her apartment at six. If I had left work early, as I had planned, I would have made it. I'd had some problems with a distribution company that had been under contract before I came to HE. This company had been guilty not only of overcharging us but was late on picking up from the manufacturers on a regular basis. After speaking with our legal department, I called the owner and threatened legal actions. If we did not receive a retroactive reimbursement for the overcharging, which had been documented in our logbooks for the previous eight and a half months, I promised to have them in court for breach of contract. I also cited thousands in damages for the late pickups, which had resulted in late deliveries of our products.

What had kept me at the office even later was Jamison Hakito's return phone call. After he thanked me over and over again, he said, "Cory, you are the best thing to happen to this company since me." At first I thought that he was attempting to be funny. But he was serious. He added, "When I hired you I had no idea that you would be so proficient. This is the third time in six months that you have found mismanagement by your predecessor, Herbert Richman, and by myself as well. I am going to have accounting here in Manhattan do a cost-benefit survey of just how much you have earned and saved for this company. I already know that it is substantial. Therefore, if I have anything to do with it, you will be able to look for some type of bonus. Of course, it has to go through the board of directors, but you can rest assured we will show our appreciation for your dedication." When I told him that I was merely doing my job, he replied, "Nonsense. You have more than enough to do just running your divisions. I haven't a clue how you find time to check up on things like that, which aren't even your responsibility." Before he hung up he described some problems he was having in the New York–New Jersey area. I guess he wanted my spin on them. As the clock ticked, I started watching my chances of meeting Nina on time dwindle.

Finally, he closed with, "Expect a call from my uncle tomorrow." I hadn't heard from his uncle, the founder of Hakito Electronics, since I was hired, and I had to admit I instantly became anxious.

As I finally cleared the accident my phone began to vibrate. It was Nina. I flipped open my cell.

"Hello," I said calmly.

"Where are you?" Nina shrilled through the line. "I am hungry, and we have reservations for six-thirty. It's close to six now. There's no way you'll make it here in time."

"Calm down, baby. There's been an accident on 270. I'm just clearing it now."

She interjected, "Why did you come that way anyway? Why didn't you take Old Georgetown Road? I swear, Cory, I'm going to call and cancel the reservations. You don't listen."

"Hold on. Who in the hell do you think you're talking to? You can cancel the reservations if you want to. I'll turn my car around and go on home."

Silence.

"Is that what you want?" I asked.

More silence.

"Hurry up," was her way of apologizing, then she hung up.

I had learned that occasionally I needed to keep Nina in line. Letting her come out of her mouth any kind of way she wanted was out of the question. That was how women operated. It seemed odd that they still had to try to wrestle with a man for control. If they won that control, the man no longer seemed like a man to them. Once a woman loses respect for a man, he can hang it up. Wasn't happening here.

•　•　•

The restaurant was located on Columbia Road in northwest D.C. a section of town known as Adams Morgan. We arrived half an hour late for our reservations but were still able to be seated. It was a Brazilian restaurant called The Grill from Ipanema. It was my first time there. Shelly had told me about it many years ago. She had tried to get me to come there with her and her parents the summer before we broke up, but an argument had sent us our separate ways that night. I nearly slipped into a trance thinking about that summer night, probably six or seven years ago. I was trying to remember what we had fussed about.

My thoughts were interrupted when Nina asked, "Cory, what are you thinking about?"

"Nothing," I said, realizing that I had been staring into space instead of at the menu.

"Yeah, you are." Nina pinched my arm. "What?"

I knew she wouldn't be satisfied unless I told her something. So I went into a whole spiel about Jamison telling me that Mr. Hakito would be calling me tomorrow. Then I asked, "So, have you been here before?"

"Yeah, plenty of times. This is my mother's favorite restaurant. We used to come here a lot back in the day, as a family." She wiped her silverware. "Why, you don't like it?"

"No, it's nice, and the whole color scheme thing . . . I'm feeling it. It has a real tropical feel to it. It's a real nice atmosphere, and being here with you makes it even better." I meant that.

"As opposed to being here with whom?" she said slyly.

"As opposed to being here without you." I smiled back.

Nina squinted her eyes and then bit her bottom lip slightly before saying, "Good answer. As a matter of fact, that is the only answer, Mister Dandridge." Then we both laughed.

The waiter came to the table, and Nina greeted him in Spanish. His eyes brightened some, and he asked what were we drinking. I let Nina do all of the ordering while I played the silent, non–Spanish speaking boyfriend. When he left I said to her, "I am going to have to brush up on my Spanish. For all I know you two could have been talking about me."

"Don't worry. He just asked me what I was doing with such a stupid-looking American. And then he asked if he could take me out this weekend. I, of course, told him that I would have to ask my stupid-looking boyfriend."

I didn't laugh. I just cracked my knuckles as if I was ready to do some damage.

"So, boyfriend, am I free this weekend?"

"No, sweetheart. You won't be free this weekend or any weekend after," I said.

"And why is that?"

"Because you belong to me." And I meant that. It was just a matter of making it official.

The food was off the hook. I had a spiced shrimp and black bean stew filled with sausages and spooned over rice. I also ate off Nina's plate until she finally had to smack my hand away from her marinated grilled fish, shredded collards, and something grainy called *farofa*. She really enjoyed her food, and it was fun trying something new with her. I would have never thought to come here for dinner, nor had the creativity to suggest it to a date. Women are different. They know how to come up with ideas to keep a relationship going. I was thankful for Nina's creativity. I was going to have to come up with something creative real soon, though, because I had something planned for Nina. I was far from a McDonald's kind of guy, but like most other men I could use a little help in the romance department.

I read in a magazine, *Essence*, I believe, that women say that a lack of romance is one of the top five complaints they have with their men. I wouldn't fall victim to that trap. I was reading in my spare time. My mother told me a long time ago that if I wanted to be able to relate to a woman I needed to be able to see things the way she does sometimes, because a woman will *never* see them the way that men do. She said that I should read the same things that women read, which I do— *Essence*, *Honey*, and on occasion I'll grab *Sister 2 Sister*. Jamie Brown always gets the scoop like she's the black Barbara Walters. Moms also had told me that I need to watch *Oprah* every chance I get, and of course I do that.

• • •

We went back to her place after dinner. I didn't have any work clothes at her apartment, so I would have to get up at about seven in order to make it to my crib to get dressed properly. We got back to her place in time to catch *Soul Food* on Showtime. I loved that show.

Nina turned the television set off as soon as the show went off and told me to come to bed. I thanked my lucky stars to have found myself such a hot-blooded woman.

When I told her that I needed a quick shower before getting into bed, she joined me. While we did start making love in the shower, we finished in her bed. Our lovemaking had been just as delicious as the food we had eaten earlier, and even more satisfying. While I lay there next to her in the afterglow I couldn't get the idea out of my head that I wanted to be tied to this girl forever. If only God could help me find a way to tell her sister.

Nate was neatly placing his clothes into the garment bag. He checked and then double-checked to make sure he had some fly gear packed. It looked more like he was the one making a video, with all of the outfits that he had packed. He was only staying for three or four days, but he had seven pairs of pants and a couple of sweat suits. Nate had spent the morning shopping in Georgetown and Tyson's Corner. He'd purchased a couple of linen shirts from Armani Exchange, some Iceberg gear, and two Hobo sweat suits. He was ready for his trip to the city. Someone would have thought it was his first trip to New York, as excited as he was.

It didn't take an expert to figure out that all of Nate's excitement was due to his impending contact with the one and only Shawn Simmons. Shawn was only the hottest R&B female singer for nearly four years running. The fact that she was a raving beauty with the body and sex appeal of a goddess was only half of the secret to her success. Her voice was a cross between Anita Baker and Kelly Price, plus she had the hip-hop flavor of Mary J. Blige and the stage presence of Patti La-Belle. When she performed women cried and men breathed heavily. She had seduced a nation in her videos, one of which she had shot entirely nude. Of course the viewers never saw her private parts, but it was just the suggestiveness that had driven people wild. On top of everything else, the girl had class. What seemed risqué for other folks seemed chic when Shawn did it.

Her star had shined just a bit brighter than the rest from day one. She recorded one album as part of a girl group out of Los Angeles called Plain Jane. Plain Jane's album made it to the top the charts, and the group was poised to do well.

What happened after that was the same thing that had happened to so many other groups. It seemed that all of the Plain Jane videos put Shawn on the map without doing anything for the other members. It wasn't long before dissension and jealousy set in. Two of the three other members of the group, including her sister Sharon, began plotting against Shawn. Terrible rumors about Shawn's private life were leaked to the press, sending her into a rage. Needless to say, Shawn left the group, leaving a fierce legal suit in her wake. The rest of the group disbanded to pursue solo careers, none of which succeeded.

Four years and two multiplatinum selling albums later, and Shawn was the hottest R&B voice around. All of the key record executives were saying that Shawn's next album was a lock to be even bigger than the first two. Accomplishing that goal would be no small feat, though. She'd sold nearly twenty million units worldwide in four years. In order to live up to such high expectations, she was following in the footsteps of icons such as Mariah Carey and Janet Jackson. She went out and got the best producers to work with her in the studio. Everyone from Dr. Dre, Timbaland, and the Neptunes had worked on songs for her CD. Even after his scandal, Shawn voiced her support for R. Kelly and insisted that he do a song with her. "Innocent until proven guilty," she said, when asked in a *Vibe* interview about her decision to work with him. She had been through scandals, and she felt as though the brother needed somebody to ride out the storm with him. Plus, it had people talking about her CD before it hit the shelves. There were also duets with Maxwell and Lil'Kim. People in her camp were predicting a clean sweep at the Grammy, Soul Train, and MTV awards shows in the coming year.

Nate had just dropped three goldfish into the tank with his piranha when the phone rang. He looked at the caller ID. It was Sahleen.

"What's up, baby?" Nate asked.

"Are you on the way?" Sahleen asked. " 'Cause I want you to pick up some Chinese food for me."

"Why don't you just have them deliver it?" Nate didn't feel like stopping, but he would do it for her.

"I don't have any cash in the house at all. If you're going to be here within the hour or so, I can just order it when you get here." She paused, then said, "But I am famished."

"Okay. I'll tell you what," Nate spoke, while carrying his bags to the door. "I'll call you when I get on 395. Then you can call in your order; that way it won't get cold before I pick it up."

"Sounds good, baby, thanks." Sahleen sounded as though she was in a really good mood. Nate figured that maybe she was looking forward to their getaway as well. They hung up, and Nate turned on the clock radio in his bedroom. He turned on the timer on the TV so that it would be on each day from nine at night until six in the morning. He put his bags on his shoulders and headed out the door. He was sleeping at Sahleen's apartment so they could get an early start in the morning, and he wanted to make sure that his place would not welcome any break-ins during the subsequent four nights.

When he got into his car he called India's house, but there was no answer. He needed her to be there. He had come up with a nice alibi for the long weekend. He was going to tell her that he was taking his grandmother to her sister's house in Newport News. His grandmother actually had gone down to her sister's home, but she had taken the train. He could have left a message, but Nate preferred to lie to a woman directly. A lying message was so tacky and impersonal. Plus, a message gave no way of judging one's delivery and the reception of the message. Then he would have to spend energy over the weekend wondering if she had bought his story or not. No, he wanted her home. He called her cell.

When India's cell rang she caught her hand midair. She had been just about to honk at Nate, who was driving in the next lane, but he hadn't yet noticed her. She decided to have some fun and humor him. She sucked on her chocolate shake and placed it back into the cup holder.

"Hey, silly," India said when she answered.

Nate had no idea why she was calling him silly, but it didn't matter. She was in a good mood, and he hoped that she would stay that way after he told her that he was going out of town. He had known for two weeks that he would be leaving this weekend, but it would have been foolish to announce it to India any time before tonight. It would only have given her ideas about wanting to go with him, or time to come to the realization that she should be offended about not being invited. Nate knew that women always wanted to come along, or at least to be asked. He could have been going to an all-nude mud-wrestling tournament and she still would have wanted to come. Some women would want to come just because they weren't invited. Just like the Million Man March, when Minister Farrakhan had told women for nearly two months to stay their butts at home, lo and behold if there weren't at least twenty thousand sisters down there with their club gear on. I guess sistahs just liked those odds.

"Hey, baby," Nate said, trying to sound loving. "You on the road?"

"Yeah, as a matter of fact I am," she said. Nate could tell that India had a grin on her face while she was talking.

"You sure sound like you're in a good mood, girl," Nate said, turning down the radio. He was missing the Rane and Flex countdown on WPGC.

"I am in a good mood. I just left Victoria's Secret at Union Station, and I have a surprise for you," India said seductively. "You'll be in a good mood too, when you see it."

Nate cleared his throat and prepared himself for his delivery. "I can't wait, believe me, baby, but unfortunately it's going to have wait a few days. My great aunt is sick, and I have to take my nana down to see her."

"Oh really, are you leaving tonight? I could see you for just a little while." India was concerned, but she still wanted a little piece of Nate tonight. Even if it was only a quick piece. He had spent the entire week wining and dining her, and she was feeling very much in love. She had just finished telling her girlfriend that she felt as though Nate was ready to define the future of their relationship. That was what she thought up until Nate answered her with a serious tone . . . too serious to be delivering what had to be a joke. She had called him silly because she had thought that he was playing along with her from the start. But he wasn't playing.

"As a matter of fact, India, we're about to leave now. My nana's in the passenger seat now. She's dozed off, and I guess it's for the best. That way I can listen to some real music. Ya know what I'm sayin'?" Nate was lying, and India knew it.

"Is that right? So when are you coming back? Maybe you could stop by and pick me up. I could easily take tomorrow off." India couldn't believe that he was lying right through his teeth. Maybe he was playing. She was hoping that he was kidding. He had to know that her car was directly beside his as he drove down New York Avenue. Her heart began to swell up and fall into her stomach as Nate began to pile up lie on top of lie.

"I would, but Nana really wants to get there quick. If she woke up and we were in Forestville instead of on I-95 South she would go off."

"So, where are you now, Nate?" India asked, as she dropped her car seat back a little. She realized that Nate hadn't seen her because there was a garment bag hanging in his back right window creating a blind spot.

"We're on 395 south. It's about to turn into 95," Nate said, while he stopped at the light. When Nate came up with an excuse to get off the phone, she let him off reluctantly.

India was getting hot. She started to get out of her car at that light, knock on Nate's window, and bust his ass right there. But she figured that by keeping her cool she could see what he was up to, and that is exactly what she did. She kept her cool as he went into the tunnel leading to 395, then as he crossed the 14th Street Bridge right into Crystal City. All of this without a trace of his grandmother in the car. India was pissed to the highest level by the time he walked in and out of the carryout with a bag obviously big enough for two. Definitely too large for one. By the time he pulled into Sahleen's complex, India was so angry she was ready to fight. And if some bitch had come out, that is exactly what she was prepared to do.

India took a space a little farther down the walkway. She watched Nate walk toward a side entrance of the building. When the door swung open, she saw a woman there. She handed something to Nate, and he ran back toward his car. He hung the paper, a visitor's pass, on his rearview mirror. He grabbed his bag and the food from the seat and walked back toward the building where the woman was still standing. For a minute India thought that Sahleen was a white woman, until she focused her eyes harder. She was a sister, all right. She just looked like a slightly darker version of Alicia Keys. India wanted to get out of the car, but she was crying too hard. Her tears had paralyzed her. Nate was a liar. He was going upstairs to eat and fuck, probably for the entire weekend. He probably wasn't going anywhere.

India sat there thinking a thousand thoughts while her heart broke into just as many pieces. "That no-good dog. Nate is a lying ass son of a bitch. I can't believe he did this to me," India thought. Then she yelled out at the top of her lungs, "I'm going to kill this motherfucker. He's fucked over the wrong one this time." She said it over and over again, just like so many others had before her. Nate had no idea that India was sitting in her car at that moment, and he had no idea that she sat there until almost four in the morning, waiting for him to come back out, before she finally put the blade back in her purse and drove off.

Chapter 23

8 MILLION STORIES

There is something serene and jazzy about seeing the skyline of New York City. It pumped Nate up and made him want to do big things, just looking at it. He thought for a second about how the Twin Towers were missing but how the city's skyline was still alive.

His system was pumping a DJ Clue mix CD that had annoyed the hell out of Sahleen for the last half an hour on the turnpike. Normally, when Sahleen made a request, Nate would comply, but not today. He was listening to the *Welcome to Atlanta* remix, where all the rappers were representing for their cities. She had asked him at least three times to put on something else, but Nate wasn't having it. Now Sahleen was claiming to have a headache.

"Do you know which exit to take?" Sahleen asked.

"We're taking the GW Bridge, right?" Nate answered with a question.

"No. Take the Lincoln Tunnel to Midtown. Then take Eighth Avenue. We're going to the hotel first. Franco is going to meet me there at two o'clock. We have a meeting with some clients, and we need to interview two young models. After that, it's me and you, okay?"

Nate smiled.

"We're going to have dinner with a few friends of mine at this restaurant called Bond Street. You'll love it."

"What kind of food do they serve?"

"It's been described as designer food, for a designer crowd. You'll fit right in. Do you like sushi? Because they have a sushi bar in the back. You're liable to see anyone in there. Regis Philbin and David Letterman frequent it."

"Why in the hell would I want to see Regis?" Nate laughed.

"Well, Elizabeth Hurley and Pam Anderson show up there often, too."

"That's a little more like it." Nate nodded his head. "But how about the sisters? Do any blacks eat there?"

"That's not the point. The point is, it's a nice place, and you'll like it." Sahleen hit the eject button and yanked Nate's rap music out of the CD player before Nate could complain. Within seconds, Faith Evans and Carl Thomas were singing to them.

Traffic moved at a steady pace, although the midday Manhattan traffic was thick. Nate crossed over to Eighth Avenue and dropped his window. The early May air felt good, and since Sahleen's hair was pulled back, he let her window down, too.

Nate pulled up to the Marriott Marquis and waited for someone to come and park the car. Sahleen had been touching up her makeup for ten minutes. "You have got to be right in this town. No second chance to make a first impression," she said.

As soon as the valet came to park the car, Sahleen got out and signaled for the bellboy to come and retrieve the bags from the trunk. Nate reached under his seat and pulled out a small package and put it into his pants pocket, and then quickly got out and handed the keys to the valet. He gave the valet a fifty-dollar bill. The valet held the bill up as if to ask if he wanted change, but Nate waved him off. The hotel room they were in was eight hundred dollars a night, and all of the staff members, from the busboys to the guy playing the piano in the lobby, were paid handsomely, but the fat tip made the valet's day and he was definitely going to take care of Nate's ride.

Nate walked into the lobby to find Sahleen talking to Franco by the desk. They were looking over some papers Franco was holding. When they saw Nate they began to walk toward him.

"Hello Nathan, good to see you." Franco held his hand out and gave Nate a firm handshake.

"You too, man," Nate replied.

"Sahleen, I'm going to grab a cab out front. Hurry," Franco said, looking at his watch.

Sahleen nodded to Franco, and then turned to Nate. "Here's your key, baby." She handed him a plastic card. "I'm leaving now. I'm going to be back here, hopefully, by five or so. So I'll look for you then. Why don't you do a little shopping?"

Nate nodded as he said, "Yeah, I probably will do that."

"I wouldn't advise that you take your car, though. Parking will be ridiculous."

"Oh, no. Believe me, I'll be cabbing it right now if I decide to go anywhere at all," Nate said. "You better run, baby."

"Yeah, okay." She kissed Nate on his chocolate cheek. "Oh, yeah, you know the video shoot starts at ten tonight. They're shooting some of it over in Times Square and Rockefeller Center, and some of it in the St. Loren Museum lobby. I think they have finished shooting at the Davis mansion out in the Hamptons."

"All of that in one night?" Nate asked.

"No. Some tonight, some tomorrow, and the rest Sunday afternoon," Sahleen said back over her shoulder as she walked away.

Nate visualized the shoot as he walked toward the elevator. He couldn't wait to see Shawn Simmons and the other models who would be in the video. Nate was wishing that Brendan were there with him, because he knew that Brendan was really into Shawn Simmons.

Nate checked out the room, which was fabulous. There was a Jacuzzi tub in the bathroom, which became the only thing Nate cared about after he saw it. The living room had a fully stocked bar, a flat-screen television set, a marble fireplace, and a vibrating easy chair. When Nate walked into the bedroom he saw a basket on the bed with champagne, assorted chocolates, and bath and body oils in it.

"Phat," Nate said aloud to himself. Then he got naked and jumped into the Jacuzzi while it filled with hot water and bubbles. There was a remote next to it, which he fiddled with until he saw a cabinet open in the bathroom. "Of course." Nate laughed when he saw a nineteen-inch television in the cabinet.

Nate had been soaking for almost an hour when the phone rang.

Nate figured that it might be Sahleen, so he got out of the tub still dripping wet. "Hello," he answered.

"Hello. Is this room 1622? I'm looking for Sahleen Austin. Do I have the right room?" the voice on the other end said.

"Yes, you do, but she's not here. Who, may I ask, is calling?"

The person on the other end paused, and Nate could hear someone yelling at him in the background. He heard the voice say that Sahleen's not there. Then he spoke into the phone. "Yes. Tell her this is Gus calling from Excite World Video. We're shooting the video for Sony. Is this one of her models?"

"Actually, I'm a friend who came up for the shoot with her. But I am just vacationing."

The guy had a thick accent. He sounded like he was a New Yorker. "Yeah, well, how's your skin?" He heard more yelling in the background.

"What?" Nate asked. He readjusted his towel.

"Your skin. How is it? Do you have nice skin?"

"Yeah, why?"

"What's your complexion . . . you dark or light?"

"Dark, like a Hershey bar. Why?"

"He's dark," Gus yelled, pulling his mouth from the phone. The voice yelled something back. "How tall are you? Are you slim, muscular, or what?"

"Look, my man, what's with all of the questions?" Nate was about to hang up.

"C'mon, man," Gus said. Then after a break a new voice was on the line. "Hello, this is Shawn Simmons. What time will you be expecting Sahleen?"

Nate was slightly shocked but he was still cool. "Um. She's probably going to be out until around five."

"Well . . . I didn't catch your name."

"My bad. I'm Nate Montgomery."

"Well, we're having a bit of a problem with a couple of the models in the video. The problem is that two of the men and one of the girls are stuck in Tokyo. They won't be back in the States until Tuesday, and of course we will be done shooting by then. The reason why Gus was asking you those questions was because we were hoping that Sahleen could help us out with a couple of replacements."

Nate was just listening to her voice. When he realized that she had stopped talking, he said, "Well, actually I'm not really a model. I am just here with Sahleen on a personal level."

"Well, that's even better. I know what you must look like. If Sahleen brought you up to the shoot, there's no doubt in my mind. How tall are you?"

"I'm six-feet-one-inch, but . . ."

"No, no, no, but nothing. Look, I need you over here at wardrobe." She yelled something at Gus about a car. "I am sure that Sahleen would have you do this for me. We're pretty tight. I'm going to have Gus send a car for you. Just slip on something and be downstairs in fifteen minutes. Thanks, Nat."

"Nate."

"Sorry. Fifteen, okay? Toodles." As she hung up Nate heard her say, "Now, get me one more body. Try that guy from the Sprite commercial." Click.

Nate couldn't believe what had just happened. Had Shawn just told him she needed him to be ready in fifteen minutes? Was he actually getting dressed to go downstairs and be picked up?

Nate was standing in front of the hotel wearing a pair of loose-fitting black linen slacks. He had a Versace T-shirt on and a linen blazer draped over his shoulder. He was looking the role of New York fashion model when a white Cadillac DTS pulled up to the curb in front of him. A white guy got out and stood with the door still open.

"You Nate?" he asked.

"Yeah."

"Okay, I'm Gus," he said, nodding his head approvingly. "Not bad. Hop in."

Not bad. What the hell? Nate thought, as he hopped in. They drove off and headed away from Midtown.

"We've got to run down to the Village for a quick second and pick someone else up. Here's the deal." Gus started with a bunch of producer talk. He was under the impression that Nate had done this before. Gus went on and on, talking about lighting, angle shots, and crowd control. By the time they reached their destination, where another brother walked out of a building, Gus had filled Nate's head with so much mumbo-jumbo he didn't know which way was up, let alone what he was supposed to do next.

They wound up at a studio off Forty-second Street near Times Square. The guy in the back seat was quiet the whole way, listening to an MP3 player. As the three entered the building, a bum walked up to them asking for change. It was then that Nate realized that he didn't have any money or ID on him. "Well, piss on you too," the bum yelled when they walked into the building without giving him anything.

The elevator stopped on the third floor, and as soon as they got off there were two sets of double doors. A girl with a headset on was seated at a desk in front of a wall. Just beyond the wall Nate could see that the entire floor was like a warehouse.

A woman who had been talking to a couple of people near a plate-glass window headed over toward Gus, Nate, and the other guy.

"Well, it's about time," she said. "Hello, you must be Nate, and you're Damien, right?"

Nate nodded and Damien said, "Yes, ma'am."

"You do look young, Damien, but Trish says that you can dance. How old are you?"

"Seventeen, ma'am," Damien said.

"Oh, stop it with the 'ma'am' stuff already. Show me what you got."

"Well, I need to warm up first, and change, if you don't mind."

Shawn smiled. "Oh, but of course."

"Did the permits and guarantees come while I was gone?" Gus asked.

"They're on the table over there," Shawn said, and Gus marched off, directing Damien to a corner where a mat was laid out.

"Come with me," Shawn said, smiling, and she took Nate by the hand. "Nice," she mumbled.

"Nice too," Nate said with a smile, as he looked Shawn up and down while bobbing his head.

"You weren't supposed to hear that." Shawn was still grinning. She took him over and introduced him to Trish, whom Nate recognized from the party at Amir's house the previous fall. Trish had been with Sahleen the night he had met her. Trish's hair was different now, though. It was still extremely long but was a little more tame. It looked almost wet.

Trish was a director. She had worked with Sahleen on hundreds of shoots and was a favorite in the fashion industry. She had consulted on videos for Kenny Lattimore, Eve, and Christina Aguilera the previous year. Now she was sought after for music videos in every genre. While Sony insisted on Excite World and Gus for the production, Shawn demanded Trish direct. The rest was history, because everybody knew that what Shawn Simmons wanted, Shawn Simmons got.

Trish was now schooling Nate on what he would have to do. Within seconds Nate had his shirt off and his upper body oiled up. The staff was trying to see what degree of lighting was going to accent him the best. It had been explained to him that he would play Shawn's lover in the video, which was for the song "One Too Many Lovers." It was her title track. It was a medium tempo track that had been remixed by Bad Boy. P. Diddy had already shot his portion of the video. He only had a cameo as Shawn's brother, where he warned her that her exploits with too many lovers would catch up to her.

Trish also had Nate trying on different outfits, silk pajamas and robes. While clad in a brown silk robe and silk leopard-print boxers, Trish had Nate walk around the corner to a set. There were three sets of bedrooms side by side. The first one had a canopy with a sheer drape on it. Off to the left of that was one with a brass bed, and the third was an extravagant ivory bedroom suite with a screen behind it showing a video of a waterfall. Each set was decorated to the tee, and looking at them it would be hard to tell that they weren't rooms in someone's home.

Trish had just finished giving Nate his final instructions when Nate asked, "Do they know that I have never done any modeling or acting before. I mean . . . I really don't want to waste their time."

Trish took her pencil out of her mouth and stuck it in her hair. "Look. It's a little late now, and it doesn't really matter. I've taken people off the street and had them in a video within an hour. It's not hard. You don't even have to say any lines. Let's see . . ." Trish looked at a clipboard. "All you have to do is walk hand in hand in Times Square with Shawn." Nate was hearing her but at the same time he couldn't believe what he was hearing. He was never one to get star struck, but the one and only Shawn Simmons . . . Trish continued, "no, the museum scene is with Andrew." She was mumbling. "Da, da, da . . . Okay. You have to go out to the Hamptons either tomorrow or Sunday and do a scene where you greet her at the door of a mansion and have a romantic dinner. You also have to roll around in the sack with her. One of these three . . . I haven't decided which one yet."

Nate's mouth dropped open.

"It's simple. And close your mouth before you catch a fly." Trish didn't smile. She was all business.

. Gus popped his head around the corner. "We're about to set up in here. Which bed?"

Shawn walked around the corner in a black satin-and-lace teddy. She was putting on a terry cloth robe as she spoke. "Let's do the ivory."

"Okay," Trish said. "Then change wardrobe and do the canopy, too, just in case we need it."

Gus was nodding his head. "Sounds good. Be back in a flash."

"You ready, Nate?" Shawn asked.

"So, you guys are ready to shoot now?" Nate asked.

"Yes. Is that a problem?" Shawn asked, and walked up to Nate.

Nate was nervous, forgetting everything about being smooth, a player's player, a Mack daddy, and a pimp. The nigga was nervous, and Shawn could sense it.

"Excuse us for a moment, Trish," Shawn said politely. Trish walked off. "You, too, if you don't mind." The stagehand bolted around the corner after apologizing.

"Come here, Nate," Shawn said, as she walked over to the bed and sat on it. "Come on."

Nate walked over and stood in front of her. "No, sit." Nate sat. Shawn began to say that she hated putting him in an awkward situation. She told him how nervous she had been in front of the camera at first. She went on for five or ten minutes about how confident she was that he would do fine, and that the production team was so good, the actors were almost a nonfactor in the video's success. "Nate, they are going to make you look like you've been doing this for years, okay. I really need you."

"Look, I'm sorry. I don't mean to trip or anything." Nate struggled to get the words out.

"No, don't worry about it. Look, I know you're not an actor or a model. But, you see, that makes it even better."

"How is that?"

"You're fresh. Like that kid, Damien. He's going to blow up, but this is his first video as well. I love to give people a chance to do their thing. This might be your thing. You've been here since three-thirty. It's five-thirty now. You've already made six hundred dollars. That's not to mention what you get after the approval and release of the finished video. Not bad, huh?" Shawn's eyebrows went up.

"Well, I'm not tripping off of the money," Nate said.

"So what are you tripping off of?" Shawn asked.

"Maybe you. Maybe I just don't want to mess up."

"You won't. I assure you."

"Well, just don't get pissed at me if we have to do a couple of takes of this bedroom scene. I'm usually very . . . no, I'm usually beyond comfortable. As a matter of fact, I am most comfortable in the bedroom." Nate smiled.

"Well, I have a surefire method of helping you so that your acting doesn't cause you or me any trouble," Shawn said, as she stared at Nate right in his face.

"And what is that?" Nate asked softly, as his normal stature and poise began coming back to him.

"Don't act. Let your mind run away when we get in this bed." Shawn let the robe slip off. Then she moved an inch away from Nate's face and whispered, "Practice." Then she placed her lips on his.

Nate's hand found her waist and he leaned her back on the bed. He kissed her like he was kissing a star. Like he had never laid his lips on anything more precious than them. He sucked on her lips as if they tasted like honey. He caressed her sides and his hands glided up and down her teddy. Shawn's hands were moving up and down Nate's back and neck. His mouth then moved from her lips to her neck as his hands cupped her breasts and pinched her nipples through the smooth fabric.

"Ooohh" Shawn moaned out. "Yessss. That's right." Shawn's right hand found Nate's crotch and slipped inside of his boxers, finding him rock hard. She began to rub him slightly as she then said, "Nate, you are so big and hard."

Nate continued kissing her, and soon his fingers had slipped up Shawn's thighs and into her teddy. Nate had barely touched her moist lips when she pulled his hands away and said, "Save it for the video. I want it just like that. If you do a good job for me now . . . I will be very grateful. You can ask Sahleen if I show my gratitude to those who do a good job for me."

"Oh shit. Sahleen." Nate put his hand on his head. "I was supposed to meet her at five for dinner. I need a phone."

"Don't worry. I had Trish call her already and push dinner back until later. We have to finish. Trish told her that you were here."

"What did she say?" Nate asked.

"What could she say? She doesn't own you. You're working. She understands that. Did you ever wonder why she brought you up here to New York? This could be your big break. You could make her company a lot of money. A pretty black man like yourself with such a sleek body is a hot commodity."

Nate was still hard, but he was calming down quickly. He thought about what Shawn had just said, and then dismissed it just as quickly. Sahleen knew he wasn't trying to become some damned model. It's not like he was a teenager, nor was he hurting for cash.

Shawn called for Gus and the rest of the crew to come back in so that they could begin shooting. It didn't take long for them to shoot both scenes from all the angles they needed. They had actually gotten completely naked for the second scene. Nate assumed that nudity was Shawn's fetish. She was probably some type of closet exhibitionist. By the time they finished shooting at 8:00 P.M. Shawn's booty was soaking wet from the scenes that they had filmed under the satin comforter. Nate had taken the opportunity to let his fingers massage

Shawn's womanhood. She had even reached an orgasm from Nate's constant fingering. Gus had praised the realism, thinking that Shawn was just a great actress. Trish knew better, and was slightly disgusted. Trish knew that Nate and Sahleen were dating. But in the industry, shit happens.

Once the shoot was over, everyone dressed and headed down to the Bond Street restaurant for dinner. Nate called Sahleen and had her bring his wallet. She and Franco, along with several other model types, met Gus and his Excite World people down at the restaurant.

While they ate, the rest of the crew set up to record outside, at Times Square. Dinner was quick and not the least bit tense. Nate and Sahleen sat next to each other. When Shawn told Sahleen how well Nate had "performed" Nate swallowed hard and Sahleen beamed with pride. Trish and Gus had both cosigned Shawn's stamp of approval. Nate, meanwhile, was staring at Shawn, trying to make eye contact.

It seemed as though every time he looked at Shawn she was staring at Sahleen. He began to get a little uncomfortable, thinking that Shawn was going to flip the script, saying he had made a move on her. He wondered then if he should tell Sahleen everything that had gone down. At least, his version of everything.

The shoot at Times Square went so smoothly and quickly that the group ended up at the Metronome before midnight. Trish, who seemed more at ease after finishing up her work, really let her hair down in the club. The DJ was pumping a nice mix of music. There was a mixed crowd in the house, and everyone was dancing, having a real nice time.

Nate was sipping on some champagne on a couch with a couple of his new friends, a Dominican model named Monte and a seventeen-year-old white girl named Kristen. The rest of the party was either dancing or sitting in a booth with Gus and his crew.

Sahleen was still sitting with Franco and Trish. Shawn was dancing with everyone in the place, and a bodyguard was standing right behind her making sure no one got out of hand.

It was nearly three in the morning when everyone headed in for the night. Everyone went his or her separate way, some of them doubling up in cabs. Nate and Sahleen went back to the room and fell asleep without so much as a good-night kiss.

Saturday's shoot was more intense. It started at three, and Nate wasn't needed, so he left the set early to do some shopping. He hit the Gucci store, Bloomingdale's, and everything in-between. Macy's seemed to go on forever. It was one full city block long. The Moschino section was at least five times bigger than anything Nate had ever seen back in D.C. The Versace section wasn't too shabby either, but since he had already hit the Versace store he wasn't impressed. He ended up on Broadway in SoHo. Before Nate knew it the package he had brought along was halfway depleted; he had spent nearly five grand in the five hours since leaving the video shoot.

There had been only a small bunch of people standing around at the St. Loren Museum when he left. They had been preparing to film the dance scenes. The scenes that they were filming after that had Shawn loving her other costar, Andrew Clark. Sean and Nate didn't have any more love scenes together, though, and Nate didn't care to spend his last full day watching the models posing. The models were mostly for visual effect. Sahleen was only in one scene. She was play-ing the part of a chick who had caught the eye of Andrew, the other lover, causing Shawn to get jealous.

Nate preferred to see some real sisters out in the streets, and he did indeed meet a couple of New York honeys. He managed to get a few numbers while shopping. He didn't anticipate calling any of them, but he took them for the sport of it. Marie from Brooklyn was really cute in her Jeep; Jennifa, the Spanish chick from the designer warehouse in Manhattan, was sexy; and Faith from Queens was a real hottie. It was what used to be a typical day out for Nate. The thing was, over the pre-vious five months he hadn't had a real desire to meet a bunch of women. He really didn't have time to entertain them even when he did meet them. He had been so involved with Sahleen and India, he had been passing on a hell of a lot of women.

Nate thought long and hard about the change in his behavior as he walked up the avenue with his arms full of bags. *No regrets*, he thought, *A man has to slow down eventually. Look at Cory.* He knew he loved Sahleen, and he also recognized that India had a special place in his heart. Because of that he had bought gifts for both of them. He also had a bag full for his grandmother. He crossed the street and hailed a cab to go back to the hotel.

"Where to?" the cabby yelled back.

"Marriott Marquis, it's in Midtown at . . ."

"Yeah, I got it," the cabby said rudely.

Nate started to curse him out for cutting him off, but he remembered he was in New York. Nate looked at his watch. It was close to nine o'clock. He got out of the cab at the hotel and went straight to the garage with his bags. After he secured his car he jumped on the elevator and rode straight to the sixteenth floor. He was a little beat, and hungry, too. He was going to order some room service and chill until Sahleen got in. He was trying to decide if it would be fish or steak for dinner as he entered the room. When he walked in he heard the radio on in the bedroom and immediately noticed the champagne basket had been opened. It was sitting on the coffee table along with two empty glasses. There was also a half bottle of Courvoisier sitting on top of the bar. Nate headed toward the French doors that led to the bedroom and walked in.

When he saw what was going on he almost fell straight to the floor. His eyes focused in on the two bodies that he saw. Shawn Simmons was on her knees with Sahleen's legs pinned up. Shawn's face was buried between Sahleen's legs. Sahleen had a pillow over her face, attempting to muffle her screams. It wasn't working, though, as Nate could hear his woman moaning in pleasure as her bottom writhed from Shawn's tongue lashing.

"What the fuck," Nate finally said. And the pillow flew from Sahleen's face. And Shawn turned around slowly. When Shawn saw Nate standing there, she smiled, turned back around to Sahleen, and continued. Sahleen's eyes were watering; they always did when she was about to reach an orgasm. Nate stood frozen. He was far from being in touch with how he was feeling right at that moment. He didn't know if he was excited, disgusted, or plain hurt. He couldn't focus on his body at that instant. He felt as though he was standing outside in the cold and a bucket of water had just been poured on him. Then, in the next moment, he felt like he was standing at the equator with a fur coat on. He was motionless. He watched as Sahleen looked around Shawn, who was really into what she was doing. Their eyes were locked until her body began to shake, for the third time in an hour. Then Sahleen's eyes closed. Shawn had been giving her orgasm after orgasm. Each time she came harder than the last, and this time was no different. Nate just shook his head "no" as he turned and walked back into the living room.

Nate sat on the couch drinking the cognac straight out of the bottle. He was in a daze. He couldn't believe that he was in love with a lesbian. How could he have not known? To put it bluntly, his head was totally fucked up. His mind raced for what seemed like an hour.

He took a few more gulps and finished the bottle, and his body began to go limp. Nate's head was leaning over the back of the couch and his eyes were closed when he felt the bush from a vagina brush up against his face from behind the couch. When he tried to push her away, Shawn said, "No, lick it." She began to grind her crotch into his face. Instinctively, he began to lick.

At the same time he felt his pants being unfastened. Within seconds Sahleen was sucking him and had him hard. Sahleen switched places with Shawn and they both had their way with Nate. A part of him was loving it. Before he knew it he was fucking Shawn from behind on the couch, and she was screaming out his name while he tongue kissed Sahleen. He pulled violently at her hair and smacked her across her ass. She was getting off on every bit of it.

"That's right, Nate, punish me," Shawn yelled out. When his dick slipped out Shawn quickly got on her back and asked Nate to dive back in. Nate was getting caught in the moment. "Come here, Sahleen," Nate heard Shawn pant out.

She commanded Sahleen to lick Nate while he penetrated her. When Nate felt Sahleen's tongue touch his backside he felt shivers run through his body. He couldn't believe Sahleen was going out like this.

Sahleen began talking to Nate. "Hit it harder, Nate. She likes it rough."

"Yeah, Nate, I like it rough." The couch was sliding across the floor with each powerful slam into Shawn. "Now, Nate, put your hands around my throat. I . . . I am . . . gettin' ready to come . . ." She was moaning loudly.

"What you want, baby?" Nate asked, making sure he heard her correctly.

"Choke the bitch, Nate. Don't be scared, baby. That's what she wants," Sahleen said, with a devilish look on her face. She kept pulling at Shawn's nipples, and at the same time she was masturbating watching them.

Shawn's head was thrashing back and forth as Nate wrapped both hands around her neck and began to choke her. Her eyes rolled up in her head and her body began to shake like she had been electrocuted as she came with flaming intensity. She passed out for a few moments, but it didn't stop Nate from punishing the punany until he came. In the bedroom, both women rubbed and kissed his body. They sucked him until he came once more, then they all sucked and fucked some more. It was every man's fantasy, and at the same time, his worst nightmare.

Finding out the woman you love is freak is a defining moment for a man. If you don't embrace it, it will repulse you. Nate had always held such high regard for Sahleen. He never imagined in his wildest dreams that she would go out like this. While he was recovering from reaching his climax he watched as Sahleen went down on Shawn. He thought about meeting Sahleen at that gay party and realized that she had probably been lying about her sexual preferences all along. *It all makes sense*, he thought. *Both times that I've seen Trish there is some gay shit going on. Trish is gay, and she is the common thread between Sahleen and Shawn . . . that has to be it*. Then he wondered how Sahleen would have taken it had she walked in while he was fucking some dude up the ass. Though he never would do anything like that, she hadn't given a damn how he felt about walking in as he had. She had lied all along, then just sprung her gayness on him. What a bitch.

Sahleen and Shawn finally fell asleep. Nate got up to use the bathroom, and decided to take a shower. He then threw on some clothes, gathered up his belongings, and started to leave. He sat down in the easy chair instead and let it vibrate. It shook him asleep, and when he woke up it was Sunday morning and Shawn was gone. Sahleen was getting dressed and had her bags together. They both seemed to be pretending that nothing had happened, and Nate was fighting the repulsion, jealousy, and pain.

The Shark Bar is famous for its food and atmosphere. The Sunday brunch was out of this world. Nate had three plates. One was piled high with waffles. Another had the freshest, sweetest red grapes he had ever tasted, along with melon slices and cantaloupe. His third plate had grits, eggs, bacon, and home-fried potatoes on it. The syrup was served piping hot, and Nate's mind was temporarily focused only on food. Sahleen, Franco, and the two models that they had signed were eating, too.

After leaving the Shark Bar everyone headed out to the Hamptons to finish the video. Nate was no longer in the mood but didn't want to let on to either Shawn or Sahleen how shaken he had been by what had transpired. He shot his scenes and was handed a check by Gus when he was preparing to leave. "Twenty-seven hundred dollars," Nate said, shocked to be getting paid so handsomely to frolic in a bed with Shawn. Most men would have paid that for the privilege.

Gus misinterpreted Nate's look of surprise, and said, "Oh, you'll get another check for at least twice that when the video is released. The nude stuff was great. Sign right here, Nate." Nate signed. "Oh, and I need your address, so I can mail your check. Who's your agent? Because if you need . . ."

"I told you, Gus . . ." Nate was about to tell Gus again that he was not a model. Franco butted in. "Mobley represents this young man, thank you," he said, as he patted Gus on the shoulder. The two walked off.

"Thanks again, Nate," Gus yelled. "You got the goods, baby. Indeed you do."

Nate turned around to see Shawn standing there. She was so hot, but he hated her at that moment. She had stolen his woman. It wasn't that he feared she and Sahleen would run off together. She had stolen her in the sense that he would never be able to view Sahleen as perfect anymore. Before this incident, he had felt as though he had found the perfect combination of beauty, class, and intelligence in Sahleen. Secretly he had wondered what their kids might look like. Now it would be impossible for him to trust her as a wife and mother to his unborn children. She was just another whore, albeit for another woman, but a whore nonetheless. Nate cracked a phony half smile and made an excuse to walk off.

Nate went to Sahleen and told her that he was about to leave. He didn't ask her if she was ready. "Nate, what's the rush? I need to tie up some loose ends here."

"Well, you do that. I'm gone," Nate said, as he walked out the door.

As he headed toward the car, Sahleen caught up to him. "What the hell is wrong with you?"

"What the hell do you think?" Nate said, as he got into his car. Sahleen stood there while he rolled down the window.

"I know you're not talking about last night."

"You know damn well that is what I am talking about," Nate said, glaring angrily.

Sahleen saw the pained look on his face and her demeanor changed. "But I thought that was what you wanted. I heard about what happened at the shoot on Friday. I heard that you two couldn't keep your hands off each other."

"That's bullshit. You've been lying to me all of this time. You told me when I met you that you weren't gay."

"I'm not gay," Sahleen said, clenching her fists.

"Well, I sure as hell couldn't tell last night. Shit, you lick pussy better than me," Nate huffed.

"Are you jealous?" Sahleen was getting defensive. "Look, Shawn has done a lot to help me and my career. I just . . ."

"Look. Fuck it, okay. I . . ." Nate paused. There was an unfamiliar lump in his throat. He swallowed hard to get it out, but it wasn't going anywhere. "I don't need this shit," Nate forced it out. "I thought you were the one. I thought you were perfect. I, I . . ." Nate stuttered out. "I felt like . . . like we were in love and shit."

Sahleen had a tear in her eye. "I'm sorry, Nate."

"I thought that we were going to be together, maybe have some kids one day." A tear welled up in the corner of his eye. Nate felt it, but prayed it wouldn't fall. Crying in front of women was for the weak.

Sahleen shook her head. "Nate, I didn't know you felt like that. If I did I would have been totally honest with you. I swear I didn't know. But hell, you knew that with my career and business in its prime that I wasn't ready for a commitment."

Nate erupted. "Well, what do you call what we've been doing for the last five months?"

Sahleen didn't answer. She just stood there staring at Nate. He stared back. After a few seconds Sahleen said in a loud whisper. "I'm sorry. I really am, but I'm not in love with you, Nate. I thought we were just having a good time, taking things as they came."

Nate shook his head and gripped his steering wheel. "Yeah, we were, but things changed. I thought we were on the same page."

"I must've missed out on something. If I sent you mixed signals or led you on . . ."

"Led me on? The time we spent together, all the love we made? And how could you be carrying on with Shawn like that?"

"Who are you to judge me? I guess if you had set the whole thing up it would have been fine. I'm sorry, Nate, but I'm just not the type to be led around by the nose. My career comes first. In case you're wondering, I don't have feelings for Shawn, but if she gets what she wants then I get what I want. That's simply how it works in the industry."

"Just tell me one thing," Nate shot back.

"What's that?"

"Did you even care for me?"

"Of course I did. I still do. Obviously, not the same way you do for me." Sahleen paused. "I'm just not ready to be tied down or judged by a man for doing what I have to do. I'm sorry, but that's just how it is."

The tear fell and burned Nate's pride. And at the same time his stomach began to churn. He felt every emotion that he owned swirling about inside of him. Before he totally lost his composure he yelled out, "Okay, well then fuck you, Sahleen, you slut." Then he drove off. At the end of the driveway he jumped out of the car and placed Sahleen's bags in the grass, and just as quickly jumped back in and drove down the road with her watching.

Nate sped down the turnpike, trying to get as far away from Sahleen as possible. His thoughts soon turned to India. His baby, the one he should have been with the entire time. The one he should have done right by from the start. He began thinking about how wonderful she was, how he had taken her for granted the entire time, all because he had met Sahleen the very same night. He was glad that he hadn't broke things off with her and that she cared so much about him. He thanked his lucky stars that it wasn't too late for the two of them.

Chapter 24

A ROCK AND A HARD PLACE

Nate stood knocking at India's door. She wasn't answering, though her car was parked out in front of her duplex. He saw her Club still on the steering wheel, which to Nate meant that her car probably hadn't been moved the entire day. It was nearly four in the afternoon, and by this time India had usually been to church, done her grocery shopping for the week, and more often than not, started her laundry. He knocked some more and rang the bell before he leaned over and looked into the bay window through the draperies.

"Shit," Nate exclaimed as he huffed. "Where the hell is she?" he said, as he backed away from the door. He walked to his car, which was parked in a visitor's space across the lot, and sat in the seat with one foot on the ground. He reached into his glove compartment to get a piece of paper so that he could write a note. He started the note with: "Honey bun, I missed you, so I came straight over. I have a couple of surprises for you, so call me as soon as you get . . ." but before he could finish, he got a surprise of his own.

A gray jeep pulled up and stopped right in front of India's door. Nate immediately spotted India in the passenger seat. He also noticed the pleasant look on her face as she laughed with the driver. He was a light-skinned brother wearing a pair of shades. Nate was instantly jealous and was about to run up to India and her date. He then decided to chill and wait and see what was going on. Nate watched as the driver leaned over and kissed India on the cheek before she stepped out of the jeep. She had what looked like a doggie bag in her hand; she laughed some more. *This guy must have been a real comedian*, Nate was thinking. India was taking her time walking away; she stood beside his jeep. The next thing Nate knew, the brother was looking at his watch and nodding his head.

Within seconds, the brother put his vehicle in reverse and parked on the island near the mailboxes. Nate realized that India had invited him in, and that was it. Nate stood and got out of his car as he and the guy slammed their doors simultaneously. India was watching her date, still grinning. She had on a yellow and blue sundress that was showing off her pretty legs. Nate noticed as well that her hair had been freshly done. Nate was ten feet away from her when she turned and saw him walking toward her.

India's mouth fell open when she saw Nate. Shock was her first reaction. She was only thinking about the embarrassment she assumed was coming for everyone. She wasn't focused on her anger at Nate, which had come to a boil a few nights earlier. She wasn't thinking about how she had been ready to stab him in the parking lot of that woman's apartment complex, or how she'd driven back over there each day this weekend to see if she would find his car there. She had planned to slash every tire and bust each window. She knew how much Nate adored his car, and she had planned to make him pay the best way she knew how. The fact that she had cried all day Friday, and that her best friend, Lynn, had come over to spend the night with her because she had been so worried about her wasn't on her mind.

India's date walked up to her with a puzzled look when he saw Nate standing there. The look on her face gave away the only question that she had at the moment, which was, "Why?" Why had Nate shown up now after not calling all weekend? India had left at least fifteen messages on his machine, some cursing and some crying. Some were threatening, but the last one, which India had left on his machine that morning, had taken the cake. But Nate had yet to check any of them. He had no idea what was waiting for him on his answer-call service.

"Hey baby, what's up?" Nate asked, nodding his head toward the stranger. India cringed when Nate touched her arm. She pulled back. She actually thought that Nate had come to hit her.

"Get off of me, Nate."

Nate's face showed confusion. He had no idea what was going on.
He had no idea that she had busted him. He also had no idea that she
had left a message on his voice mail giving him a step-by-step descrip-
tion of how she had gotten herself together after he had devastated
her. Her message described how she and Lynn had gotten up on Saturday morning and gone to the hair salon. How they had gotten man-
icures, pedicures, and massages. It went on to describe how she had
gone on a date with the guy in the jeep the previous night and how he
had spent the night with her. She had gone on to describe every detail
of the kissing, sucking, and fucking she had done with her date. Finally,
she had said that what she had thought was going to be payback sex, a
little "wham, bam, thank you ma'am," had turned out to be the fuck of
a lifetime for her, and that she had found a replacement for Nate's
sorry ass.

Nate stood there, shocked. "What's going on? Who the hell is this?"

The stranger said, "I'm Cooper. Who are you?" He poked his chest
out.

"I'm her motherfucking boyfriend and an ass-whooping waiting to
happen, nigga. I sure as hell hope that you are her cousin or some
shit," Nate said, pointing a finger in Cooper's face.

"Hold up, man. You need to calm the fuck down. She didn't say
nothing about no boyfriend to me."

"Nate, you need to leave," India said.

"What?" Nate said, with a stunned look on his face.

"You heard me. Nigga, you need to go." India was starting to focus
on her pain. "You didn't call me all fucking weekend when you were
off with that bitch." Nate's eyes gave away his guilt. "Yeah, motherfucker. I followed your ass on Thursday night. When you were spitting
all those lies about your grandmother being in the car, and taking her
out of town and shit . . . I was right behind you on my cellphone. I had
just left Union Station and had come straight to your apartment. I saw
you pulling out of the gate, and I was going to pull up next to you, but
you were driving too fast. By the time I got close enough to you to
honk my horn you had called me. The next thing I know . . . you were
telling me all of these fucking lies. When you said your grandmother

was in the car, I thought that you were just playing with me, and that
you had seen my car. When you kept on lying, though, I decided to
follow your ass . . . and . . ."

Cooper cut her off. "I don't want to get in the middle of this shit.
India, you two obviously need to talk. You can just call me later, okay?"

"No, Cooper, you stay. He's about to leave. Here." She handed
Cooper the keys. "The alarm isn't on. Go in and wait. I'll be right in."

"Are you sure?" Cooper asked. India nodded. "Are you alright out
here?"

"Nigga, go on in the house before I fuck around and whip your ass
out here," Nate yelled.

Cooper shot a nasty glance at Nate, but the one Nate shot back was
meaner and more threatening. The shit was getting too real for
Cooper, so he walked into the house. "I thought so," Nate said.

"Look, I don't know what gave you the nerve to come around here
after the shit you pulled, Nate. I know that you've probably been fooling around with other women the whole time. I should have left you
alone a long time ago. I saw the signs a long time ago . . . I just didn't
listen to them."

"India, you don't know what's really going on."

"Oh, but I do. And you know what?" India's big eyes looked straight
at Nate. "It doesn't even matter anymore. I've had enough."

"So you been fucking around on me the whole time, huh?" Nate
asked. He was hurting. He was talking to India, but he was seeing
Sahleen's face in front of him.

"No, I swear. I'm not like that. I'm not like you."

"So who the hell is this faggot?"

"Cooper is a friend."

Nate interrupted with "How long have you known this nigga?"

"A month, two months, what difference does it make? Bye, Nate."

"So you been screwing this nigga?"

"Look, I know I shouldn't have left that message. It was tacky and
beneath me. I'm sorry. But it was the truth. Last night was the first
time I was with Cooper."

Nate's heart dropped. For the second time in twenty-four hours he had been the victim of a bomb dropping on his head. "What the fuck did you say? You left a message on my machine. You left a message on my machine telling me that you sexed that nigga?"

Nate put his hand on his mouth and then moved it up his face, massaging his mouth first and then his temples. He was seeing Sahleen's face again. India was backing away when Nate reached out and grabbed her neck. "Bitch, you must be fucking crazy. How are you going to do some shit like that to me? Just because I was gone for the weekend, you go and fuck somebody else."

Nate was oblivious to how hard he was choking India. "Girl . . . I was about to make everything right between us. But you went and did this dumb shit."

"Let me go," she tried to mumble out, as she started to scratch Nate's hands. His grip was secure, though. Tears were running out of India's eyes.

"I bet you like women, too," Nate growled out. Then he realized what he was doing and let her go.

India was coughing and crying. Nate was about to apologize when he saw India's front door open and Cooper come running out of the house with a bat. Nate saw him and ran toward his car. "Cooper, noooo, please don't," she yelled, as he ran past her with the bat, toward Nate's car. By the time he got to Nate's car, the top half of Nate's body had reappeared out of the car. He was holding a black nine-millimeter in his hand. It was pointed in Cooper's face. Nate was standing still, his face was like ice. Cooper stood with the bat cocked over his shoulder.

"Do it," Nate said in a low voice. "Give me a reason." Nate saw fear in Cooper's face. His bottom lip was trembling.

India was screaming in the background, begging Cooper to come back and go into the house. Just then India's neighbor pulled through the lot and parked. India was frantic and ran to the door of the Cadillac to ask Mr. Watkins, who was at least sixty years old, for help.

Meanwhile, Nate had eased his body from behind the door of his Lexus and was separated from Cooper by only a few feet. "Bitch-ass nigga, once you put that bat down, I'm gonna whip your ass, and I mean bad," Nate said, as he moved threateningly toward Cooper. "After I beat the shit out of you, I'm going to give her the gifts that I have in my trunk, make up to her, and then go in the house and fuck the shit out of her."

Cooper's face tightened as he rocked his body back slightly to keep his balance and said, "Like I did last night . . . and this morning."

A sudden flash of anger shot through his body at Cooper's mocking words. Nate instinctively cocked the pistol, and out of fear Cooper swung the bat. India and Mr. Watkins's bodies both shook when they heard the deafening crack of Nate's pistol followed by crashing glass. India ran toward Cooper as Nate went into his car and was pulling off within seconds. Mr. Watkins dropped his bowling bag and sprinted toward his door. India called out to him, but Mr. Watkins ignored her and nearly broke his screen door trying to get into his house.

India was hysterical when she reached Cooper, who was trying to get up. He was holding the side of his head, especially his ear, which was ringing loudly.

He stood and removed his hand from his head. He stared at his hands, which revealed no blood. India inspected him thoroughly and assured him that he hadn't been hit. Although he couldn't hear out of his left ear, he was fine. He was shaking and his pants were wet, which he didn't realize until India pointed it out to him. She offered to drive him to the hospital to get his ear checked out, but he refused and headed toward his jeep.

India didn't put up a fuss as she watched him pull off even faster than Nate had. She was still a wreck herself and barely made it to the house. As she walked toward her door she could see Mr. Watkins on the phone, staring out of his bay window. She walked into her house, grabbed her keys, and prepared to leave. She suspected that he was talking to the police, so she left a note on her door that read "Angie, I am running to the mall. I'll be back in a couple of hours. 4:15."

Never mind that she didn't know anyone named Angie; the note was for the police, whom she didn't feel like dealing with. She passed the cops and their flashing lights as she drove out onto Ritchie Road. She silently prayed that her note would keep them from bursting through her door in search of survivors. Although she was through with him, she wasn't mentally prepared to turn Nate in to the police, nor was she ready to be berated by detectives. It probably wasn't a

good idea for her to leave the scene of the crime, but she hadn't com-
mitted one. She had been the victim . . . in more ways than one. On
top of it all she felt as though she had provoked Nate by leaving the
nasty messages on his voice mail.

So India just drove and thought. She came to the conclusion that
Nate was crazy, as well as a dog. There was no way that she would ever
have anything else to do with him. She did enjoy Cooper's company,
and even hoped that they might start something, but she doubted that
he was ever coming back around.

At around six India wound up at her cousin Monique's house in
Clinton, where she found Monique and her live-in boyfriend cooking
outside on the grill. There was another couple there, and India spoke
to them before she pulled her cousin to the side. She chose not to confide in Monique about the events of the weekend. She only told her
that she needed somewhere to stay for a night or two. Knowing that
India had her own place, Monique found her request a little strange,
and though Monique was a little worried, she quickly agreed without
asking questions. The two of them had been close since childhood, and
Monique knew that if India wanted to talk about something she
would. So she went on about her business entertaining and didn't
think twice about bothering India when she went into the guest room
and closed the door behind her.

Chapter 25

A KISS AND A SLIP

Brendan had been at odds for a month. He had been trying hard to regain some type of footing in his life. He was wrestling with issues in his social life as he had never before. He spent so much time envisioning how things would be once they all were smoothed out, but he realized that he had entertained the same vision ten years before. Before, it had been, wait until I get my driver's license, wait until I graduate high school, wait until I get my own place, or wait until I get a nice car and a good girlfriend. Everything was supposed to signal the change in his life. Instead, every change brought more anxiety, and every woman brought a new set of dilemmas to his world.

He and Renee had been trying to fix the friendship that had made a wrong turn and landed the two of them in bed together. It was almost the Fourth of July, and they had only slept together once in the previous month. He was sleeping in his own room again, and even the one night they had slipped up and wound up in bed together, it was Renee who had come into his room waking him up. Even though neither of them had mentioned it the next day, there was obvious tension.

Brendan feared that the relationship had changed for good. He no longer felt comfortable talking to Renee about other women. Specifically about Laney or Trina, who had started calling him again and talking about their nonexistent future. Around the middle part of June Laney had come back to town after taking care of her nephew for almost two months. Things had been up in the air with them since

Brendan had apologized to her for being so judgmental and had started spending time with her again, though only at her apartment. Laney hadn't questioned not being invited to Brendan's place.

Laney had been suspicious about Brendan and Renee's relationship since the night she had paid him the surprise visit and found them both in nightclothes at eight-thirty. It had taken much restraint but Laney had held her tongue on the matter, since she was still trying to weasel her way back into Brendan's life. She was too tactful to come back into his life and start accusing him of fucking his best friend after all of the things that she'd held from him.

Trina, on the other hand, often came right out and told Brendan that she wanted him back. She didn't seem to understand the word "no" and continued to push and pressure Brendan to see her. The two had bumped into each other in Miami during Soul Fest on Memorial Day Weekend. Brendan was in shape and looking better than she had ever remembered.

Brendan's hormones had gotten the best of him while in Miami. The vacation had been coming to a close and Brendan had been frustrated that he had not gotten laid during the trip. On his last night there Brendan had gotten drunk and foolishly begged Trina to come back to his room with him. Trina had been drunk as well and all too willing to oblige him. She knew the effect that her sex had on Brendan. She knew that it always forced him to open up his heart, mind, and sometimes his wallet to her. Miami had been no exception, and Brendan had felt as though he had shot himself in the foot the next morning.

Brendan had no problems confessing that during the past year he had made more than his share of mistakes. He had allowed himself to be crushed by Trina, betrayed by Laney, but worst of all, he had used Renee. He was trying to navigate his way through situations with three women who couldn't have been more different. Although he'd somehow flipped the script with Trina, and was actually learning to enjoy her begging, he was still dealing with the mistakes he had made with Laney and Renee. He still viewed the situations with them as fixable, though. Laney seemed to be happy that he was spending time with her again, and at times Brendan couldn't tell who was forgiving whom. It was obvious to him that he had been a tad too harsh in judging her, but she had lied terribly, and getting over those lies wasn't easy for him. Every now and again images of Laney bending over, showing her ass in a smoke-filled club for tips, flashed through his mind and sickened him. When he was with her he wondered if he would ever be able to get past it all.

What he felt was most important was his hope that sooner or later things would get back to normal between him and Renee. Brendan somehow had not picked up on the fact that for the last couple of months Renee had begun to shut down and hold in her true feelings for him. While he walked around thinking that the sex had merely been a result of the two of them living under the same roof, as if it was some sort of a side effect, Renee was dealing with feelings that ran deeper than merely friendship. Had Brendan actually thought more seriously about the situation, he would have realized that he should have known her better, and that Renee wouldn't have been the type to screw him simply because he was there. Instead, Brendan walked around in his own world, believing that as rough as things had gotten, they could get no worse.

Chapter 26

FIREWORKS

I t was way too hot to be outside, but my mother had insisted that we eat outside. "It's a cookout, everybody, not a cook-in. Now get out of my basement," she told everybody who kept trying to sneak in and soak up some of the air-conditioning. Even at 6:00 P.M. it still was at least 90 degrees and as muggy as ever outside. It was, in fact, typical D.C. summer weather.

My mother was enjoying her annual Fourth of July gathering. It was the first one that I had made it to in five years. I had never bothered coming home for the Fourth because there had always been too many other dates that I had had to come home for during the rest of the year. I had had to pick and choose. I couldn't have missed Mother's Day, Christmas, or Kyle's birthday, and I had come home each year to accompany my mother to my father's gravesite on his birthday. He would have been fifty-seven this August. Time was flying.

As I sat in the shade sipping on a Corona, I remembered my father working the grill every Fourth of July and cooking enough food to feed an army. He had been a good cook, too. Nobody could come near his grill when he was working. He was always accusing somebody of trying to steal the recipe for his secret sauce. During his days on the grill he never told anyone how he made it, not even my mother. But the day we went to the reading of his will the lawyer handed Freddie an envelope that contained the deed to their parents' home in North Carolina and, to everyone's surprise, the recipe for his secret barbecue sauce. Since that day my uncle Freddie has taken over the grill. Now

Freddie guards that recipe with his life. It was almost like having my father back one day a year.

There were at least thirty people at the house this year. Nina, who was helping my mother host, was busy running back and forth to the kitchen until she started to complain about the heat and feeling dizzy. Her allergies hadn't bothered her in a couple of months, but Moms ended up making her lay down upstairs in the cool confines of my bedroom while Brenda took over. All of my crew was there as usual, plus I had invited a couple of other folks. My barber, Dee, had shown up, accompanied by two honeys, neither of whom looked older than seventeen. My cousin James had come, and he had brought his wife, Gina, and their two boys, James Jr. and Manny. Brendan had come, and he had brought Laney with him.

Nate had shown up with a honey no one had ever seen or heard of before. She was, of course, nice looking, but there didn't seem to be a lot of chemistry between them. I noticed that she wasn't much of a conversationalist. She was the type who answered questions with as few words as possible. I knew from the look on Nate's face that she was driving him crazy. When she went inside for a minute to use the bathroom and left Nate alone, I jumped at the opportunity to ask.

"What's up with her, Nate? She doesn't talk a lot, huh?"

"I know. She's acting all stuck-up and shit. I'm about to run her ass home. I'm not even pressed to crush it now," Nate said, twisting his lips as he pulled the Corona from them.

Dee heard us talking and leaned back on the bench toward us. "Nate. Is that the broad from South Beach . . . the one with her belly button pierced?"

"Yeah."

I remembered her then. "Damn, you're still talking to her. I thought you said . . ." Dee joined in with me and we said it at the same time: "What ever happens in South Beach stays in South Beach." And then we laughed.

"I know, but I didn't fuck her, though. She was on her period when I met her. And when she left she was still on it. She has been trying to hook up with me ever since we got back."

"Damn, we been back for a month and you been that busy." Dee laughed. "She should have given up by now."

Nate laughed, but I knew better. Nate had been acting strange for the last two months. Ever since he had come back from New York in early May he had been tripping. He hadn't so much as mentioned Sahleen. When I had tried to ask him about her he just said that she was overseas for the summer working, and he wasn't going to sit around waiting for her. But knowing Nate the way I did, I sensed something else in his tone and in his eyes, but I hadn't bothered to question him.

He had told me that he had broken it off with India as well, simply because she kept pressing him for a commitment. That sounded about right. For as much as I had gotten a chance to know her, I did take her to be the serious type who would want a commitment from a man who she was sleeping with.

Nate's date, Monica, walked back over toward us and sat down next to Nate. It was too hot for the tight jeans she was wearing, and they were black on top of that. Some sisters will do what they must in order to properly flaunt their asses, I guess. I couldn't help but take a good long look at it before I got up and left to go check on Nina.

I pushed open the door to my room and peeked inside. My princess was lying on her side, fast asleep it appeared, and I started to slip back out when she spoke: "Cory." She rolled halfway over and looked up at me.

"Hey, baby, I thought you were asleep. You feeling okay?" I walked over and sat down on the bed next to her.

"I'm fine. I was a little dizzy earlier, but yeah, I'm fine now. It feels so good in here," she said in a whispery, sleepy voice.

"Do you want something to eat or drink? I'll bring it up," I said. I walked over toward the window and I could see into the backyard. I was watching my mother as she sat with a group of her good friends. My aunt Earline was next to my mother, and they were laughing, having a real good time. Mr. Fields was on her other side and was glaring at her.

I had noticed the way he looked at my mom whenever he was

around. It was obvious that he had a thing for my mom, but I think he was afraid to pursue it for one reason or another. I had no problem with it. As a matter of fact, I'd mentioned it to Brenda, and we shared a good-natured laugh about the two of them hooking up. I even hoped that he might get up the nerve to finally ask her out.

"No, I'm not really hungry." Nina paused, as she was now staring right up into my face. "Not for food anyway." She smiled.

I knew what that meant, and I leaned down to kiss her before I got up and locked the door to my old bedroom. Nina was a perfect match for me. She was the kind of woman every man dreams of having. It wasn't just about her looks, either. It was about how she complemented me in every way and, just as important, about how she was always in the mood, just like me.

I pulled off my T-shirt and shorts and was naked in seconds. She was almost as fast coming out of her halter top and wraparound miniskirt. My face immediately dove down between her thighs, but she stopped me.

"No, Cory. I'm already wet. I want you inside of me, now," she said, pulling me up by my ears.

I put up no arguments as I quickly slid my body up hers and slowly worked inside of her. She began to moan and rhythmically lift her hips off the bed to meet my every stroke. My upper body was suspended over the top of her as we looked into each other's eyes between moments of rapture that made us high off one another. I began to shower her face with kisses. I kissed her eyebrows, her nose, her cheeks, and her lips. I could feel the slight pinch of her fingernails as she squeezed my butt while she attempted to pull me deeper inside of her.

"Oh, Nina," I heard myself say when I felt her body begin to quiver. "I love you so much. I love you so much, baby."

"Do I make you feel good? Huh, Cory. Do I?" she said.

"Oh, yeah, you do, baby . . ." I was cut off when she screamed out.

"Baby, I'm about to come. Ohhhhhh . . ."

Her body began to buck and her back tightened up as her moans increased. Neither of us seemed to care that there were people out back or possibly in the basement. She flung her head to the side as she reached her peak. I could feel her muscles contracting and the sensation caused me to reach my orgasm as well. We both panted our way through the sensations and tremors, and I collapsed on top of Nina's golden body.

We weren't sweating, but there was a light moist shine on our skins. I rolled off Nina and she placed her head on my chest while her hand fondled my manhood. She always did that after we finished.

"You better get up and go back outside with your friends before they come looking for you," Nina said.

"Or send my mother to do it." I laughed out as I stood up. I looked at Nina lying naked on the bed, and I knew I would be ready to take her home soon. I wanted to finish what we had started.

She grabbed her clothes and walked out of the room and into the bathroom, after grabbing a washcloth from the linen closet. I didn't bother washing and just put my clothes back on. I knew that my underwear would be stuck to me later, but I didn't care. I fixed the covers and looked outside and saw that no one had missed us. Brendan and Laney were sitting across from Nate and Monica, and they were all playing cards. Everyone else seemed to be enjoying themselves.

Nina walked back into the room and took her spot back on the bed. I tied up my tennis shoes and was about to head back outside when Nina said, "I'm going to stay in here. It's just too hot out there for me."

I nodded my head and said, "Okay." I looked at my watch. "It's almost seven. We can leave in about an hour if we're going to go watch the fireworks."

"I'm not really pressed. I enjoyed the best fireworks in town just now." She smiled.

I smiled back. "I bet you did."

"Cory."

"Yeah."

"If I tell you something . . ." She paused and tilted her head. "Can we agree not to discuss it any further right now?"

"That depends on what it is."

"No. It is a yes or no question. So, can I tell you something?"

"And I'm not going to want to discuss it right now?" I asked.

She shifted her body so that she was completely on the bed. "I didn't say that you weren't going to want to discuss it."

"Look. Just spit it out."

"Who are you talking to like that?"

"Pardon me, Nina. Please just tell me what it is." She was beginning to irk me. I knew that whatever it was it wasn't going to be all that important. She just liked to rile me up because she could.

"Okay, that's better. So you agree that when I say what it is that you will walk out of the room and not bother me about it until at least tomorrow." Her lips were turned up as she smirked.

"Deal," I said, as I stood by the door. "You haven't cheated on me. Because if you have the deal is off."

She laughed. "No, stupid. I haven't cheated on you." Then she was silent and just looked into my eyes.

I looked back. "Well," I said.

"I'm pregnant." There was silence. "Now go outside," she said, and turned back on her side.

I stood there motionless for about fifteen seconds before I walked back over to her. I didn't say a word. I just kissed her long and hard, held her tight for a long while, and then I was so overwhelmed with emotion that I made love to her once again.

After we finished she kissed me on the forehead and whispered into my ear, "That was the correct response. Congratulations, Cory, you're going to be a wonderful daddy."

"And husband," I added.

"What?" she said, as she leaned her face back to look at me.

"I want you to marry me." I swallowed. "I mean, will you marry me, Nina?" I corrected myself.

Without hesitation she said, gleaming, "Of course I will marry you, baby, but you're going to have to propose to me a little better than this." She laughed.

I nodded my head and responded, "Tomorrow we will go pick out your ring, and I promise that that will take care of the real proposal."

"Are you sure that you're ready for that? We don't have to get married just because of a baby, Cory."

I shook my head. "You know better than that. You know I love you, and you love me, too. There will never be anybody else for me, and no one is going to love you the way that I do." She smiled.

She was about to speak when I put my finger on her mouth. "You know I'm right. This is what I've been waiting for all my life. This is it." I got up, put my clothes on, and headed toward the door after having spent the last hour inside with Nina. She called my name and stopped me at the door.

"Cory . . ."

I stood there looking at her.

"Are you sure that you're happy about this?" Her big brown eyes were staring into mine. "I mean . . . really?" she asked.

"Yeah, baby . . . really." I smiled, because I truly was pleased at the thought of bringing a life into this world with Nina. Then I turned the knob and walked out of the room.

I had just walked back to the picnic table where Brendan and Laney were whipping Nate and his date, Monica, in spades.

"Where you been, boy? You missed this clinic in spades," Brendan said, as I sat down next to him.

"I was inside checking on Nina. She's not feeling too well. She's got bad allergies."

Brendan nodded. Laney said, "Maybe she should take that prescription stuff."

"Claritin? Yeah, she already does, but sometimes it works, sometimes it doesn't."

"That's a shame," Laney said.

"C'mon, Nate, throw something out," Brendan yelled.

"Man, shut up. Don't tell me how to play my hand," Nate barked back.

"Is that what you call yourself doing? Monica, I understand if you want to get a new partner." Brendan laughed.

Nate finally threw out the king of spades, and Laney took the book with the little joker.

"They're going to renege, Laney." Brendan laughed out. "They're going to renege."

Nate shouted out, "Shit." But not loud enough for the older peeps to hear. Then he said, "That's it, then. I quit." Nate huffed.

"Don't quit, Nate," Monica said.

"Look, we were only playing to five hundred. They have four hundred now, and we've got . . . What do we got, Laney?"

"Minus thirty-seven," she answered.

"A fucking minus thirty-seven." He shook his head. Then he yelled at Dee, who was sitting on the deck drinking a beer and talking to my cousin James. The two young ladies whom he had brought with him were playing volleyball with James's two sons. "Dee. It's your game if you still want to play."

Dee just waved. He was drunk.

As I popped open another ice cold Corona, Tory came running out of the house. "Hey, everybody . . . Nate is on TV."

We all just looked at her. "He's on a video, with Shawn Simmons. You better hurry up," she yelled, and then disappeared back into the house.

Brendan was the first one up. I followed, with everyone else who was at the table. I looked back to see Nate moving coolly in the back of the crowd. I was expecting to see someone who looked like Nate, but when I entered the basement and took a look at the screen, there was Nate's black ass walking hand in hand with Shawn Simmons. I turned and looked at him. He looked like he was holding in a smile.

"Y'all move over," I heard my mother say, as everyone moved out of her way. "Well, look at that," she said. "Nate, I didn't know that you were an actor." He was sitting at a table in a silk robe with a glass of champagne watching Shawn sing. Nate was now smiling. He was feeling proud of himself. He really looked like he belonged on that screen. The people at Excite World Video had done a superb job with the special effects. There was a haze, and the glow from the candles seemed to reflect off his body.

My mother's basement was filled with oohs and ahhs as we watched the dance steps. Nate hadn't watched them film that scene. He had gone shopping. He still had the clothes that he had bought for India and Sahleen in his closet. At that instant, he decided what he was going to do with all of the stuff he had bought. There was at least two thousand dollars worth of fine clothing in the bags, all of it sizes four and smalls. Otherwise he would have sent it to his mother.

Nate was taking notice of the sequence of the video. The scenes had been shot in almost the complete opposite order, which meant that . . .

"Oh my God," I heard Laney yell out. "Look at you, Nate." Nate was in bed with Shawn Simmons, kissing her on the mouth. He looked like he was completely naked and so did she. I couldn't believe it. I watched as their bodies writhed underneath the satin sheets.

"Kyle, cover your eyes. Tory, you too," my sister Brenda said. "I can't believe these damn videos today," she said, as she shook her head and looked at Nate. Even though she was three years older than Nate, she acted as though she had always wanted to screw him . . . if she hadn't already.

The video went off and everybody, including me, began asking him a thousand and one questions, as though he were at a press conference or something. It was incredible. He hadn't said anything about being in a video, let alone with Shawn Simmons. The chick Monica who he was with looked as though she was ready to rip his clothes off right there and take him in front of everyone. His new star status had done a number on her head, and the two girls who were with Dee as well. It was no surprise when Dee quickly rolled out, taking his two hotties with him.

As the sun set on the cookout, every one began to leave one by one, and soon there was only Nina and myself in the house. Brenda had convinced Mr. Fields and Momma to ride downtown to see the fireworks with her and the kids.

Brendan had left with Laney to take advantage of a rare opportunity to have the townhouse to himself. Renee had gone out of town, to Virginia Beach, for the Fourth, with one of her Delta sorors. On the way home he and Laney joked about the "fireworks agreement" that they had made on New Year's Eve. Then they talked about how they almost hadn't made it this year, but how glad they were that they had. I didn't even see them leave, but I knew that Nate and Monica undoubtedly had headed back to his place to make their own fireworks.

Nina and I ended up staying the night at my mother's in my old room. We stayed up until about eleven talking about our wedding, our baby, and our future. Nina cried at least twice, saying that she had had no idea that I would be so good about it. She said that she had thought that my career was my only focus, and that I wouldn't want a baby or even a wife to interfere. She had been wrong, because we were definitely getting married and having a baby.

Everything was looking good. The future was set. The only thing I had to do was find the right time to tell her that Mr. Hakito was going to need me in New York for about six months or so, starting in the fall. I knew that Nina wouldn't want to go, but it was only temporary. I had to go and take over the New York/New Jersey production and keep it on track while the Hakitos went back to Tokyo for a short time. I was told that I was the only one they trusted to handle things while they were gone. I had no choice. Six months wouldn't be that rough.

We drifted off and fell into a deep sleep. When I woke up at 4:00 A.M. and got up to relieve myself, I saw that my mother's door was still open. When I stuck my head in I saw that her bed was empty I almost freaked out. I woke Nina and called my sister.

"Cory, Mom is fine."

"How do you know?" I asked. "What if they got into an accident on the way back here?"

"Back here . . . where are you?" Brenda asked in a sleepy voice.

"I'm still at Mom's house."

"Well, Mr. Fields drove downtown in his Lincoln. I left my car there, so he had to bring us back there to get my car. We didn't see your car there when we got back. We thought you were gone."

"We came in Nina's car."

"Oh," she cleared her throat. "Look outside. Is his car in his driveway?"

I walked to the bay window in the kitchen and looked in his driveway, and sure enough his car was parked. "Yeah, it's there."

"Well then, Cory."

"Well then, what?" I still didn't get it.

"Cory, Mom never told you about her and Mr. Fields?"

"What?"

"Never mind," she said. "Cory."

"Yeah."

"Go back to bed. Moms is fine. Believe me." She laughed.

It all came to me, and it made my head swim. I couldn't believe it. But I said okay and went back up the steps.

"Is everything okay?" Nina asked.

"Yeah," I said, sounding dejected, or maybe embarrassed was a better word.

"Where's your mom?"

"Across the street, at Mr. Fields's crib."

Nina laughed. Then she said something in Spanish.

"What did you . . . never mind."

"I said that your mother has to get busy too every now and then. She's only fifty-something, not a hundred."

"Leave me alone," I grumbled.

"Don't playa hate con-grat-u-late, Pappi," she laughed out and rolled back over. "Goodnight again."

I just lay there and tried not to imagine my moms getting her freak on as I drifted back to sleep. I had enjoyed an eventful Fourth of July, and now all of my tomorrows were coming quickly, all at once, it seemed.

Chapter 27

TRUE TO THY OWN HEART

Brendan never even heard the front door. Maybe Laney's passionate screams had been too loud, or maybe he was just too comfortable. His bedroom door was standing wide open, and it took no more than a few seconds for Renee to witness more than she could stand. When she flipped the hall light on, partially exposing Brendan's nakedness as he moved on top of Laney, Brendan's face turned toward where Renee stood in the door, and his eyes grew to the size of golf balls.

Laney looked around Brendan to see Renee standing in the doorway wearing a scowl that would have massacred them both if looks could kill. Laney didn't know what was going on, and was even more confused when she saw Renee burst into tears and run off into her room. Brendan climbed off her and sat on the bed with his head in his lap.

"What's going on, Brendan?" Laney sat up and pulled on Brendan's shoulder. "What the hell is wrong with Renee?"

Brendan huffed deeply and reached for his shorts. "It's a long story. Put your clothes on. I'll explain on the way to your place."

"What . . . Why do we . . . ?" Brendan stopped her.

He turned and looked at Laney with the sternest of looks. "I said put your shit on and come on."

Laney was taken back by Brendan's harsh tone. She had only seen him become like that a few times. Brendan was becoming colder through all the abuse he'd suffered in the name of love, and he was quicker to snap than he had ever been before. Trina had brought out that side of him. Brendan, though, was unaware of how he was changing, from the pushover that he had been a few years back into a brother who wasn't putting up with foolishness. Every experience he had weathered in the last couple of years had seemed to intensify the effect.

Laney was now moving in fast motion. She slipped her sandals on, grabbed her purse, and headed down the steps. Brendan looked up at Renee's closed door as he walked behind Laney. As they left the front door and headed toward the car, Brendan wondered why Renee had come home. She was supposed to be in Virginia Beach until late the next afternoon.

It was a little past midnight, and he had just been caught literally with his pants down. Not that he had a commitment to Renee other than friendship, but Brendan knew that his sexing Laney under Renee's roof had added insult to injury.

Brendan quickly reviewed the first night that they had slipped up and made love. Then, after deciding to end their trial relationship and go back to being friends, there had been a relapse. Watching a DVD one night together in Renee's room had ended up with them bumping and grinding on her floor. The sex had been passionate. Before, during, and after her orgasm, Renee had told him that she was in love with him and always had been.

Though neither of them had mentioned it since, Renee had made her true feelings known to Brendan. Lying to himself had now gotten him in a precarious position. The girl who once had been a form of inspiration now seemed more like a gloomy cloud of guilt looming over his head. He had hurt her already, and now he'd added disrespect on top of it. Even as unintentional as it had been, it was done.

As Brendan drove around the Beltway toward Laney's apartment, he explained everything to her. Coming clean to Laney wasn't hard for him, and he felt stupid for not having done it before. He could have avoided the whole scene that had just transpired. When Laney asked him why he had held back and not told her, Brendan replied honestly, "I guess I was trying to make up my mind."

"About what?"

"I guess about whether I was going to give you and I another try or if I was going to see how things worked out with Renee," Brendan said softly. Laney shifted her body toward Brendan, and he noticed that she didn't have her seat belt on. "Put your seat belt on."

Laney complied, and the two rode in silence the rest of the way. When they reached Laney's complex, Brendan parked and the two of them began to talk. Laney turned to him and said, "I'm glad you chose me." Then she kissed him on the cheek. Then she said, "Look I know how much you care about her. So I won't ask you to stay . . ." She opened her door. "I mean, you can if you want to, but you probably should go home and deal with her . . . you know, apologize for hurting her and everything."

"Yeah, I know," Brendan said, looking straight ahead.

"Do you want me to call and talk to her? You know, like, to apologize."

"Hell, no. For what?" Brendan shot back. "No."

Laney waved her hands in front of her chest. "Okay, okay. Calm down." She leaned back into the car and kissed Brendan again. "Call me if you need me, okay?"

"Okay."

"I love you, Brendan Shue."

"I know. I love you, too." He said, while his eyes asked if she was worth all of this.

"Are you sure you don't want to come in for a minute? You know we didn't get to finish." Laney offered a naughty smile, and Brendan folded.

It was almost noon when Brendan returned to the house. Renee was sure to be at church. Brendan parked his car in the lot and noticed people washing their cars and little kids playing as he walked to the front of the townhouse. As he approached the front door, he noticed that it was open. He made it to the foyer before he saw Gladys and Andrea sitting in the kitchen sipping iced tea while they were blasting his Luther CD. There were two boxes stacked in the dining room, and there were garment bags on top of them. Next to those were two large suitcases and his duffel bag.

"Good morning, ladies," Brendan said, as he walked up the five steps into the living room and headed toward the kitchen.

Gladys rolled her eyes and walked upstairs. Andrea stood up. "Hello, Brendan."

Brendan looked up the steps. "There's no reason for you to go up there, Brendan," Andrea said. As they both turned to the door in response to the tapping at the front door. Andrea waved her hand to signal for the two men to come in.

Andrea walked over to the two men and took a receipt and a key and handed them a hundred-dollar bill. "Thanks, Ms. Carter."

"No. Thank you," Andrea said, and turned back toward Brendan. The two young men turned and walked back out of the door as fast as they had come in. "Here, Brendan. These are for you."

"What's going on?" Brendan asked.

Andrea took a seat on the steps. "Listen here, Brendan." Andrea fumbled through her purse. "Renee no longer wants you here. Here is the rent that you paid for the month of July. It's only the fifth, so she's not charging you for the days that you've been here. This is your receipt for the storage."

"What storage, Andrea?"

"All of your things have been moved professionally into storage. It's located right up the street on Central Avenue, just past the McDonald's, on the opposite side of the street. Renee has paid for two months' storage in advance. Anything after that, you have to pay for. These are the keys." Andrea could see that Brendan didn't have a clue what to say, so she kept talking. "These are the only things that she figured you would need right away." She pointed toward the boxes. "Those are personal items, shoes, and underclothes, etc., etc. I think you can fit the rest of that stuff in your car. If you need me, though, I can follow you wherever you need to go."

"I don't believe this shit," Brendan said, as he started up the stairs.

"He's coming upstairs, y'all." Andrea yelled out.

Renee's door slammed shut, and Brendan heard the lock. He walked past his room. It was naked except for the picture on the wall that had been there already when he moved in. The floor was freshly vacuumed and incense was burning on the windowsill.

Brendan knocked on Renee's door. "Open the damn door, Renee. Why are you acting so petty?" No answer. "Renee. We really should talk about things. I'll leave. But we still should talk."

Brendan knocked again and again before he finally turned and walked past Andrea.

"Do you get it, Brendan?" Gladys said, as she popped out of the door and closed it again behind her. Brendan turned around and started back toward the room. "She doesn't have shit to say. You ain't shit. You're just like Nate and Cory."

"How could you be so damn trifling, Brendan?" Andrea joined in. "In her own house, on top of it all. That's so wrong. I thought you were different, and I told her that by letting you move in it would mess up a good friendship, but I never would have guessed it would be something like this."

"She's in there still crying," Gladys added. "She said to tell you that when and if she decides to talk to you again, that she'll call you. So if you were ever her friend . . . if you ever cared about her . . . don't call her or come around, because you are no longer welcome."

Brendan's face held back the sting that it felt from those words. He knew that they had come straight from Renee's mouth. He knew her. He knew that those would be her words had she spoken to him. So with that, he turned around and went downstairs, packed his car, and drove back to Laney's.

Chapter 28

DOG DAYS OF SUMMER

On a Friday night in mid-August, Nate, Brendan, and I decided to get together and have some drinks at one of our usual hangout spots. Brendan and I were sitting in one of the booths closest to the backgammon tables in Jasper's Restaurant in Greenbelt while Nate was at the bar getting us our third round of drinks because our waiter was moving too slowly. It was packed as usual for a Friday night. There were people everywhere enjoying the happy hour, as they had for the last fifteen or so years that the place had been open. In addition to our waiter's slow service, Nate had said that he didn't want the bill at the table to go over one hundred dollars, because then they would automatically add the gratuity in. He said he always liked to decide what to give his waiter or waitress himself.

While we waited for the drinks and the champagne we talked about everything from sports to politics. We argued over which had been more live, the Soul Fest, in Miami, or the Essence Festival the prior year, in New Orleans. Brendan talked smack about how good the Skins were going to be this year. All of the magazines were picking them to finish over the Cowboys but behind the Eagles and Giants again. "Yeah, right," I had yelled in response.

When Nate came back over with the drinks, he nearly bumped into Bob, who had finally brought out our Buffalo wings and barbecued shrimp. Nate began pouring into the glasses as we each slammed shots of one kind or another.

"Yo man, a couple of chicken heads over there were sweating me because of that video," Nate laughed.

"Aw, nigga, you know you love that shit," Brendan said, and I nodded my head as I stuffed my mouth with a wing.

Nate, doing his best Chris Tucker impersonation, said, "And you know this, mannnnn." Then he laughed at himself. "They wanted to come over here and drink with us, but I told them broads maybe on the next bottle. This one here is just for the fellas."

"Yeah, we need to chill. We haven't had a chance to kick it since you hit us with the bomb, Cory," Brendan said with greasy lips.

"Yeah, I know. Lick those soup coolers, bro. You lookin' like a slave up in this piece." We laughed as my grammar slipped into its after-hours format. "So, what do you think? Are you going to be in the wedding or what?"

"C'mon fool, what kind of question is that? I'm going to give your punk ass away," Nate laughed out.

"So, when is it? When you gonna do this thing?" Brendan asked.

"October. The first weekend," I answered, and grabbed another wing.

Nate sat back. "You lying. That soon? What's the rush, nigga? Is she pregnant?" Nate said jokingly.

"Yep."

I watched and smiled as I saw both of them stop chewing. Then together they both asked, "For real?"

"Yeah, for real. She won't be showing that soon. She wants to do it before the baby comes," I commented.

"Damn," Nate said.

"What's all that for?" Brendan said. "It's a wedding, not a funeral."

"I know, that's good shit and all. It's just soon. But fuck it . . . y'all grown. Congratulations, dog." Nate extended his hand. "I mean that, man, from the bottom of my heart. And it don't hurt that she's a fine sumthin' sumthin' too. Gonna make a pretty-ass baby." Nate rambled on. "If it's a girl, I want to be the godfather, so I can spoil her."

"What if it's a boy?" I asked.

He pointed at Brendan. "Then Mr. Nice Guy can be the godfather. He'll be a better example for a boy."

"Hell, I don't know. All the shit he's been going through lately. He getting more like you every day."

Brendan smiled. "Whatever, nigga. If I was like him, I wouldn't have gotten caught, and I wouldn't be living with Laney's ass right now."

Renee had thrown him out of her townhouse on the Fourth of July weekend. He had been staying with Laney for the last five weeks. He hadn't had the time to give moving in with her any thought, but he figured that since it was Laney's fault that he had gotten kicked out, why should he even consider moving in with his parents? When he'd shown right back up at her house with his bags and boxes, an hour after leaving, Laney had secretly rejoiced. She finally had Brendan all to herself, at least in body.

"How's that going?" I asked.

"Not bad. Just not much space. I'm just getting used to it . . . but sometimes I still think about all that stuff that went down in the spring, and then the sight of her pisses me off. But other than that . . . everything is cool."

Nate pointed a finger and waved it at Brendan. "Your ass ain't in love no more now that you stuck with that same ass every day," Nate said while chewing. Brendan didn't say anything back. "I know what it is, though, for real," Nate said, like a courtroom lawyer addressing a jury.

"Nigga, you don't know Jack." Brendan slurped down his second glass of champagne.

Nate turned to me. "Cory, this fool is still in love with Trina." I turned and looked at Brendan, whose face had gotten tight. He didn't deny it, and I just shook my head.

"Believe me. I know," Nate said. "I've been messing back with Kim, and she's been telling me shit . . . B's ass be creeping."

"Whaaat," I said.

"I gotta give it to this, nigga. He's startin' to get real smooth with his shit. Trina doesn't even know he lives with Laney. He keeps telling her he might get back with her if she goes to counseling." Nate burst out laughing. We were all feeling the drinks.

We sat around drinking and tripping for another hour. Brendan tried to tell us the ins and outs of what was going on with him and

Trina. He ended up admitting that he still had feelings for her. The brother was so confused it didn't make sense.

When he finished, Nate explained the details behind him and Kim's reconciliation. It turned out that he had dropped by her job the previous month, walked in, and given her flowers and the clothes he had bought for India and Sahleen when he was in New York. He said he hadn't said a word other than "hello" before walking back out. There was a card that said he had been thinking about her and wanted to make up with her. He said she had called him that night and thanked him, and told him how shocked she had been that he'd come by. She had told him regretfully that she had a boyfriend, and that they could be only friends.

That had been a month ago, and Kim was at Nate's apartment tonight, where she had spent the last three nights, waiting for him to come in from Jasper's. "So much for her boyfriend." Nate laughed. He was probably a nice fellow, too. But too many women would rather have a "Nate" than a nice guy.

We finished a second bottle of Moët and I finished my strawberry shortcake and then I had to go to the bathroom. As I stood up I began to truly feel the effects of the alcohol, and I staggered toward the restrooms. I realized that I definitely had a nice buzz when I looked at myself in the mirror while washing my hands. When I walked back out of the restroom I thought I heard someone call my name, but when I looked around I didn't see anyone. I didn't want to look stupid by looking around the room, so I headed back toward my seat. As I made my way past the bar, I felt someone grab my shoulder from behind.

I turned around and heard "So, are you gonna just play me like that? How are you gonna ignore a sistah like that, Cory Dandridge." Then she said something in her native Spanish as her head bounded back and forth.

She was still beautiful. It had been so many years since I had seen her last, but those years had obviously been good to her. It was amazing how much she and her sister, my fiancée, looked alike.

"Shelly," I said, with slightly slurred speech. "I thought I heard someone calling me. How have you been? It's good to see you," I continued on, before waiting for her answer.

She started to smile when she realized that I truly hadn't heard her and had not intentionally dissed her. "It's good to see you, too."

We both just nodded our heads, smiled halfway grins, and looked for something to say. I had plenty, but I just wasn't prepared. Nina had decided to have a talk with Shelly herself about what was going on between her and me. She figured that it would be less of a blow to Shelly's pride if it came from her. I knew that by this point things had gone on too long and too far for it not to cause tension between them. They were sisters, and they loved each other; however, they were four years apart, and they weren't as close as one would expect sisters to be. Nina had always been closest to her brother, Juan.

Finally, Shelly asked, "So who are you here with . . . your girl-friend?"

Damn, she knows, I thought. Suddenly I got a grip and realized she was attempting to be cute, as if she had needed to *attempt* to be cute. "No, actually I'm here with Nate and Brendan," I said, as I looked her up and down and noticed that her hips had gotten a little wider and her breasts a little heavier. Every pound had found the pefect spot.

"The Three Musketeers still rolling together, huh? Or should I say, the Three Stooges?" she said, as she flashed her award-winning smile. Both of those Sanchez sisters had themselves a mouth full of pretty teeth.

"Very funny," I said, looking away from her eyes.

"Where are you guys sitting, because I'm here with Mia and a couple of other girls, and we're still waiting for a table. They're over there at the bar. You should say hello."

"I will." Then I pointed across the room to show her where we were seated. We stood there and made small talk for about ten minutes, updating one another on our careers and where we had been hanging out. I carefully avoided the subject of family, not wanting to have to pretend that I didn't know every detail of her family life. We eventually went on about how tired we were of the club scene, and both agreed that "happy hour" was only an every-now-and-then–type thing. When it seemed as though the conversation had come to a comfortable break, she assured me that she was going to come past our table with Mia, her best friend since high school, to say hello to Nate and

Brendan. Just as she turned I grabbed her arm before she could walk away completely. "Hey, Shelly," I said meekly.

"Yes," she answered, as she turned back to face me.

I had the feeling that I wanted to swallow deeply, but I didn't. I simply muscled up the strength to say to her, "I need to talk to you about something really important. It's been going on for a while, and I don't know any other way to go about it . . . other than to just come right out and say it." I watched as her eyes widened and began to water instantly. I was puzzled at why she was reacting already to something I hadn't even said.

All of a sudden she looked really nervous. I noticed that she was biting her bottom lip, so I asked, "What's wrong?" Her eyes were now looking at the ground, so I said, "We don't have to talk about this here if you don't want to." I paused. "Why are you so upset?" I asked her, with my hands on her shoulders.

She looked back up at me. "Can we go somewhere?" she said.

"Yeah, sure," I said, not knowing why I had agreed. "Do you want to come by my table when you finish?"

"No," she said, seeming calmer. "I rode with Mia. Do you have a car here? Do you have anyone riding with you?" she asked.

"Uh uh. We all came in separate cars."

Shelly looked at her watch. "Can we leave now, if that's alright with you?"

"No problem. I'll tell Nate and Brendan . . ." She started talking again before I finished.

"Okay. Pull up to the front, and I'll be out there in a minute. I just want to tell the girls that I'm leaving." When I nodded she walked back toward a crowded group by the bar. I went over to leave a fifty for the bill and to tell Brendan and Nate what was going down. They took a look at Shelly from where we were seated and wished me luck.

"This is nice, Cory," Shelly said, as she looked around my living room.

I had to admit I had been a little disappointed that she hadn't said anything about my car. I had thought that she might have been purposely holding back any compliments she had for me. When she gave me one on my apartment and its furnishings that idea flew out of the window. She had either been proccupied on the drive over or actually unimpressed with my car, which I found unbelievable. I had new rims on it, and two TVs in it. I knew she wasn't used to riding in a whip like mine, because neither she nor her man could afford one.

"Thanks," I said. "Have a seat. I'll be right back." I walked into the bathroom to once again relieve myself from the effects of all the drinks I had downed at Jasper's. I quickly brushed my teeth and walked into my bedroom. I grabbed the picture of Nina and myself from our ski trip, and the one of her by herself, and put them both in the drawer of the nightstand. I didn't expect Shelly to come into my bedroom, but just in case she asked to see the place I wanted the pictures out of sight. When I made my way back out into the living room, Shelly was sitting Indian style on my sofa. She had taken her shoes off and was looking very much at home. I sat on the reclining leather chair and grabbed the remote to the stereo. I turned on the CD player, and Musiq came on. We listened to the first song before she asked me, "Do you have the new Jaheim CD?"

"*Still Ghetto?* Yeah, it's hot."

"Put it on after you play Musiq's slow jam, the one that they play on the radio."

"The one that goes 'I will love you when you're old and gray/I'll still love you if you gain a little weight' . . . I can't remember the name." I tried to sing it but sounded nothing like Musiq.

"Yeah," she breathed out. "That's the joint, ain't it. Excuse my English."

"It's alright. School's out right now, and plus, some of my best friends speak Ebonics."

"Yes, but I try not to master the language of Ebonics, which reminds me: As a black man you should be offended that they take a language that uses broken English, throw in some of the hood slang, and attribute it to your culture. And then they go as far as to name it after black people. Ebony-phonics. E-be-ony-fo'-nigs."

"Huh?"

"Get it. It be only for niggas." She shook her head.

I laughed. "Girl, you know that you are still sick."

"You made me that way. Now put that Jaheim in."

"Yes, ma'am," I said, as I complied.

Shelly got up and walked into my kitchen. "This kitchen has a woman's touch. Who helped you decorate?" I didn't answer, as I heard her open the refrigerator. "Can I have some of this wine, Cory? It's unopened."

"Of course," I said over the music, which was flowing out of the speakers. I was leaning in the chair when she walked back out of the kitchen with two glasses of wine and the bottle. She also had a bag of baked Lay's potato chips under her arm. She handed me a glass, which I didn't need, because I was still tipsy from the drinks at Jasper's. I was disappointed with myself for even driving home under the influence. When I drink like I had earlier, I usually stay wherever I am for at least a couple of hours, drinking water until my buzz wears off. In this case the alcohol felt like a blessing. I was dealing with a potentially loaded situation. I was wrestling with thoughts and memories that I had supposedly put behind me. The alcohol masked my nervousness, but was beginning to dull my resistance.

As I took my first sip of the white zinfandel, I stared right at Shelly, and she stared back. I wondered what she was thinking. I was thinking about Nina. She was probably home sleeping or waiting for me to call her when I finished up with the fellas. I wondered how she would feel knowing that her sister, who I had loved, and always would love in some kind of way, was sitting in my apartment.

I hoped that I was doing Nina a favor as I was preparing to break the news to Shelly for her. It had been obvious that she either wasn't looking forward to it or was scared. As a matter of fact, it was apparent that she had been avoiding it. If there was nothing wrong with what we were doing, then why hadn't we been open with Nina's family? A baby and a wedding were supposed to be happy events that you share with your family. Instead, we were keeping it on the down low like a couple of adulterers. I had had enough of keeping secrets with Paula. It was time to come clean. And those were the exact words I said as I got out of the chair and sat down on the couch next to Shelly.

Chapter 29

BOMBS AWAY

I thought I was the one who was supposed to be dropping the news, but I sat on the couch with my mouth partially open and my eyebrows curled and twisted as Shelly continued to speak.

"Listen, Cory," she said, placing her hand on mine. Her touch was warm and inviting. However, at the time it was only meant to be apologetic and calming. "I know I should have told you sooner. I just didn't know how . . . or when would have been the right time."

I shook my head no, finding it hard to believe what she was telling me. As the tears were running down Shelly's cheeks she continued with her explanation. "Cory, you had made your mind up that you were leaving for school, and we hadn't been getting along all that great, anyway. The last thing I wanted to do was slow you down. I knew . . ." She paused, sniffed, and then wiped her eyes. "I knew that if you knew that I was pregnant with your child that you would have changed your plans about going. You had so much going for you with all of those grants and scholarships. I didn't want to stand in your way . . . I couldn't have. I knew that I could take care of Amani on my own, and I was prepared to. Then I met Eric. I was so vulnerable, and he was just there for me at a time when I was really afraid."

I was in shock. Shelly. There couldn't have been a bigger bomb. I sat back into the couch and covered my face. Thoughts raced through my head. I ran over the last six years in my mind. I had been walking around living my life as a single man with no responsibilities except to myself. In a matter of seconds I realized that six years of parenthood had been stolen from me. In the next instant I felt hurt for my child. *Had she been okay all these years?*

The first words I said were "Are you sure that she's mine?"

"I'm positive. I was already a month and a half pregnant when I met Eric."

"Does he know that he's not her father?" I asked.

"Apparently he knew all the time, but he just never wanted to admit it to himself. Last Christmas his mother got angry during dinner and announced at the dinner table in front of everyone there, including Amani, that he had had an accident as a child that would prevent him from having any children, and that he was obviously in denial." I was all ears as she continued to speak. "After that, he was never the same around me or Amani. It was such a coincidence that you had called the house that morning and asked for Nina. No one had so much as mentioned your name for three or four years. It was like a forbidden word. But after that incident at dinner, he never let it go." She had stopped crying and was sipping from her second glass of wine. "We finally had a blood test in March. He said that he just needed to know before he walked out of our lives for good. I told him that he didn't need one and that I knew Amani was your child, but he insisted anyway." Shelly paused while she sipped her wine. "We've been broken up since then, and I haven't heard one word from him. He mailed me a letter telling me that he had had his name removed from her birth certificate and that the Pennsylvania Department of Vital Records and Statistics would be sending me a new one for her."

"Damn, Shelly. How could you do this?" was all I could say.

"Don't worry, Cory. I don't expect a thing from you." Shelly stood up and walked to the balcony. While she stared out into the August night, she told me she'd wanted to tell me for a long time but she hadn't because of Eric. She said that the funny thing about it had been that Amani never bonded with him the way that most little girls do with their fathers. She said that she had been surprised at how little Amani had asked about or mentioned the man whom she had always thought was her father.

"That's not my concern. I don't care about the money. What about her? How is she handling it? Hell. How am I going to handle it?" My face was down again. I then assured her that I would take full financial responsibility for Amani.

"It's not necessary, Cory. Really. We're fine," she responded.

"Nonsense. Dandridge men take care of their responsibility. I owe you money. And Eric, too, I guess."

"He'd probably take it right about now," she laughed. "I know you're probably making megabucks right now, Cory, but believe it or not, I do okay for myself. I have a master's degree in guidance. I'm second in charge at the school I work at. I'm not hurting at all."

She was so confident, even when she was putting herself on the line. I was dealing with the shock of the news that she had given me, and at the same time preparing to tell her about Nina and me. I contemplated putting off telling her about us. This had been a traumatic evening already. I thought about her claiming that she wouldn't want any money from me after she heard my confession. "You might change your tune after I say what I need to say to you."

She turned, looked, and walked back toward the couch. She stood in front of me with her arms folded. "What is it?"

"Sit down. Please."

"I'll stand," she said, and turned back toward the window as I started my story, from the night at the party when I had seen Nina and thought she was Shelly. I told each detail of how we had just started out catching up on old times. Before long, Shelly was sitting on the floor by the table. Her third glass of wine disappeared, then her fourth, as she listened attentively. Her expression changed dramatically when I got to the part about sleeping together.

"I can't believe this shit. How could you be with her, Cory?" I recognized the words that followed it as profanity in her native tongue.

"I . . . I'm . . . sorry. I didn't think that it would make a difference after all of this time."

"Bullshit. How could you think that? She's my sister, Cory. Were you that hard up to be with me? You had to go after the next best thing, huh?"

"Shelly, that's not how it was. It didn't start out like that."

"I ought to kick your ass, and hers. That's foul."

"As foul as you denying a child her father?"

That comment stopped her in her tracks, and she sat down on the couch. "Take me home, Cory." The tears started, and I felt my heart sinking. I had caused so much pain. It was like the old days when I had said something to hurt her feelings.

She had always melted me with her tears. Things hadn't changed, and I sat down next to her and began to stroke her back, trying to stop her from crying. To my surprise it didn't take long for me to calm her down. Amid her tears she began to speak. She said, "Nina isn't worth a damn, and you are just a typical man . . . my sister, Cory?"

She went on about how low down Nina was. She went back to the days when we first dated as undergrads, telling stories of how she had suspected Nina of having a crush on me back then. She even recalled finding a letter Nina had written to her fantasy man about how she wanted him to be the first to make love to her, but that Nina hadn't put a name on the top. Nina had described how she felt whenever her mystery man came by the house, and how wonderful she had felt inside when he hugged her. Nina was only seventeen then, and no boys were coming by the house, but I had hugged her most of the times I went by to see Shelly. Shelly said that she had always known that Nina had written it about me.

Shelly just shook her head. "You know what's funny?"

"No, tell me."

"When I looked in your fridge, I said to myself, 'What in the world is Cory doing with that butterscotch yogurt. He never liked yogurt. The only person I know who eats that is Nina." She looked at me. "So are you still seeing her?"

"Yes."

"Is it serious."

"Yeah, it is," I said.

Shelly's lips tightened. "How serious?"

"Very."

"Do you love her?"

"Yeah, I do," I said, surprising myself.

"No, you don't," she said, getting up off of the couch and sitting next to me, forcing my body to slide over. "Because if you did, you wouldn't have been looking at me the way you have since I've been over here."

"Shelly, what are you talking about?" I said, as I leaned back and tried my best to look unfazed.

"This is what I'm talking about." She stood up. "You don't love her. The only reason why you have been with her is because you thought that you couldn't have me." Shelly had on a peach-colored silk blouse, which her fingers began to unbutton. "But guess what? You can still have me. I still want you. I never stopped loving you." Her words overwhelmed me. I couldn't believe she had said that. I was overjoyed to hear her say she still loved me, but sad at the same time. I had spent many nights dreaming of hearing her say those words, but I never heard them again until now. She still loved me, but I was with her sister now. I loved Nina and had to show it by being strong enough to resist Shelly.

"Love me, Cory," she said, as her blouse slid off her shoulders and fell to the floor. My head felt light, as if all of the blood had rushed away from it. I couldn't believe I was staring at Shelly, whose beige Miracle bra was getting paid for nothing. Believe me when I say it: This woman needed no miracles up there. "Tell me you don't want me, Cory, and I'll put my shirt back on. Tell me." Then she started talking in Spanish, and my dick grew even harder.

"Just as I thought," she said, as she unfastened her black linen slacks. And I watched them fall and hit the ground, revealing a sexy pair of thong panties. "Now, what are you going to do?" she said in Spanish, and sounded even sexier. I just sat there in a trance staring at Shelly. I watched her hips as she moved toward me. My mind began to race with indecision. I couldn't do this to Nina. I shouldn't even want to. It shouldn't have even been up for debate.

The little devil on my shoulder was telling me to go ahead. She was standing over me with nothing on but her panties, bra, and Via Spiga sandals. One time for old time's sake wouldn't hurt anything. At the same time, the little angel on my right was warning me not to do it. I just closed my eyes and tried to be strong. The last thing I wanted was to hurt Nina in any sort of way. Shelly was only a breath away, and now what was I going to do?

Chapter 30

LOVE OVERBOARD

Finally, after all of this time, Kim believed that Nate was getting the picture. He was lying still in Kim's bed at two in the morning, listening to her as she continued to talk. She had been pouring her heart out to Nate for twenty minutes.

"Nate, do you love me?" Kim turned on her side and asked him.

Without even the slightest hesitation Nate answered, "Yeah, baby, I do."

"Why do you love me now when you didn't before?"

"I did. It was just different . . . I mean, I just wasn't able to express . . ." Nate paused. "Why are you asking me all of these questions? What's wrong, Kim? . . . I'm here . . . right, baby?" Nate propped his head on his pillow. "All of that stuff is in the past. You have to let it go."

Kim sniffed. "I know. I know, but it still hurts. You disrespected me. You didn't love me then, even though I loved you. I just don't understand why. It's like I wasn't good enough then."

Nate turned back toward Kim and kissed her forehead and began to rub her stomach and her breasts. Not in a sexual way, though. He was simply trying to ease her, and it always worked. After a few minutes she was silent, and her eyes closed as she tried to think things through in a state of semiconsciousness.

Kim smiled to herself. Nate was taking care of her the way a man was supposed to. She had been upset a few moments earlier, and Nate had taken responsibility for her emotions. It couldn't have been any better had she written the script herself. Kim felt a quiet sense of self-satisfaction. Nate had not only come *crawling* back to her, as she liked to explain it, but it made her feel good to think that she obviously had been worth enough to him for him to make major changes in his outlook on relationships.

Since they had started seeing each other again there had been several noticeable changes in the way Nate now treated her. After making love to Kim, instead of jumping up to play video games, or rushing her off when she was at his house, Nate had begun to simply lie still and listen. Sometimes he would just listen to her breathing as she calmed down. Other times he would go as far as running his fingers through her hair and holding her. Kim had been forced to admit to herself and her friends that even she didn't know where it had all come from.

Trina, portraying the wise and experienced best friend, had taken in the facts and given Kim her analysis over lunch at Crisfield's one afternoon in September. "Honey," Trina said, "maybe that negro has changed. Brendan told me that Nate had been seeing some model for a while and that he treated her good. . . . Hell, I didn't believe that a model worth anything would date Nate's ass until I saw him in that Shawn Simmons video. But maybe she taught his ass how to treat a lady. I mean, damn, look at me. . . . I know that now, since Brendan is giving us a chance at working things out, I know I'm not going to blow my opportunity." She'd gone on to insist that perhaps Nate had come to realize that Kim was everything he needd, and that he was going to do whatever it took to make things work, too.

The next morning, Nate woke to the smell of bacon and eggs coming from Kim's kitchen and the sound of his phone vibrating against the belt on his jeans.

"You hungry?" Kim asked, as she poked her head inside the doorway and saw Nate putting on his jeans.

"I could eat a horse right about now," Nate said, pulling the laces on his Jordan's.

"That would be a lucky horse," Kim said. "I hope we're talking female horse, too."

"Real funny. I'm going to have to get you an audition for *Comic View*. But yeah, make me a bacon and egg sandwich."

"How do you know that's what I cooked?" Kim asked, sitting on the bed.

"I know what pork smells like."

"You got a problem with pork, sir?"

Nate stood and headed for the bathroom. "Nope. As long as the pig ain't still wiggling. Ya know what I'm saying?"

They both laughed while Nate washed his hands, and then they headed for the kitchen. Nate felt his phone ringing again, but when he looked at the number he didn't recognize it.

"Do you need some privacy?" Kim asked him sarcastically, when she heard his cell vibrating.

Nate flipped open his phone and dialed his grandmother's number. "Hey, Nana. What's going on? Did you need anything?" Even though his grandmother hadn't called him, he knew she would always jump right into a conversation with him and tell him of at least two items that she needed from somewhere. It was an old trick that had always worked to quell suspicions that arose when women saw he was reluctant to answer his calls.

"Okay, I'll stop by in a little bit," Nate answered. "Okay. All right. Bye bye." He hung up. While the two of them ate Kim occasionally looked across the table at Nate, staring with admiration for the dedication that he showed his grandmother.

Nate left Kim right after he finished eating with the assurance that he would be back to pick her up to take her to the doctor's office at three. He didn't know it, but Kim had been having sharp pains in her side and she feared she might have a bladder problem, or worse. She'd had some tests run the previous week, and today she was going to get the results.

As soon as Nate got into his car, he pulled out his cellphone. He was so preoccupied with returning the call that he pulled too far into the road and had to back up to keep from getting the front of his truck smashed.

"Yesss," the voice on the other end of the phone answered.

Nate didn't recognize the voice on the other end of the line. "This is Nate. Someone called me from this number."

"Nathan, how are you, my dear? Long time no hear from . . . this is Shawn."

"Shawn? Shawn from . . . ?" Nate asked.

"Very funny. Shawn Simmons."

Nate grew silent while he gathered himself. He couldn't guess why she would be calling him now. "The one and only. How are you?"

She didn't make him guess. "I'm good. Look, sweety, I'm in town on the way to New York this afternoon to do *106 & Park*, and I was wondering if you would come with me. I would really appreciate it."

"Well, I kind of have something to do."

Shawn huffed into the phone and told her driver, "Turn here." Then she continued. "Look, Nate. I need you to do this. I don't have an escort and I need you to go. Image is everything. All you have to do is stand around and look like you're waiting for my every request."

"I don't know," Nate began.

"Nate, I know that you're not still upset with me about that stuff in New York with Sahleen. As I understand it you two still aren't speaking, but hey, this is business. Besides, I'm through with her as well."

"Oh, is that right?" Nate asked.

"Yeah. She's not to be trusted. She'd screw her brother if she thought that it would help her get somewhere." Nate didn't reply. He truly was still stinging from what had happened. Shawn went on. "Shit, I found out that she'd slept with my sister's husband in *her* house at a party we had there on the Fourth of July. Her husband is Phil Jeffery. He hires actresses for a couple of soaps, and he probably promised her a part. Sahleen is a real tramp.

"Anyway, what do you say? Can you help me out or what? I promise that if you do I will take *real* good care of you for the rest of the evening. I don't go back to LA until Thursday. And I know that I'll be lonely in that big old room down on Park Avenue. It could be just me and you . . . you know? Taking care of some unfinished business. We could even send Sahleen a picture thanking her." Then she giggled.

Instantly Nate remembered Shawn's naked body, and he began to cave in. As he drove toward his apartment Shawn filled his head with promises of a great time. It wasn't long before he was gung-ho. The idea that he had put a little "come back" on the sex that he had given her made his chest poke out. Shawn explained that she wasn't into women anymore, and that it had been the devil in her. She insisted that she was over it completely. She told him that she had thought about him often since that night but had been afraid to call him for fear of rejection. Imagine that.

Before Nate realized how much time had passed it was after six o'clock in the evening and he was in Harlem at the studio with Shawn. He had ignored at least ten of Kim's calls.

After being forced to go by herself to the doctor, she had been diagnosed with tumors on her ovaries and had been told that she wouldn't be able to have children. Even worse there was the threat that they might even be cancerous. And as Kim lay across her bed in tears watching *106 & Park* on BET, she saw Nate sitting in the front row as Free gave him a shout out for his appearance in the video. At that moment she knew why Nate had stood her up.

Kim never answered the phone when Daphne called her from the salon, where BET was on the tube as well. Kim continued to cry as she took tablet after tablet of Percocet, a strong medication prescribed for severe pain, and washed them down with gin. She barely had enough energy to whimper, as her body grew limp when she drifted off. She thought she was speaking out loud, but then realized that it was only in her head that she heard herself repeating the words, *Nate doesn't love me . . . He never will . . . I wish he would die . . . I wish he would die . . . I wish he would . . . I wish . . . he wool die . . . I . . . wush . . . he . . . woo . . . die . . . I . . . wus . . . he . . . wud . . . die.* She murmured inside of her own mind until all conscious thoughts had escaped.

Chapter 31

IN TOO DEEP

Nate spent the night with Shawn Simmons after leaving the show
at BET. It was so good that he ended up spending the next one
with her as well, which was her final night on the East Coast.
They seemed to genuinely like each other. Nate found the down-to-
earth attitude Shawn had in spite of her wealth and fame intriguing.
Likewise, Shawn liked Nate's relaxed attitude toward life and his
"street edge." She wondered out loud a few times how he could afford
to just hang out with her and never once mention so much as a job. It
was obvious that he had money from the clothes he wore and the car
he drove. In the back of her mind she suspected that he was a big-time
drug dealer, and the notion only seemed to turn her on more.

When she invited him back to LA with her the next day, she acted
surprised when he accepted. He didn't leave a number anywhere, nor
had he bothered to check his messages until he had been in LA for
three days. He knew that he would hear Kim cursing him out about
standing her up. He wanted to enjoy his little getaway before he dealt
with the guilt trip he knew was coming.

It wasn't every day that a brother off the streets of D.C. got to come
out to LA and screw the hell out of one of the top R&B divas in the
music industry, her treat. Shawn was like a kid with a new toy, and she
took Nate out to all of the trendiest restaurants and clubs in town. Not
to mention the shopping. Nate hadn't been spoiled by a woman with
any money before . . . real money, that is. The brother was in paradise.
That is, until he checked his messages.

"You have thirty-seven new messages and three saved messages. Message number one is marked urgent. Press one to hear the message."

Beep, as Nate pressed the button. "Nate, you motherfucker. Kim killed herself last night because of your black ass." Daphne was hysterical. "You left her alone after she found out that she might have cancer. How could you do that shit? Everybody saw you on BET, you sorry bitch." Click. Nate replayed the message because he was sure he'd heard wrong. He started to feel sick when he realized he hadn't.

Message two was urgent as well. "Yo, Nate. Where you at?" It was Brendan. "Yo, man. I need to tell you some shit. Call me. Everybody has been calling and paging you like crazy."

The message that I left was marked urgent also. "Nate, this is Cory. Where are you, bro? Your girl Kim overdosed last night. I need to holler at you and find out what happened. Your grandmother has been worried."

Urgent. "Nigga, my cousin died." A male voice on the line spoke. "You dogged the wrong one this time, boy. Say your prayers . . . 'cause when I see you, I'm going to lay your ass down to sleep."

"Nate." Kim's voice was groggy. "Call me back. I'm going to be late. It's two-fifteen." Click.

"Nate, I'm going to drive myself. It's twenty minutes 'til three. Meet me at the doctor's . . . Columbia Hospital for women. My doctor's name is Herschel, and his office is on the third floor."

Kim was crying. "Nate, I need you. Call me." It was four o'clock.

Four-thirty. "Where are you?" She was still crying. She left five more messages before she saw him on television at six-fifteen.

"Everyone knows that they record this show live. You were at a video shoot when you were supposed . . ." She couldn't even finish. She just cried into the phone. It was her second-to-last message.

At eight o'clock Kim called back. "Nate, I hate you. How could you do this to me? I loved you. I hope you die. You will never change . . . you have dogged this bitch for the last time . . ." Her voice was wavering in and out in degree of strength. "Good-bye . . . Good-bye forever."

Nate was alone in Shawn's apartment. He hung up the phone after the last message and called me. When I didn't answer he quickly dialed Brendan, who was at work. Brendan went into the office and took a break when he heard Nate on the phone.

"Yo, B. Did she really do that shit?" Nate's voice was cracking.

"Yeah," Brendan said solemnly. "She did."

There was silence until Brendan asked, "Man, where are you?"

"I'm in LA. Been here since Thursday."

"You with Shawn Simmons?" Brendan asked, not knowing whether or not to sound excited under the circumstances.

"Yeah."

Nate asked for details, and Brendan gave him as many as he could. They talked for a while, and Brendan called Nate's grandmother on a three-way phone for him. His nana was fine, and she chastised Nate for not calling in five days. He got her off of the line and resumed his conversation with Brendan. Nate asked about funeral arrangements.

"I hope you're not going to consider going," Brendan said. Then he went on to tell him all the things that Trina had said she had heard about Kim's cousins being out for Nate's blood. Plus the fact that it would've upset Kim's family. They had already joined forces with the women in the salon in a crusade to pin the blame on Nate. Brendan told her that Kim's family was even considering suing Nate for wrongful death via emotional and mental torture.

Nate was overwhelmed. He sat on the bed with the phone in his hand for a full minute as the gravity of the situation came crashing down on him. He realized that he had gone too far. He had treated someone so badly that they had no longer wanted to live. He had destroyed a life and a family. The room began to spin along with his mind. For the first time he literally lost it. After he got off of the phone with Brendan, he threw up before he could make it to the bathroom, and he collapsed right in the hallway. He had finally done something that money couldn't smooth out. He called back and listened to his messages again, hoping that it was all a bad dream.

Nate had never hyperventilated until this. His breath kept leaving his body. Thoughts of Kim dying alone dominated him. He didn't know what to do or who to call. Cory didn't answer when he called. Nate was panicking, wondering if he was criminally responsible. He even wondered how serious the threats were that had been levied against him. He planned to find out soon.

When Shawn came back to her apartment she found a note from Nate: "I'm headed back home. A friend of mine passed away and I need to go face the music. I took a cab to LAX. Thanks for everything. I'll call you."

Shawn had no idea what he meant by facing the music, but she knew that it didn't sound too good.

"Oh, well," she said, as she picked up the phone. "Hey, Steve. My cousin is gone. Why don't you come on over and rub my back. I would really appreciate it . . . and if you do, I promise I'll make it worth your while."

Steve answered with an affirmative.

Shawn shot back, "An hour sounds great. It'll give me a chance to shower. . . . Oh, by the way, Stevie, baby . . . bring your girlfriend, too, if you can. I'm in one of those moods. Peace." Click.

Chapter 32

ALL IS FAIR IN LOVE

My day of reckoning had come quickly. Nevertheless we had a date with destiny, and it was time to dance. I sat there looking up at the sky, and I noticed that indeed it was the type of day that God had created for a wedding. The sky was powder blue, and the sun seemed to be shining from every angle. It was nearly 70 degrees, the breeze was blowing through the windows, and the sunroof was intoxicating. It was taking my mind off of what I was about to do. And I had to admit that I was a little nervous. Hell, I was a lot nervous. My life was about to change forever. There would be no turning back after today.

As I pulled into the parking lot I hoped that I was making the right decision. I hoped that *we* were making the right decision. I couldn't help but feel guilty about how selfish I had been in the last year. Love had taken me through some serious changes. But through it all, it had been all about me. I had only focused on what was going to make Cory happy or bring Cory the most satisfaction. I hadn't once thought about whose feelings were being trampled in the process. I didn't want to end up like Nate, all caught up out there in the game that he seemed to live for. He had come into town and left just as quickly to avoid Kim's relatives and friends, who were looking for him.

We all talked him out of going to her funeral. He would have surely died that day. I wasn't too convinced that he still wouldn't face some repercussions if any of Kim's people caught up with him. Kim had had a big family, and they were plenty mad at Nate. He wisely decided to leave D.C. for a while. He told me that he would call me after he had gotten situated somewhere. When I dropped him off at the airport he was headed to Chicago to spend a few days with his cousin Lowe. After he left there, he said that he didn't know where he was headed, probably Houston or Miami.

He knew that I was transferring to New York in a couple of months and he told me not to be surprised if he popped up there. I told him that he probably just needed some time to get his head together after what had happened with Kim. He'd agreed. The last thing he said to me when I told him about my plans to get married was, "Good luck, Cory. You're doing the right thing. True love comes only once. When you see it, you know it. Go after it, but always be prepared to deal with the consequences." Then he shook my hand as he got out of the car. "You two make a great couple. Treat her good. Keep the dog in you locked up . . . but not all of the way." He smiled. " 'Cause you have to remember that . . . nice guys finish last." Then he turned and walked away. I just laughed as I walked out of the terminal at Reagan National Airport with the keys to his Lexus in my hand.

The scariest thought that entered my mind on my wedding day was that I still considered myself a nice guy. Paula's husband wouldn't have agreed with that notion, however. Paula didn't either when I left Atlanta, and her behind with it. In fact, my one-time-no-strings-attached partner, Darlene, had even cursed me out for not returning her phone calls after the night I had spent with her in April. Worst of it all, though, had been the lack of consideration that I had shown Nina. By pursuing a relationship with her I had put her in a position where she had been forced to choose between her family and me. Ultimately, she had chosen me . . . and so had I. I felt bad about it, but it still hadn't stopped my pattern of selfish behavior. Today was just another example . . . It didn't matter who got hurt as long as I was still standing at the end of the day.

I looked over in the passenger seat at my bride-to-be and my heart skipped a beat. Her expression was calm. It was almost as if she had planned it this way. Never showing any sense of disappointment about getting married in a courthouse, especially knowing that I could afford a big wedding. I knew that every girl dreamed of a big wedding, but I'd

insisted that we go to the justice of the peace. I didn't want a big production or to face the possible commotion at a ceremony. I hoped that
the tickets for an all-inclusive trip to the Cayman Islands, which I'd
hidden in the glove compartment, made up for the shoddy wedding.

As I got out of the car, I pulled a picture out of my pocket of
Amani, my daughter, and I felt a lump in my throat. She was so beautiful and innocent. She had my smile and a pair of dimples that were
as deep as the ocean. In the picture she had her hair in curls, and she
looked like a doll baby. I was so sorry that I had missed the first six
years of her life. Just thinking about another man raising her all of this
time stung deeply. I couldn't believe that Shelly kept everything from
me like that. The more I thought about it, the more difficult it was ac-
cepting her reasons. I kept feeling as though she should have been
more selfish and not considered how it was going to affect me. It was,
after all, my responsibility. Deep down inside, even though I didn't
want to admit it, I knew she was right about how I would have reacted
back then. Had I been faced with the responsibilities of raising a child
five years ago, I doubt that I would have left for Atlanta. I also doubt
that I would have done as well as I had. Shelly had told me that it was
easier for her to act as though I no longer existed than it would have
been for her to live with my resentment.

We approached the courthouse hand-in-hand. I looked over at her
face, and I started to feel as though I was dreaming. Everything was in
slow motion as we made our way through the doors, past the metal
detectors, and off into the judge's chambers to the right. We took a
seat right outside on a bench as we waited for our names to be called.

We hadn't even warmed the bench when Brendan walked around
the corner. Trina was with him. He was going to be my witness. I had
figured that Trina would be with him. They'd gotten back together.
They were getting relationship counseling, and Brendan was happier
than he had been in a long time.

It turned out that Brendan had caught Laney in yet another lie
when her uncle had called looking for her from Philly. I couldn't remember every detail, but it was something about Laney lying about
everything from having a deceased sister to a mother on drugs. It
turned out that Laney's mother was a nurse who was raising Laney's

son because Laney had been an abusive parent. Brendan hadn't gone into every detail. The only important detail had been the one where he had gotten off of the phone with her uncle and immediately moved his things out of her apartment before she had even come home. He had written her a letter telling her that she needed help that he couldn't give her and that she was never to contact him again. Finally, he'd had enough. It seemed that for some reason Trina was the only woman whose lies he could forgive.

Brendan had been staying in Nate's apartment for the last month while he was waiting to close on his new condominium. I didn't have to ask if Trina would be moving in with him. They looked like two kids in love for the first time. I guess Trina had finally realized that she had a good man, and she was not going to be the same fool again.

The door opened and an older couple emerged looking freshly married. The bailiff called our names and we walked in. At that instant I finally felt the confidence and sureness of heart that I had been looking for. Suddenly things seemed like they were always supposed to have been this way. I looked at her. She had been quiet until a bailiff sitting off to the side with a small boom box asked if we wanted music playing in the background.

"Yes, please."

She held two CDs. "Luther Vandross, Johnny Mathis . . ."

Brendan pulled a CD out of the pocket of his blazer. "Play this please. Number six." It was Kenny Lattimore's "For You." Perfect.

"No problem," the bailiff said, as she took the CD and fumbled with some papers.

The judge was young. He looked to be in his late thirties and seemed more jovial than a judge was supposed to be. He cracked a couple of jokes about Brendan bringing his own music with him before he got down to business.

Maybe it wasn't the big wedding I had hoped for, but I was glad we were doing it. The ceremony was over as quickly as it started: "Cory, you may kiss the bride." But it was special and moving in its own way.

I couldn't believe it . . . I was married. We had eloped. When I pulled my lips from hers, she just smiled. I saw tears of joy running down her cheeks. I heard Trina blowing her nose. When everything came to a stop we headed out of the same doors that we had entered from and proceeded out of the courthouse and back into the inviting sun, but only now as man and wife.

Brendan was hugging me and telling me how happy he was for me when Nina walked up and stopped right in front of us on the steps. Shelly had been talking to Trina about the honeymoon surprise and didn't see Nina approaching either. We just stared at her, and she stared right back.

"So you two really did it?" Nina said. "You really fucking did it." There was silence. "I had a miscarriage not even four whole weeks ago, Cory. . . . Your baby, Cory . . . the baby you claimed you wanted and grieved over with me. We were supposed to be getting married tomorrow, but instead you ended things with me. . . . No excuses . . . nothing. Then here you turn around, and you marry my sister." Nina began to rant in both English and Spanish, and people were starting to stare. "I stopped past the house to drop some things off for Momma. Juan was over there cutting the grass and babysitting Amani. He said that Amani had been telling him all morning that you were getting married to her real daddy today." Nina shook her head and looked at me. "What kind of shit is that?" Nina paused and covered her face. "Oh God, I can't believe you did this to me, Cory. You said you loved me."

Shelly, who had listened while Nina said her piece, finally spoke up. "You have a lot of nerve, Nina. You knew the whole time that Amani was Cory's daughter. If you loved him so much, why weren't you honest with him?"

I saw Nina's face fill with shame, and I said, "Shelly, no," hoping to save Nina from Shelly's onslaught. I knew that Shelly was prepared to verbally crush her sister.

"No my ass, Cory. This is my sister. I know why *you* were with her, but she was my own flesh and blood. She was never supposed to fall for you . . . not in a million years."

Nina was in tears. "You don't know how it was with Cory and me. You don't know."

Shelly's eyes turned cold and cut into her sister. "Well, here's a news flash, you conniving little slut. It's over, and if I ever catch you around my husband, my daughter's father . . . I swear I will . . ."

I grabbed Shelly. "Come on, Shelly." I turned and looked at Nina and said, "Nina . . . I'm sorry. I really am. But I never stopped loving Shelly . . . and I never will."

"You can take your apologies and just keep it." I saw Nina's nose running when she wiped it. "I hate you both, and I swear . . . I hope you burn in hell."

"Save it, Nina," Shelly said, as she took my hand and we turned and walked away. Brendan and Trina followed us, and I did my best not to look back. And it seemed that my best was good enough, because by the time that I succumbed to the urge and turned back . . . Nina was gone.

Excerpt from Darren Coleman's sequel

Don't Ever Wonder

COMING SUMMER 2005

chapter one

Once Upon a Time

J immy's Downtown was already packed at 6:00 P.M. I should have
known it would be mad hectic like this. People piled in for happy
hour during the work week but ended up leaving at a pretty decent
hour. But on the weekends, it was a whole different story. That was
when the party *really* got started. Folks always ended up staying until
three, four in the morning. I hadn't come for networking or a party this
time. I came for one quick drink with one special person. My fingers
were crossed that my meeting wouldn't turn ugly, even though she assured me that we were adult enough to handle this.

I made my way past the bar and headed toward the rear of the café.
I had told the hostess I wanted to sit away from the crowd. As soon as I
passed the couches I saw my date sitting off to my right. A mix of emotions flared up, and I swallowed hard as I made my way to her. Our eyes
locked, and she stood up as I reached the table. She extended her arms
and gave me a tight hug. The warmth was familiar, and when Nina
pulled away she was sporting a smile as wide as the Hudson River.

"Mr. Dandridge. How nice to see you after all this time," she said,
both sarcastically and seductively. She reminded me how few women
can actually pull that off.

I smiled at her. "It's good to see you, too. You look well." I couldn't help but notice that she was looking exceptionally beautiful. Not that I had expected anything less from her, but when you don't see someone for a while you tend to forget some of what you loved about them. She was wearing a copper strapless dress that showed off some serious tan lines, and she had on the necklace that I had gotten her from Tiffany's. She had obviously been on vacation. "Nice necklace," I mentioned, and then added, "Nice tan, too."

"Oh, thanks." She was grinning. "An old friend picked it up for me a while back. As for the tan, I picked that up in Puerto Rico at my family reunion."

I knew about the reunion because my wife Shelly had contemplated for weeks whether or not to attend. She was really torn. She had decided not to go once her mother had confirmed that Nina would be there. We sat, and the waitress came back for our orders. I pointed at Nina and asked the waitress to take her order first. "I'll take a glass of the house wine and the adobo-roasted chicken for my entrée."

"I'll take a vodka martini and the shrimp dish."

She took the menus and headed off. There was a moment of uncomfortable silence that I tried to fill by observing my surroundings. I was interrupted with, "Cory, are you okay?" My hands were on the table and she reached for them. "If you are uncomfortable we don't have to do this. You can leave." Damn. She could always read me like a book.

I lied. "No, I'm fine. I was just thinking about work. I have to stop doing that." I paused. "So, what did you want to talk about?" It came out more hurried than I wanted it to.

"Whoa. I wanted to have a drink and relax with you first." She released my hands. Her touch had been so subtle I had forgotten that she had held them. Her hands has always been the softest I'd ever felt. "I must admit that I am surprised that you even agreed to meet me."

I nodded my head, because I was surprised as well. But I guess that deep down inside I had wanted to see her months ago to be sure she was okay. Now that I was here, it wasn't as bad as I thought it was going to be. I mean, I've been happily married to Shelly for years; our baby girl Amani was the apple of my eye. So what in the hell am I doing here? I chalked it up to settling old debts and burying old ghosts. At least that's what I told myself. I relaxed a bit while we ate and ordered our second and third drinks. It was a quarter past eight when my phone rang. I excused myself and went to the restroom.

"Hey, sweetie," I said to my wife on the other end.

"Hey, do you think you can pick up Amani from the sitter's? I need to run to the store with Rockelle to pick up a few things for Christina's baby shower tomorrow." Shelly had been planning a shower for her best friend who lived in Brooklyn.

"Why don't you call and ask Mrs. Lamar if she can stay a little late. I am in the middle of something and probably wouldn't make it there for at least two more hours." I didn't want to leave yet.

"Fine." I heard the disgust in her voice. "You always do this, Cory. I'm sick of this." And she hung up. I knew I was headed for attitude city when we met up at home. There was nothing new about that these days. Nina had the wine glow on her face when I got back to the table.

I was feeling way too relaxed at this point. Relaxed enough to want to sit and talk for another hour with my sister-in-law, who also happened to be my ex-fiancée. Relaxed enough to give my wife the impression that I was probably still working on some important project. Relaxed enough to come out of my mouth with the truth: "Nina, you are so beautiful. I am so sorry for hurting you the way I did. If I could take it all back I would." I began rambling. "I didn't even realize how much I loved you. I have to admit that I think I made the biggest mistake of my life." She looked down at the table for a second, dodging my eyes. On a roll now. "I don't expect you to forgive me. I just want you to know that . . ." I shook my head in disgust at myself for spilling my guts like a loser. I went on. "I just want you to know that I am sorry and have been miserable without you." It was like a dam being released.

While I spoke I hadn't noticed that her eyebrows had raised and her lips had parted. She would have interrupted me if she could have, but I had stunned her with my confession. She was speechless. She placed her hands over her face, stood up, and walked away. I could have sworn I saw tears.

I waited in confusion for about ten minutes, wondering what was going through her mind. While she was in the restroom the waitress came back; I paid the bill and continued to sit patiently, waiting for her.

"How much do I owe you for the bill?" She whispered it. I looked up and saw her standing there.

"C'mon, now. You know better than that." I motioned for her to sit down, and she shook her head no. My heart was sinking as I asked, "You are ready to leave?"

"Yes." Her demeanor had changed. She was no longer relaxed. Her arms were folded and she was clutching her purse as if I was going to steal it. She sounded like she was in a meeting. All professional and whatnot.

"Let's walk." I led her toward the door. The spot had gotten packed. Everyone was piling in, trying to get the last taste of summer before September rolled in. We hit the street and moved toward the curb. "I'll get you a cab."

"No, wait. Walk a little up the block with me. I want to respond to what you said in there." We started walking. The air was warm and people were moving about on both sides of the street. We made it halfway down the block before she turned and said, "Cory." I was still. Hands in my pockets. I looked directly at her. "I want you to know something."

"I'm listening."

"I was wrong, too. Not just you . . . the whole thing was wrong. I should have never dated you. A crush is one thing, because believe me, brother, you are *fine*." She punched me in the chest softly and laughed. "What we did, though, was wrong. You and my sister were together and made a child. I still think that she is ignorant as all hell. Keeping you in the dark for five years about the child you had together will never make sense to me, and I hope that it never makes sense to you."

I digested what she had said but wasn't sure if she wanted a reply. It became obvious that she didn't because she went right on. "But two wrongs don't make a right. I should have been better and so should you." She sounded more normal now.

I cut her off. "But, baby girl . . . *you* are so damned fine. How could I resist you?" I pinched her cheek, lightening the mood, and we both laughed. "You're right. No doubt about it. I have lost many nights of sleep over the way I have handled things."

"As well you should have."

"But what does it mean to be here now? Everything that has happened can't be undone. These feelings can't be turned off." I looked down at the sidewalk. "I do still love you, though."

I felt her fingers touch my chin. "Poor Cory. You love me today. Shelly tomorrow. Whoever ain't there . . . that is who you will love, Papi. With you it's never the here and now. You are a faraway love."

"What?" Was she for real? I come out with this confession and she's talking this junk?

"You're a faraway love. Not good at loving up close and in the present. That's the funny thing about men. Something most women will never understand." I was all ears. "When a sistah leaves your ass, you all of a sudden gain all of this clarity. But by then it's too late. She has picked up the shattered pieces of her heart and moved on."

"So, it's too late." I had been thinking that I could end my marriage to Shelly and make everything right. Nina and I could move somewhere far away and be happy and never worry about anyone judging us because we had fallen in love. But I didn't say it.

"It's way too late," she said, backing toward the curb. She turned and hailed a cab.

"So how long are you in town for?"

"I leave on Sunday."

I slipped her a card. "Call me tomorrow. The afternoon will be best."

"I'll think about it." A cab stopped and she opened the door. "I won't make any promises." Her tone stung a bit.

"Hey."

She looked back. No smile.

I couldn't believe I asked her. "Do you still love me?" I was willing to hold on to anything at this point.

As she backed into the cab she said, "Once upon a time." The door shut . . . and Nina was gone again.

chapter two

What a Difference a Day Makes

He was in the fetal position sleeping like a baby. The sheets were all twisted up between his chocolate legs and slob dripped slowly out of the corner of his mouth. As usual only the aroma of bacon, eggs, and fried potatoes were enough to cause him to stir from his slumber. Like clockwork Janette came into her bedroom with breakfast on a tray.

"Wake up, baby." She nudged his slow-moving body to sit up.

"I'm up." Nate stretched and propped the pillows up behind his back. "Where is the remote?" Janette pointed to the covers next to him and he nodded his head, letting her know he wanted her to hand it to him.

"So, are you going to come down to the office today and join me for lunch?" Every day she asked, and every day he gave her the same answer.

"We'll see." Nate flipped the channel to ESPN. "I told you I was going to go down to the Run 'n' Shoot today to renew my membership." While hiding out in Charlotte he had gained fifteen pounds. He seemed to meet one great cook after another, but Janette was a triple threat. She fried, broiled, and baked her thick ass off. Although he would never admit it, she was the only woman whose cooking topped his grandmother's. Now, he didn't mind his new life in Charlotte one bit.

"You said the same thing last week and the week before." Janette was in the closet grabbing a shirt to put on. "I don't know why you need to go to the gym. No woman wants a man that is skin and bones. You look great."

Compared to you I look great. "Nah, this isn't me. I don't feel right. I have never weighed over two hundred pounds." He had a mouth full of food and was talking at the same time. "And you *are* going to stop making me all of this fattening food. I know what you are trying to do."

"And what is that?" Janette said, sticking her head out of the closet.

"You want me all fat so nobody else will want me." He was spreading Country Crock on his toast.

"Negro, please. I'm a thick sistah, and brothers are constantly pushing up on me."

"Yeah, that's because you are two-hundred-pound goddess." He puckered his lips up to get a kiss. Janette walked toward him and gave him a smooch on the lips and turned away to continue getting ready for work. "And that 500 CLK you pushing don't hurt either." He started laughing. Janette walked back over to Nate, punched him softly in the arm, and snatched a piece of bacon off his tray. "Hey, now. Don't mess with a dog's food while he's eating," Nate growled.

"And don't bite the hand that feeds you."

"Speaking of biting, come here." Nate placed the breakfast tray on the floor. He reached for Janette, and his hands caught hold of her waist.

"No, sweetie. I am going to be late for work. We don't have time." She didn't try hard enough to pull away.

"Work. I got all the work you need right here." Nate slid his Calvin Klein boxer briefs down to his ankles and kicked them off. His dick was halfway hard, and when Janette took a look she couldn't fight the arousal that washed over her body. From the first time she had laid her hazel eyes on Nate she had wanted him. The tricky part had been getting him to do more than sex her. Her weight was distributed mostly on her hips and ass. Although they sagged a little, her 40DD breasts made most men drool, and she kept them encased in the most beautiful brassieres money could buy. Janette had no problem with her size, nor any problem enticing men with her appearance. She did, however, harbor deep fears of a man straying and wanting a smaller woman once she had become attached and decided she wanted him all to herself.

Nate had noticed Janette heading to her car after a jazz concert at Marshall Park on a Sunday afternoon. He had been intrigued with her walk. He had never seen a full-figured woman move with the grace of a runway model. He had had no intention of stopping to talk to her until he moved past her car and saw her smile at him. He smiled back, and then he heard her laugh and ask him if he was too scared to stop and talk. Janette was confident and beautiful. Her hair, nails, and feet were always done. She had been showing off at the concert in a tight pair of capri pants and a linen shirt with no bra underneath. He had ended up standing at her car talking and putting his mack down until every car had left the parking lot.

They had spent the next few days talking on the phone before Nate had decided to give thick loving a try. He had not regretted it. Janette had ended up breaking him down with a massage that had left him weak as a lamb. Before he met Janette he hadn't slept soundly since leaving D.C. almost a year before. After Kim's suicide Nate had succumbed to guilt and shame, to the point that he had had nightmares and anxiety attacks that had left him short of breath. It wasn't as if Kim had been his lady, but her death had scared him shitless. He vowed to treat women much better after that. In fact, he thought he'd just swear them off for a while. Eventually, the cooking and pampering Janette had provided softened Nate, and he had been able to fight off the guilt and depression that had haunted him almost every night. As time wore on he had become dependent on Janette, and had all but abandoned his old ways of running the streets. Although he was officially living in his aunt Marion's basement, he slept at Janette's almost nightly. He had gained weight and had stopped getting his hair cut regularly. He would have looked like a broken man to anyone who truly knew him. But to Janette, he was a dream come true.

She took a glimpse at her clock and knew she would be late for her first patient. Still, she leaned over and took him in her mouth. For some reason, as she began sucking Nate, she thought long and hard about getting married one day. She had an idea of what it would take to keep a husband happy, and this was her version of it. Feed him, fuck him, and suck him. Nate's head instantly fell back and his mouth dropped open. She was sucking him so well: He knew that she was trying to take him out fast so that she could get to work. He wanted to slow her down so that he could show her that he was the boss. He attempted to pull himself up, but one of her hands slid up his chest and pressed him back into the bed. With the other hand she began to pump his shaft while making loud slurping and purring noises with her mouth wrapped around the tip of his manhood.

"Oh, Nett. Oh, Nett," he moaned out. "No, baby, not like this."

She knew she had him. She started bobbing her head up and down, using her tongue and the roof of her mouth to drive him over the edge. She had one hand on one of his nipples, pulling and caressing it. With the other hand she gripped his balls and massaged them, never stopping the suction she had going on.

Nate felt the room spin. He was flat on his back, amazed, trying to watch as Janette used her tongue like a weapon of mass destruction. Just as Nate was about to reach his orgasm, he regained his composure and caught her head on the upstroke. He pushed her head back and rolled away.

"Take those pants off," he demanded. She was disappointed that she hadn't made him erupt, but she knew her body was in for a delightful pounding. She grabbed her Nextel and smashed a button.

"Liza," she said into the walkie-talkie.

"Hey, Janette. What's up?"

"Are you at the office?" Nate was standing behind her sliding her pants off. She stepped out of them. He then grabbed her thong and slid it down as well.

"I just got in."

"Okay. I am running about a half-hour late. Call Mrs. Tucker and see if we can push her down to three-thirty. What is she getting, anyway?"

"Fillings. Two of them."

"If she can't make it then . . ." Janette stopped when Nate's fingers found her button and he penetrated her at the same time. "Whoo," she said aloud. She mouthed "stop" to Nate but didn't mean it. "Just do what you got to do. S . . . s . . . see you in a little bit."

"Girl, you alright over there?" Liza had a feeling she knew what was going on. Liza was Janette's first and only receptionist, and she had noticed that Janette had been running late more often in the last three months than she had in the previous four years combined that she had been practicing dentistry.

The phone was already on the floor, and Janette had leaned over the bed. Nate had slipped on a condom and was entering Janette an inch at a time. "Mmmm," he said. "Slippery when wet."

Janette's breath quickened in pace as Nate locked onto her hips and began banging away. Sometimes he hit it slow, but that was more for him than for her. She loved to be licked slow but fucked hard and fast. "That's right, daddy. Bang it. Bang it!"

The bed was shaking as Janette used it to hold her up. "You like that? You want it harder?" Nate quickened his pace, and was pulling all the way out and slamming it back into her. He worked a nonstop pace on her from the back for five minutes, until sweat was pouring off his chest.

Janette's eyes rolled up into her head, and she thought about how lovely life had been since Nate had been around. All the women who said size didn't matter obviously had never been hit by a Mandingo like

Nathan Montgomery. She was bouncing back against him, enjoying the feeling of him thoroughly working her middle. "Ooohhh, baby. Don't stop." She felt electric sparks start in her toes and creep slowly up past her ankles. Her thighs began to tremble to the point that she feared she wouldn't be able to keep her balance.

Nate felt her orgasm nearing and decided to send her over the edge. He took the thumb that was gripping her right cheek and let it slip into her ass. When he did this Janette growled like a grizzly that had been shot with a dart gun. She tried to stand as the tides of her orgasm crashed through her body, but she was too weak. "Are you coming, Nett?"

Why he had to ask she never knew. "Yes. Yes. Yessss." And she let out a series of short screams. His breath quickened, and she knew what to do. She summoned all the energy in her body and pulled away from him, spun around, and dropped to her knees. In one motion she had the condom off and Nate in her mouth.

"Oh, yes." His body stiffened and the veins in his neck seemed to pop out at the same time he released into her mouth. She took him all in until she was sure he had finished. *This is how to get a man, and that food I cook is how to keep one,* she thought, as she swallowed his juices. "Girl, you so nasty," Nate said, as a smile slowly formed out of the fuck face he had sported moments earlier.

Janette wiped the drops that had run on her chin and licked her fingers clean. "You love it. You love it," she repeated.

"I can't get enough of it." He began laughing. He pointed down to his penis, which was still hard. He walked into the bathroom singing, "It's the remix to ignition coming hot out the kitchen . . ."

He could see that Janette had picked up her cell. "Liza. Cancel and reschedule all of my appointments. I'll work late all of next week." He stood in the door of the bathroom and shook his head.

"Girl, you are crazy."

"Nasty, crazy, whatever. Just come eat me."

chapter three

It Takes a Fool to Learn

H e was the last person Brendan expected to bump into in Dr. Harmon's office.

When Brendan saw his face he was wishing he could turn around and walk right back out the door. Mr. Shoreham put the *U.S. News* & *World Report* down and immediately noticed Brendan.

"Hey, fella," Mr. Shoreham said. Brendan was surprised that there wasn't even the slightest hint of hostility. He leaned across the magazine table to give Brendan a handshake. "Where you been? Just because Renee moved out of town doesn't mean you can't stop through and say hello once in a while."

Brendan swallowed hard and tried to digest what Mr. Shoreham had just said. "Oh. I have just been working hard, you know, trying to put those hours in." Sensing that he needed to keep the conversation moving, he added, "I will try to get by there one day to see you and the missus." Brendan was stunned that Renee had moved out of town and not so much as said good-bye.

"You need to do that. How is your family?" Before Brendan could answer, Mr. Shoreham went on. "As a matter of fact, I saw your mom a few weeks back out at Arundel Mills."

"Everyone is fine." Brendan shot him a few questions about his grandson, followed by a couple of comments about the weather, before he came up with a way to ask him about Renee. It was obvious that she hadn't told her parents about the way they had fallen out. If he had known Brendan had broken his beloved baby girl's heart, Mr. Shoreham might have tried to put a chokehold on Brendan right there in the waiting room. "So, how does Renee like it down there," Brendan faked a yawn. "Excuse me."

"No problem. She said she loves it in Houston. She complains about the heat, but it's Texas. I mean, what did she expect?" Mr. Shoreham laughed. "I think I am going to make it down there this fall. You ought to come with me."

Brendan imagined himself showing up at Renee's door. His face tightened when he thought of the drama that might unfold. "Yeah, I might do that." He said, knowing full well there was no chance of that.

"Yeah, her fiancé is a really nice guy. He reminds me of you, to be honest. Just a clean-cut, decent guy. Just like you, as a matter of fact." He patted Brendan on the shoulder. "When I met him on Easter, I joked with her. I said you didn't have to go all the way to Houston to marry Brendan." He burst into laughter, and Brendan's face got the kind of look you get when you pass gas out loud in a crowded elevator.

"Wow, that's really something," is all he said, in a low tone, but really wanting to scream out, "That's some bullshit."

The receptionist called Mr. Shoreham up to the counter and gave him a prescription. He gave Brendan a handshake as he left. "Don't be a stranger, son. I mean that." Brendan nodded and Dr. Harmon came out and told him to go to the room in the back. Brendan's mind was racing with thoughts from all the news he'd just gotten. His best friend since middle school had cut him off. He had played with her emotions. Unintentional as his actions had been, a lifelong friendship had been ruined by passions gone awry. Now she had left town, which seemed to be a new trend for everyone he knew. First Nate, now Renee. Brendan wondered about her getting engaged so soon after leaving, and assumed she was on the rebound. His mind was completely blown by it all.

As he sat on the examining table he tried not to wrinkle the white paper on the table. He thought about calling Cory from his cell to tell him what he'd heard but decided to wait until his appointment was over. Dr. Harmon walked into the office. "Hey, dude. How are you?"

Brendan considered telling him the truth, but instead gave the traditional, "Fine."

"Great. Listen, I called you back in for two reasons." Dr. Harmon was looking at his charts. "Like Yvonne told you, your sodium levels were a little abnormal, but that is nothing to really worry about. Just start drinking some more water, and I will check it for you in two weeks." He placed the chart down on the table.

"Okay. But what was the other thing?" he asked, thinking he'd heard the worst.

Dr. Harmon took a deep breath, which Brendan realized couldn't be anything good. "My friend, from looking at your blood work, it seems that you have contracted a case of chlamydia."

"Say what?" Brendan shot back.

"I can't say one hundred percent without a culture, but I tested you for everything in your physical." Dr. Harmon picked up the file and started scribbling. "I don't want to say it's no big deal, but it is easily treated. I will get you a quick shot and a prescription." He grabbed a needle and told Brendan to drop his pants. A few seconds later, and the needle was pulled from his hip.

"So what does this mean?" Brendan was trying to make sense of it all. "Has my girlfriend been cheating?"

Dr. Harmon smiled. As far as Brendan was concerned there wasn't anything to smile about. "Not necessarily." He handed Brendan the cotton ball doused with alcohol and a Band-aid. "You may have contracted this any time after your last checkup, which was . . ."

"Seven months ago, and Doc, I haven't had sex with anyone except for her since then."

A frown came over the doctor's face. He nodded his head to show that his heart went out to Brendan. "Then there's a pretty good chance she has some explaining to do." He scribbled on his prescription pad. "Tell her she needs to get checked out. Also, I would advise that you don't have any unprotected sex until she does so." He handed Brendan the prescription. "Two a day for ten days. Take care of yourself." He shook Brendan's hand and headed out the door.

Brendan moved up the short hallway, through the lobby, and out of the office building. When he walked outside, he was blasted by the heat. Instead of lifting him up, the sun felt like the decisive blow in a heavyweight fight. As he moved toward his car he thought, *Some days it doesn't even pay to get out of the bed.*

Brendan exited the parking lot and put on the *Kindred* CD as he tried to pull himself together. As he drove toward the CVS he contemplated all of the possible outcomes to his situation. Trina would be coming home from work in a couple of hours and had no idea how angry he was. But she was sure going to find out. Renee was two thousand miles away and engaged to some clown who was "a lot like" him. He wondered if he would have been happier if he and Renee had tried to work things out.

It was water under the bridge, and he needed a plan.